**Keep up to date
with Walker Fayt:**

www.walkerfayt.com

THE WORLDWIDE SEXUAL ADVENTURES OF WALKER FAYT

MITCH RHODES

a novel for men

Copyright © 2000 Mitch Rhodes
New World Solutions Inc.
www.walkerfayt.com

All rights reserved. No part of this book may be reproduced in any form or by any means without the written permission of the publisher, except by a reviewer who may quote passages in a review.

Canadian Cataloguing in Publication Data

Rhodes, Mitch, 1957–
The worldwide sexual adventures of Walker Fayt

ISBN 1-894694-01-5

I. Title

PS8585.H567W67 2000   C813'.6   C00-911124-7
PR9199.3.R4643W67 2000

Edited by Neall Calvert
Ursa Major Communications • Vancouver, BC

Designed by Rebecca Davies Design

Cover Art: Lino cut "Bathroom Nude" by Sally Sneddon Copyright © 2000
Recoloured for this edition by Rebecca Davies

First printing October 2000

Creative Connections
PUBLISHING

Creative Connections Publishing
Vancouver • Victoria • Calgary
Head Office
212–1656 Duranleau • Granville Island
Vancouver BC • Canada • V6H 3S4
www.creativeconnectionspublishing.com

Member of Affiliated Publishers
Vancouver • Milwaukee • Denver

Printed and bound in Canada

To Betty Leona Thrasher (1933–1990).
Her ambition to be a novelist migrated to her son.

chapters

1. Guiding Visions
An Odyssey Begins — 1

2. Inadvertent Touches
Warming Up on the Flight to Europe — 12

3. Red-light District
Coming to a Full Stop in Amsterdam — 20

4. Monique—A Hands-on Sex Professional
Charmed by a Passionate Belgian — 28

5. Patricia—The Remarkable Stripper
Tippling & Nippling in Shakespeare's England — 43

6. I Trust You—Will You Trust Me?
In Idyllic London, Love's Labors Heal a Painful Past — 54

7. Fantasy Meets Fantasy
'If a Swedish Woman Likes You, She'll Go To Bed With You' — 74

8. Selena—The Woman Who is Everything
Heaven & Hell in a Picturesque French Vineyard — 97

9. Havoc in the African Jungle
Gentle Gorillas & Wild Women — 129

10. Tanya—The Colors of Pleasure
   In Jordan's Deserts, Surrender to Sexual Gratification   165

11. Ancient Village Rhythms
   Full-moon Rites with a Thai Tribal Girl   207

12. Humbled in Bangkok
   Money Can Buy Anything, Including a Breast Massage   236

13. Indeara—A PhD in Lovemaking
   The Kamasutra as Pathway to Fulfillment   267

14. Going Beyond Oneself
   Rescuing Children in Chaotic Cambodia   304

15. Death of a Father
   Home Again, and a Dark Detour into Ménage à Trois   353

16. Ellie—Doctor, Healer, Lover
   In the Coast Mountains of British Columbia,
   Tracking Down the Male G-spot   385

17. Reconciliation
   Foes Become Friends in Tropical Costa Rica   411

18. Epiphany Fulfilled
   Accepting the Unfolding Universe   436

ACKNOWLEDGMENTS

The author thanks the people who helped my editing process in the early stages: Suzanne Denbak, Marline Emmal, Nancy Lewis and Jay Draper; Steve Schmidt for his preliminary legal work and continued encouragement; John Wittig and Herb Richards for supplying me with resource materials; Roger Daly for allowing me to listen to his wee Irish accent; and the Vancouver Branch of the Canadian Authors Association for helping writers make connections.

I also want to thank Neall Calvert, who as well as being a meticulous editor is gifted in creating chapter headings; Sally Sneddon of the Hunter Valley in Australia for "Bathroom Nude," which forms the cover art; Rebecca Davies for her insight and imagination in developing the text and cover design; Jo Blackmore and Paul Vanderham of Creative Connections Publishing for their expertise in helping me wade through the sometimes strange and often antiquated world of publishing; and Suzanne, my wife, whose support, patience and love have made this book-writing journey possible.

chapter 1

GUIDING VISIONS
An Odyssey Begins

There is no truth; there is only what we believe. Walker Fayt believed that his first life was ending. As he settled into seat 17A by the window, this first life began flashing before him. He had been told that such things might happen just before death. It seemed strange, but somehow appropriate, that they were occurring at this moment.

Most recent memories came first. Yesterday Walker's younger daughter, Amy, had graduated from high school. The memory of her enthusiasm for life and her belief that all possibilities still existed mingled with his pride and love for his child. Her positive attitude and lack of cynicism inspired him. He began to see that those traits in her gave him the courage to take up a different direction. Insights into Amy's influences on him vanished in a flash and new memories appeared.

Walker's talents as a teacher had made history one of the most popular subjects at Appleton West High School. Allan Jones, the principal, had been Walker's boss and friend for the last ten years. Allan had sat shocked and stunned when Walker announced that he was resigning. Allan responded by saying that he had never worked with a teacher who allowed students to excel by stimulating their imaginations the way Walker did. Allan also praised Walker's ability to connect the flow of past events with the present, a special talent that allowed Walker to challenge and excite his students.

Walker dismissed all attempts to hold a farewell party; he wished to keep his departure a low profile. He feared it might overshadow the graduation ceremony and celebrations. He wanted the teachers, parents, students and especially Amy to fully enjoy the occasion. During the graduation festivities he exchanged hugs and kisses, many accompanied by tears of sadness. There were also shared laughs and cheers.

Petra, his elder daughter, began occupying Walker's thoughts. A few days before his departure she had arrived home from Ann Arbor, having completed a successful junior year at the University of Michigan. She was planning to be a primary-school teacher. Father had pulled a few strings and arranged summer employment for her at an Appleton, Wisconsin, day camp for children.

Walker loved and cherished this daughter beyond his capacity to understand. Petra's pain and despair at his decisions suddenly became impossible to bear; he moved on to other thoughts.

The HOUSE FOR SALE sign with a SOLD sticker plastered across it and Walker's signature on the legal documents occupied his mind next. He wondered if a house could maintain memories, or if they would only live on in the family members. Could the love and emotions of twenty-two years remain in that house? He had broken a connection to a place that contained more than half of his personal history. It saddened him to think of it.

The captain's voice came over the intercom system. "Welcome aboard American Airlines Flight 54 from Chicago to New York en route to Amsterdam. The weather is clear and we're expecting to arrive in New York ten minutes ahead of schedule. We've been cleared for takeoff and should be in the air in a few minutes. Once again, welcome aboard and enjoy your flight."

The announcement pulled Walker into the present moment and he glanced out the window as the plane taxied down the runway.

"No matter how much I fly, takeoffs and landings always make me nervous," the woman in the seat beside Walker's said. Her voice brought him back to the activity within the cabin.

"Faith and trust are never easy," he responded, as he turned and smiled.

Walker noticed that she was a good-looking woman in her mid-twenties. She wore her blond hair in a French braid and her make-up light and understated. This highlighted her natural attractiveness. A blue business suit with a tight skirt flattered her figure.

"Are you going to New York or Amsterdam?" asked Walker.

"To New York—and you?" she returned, tension rising in her voice as the lights dimmed and the plane began to pick up speed. A voice on the intercom announced, "Attendants, prepare for takeoff."

Walker said, "To Amsterdam." The woman nodded as she prepared for takeoff by closing her eyes and tightly gripping the armrests.

Speaking the word "Amsterdam" aloud to a stranger had a profound emotional effect on Walker. It made his life-changing decision seem real, even though the circumstances remained dreamlike. He watched the tense young woman try to relax. He smiled to himself and resumed looking out the window. Blurred images of black asphalt and green grass mingled together and caused his mind to drift. Recent memories returned.

Walker remembered standing alone in the safety-deposit vault of his bank in Appleton and feeling warm tears run down his face and drip onto his shirt. The grayness of the room made everything in it feel empty. Locked away in the various-sized boxes were other people's most valued treasures. He had taken off his wedding ring, placed it into his small rented box and locked the box into place.

Twenty-two years of wearing his wedding ring had left a visible mark on Walker's finger. Touching his ring finger against his cheek, he had suddenly felt naked and exposed without it. A great sadness overtook him as he next remembered sitting in the lawyer's office signing the divorce papers.

After Petra was born, Walker and Marlene had had Jerry McIntyre prepare their first set of wills. Jerry had handled all of their legal work thereafter and had become a close friend. During the signing of the divorce documents, all three of them had wet the pages with tears, then shared a nervous laugh, wondering if the stains affected the legality of the divorce.

"Do you mind if I use my laptop?"

The voice interrupted Walker's thoughts and he noticed the woman beside him unzipping a black computer bag. As his head cleared and the strong emotions faded, he turned to her with a big, bright smile.

"Hello, I'm Walker Fayt. It's a pleasure to travel with you and, no, I don't mind. Go right ahead."

With his good looks, healthy physique and youthful appearance, Walker could easily pass for thirty-five rather than his actual forty-three years. This may have accounted for the woman's cheerful, "Hi! I'm Belinda. Nice to meet you."

As she finished unpacking the expensive computer, Walker noticed her smart attire and confident manner, and made an assumption.

"Do you travel a lot in your work?"

"Constantly. I'm an internal auditor for Coca-Cola. I travel over forty weeks of the year. I don't even have an apartment. I keep a room at my parents' house in Atlanta. It's hectic, but it works for me. I'm young. I travel all over the world. I save lots of money . . . I don't have the time or a place to spend it."

Walker recognized her response as a tension release and let it go at that. In his new life, he had decided to be direct in his conversational style and focus on matters of importance. He believed that earnest and honest questions and comments would reciprocate like responses. In this way he hoped to create memorable conversational exchanges.

"Belinda, how about a relationship? Is there any time in your life for that?"

Without missing a beat, and without any indication that she thought he was prying, she said, "No, nothing serious. I'm never in one place long enough to allow a relationship to develop. Occasionally I have companionship, but for now I'm focusing on building my career. Romance can wait."

"You're a young, attractive American and must get a lot of attention from foreign men. Are you attracted to foreign men?"

Belinda hesitated just a little. Her eyes twinkled and a small smile formed. "Yes. I find them more romantic—especially the French and Italians."

"*Très bien! Le français est une langue très romantique,*" Walker said as best he could.

Belinda blushed slightly. "Was that French or Italian? I don't speak either."

"My French is poor. I went to high school in Canada and took French for four terms. It seems I still remember a little." He showed a small space between his index finger and thumb: "*Un petit.*"

Many years had passed since Walker last spoke French and it surprised him that he had remembered any at all. It boosted his ego that his attempt at flirtation had made Belinda blush.

In her best southern drawl she confessed, "I'd love to listen to more of your French, but I really must finish this report before we land in New York. Remember: career first."

Walker nodded his head, widened his eyes, plugged in his headset and turned the channel to classical music. It relaxed him and he eased back into his memories.

THE WORLDWIDE SEXUAL ADVENTURES OF WALKER FAYT

He recalled decades ago having an argument with Marlene late one night and afterward, alone and upset, trying to understand what had gone wrong. Replaying the events of the evening over and over in his mind, he had had trouble connecting the dots. Then suddenly a light had come on in his mind and its brilliance had consumed him.

That instant he had begun to understand his world differently. He understood that no event or any other person controlled the emotions that were within him. Responsibility for his own happiness or sadness, from moment to moment, always remained with him. He was twenty-one at the time. The scene faded and another memory arose.

A dinner engagement with friends had been scheduled and it was almost time for Walker and Amy to leave the park. Amy wanted to continue playing on the swings and, like many five-year-olds, she refused to cooperate and leave when requested. He carried her home crying and screaming.

Walker would have preferred to stay in the park as well, but that choice would have hurt Marlene and Petra. As he held Amy, her sobbing echoed deeply in his soul and he resented having to make choices that hurt the ones he loved. In a flash, a life mission entered his awareness. It said, "Death can occur at any time. So at any given moment you must live your life with no regrets and with no skeletons in the closet." He was thirty at the time and the insight liberated him.

Three years ago, about four o'clock in the morning, Walker lay in bed awake, trying to get back to sleep, when a realization suddenly came over him. "If you don't want to be a grumpy, miserable and unhappy old man, in middle age you must resolve old issues and make peace with your past."

Instinctively Walker knew that these inspirations and insights occurred on an emotional level as well as an intellectual one, but he had stopped exploring theories as to where they came from. Instead he tried applying these philosophical concepts to the practicality of his everyday life. That often proved difficult.

On January 4, the most powerful revelation of Walker's life had occurred. A few seconds of insight left an emotional and intellectual charge that lasted several days. A constant state of knowledge, love and euphoria surrounded him; his past, present and future were one. Everything in his life cleared; there were no problems, issues or uncertainties. He hoped the condition would last forever, but he knew it could not. He realized that the human mind and body were not built to handle the energy of universal inspiration for long.

These powerful memories now flowed together in Walker's mind, creating a melting pot of destiny. They blended together to form the backdrop of his thoughts and emotions as he re-enacted the moment when Marlene had finally agreed to a divorce. The day and everything about it seemed extraordinary. Rarely did they have time together on a weekday; he was at school and Marlene was at her medical practice. It had happened on Washington's birthday and the moment remained clear and forever fused in the neural patterns of his brain.

The memory of walking in the park along the river on that sunny, crisp February day became strong. Everything seemed to resonate; the day appeared more alive than usual. As they strolled along a tree-lined path, Marlene asked him to explain his revelation one more time.

Walker hoped that his words, seen in the cold air, would come to life and she would understand. Explaining the touch of universal inspiration would not be easy and he knew difficult moments lay ahead. His words emerged to join the frosty air.

"If I'm to be happy in my old age, if I'm to die with no regrets, if I'm to live an open and honest life, if I'm to take responsibility for my well-being moment to moment, then I must pursue the vision that has come to me." Walker breathed more heavily than usual.

With each syllable, tiny crystals formed and were exhaled from his mouth. After a brief pause, he continued.

"Harmony and love filled every fiber of my body and became my entire essence. My heightened state of awareness passed, but the direction given to me during the experience remains true. It is an absolute."

"Walker, I love you, but nothing like this has ever happened to me and it's difficult for me to understand." Marlene paused and took a big breath. "To drastically change your entire life based on a few seconds of something you think is insight seems crazy. How can you be so sure? Please explain it to me one more time. What it is that you must do to complete your life?"

They had tried to discuss the topic several times previously and it had never worked out and Walker didn't want the discussion to fail again. He cautiously said, "I understand that you're feeling rejected and unloved. I don't mean to make you feel that way and it's not my intention to create those feelings in you. What I need to do will not complete my life but will allow my happiness to be shared with the ones I love later in life. Honey, I know it sounds crazy and if you didn't think so, I would wonder about you."

With tension rising in her voice, Marlene stated, "A vision that tells you to quit your job, sell the house, divorce your wife and leave your family and friends to travel around the world seeking sexual experiences . . . *is* crazy."

In his most supportive tone, Walker said, "You're right. That's your truth and it's valid."

"Where do you think your visions come from?" As he opened his mouth to respond, Marlene spoke first. "I think this is just an elaborate way for you to get some . . . some strange . . ." She let the words fade and linger before she began again. "I'm the only sexual partner you've ever had. I'm no shrink, but I believe it's just a latent sexual thing being played out in middle age."

GUIDING VISIONS

Walker calmly said, "Let's walk for a little bit."

Marlene nodded her head in approval. They both knew that in the midst of a difficult discussion it was sometimes best to take a break so they wouldn't get angry with each other.

Walker took her arm. They trudged along the path in silence until they came to their favorite place in the river. A small section where the water still flowed quickly remained unfrozen. A dozen ducks floated in this open patch of river. Despite the coldness of the water, the ducks appeared happy and thankful that they had a place to swim.

In a quiet voice he said, "You may be right. It may be a mid-life sexual crisis. If I believed that to be true, I'd go for counseling—but I don't." Slightly louder, he said, "My entire life has led me to this point. I must continue in the way I know is right for me."

Marlene shook her head slightly and looked down at the ground as Walker continued. "I don't know where the visions come from. Maybe Carl Jung is right: original thought comes from tapping into a universal, absolute body of knowledge. Or, perhaps that knowledge is sent to us at a specific time for a specific purpose."

She cut him off. "I'm not ready for a heavy philosophical discussion. I just wondered if you'd considered what was influencing you."

"From a very young age, one of my strongest abilities was to piece together seemingly unrelated information and come up with an explanation or a solution. I believe that's why I'm so interested in history and why I excel at teaching it. Yes, I have thought about it, but I've stopped—it doesn't get me anywhere. It does become too philosophical."

Tears started to well in Marlene's eyes. "There's nothing that anybody can say to change your mind . . . is there?"

"Let's move on in a state of love that we can remember and cherish. If you were to convince me to stay, I'd resent it and it would end up getting vented in many different ways. Communication between us would start to break down and our relationship would end either in a divorce or in an unloving or unconscious marriage. This is the future I see if I refuse my vision."

Tears rolled down both their faces. Marlene hesitantly asked, "What if we stay married and you go off and do your thing?"

"Thank you for loving me so much. We both know that wouldn't work." Walker held her head with both hands and kissed her on the temple. He whispered in her ear, "It would slowly kill us both."

"I know," she whispered, then continued. "This is the saddest day of my life. I don't understand and I don't think I ever will. I feel unloved and abandoned. These feelings may last forever and I can't help but blame you. But, yes, I'll consent to a divorce."

Walker kept silent as he turned to hug her and passed along as much loving energy as possible. She resisted at first, but eventually allowed it, as well as a gentle kiss on the lips. They walked home arm in arm with nothing further being said.

"Please fasten your seat belts. We have begun our descent into JFK," a voice on the intercom stated.

Walker took out his journal and wrote the first entry on a blank page.

June 22

Somewhere over the Eastern Continental U.S.A.

> *It doesn't take a day to change your life,*
> *It only takes a second;*
> *Revelation happens at the moment of creation—*
> *Time is irrelevant and has only just begun.*

These lines burn white hot in my brain. I feel compelled to use them as the first entry. They are words I remember from a poem I once wrote for Marlene. The poem was for her, but these specific words, I now know, are for me. My journey begins.

After putting down the pen, Walker gazed out the window to search out the lights of New York City. He needed to concentrate on something to bring him back from the emotional flashbacks. Next to him, Belinda had packed up the laptop and begun her landing ritual.

Slowly the distant brightness became distinguishable as buildings. As Walker peered down on Manhattan and Queens, Belinda kept her eyes closed and tightly gripped the armrests. The plane landed softly.

"Welcome to New York. Those passengers en route to Amsterdam please remain on board," the intercom voice stated.

Belinda unbuckled her seat belt. She looked a little shaken but relieved. "Enjoy yourself in Amsterdam," she said cheerfully. "It's a great city."

"Thanks. *Bonne chance! Au revoir.*"

Belinda smiled and, as she walked away, waved goodbye.

chapter 2

INADVERTENT TOUCHES
Warming Up on the Flight to Europe

Walker's six-foot, three-inch frame did not fit well into an economy seat. While the crew prepared for the New York passengers to board, in the space at the latrines he stretched his legs, arms and back. Thinking about the six-hour overnight flight to Amsterdam caused tightness in his body, and doing the isometrics helped loosen him up.

Almost as soon as the New York–bound passengers had left, Amsterdam-bound passengers began arriving. Busily the new arrivals found their seats and stored their hand luggage. Bending over at the waist, Walker let his arms hang free in front of him while he stretched his spine. Intent on finding their seats, most people walked past without looking at him. He heard a young woman's voice with a distinctive New York accent say, "Nice butt!"

In one motion, Walker quickly turned and stood looking for a visual clue as to the source of the comment. He smiled and shook his head in amusement.

"Please take your seat, sir; we're almost ready to leave," a flight attendant with a different voice requested with a perfect stewardess's smile.

INADVERTENT TOUCHES

Walker wondered if there would be any yelling babies, young children, drinkers, loud and obnoxious people, those needing to bathe, chitchatters or good-looking women aboard. While heading toward his seat, he observed the passengers as he passed them. As he did this, he found it amazing how the human mind instantly judges on so many levels with just a glance. He continued his assessments as he headed toward his seat. When he got closer, he noticed the person sitting in 17B, the aisle seat.

She looked in her early twenties. Walker caught sight of dark hair and lily-white skin. An attractive face was masked with heavy make-up—dark eye shadow and bright lipstick. As he got closer, a nose gem and a neck tattoo came into view. Standing over her, he looked down at her black, loose-fitting crinkle pants, sleeveless V-neck and platform shoes.

"Excuse me," Walker said softly, interrupting her gaze outside. "I'm by the window."

"Oh, okay," she replied as she turned her legs slightly toward the aisle.

Walker held on to the seats in front of him and contorted himself to get past her. Her refusal to get up while he slid past caused their legs to collide and his behind came close to her face.

"Nice butt," she whispered loudly. "Want to join the mile-high club?"

A little flushed and embarrassed, Walker finished maneuvering into his seat. At least he had solved the mystery of who found his backside attractive.

"Oh, hi . . . um . . . sorry about that. What's the mile-high club?"

A look at once innocent and devilish came over her. "Take a guess."

"Well . . . um . . . um. . . ." Walker cleared his throat, lowered his voice and leaned her way. "Well . . . I've lived through the Sixties, so I'm sure it has something to do with . . . taking something to make the flight more . . . enhanced." He looked around. "You know what I mean? But I'm certainly not into that any more. I'm right . . . aren't I . . . about the club?"

The young woman continued with the same look, only with a bigger smile. She slowly shook her head no and then yes.

"Yeah, I thought so," Walker said, trying to convince himself. He felt foolish about having lived such a sheltered life and tried changing the mood. "I'm Walker Fayt. Pleased to be traveling with you. Are you always this . . . shy?"

"Hi! I'm Angela. Being from New York, I have to be aggressive. I hope you don't mind . . . but even if you do—" she smiled without finishing the statement.

Walker sensed no malice in her introduction, but rather a matter-of-fact, take-it-or-leave-it attitude. They spoke no further as the plane taxied to the runway and took off. Blackness filled the window and he leaned over to look down at the bright lights of New York City. He had lived in Manhattan as a boy and it pleased him to see the city once again. It stirred boyhood memories.

Past experiences again began to resurface and Walker welcomed the opportunity to resolve old issues by remembering childhood events. These treasures came easily to him.

Madison Square Garden and the New York Rangers came first. Walker saw himself, his father and his older sister at a hockey game together. Once, or perhaps twice, per season this monumental event happened. Why did he have such strong feelings about these events? What made going to the game such a big deal? At the time, how the Rangers fared seemed to be important. Walker visualized himself watching the game. Then the interaction with his father and sister came into focus.

Walker and his sister, Tracy, had been big New York Rangers fans, but their father had no interest in hockey, or any other sport. But at the game, Walker remembered that their father had no business dealings to attend to and no social schmoozing to do. There they had access to the most precious commodity in their lives—their father's undivided attention.

A deeper understanding of himself came with Walker's now-fading visualization. The joy of going to the games masked the pain of not receiving his father's attention at other times. This connected with deeper feelings—feelings that he did not mean as much to his father as working hard and making money.

As an adult, Walker understood and accepted his father's motivations and behaviors. But Walker knew that the part of the brain that holds emotions was not affected by time and for the subconscious, it was as though the hurt had just occurred. Those childhood wounds were still a part of him and in order to heal the adult, his inner child needed to confront his father. He tried to go back to that place and express his anger, sorrow and regret to his father—as well as his forgiveness.

"Would you like something to drink?" brought Walker back to the present and he saw Angela pouring a little bottle of Jack Daniels into her glass.

Walker looked up at the flight attendant and said, "Mineral water, please."

Angela jumped in with a smile. "Oh, it's going to be a fun night."

He took his drink. "This is as wild as I get." He clinked their plastic glasses, "Cheers!"

Walker and Angela talked while they sipped their drinks. They discussed the weather, where they were from and what they did. She attended New York University and had just finished her first year of journalism. An only child, she had lived all her life in Manhattan. Angela joked that her parents had financed the cost of her trip just to be rid of her for the summer.

Despite the somewhat tough image, Walker found Angela to be bright, enthusiastic, sensible and a bit of a free spirit. He felt her magnetism and it made him feel more energetic. She did most of the talking and he enjoyed listening to her. She seemed to enjoy his unconditional acceptance of what she said.

In the middle of a conversation about journalism at NYU, she suddenly inquired, "Are you married?"

It had been a very long time since someone had asked Walker about his marital status. Quite often, women had told him that even before they saw his wedding ring, they considered him to be married. He had never really understood the comment and just accepted it, figuring that he unconsciously sent out a signal that he wasn't available. He guessed that that signal had changed.

"Divorced, very recently divorced," Walker replied. "And you? Married? Any kids?" he said jokingly.

"Funny guy. No! I don't even have a steady boyfriend, and I'm not looking for one...." Angela hesitated a little and then continued, "But I'm sure I'll fall in love a few times this summer—those French and Italians!"

"Hmmm—there must be something about that seat," Walker quipped.

"What?" she asked, looking a little confused.

"Oh, ah . . . never mind, just a strange coincidence. Forgive me."

As their empty glasses were taken away, Angela asked, "Do you have any kids?"

"Yes, two girls. Probably one older and one younger than you," Walker replied as he put up his tray table.

Loudly she cried, "Get out!" and then a little quieter, "You're joking—right?"

"No, I'm serious," he reassured her. "Really."

"What cryogenic chamber do you stay in?" Angela queried in an amazed and tender tone. Then she leaned over and whispered, "I may have to take back the 'nice butt' comment." The move placed her breast against his firm triceps. "No . . . on second thought, the comments stands," and she leaned back and the touch ended.

Angela's breast against his arm had felt wonderful. Walker pondered if she had been conscious of the encounter. Were women's breasts sensitive to an inadvertent touch? Had it been inadvertent?

Walker's mind filled with similar experiences from his past and he remembered being curious at those times too. Back in high school when such accidental yet fortuitous encounters happened, it thrilled him and his friends. They had names for such rare and delightful occasions. "Tit-of-elbow", "ass-of-knee", "twat-of-backhand" were some of the ones he recalled. He smiled at remembering them after such a long time.

Another memory from several years ago resurfaced. The incident had happened at a cocktail party, in a line-up for the bar. Walker had turned around at the same time as the woman in front of him, and he had touched her breast with his hand that held his empty wineglass. The back of his hand had gently pressed against her semi-hard nipple. They had recognized each other as their eyes met. Walker worked with Ann. Both had blushed and smiled nervously as she said, "Sorry," and he said, "Excuse me," and they had moved around each other. They saw each other almost every day at school and had never once discussed or even joked about the "tit-of-hand" incident.

Other occasions when women had touched him came to Walker's mind. There were the young women that washed his hair before it got cut. Frequently they brushed their thighs against his shoulders. While reclined in the dental chair for teeth cleaning, Walker's dental hygienist sat in a chair at the crown of his head. As she leaned over to look and work in his mouth, often her breasts pressed against his head. Once a student teacher tried to read his comments while he marked papers and she leaned over him, resting her chest against his back.

These occurrences seemed trivial and Walker had never asked Marlene about them. He didn't know if women would even notice when another woman's breast touched them. After all, they had breasts of their own, so it was not such a big deal.

"What are you thinking about?" inquired Angela.

"Oh . . . nothing really—just some old buried treasures," Walker replied hesitantly.

"Forget the past. You're going to Europe for some fun. You're single now." After a slight pause, she continued. "You are going for fun, aren't you? It's nothing serious, is it?"

"It depends on how you define serious." Walker looked at her. "I've taken some very serious steps to be sitting in this seat. Is it for fun? It doesn't feel that way to me . . . but if fun is doing what you know you must, even if you don't know why, then yes, I'm having fun."

"That sounds complicated. I'm going to keep it simple this summer and have a blast." Angela's energy level rose as she talked about the adventures that awaited her.

Walker commented, "It's strange. Somewhere along the way I've lost my ability to have fun. I have a great time. I enjoy things very much—somehow life has become interesting, but not fun. What's even stranger . . . I don't regret it; actually I quite like it this way. Fun seems to be more of a release than a purpose. I suppose I'm looking for purpose."

Angela listened intently and then asked, "What's your purpose in going to Europe?"

At first Walker explained his need to travel and experience the places he had only read about. Then his focus changed. He did not know why the urge to tell his story to Angela engaged him. Perhaps he found merit in the notion that it was easier to tell deep personal thoughts to a stranger because exposure was less risky. A burning desire to verbalize his truth and make it real overpowered his fear of inner exposure. He explained everything to her. To his amazement, his words rekindled some of the intensity of past insights.

Most of the passengers slept in the darkened cabin. Walker kept his voice low, just above a whisper, as he talked to Angela in the dimness. Deeply drawn in, she added no remarks other than to acknowledge that she understood and was still listening. Walker talked for about thirty minutes. The exchange of energy captured them both and made them tired by the end of it.

Angela placed her hand on his, and Walker interpreted this gesture as a sign of understanding and nonjudgmental love. He continued holding her hand until she fell asleep.

Feeling positive about what he had accomplished this first day, Walker got out his journal to write.

June 23

Somewhere over the Atlantic Ocean, en route to Europe

> Yesterday's disasters, misfortunes, mistakes and accidents are today's treasures, waiting to be found, examined, explored and cherished.
>
> I write these words as I look from the window of the airplane down at the Atlantic Ocean. It's the middle of the night, so I can't see the water. I assume it's down there, embracing lost sunken treasures from ages past beneath its surface.
>
> I wonder what secrets I hold beneath the surface?

chapter 3

RED-LIGHT DISTRICT
Coming to a Full Stop in Amsterdam

The sound of breakfast being served ended Walker's sleep. As he opened the window flap, his eyes were flooded with sunlight and the promise of a glorious day.

The attendant gave them their trays of breakfast and offered them coffee. Angela slowly opened her eyes and spoke in a raspy voice. "Hi—good morning. It *is* morning, isn't it?"

Walker only nodded and smiled, thinking it might be offensive to start up a conversation right away.

"Wow, did I ever have wild dreams last night, and there seemed to be so many of them. They were really vivid, but now I don't remember anything," Angela spoke softly between sips of coffee. "The conversation between you and me was wild, too—that I remember. It was real, wasn't it?"

"Yes. Very real, and thank you for listening. Other than my wife, you're the first person I've told. Verbalizing it to you made it real for me," Walker said while opening the foil cover over his food. "Oh, a cheese omelet and Canadian back bacon—looks good."

Angela rubbed her stomach in an unusual way and seemed

preoccupied. She caressed her skin directly under her loose-fitting shirt. After about a minute Walker inquired with concern, "Is everything okay? Is the smell of the food making you sick?"

"No. I'm all right. It's just a really strange sensation. Last week I got a bellybutton tattoo and it's still a little sensitive. Have a look." Lifting her top, Angela exposed her bellybutton and the colorful inked addition to her body. "It's a flying bat."

Walker leaned forward to have a look, but couldn't really see much and commented, "Nice—very nice. It suits you."

"Touch it," she said quietly, as she looked at him and smiled, while continuing to hold up her top.

"No—no, I don't think so." Walker nervously looked away and ate more of his omelet.

"Really . . . please. It's medicinal. I want to see if the sensation is the same when someone else touches it." When Walker didn't respond, Angela said, "I listened to you last night. It's the least you can do for me."

"I don't believe this," Walker thought to himself as he put down his utensils and lifted the armrest that separated them. Turning slightly, he reached for her exposed abdomen, now getting a better look at the tattoo.

Most of the bat's head showed, as well as the upper part of the wings that spread out on either side of her navel. Blues, purples, reds and oranges made it very colorful. Her pants still covered most of the design and he imagined how low the wings extended.

Walker's hand touched Angela's bellybutton area and as it did, her body quivered and she released an almost silent, orgasmic moan. With her movement, his fingertips slipped inside the waistband of her pants. Slowly and delicately he caressed the tattoo, causing her body to undulate ever so slightly. Her reaction to his touch began to arouse him, then alarm him.

Walker pulled his hand away saying, "Yeah, it sure is sensitive."

THE WORLDWIDE SEXUAL ADVENTURES OF WALKER FAYT

Angela smiled for a long while. "I can only hope it stays that way—boy, am I hungry." She unwrapped her breakfast and started eating.

The plane began its descent into Amsterdam. They both looked out of the window without speaking and Walker thought about the future. In the midst of his anticipation about what lay ahead, Walker wondered about what had just happened. Had Angela experienced an orgasm? Was that possible? Marlene was his only reference and she would not have experienced one so easily. He decided to hold the memory as a mystery to treasure.

After a smooth touchdown at Amsterdam's Schiphol Airport, they collected their carry-on luggage and left together to pick up their baggage. Walker had decided to travel as lightly as possible and had only a small carry-on knapsack and a larger one that he checked.

They cleared customs and immigration, purchased second-class train tickets for a thirty-minute ride to the city center, waited about ten minutes for the train, and then they were on their way. Angela sat next to the window and Walker sat beside her.

"I'm staying at a hostel. How about you?" Angela asked.

"I'm booked into a bed and breakfast in the old part of the city. It's supposed to be close to the train station, but I don't know where I'm going, so I'm playing it safe and taking a cab there."

They arrived at Centraal Station and proceeded to the taxi stand. A driver took Angela's bags, looked at Walker, and spoke to them in Dutch. When neither of them responded, the driver said, "Together?" as his finger pointed between the two of them. Walker shook his head and the man signaled for another taxi.

Halfway into the car, Angela stopped and came back to where Walker stood. "Maybe we'll run into each other again. It was fun, I mean interesting, on the plane." She stepped closer to him so that he could give her a little kiss on the cheek. As he did, she said, "Bye."

RED-LIGHT DISTRICT

"Goodbye. Have fun—I know you will," Walker said back.

Angela smiled at him as she returned to the taxi. That strange expression at once both innocent and devilish came to her face and she said, "Oh, by the way, you're wrong about the mile-high club."

Before Walker could blurt out a request for an explanation, the door closed and the car drove off. He got into his taxi and it pleased him that the driver spoke English and knew where to take him. As the car drove away from the extravagant red stone station, the history of the large building spoke to him: he noticed that the date "1889" was carved into the cornerstone.

Walker settled into his small, spotless and well-maintained room. Light came in from a window with a view of an alleyway. At the moment, none of that mattered. He needed a nap before venturing out.

Later that evening at a little café, Walker sat eating rijsttafel—an Indonesian dish of spiced rice, meat and vegetables—while he thought about his reasons for beginning his trip in Amsterdam. Back home when he had explained it to friends, he had said a number of things, all of which were true, but none of them the real reason. He had started here because of the Rosse Buurt—the red-light district.

The city's acceptance of prostitution made it one of the safest areas in the world to purchase sex. Having sex with a woman other than Marlene would be difficult and Walker wanted a safe, healthy and businesslike environment to start. The artistry and culture of Amsterdam provided the right setting to begin his sexual adventures and he decided to begin them shortly.

Nervousness set in just thinking about it, and Walker felt his heart pound, his palms begin to sweat and his breath quicken. To calm himself, he ordered a Dutch gin. The waiter brought the jenever and Walker finished it in one quick shot, then asked for another and the check. He paid the bill and left the café.

THE WORLDWIDE SEXUAL ADVENTURES OF WALKER FAYT

Strolling along some of the city's oldest canals, Walker tried to feel calm and relaxed, but tension mounted within him. Earlier visualizations of how it would happen did not include these emotions, and he realized now that following through would be harder than he had imagined. His fantasy unfolded and it quickly collapsed into a stark reality.

Soft, red lights emanated from open windows adorned by women clad in sheer lingerie. Some stood with their legs apart as the light shone through their translucent clothing. Others sat on the windowsills, their eyes inviting. Still others, fixing their makeup or nails, seemed bored and uninterested in potential business.

People that filled the streets did not catch Walker's attention. His focus stayed on the many women and how to choose. It was as though he were walking down an aisle in an airplane, making a complete assessment with just a glance.

From across the street, a woman wearing a short, black leather vest captured his attention. Her beautifully endowed breasts were barely covered by the open vest and her short, tight, red leather hot pants revealed a stunning figure. Knee-high black leather boots gave her that extra edge.

Walker crossed the street and as he got closer, he noticed tattoos, one on her shoulder and a smaller one around her belly button. Her pale skin contrasted with her long, wild, dark hair. Slowly he moved closer to the window she stood in. The light in the room behind her changed in a sequence of colors: blue, red, green and yellow.

While Walker watched her proposition a group of young foreign travelers, he noticed her many body piercings. The young men laughed and walked away and then the prostitute turned and looked at Walker. Without saying a word she put out her hand and moved her index finger with a "come here" gesture. Her eyes met his, increasing the intensity of the moment, and Walker found it difficult to hold the glance. A sickly, hot wave burned within his chest and he nodded his head, yes.

The leather-clad woman turned and walked away from the window toward a door at the back of the room, swinging her hips rhythmically as she walked. Walker viewed her incredible body and noticed that a partially exposed tattoo on her buttocks peeked out from the bottom of her short-shorts. He watched intensely until she left the room and disappeared from his sight.

In a few moments, a door to the outside opened and the beautiful prostitute stood framed in the red illuminated doorway with her legs apart and one hand on her hip. In a thick Dutch accent, she said, "Welcome to Amsterdam. American, yes?"

Walker nodded, nervously checked to ensure that no one saw them, then slowly stepped toward her. She turned and walked up a set of stairs, he right behind her getting a good, close look at her partially exposed tattoo and tight red shorts. Wildness flowed from her every movement.

Dim lighting along the hallway made it difficult for Walker to see and as his eyes adjusted, his heart pounded in his ears. She suddenly stopped and he lightly bumped into her, knocking his upper thigh into her tight behind. She pushed back with her ass, pressing it into his body.

Jokingly she said, "Can't you wait until we get into the room?"

When the woman opened a door, diffuse golden light surrounded them and as they entered the room, the aroma of licorice filled Walker's nostrils. She closed and locked the door, put her hands on his waist and in a deep, sultry voice said, "That smell makes me so horny."

The prostitute reached up, pulled her vest aside, exposing her firm, shapely breasts. She had small, dark, perky nipples, the left one pierced with a golden hoop. Leaning back, she let her wild hair dangle loose. As she arched her back as far as it would bend, her vest dropped off and fell to the floor.

Trembling, Walker looked this untamed temptress up and down. Sweat made his shirt stick to his skin; dryness in his throat made it impossible for him to speak. She came close, grabbed the top of his pants and pulled him tight. Her naked breasts rubbed against his midsection while she squeezed his right leg between her legs.

With her crotch pressed firmly against Walker's leg, she slid down until her face stopped at his belt. Backing away slightly, she slowly undid his belt and the top button of his pants and then pulled down his zipper. Walker looked up at the ceiling. His vision blurred, then he looked down at her as she began to speak.

"This will give you a sensation like you've never had before," she whispered huskily, and then flicked her tongue far out of her mouth revealing two studs, one near the tip and one farther back.

Walker's throat felt as if it had completely contracted. He could not swallow or breathe, and he thought he would faint, throw up or both. He reached into his pocket, pulled out about $100 in guilders and let it drop to the floor. In a raspy voice, barely audible, he said, "I have to go!"

Walker dashed for the door, unlocked it and made his way down the dark hallway. He heard laughter and the words, "Come back anytime!" Quickly he negotiated the red-lit staircase and the door at the bottom and then he was out on the street, where he gasped for a big breath of air.

Passersby stared at him, some horrified, some with concern and others with amusement. Walker stood there sweating profusely and taking deep breaths, too scared and confused to notice anyone else. After a minute or so, he realized that his pants and belt were still undone. He pulled himself together before making his way back to his room. Completely spent, Walker wrote in his journal.

RED-LIGHT DISTRICT

June 24

Bed and breakfast lodgings, Amsterdam, Netherlands

Is it possible that visions and revelations are just self-delusions? The question reverberates through my mind.

I will use "the power of the moment" to overcome my fears of living my revelations, and to sweep away the past. The notion of living just for each moment makes me stronger. I pray enlightenment will arrive and help maintain my strength.

Fully clothed, Walker crashed onto his bed and immediately fell asleep.

chapter 4

MONIQUE—A HANDS-ON SEX PROFESSIONAL
Charmed by a Passionate Belgian

As Walker took several deep breaths, the smell of coffee filled his senses. Could it have been a nightmare? He wished it had only been a bad dream. Awash in self-doubt and confusion, he contemplated his next move. Putting first things first, he cleaned up and went for breakfast.

Walker spent the morning in the Jordaan, the old French quarter of Amsterdam. Watching the water taxis float by on the canal, he relaxed and absorbed the activity around him. For the moment, he put aside the events of the previous evening. Often when faced with a problem, he would put it out of his mind by doing something either relaxing or strenuous. This usually allowed a solution to come to him and this strategy worked once again.

At the Dam, a broad square in the old section of town and the closest stop to Rosse Buurt, Walker got off the tram. Avoiding the spot from the previous night, he noticed much more about the general area. A multitude of sex shops, billboards advertising porn shows and cafés displaying a green marijuana leaf in the window lined the streets. Mid-afternoon light totally altered the ambiance of the previous evening, yet there were still women standing in the windows.

MONIQUE—A HANDS-ON SEX PROFESSIONAL

A sign advertising a "dating agency" caught Walker's attention. He observed many such places as he walked around; he decided he would investigate them. The first three agencies felt wrong—something about the decor or the initial contact person put him off the place. The next one he tried felt good. Pastel colors made it bright and cheerful, and fresh-cut flowers sweetened the air.

A striking woman in her early sixties stood behind the counter. An air of confidence and sophistication accompanied her movements, giving her a commanding presence. Walker concluded that she ran this agency.

Professionalism exuded from her as she looked at him and sensitively said, "Yes?"

Unable to break her gaze, Walker quietly said, "I need some help."

"Why, dear boy, that's why I'm here—to help you. Now, if you'd be so kind as to tell me what it is, I can see to it immediately."

Walker began to ramble. "I'm recently divorced . . . I've never been with anyone but my wife . . . I tried it on my own . . . it was bad, really bad . . . I need to do this . . . it's important . . . I'm not sure how to start . . . can I—"

"Yes, yes, yes, I understand," the woman cut in. "Calm down and don't you worry, I know just how it is. Your situation is not unique and I have the perfect solution. Do you trust my judgment in this?"

Walker nodded without saying anything. As strange as it seemed, for some reason he did trust her.

"Good! Go back to your hotel. Rest, bath, shave, have dinner and be back for eight tonight. We'll discuss more of the arrangement then. Everything is going to be perfect—okay? We'll see you at eight."

As Walker left, the telephone rang and the woman picked it up and conversed in what seemed to Walker to be perfect French. He then realized how impeccable her English had been.

THE WORLDWIDE SEXUAL ADVENTURES OF WALKER FAYT

Walker arrived at the agency at two minutes to eight and he looked very good. He had followed all of her instructions. The hostess from the afternoon, while speaking with another client, motioned for him to have a seat on the couch. He picked up one of the English-language magazines from the side table and pretended to read it. Outwardly cool and collected, his inside nervousness precluded reading, so he just looked at the pictures.

Over top of the magazine, Walker watched as the woman finished with the client and took a couple of phone calls. When she came around the counter to join Walker in the reception area, he stood to greet her and noticed her stylish, deep-green designer business suit, complemented by a crisp white blouse.

"Nice to see you again," she said, extending her hand. "I'm Madame Lisse—named after my hometown not far from here," and as they shook hands, "—and you are?"

"Walker, Walker Fayt. Pleased to meet you."

"Please follow me, won't you?" Lisse said as she turned and pushed open a door which led to a hallway beside the reception area.

As they walked, Walker noticed her style and poise. They entered a small meeting room. Walker's hostess sat down on a couch and crossed her legs, displaying bright-red pedicured toenails in her high-heeled shoes. He sat down across from her in a comfortable chair. Lisse smiled warmly and looked into his eyes.

"Let me do the talking. If I'm wrong, please correct me. You're an intelligent, sensitive man—with a purpose. You have come to Amsterdam to be with a woman because it is safe, healthy and acceptable. You need to get through this in order to move on with your life.

"Now, here's the plan. I have assigned an associate of mine to your case. Her name is Monique. She is from Brussels—young, sweet and just what you need. I spoke with her this afternoon, and she is anxious to meet you and get started with your program."

Walker sat silent and attentive as Lisse continued.

"For this to work properly, we must proceed slowly and build trust. What I'm recommending is a three-session program, with each session being one and one-half hours. You'll begin tonight at 8:30 and come back at the same time for the next two nights."

Looking at her watch, Lisse then said, "If this is acceptable to you and we can come to an agreement, your session will begin in . . . ten minutes. The agency would normally charge—" and she picked up a pen and paper that sat on the table beside the couch, wrote a number in big print, showed it to him and said, "—per hour. For all three one-and-one-half-hour sessions, I'll charge you this." She wrote a second number on the paper, displayed it, and added, "This is a thirty-percent discount from the straight hourly rate."

Finishing her pitch, Lisse said, "Of course, all of our associates are required to be checked regularly and must prove they are free of sexually transmitted diseases. The agency guarantees this, as well as complete confidentiality. I believe Monique is perfect for you, but if for some reason it doesn't work out tonight, I'll only charge you for an hour and you can try another girl or even another agency."

It all seemed reasonable—and definitely cheaper than tossing a pile of money on the floor and leaving abruptly. At this point, numbers were beyond Walker and he did not want to negotiate or think of other options. He tried to sound confident when he said, "No, no, I'm ready to go. The arrangement is fine. Thank you for your understanding and help. Where do I go?"

Lisse took a key out of her purse and said, "Go down this hallway. At the end you will find a stairway. Go up to the third floor, turn right and the key will open Room 311. Come and see me afterward. I'll be at the front desk."

Lisse dropped a key into Walker's hand. He followed her instructions and stood in front of door number 311. For about a minute, he took deep breaths and alternated between looking at the floor, the ceiling and the number on the door. Finally, he put the key in the lock, turned it and went inside.

Pale pink paint colored the walls, stuffed animals sat on shelves, photographs of colts running beside their mothers hung on the wall and classical music quietly played. The atmosphere of the room helped lower Walker's tension.

On a bed of white frilly lace, a beautiful young woman sat cross-legged with her heels underneath her. She wore a white linen nightgown covered with small teddy-bear prints. Delicately, she pushed down her nightgown so that only her legs were exposed.

"Hi, I'm Monique and you must be Walker," she said with the most exquisite French accent that he'd ever heard. "Have a seat." She patted the bed with the hand that wasn't holding down her nightie. "I'm here to make you feel comfortable. I know it's a little unusual . . . let's talk. Tell me about yourself."

Walker adored her accent and would have preferred listening, but she evaded his questions and prompted him to do the talking. After dealing with the usual topics of background, family and occupation, he eventually got to the real story and told her everything. Walker felt very relaxed.

They had talked for about twenty minutes when Monique smiled and stated, "Okay, enough talk. Now I'm going to give you a massage."

An unusual combination of crystal-blue eyes and auburn hair made Monique uncommonly attractive. Thick linen could not hide her firm, young breasts displayed prominently underneath the nightie. Reaching over, she undid Walker's shirt and put her hands inside, running them over his muscular chest. Then she slipped off his shirt and continued caressing his bare chest and shoulders while

MONIQUE—A HANDS-ON SEX PROFESSIONAL

gazing into his eyes. After this long exchange, she guided him to lie face down on the bed.

Walker became more relaxed with each muscle touched. Monique massaged his back and neck for about thirty minutes before rolling him onto his back. She removed his shoes and socks, unbuckled his belt, undid his pants and pulled them off. She then worked his upper and lower legs and by this time he had no doubts about her being a professional massage therapist.

Although the oil acted as a lubricant, the friction of skin on skin caused Monique's hands to become very warm. When she touched knots and tight spots, it felt particularly soothing. On some of the tighter spots she used her elbow to apply pressure, and when she did, Walker cried out in a good kind of pain. Next she rolled him onto his stomach and removed his underwear.

"This may hurt a bit," Monique warned. "Tension gets stored in the buttocks." She pressed firmly with her thumb into his gluteus muscle and began working on a knot the size of a golf ball. Then she used her elbow to exert more pressure, making Walker recoil, and said, "Now the other side." He mumbled a mild complaint.

Monique treated his arms and shoulders and the tension flowed out of Walker's body, causing a kind of physical and mental twilight zone. She had him roll onto his back and move so that his head rested at the edge of the bed. She caressed his face, head and ears with hands that were as hot as fire.

As she slid her hands down his chest toward his abdomen, Monique's nightgown fell onto Walker's face and he opened his eyes for the first time since the massage had begun. As she slid her hands back up his body, she stood up straight and he could see up her nightie to her cotton panties.

As Monique slid her hands back down his body, her nightgown again fell into Walker's face. This time, her reach extended to his pubic hair before she stopped and slid back up his body and stood up straight. Now she pulled him by the underarms, getting him to move until his head hung over the edge of the bed.

Monique straddled Walker's head and slid her hands slowly down his body, past his nipples, past his abdomen, past his hip bones, past his pubic hair to the base of his penis. With his eyes closed again, Walker sensed her nightie up over her panties and smelled her youthful freshness only inches from his face. His desire to taste her aroused him.

Hot, oiled hands stroking his penis brought Walker fully erect. Monique quickened her pace, which heated her hands even more and added to his excitement. With one hand she stroked the shaft of his cock while with the other she rough-handled its throbbing head.

Walker groaned loudly as semen spurted into the air with several large releases. He lay there exhausted as a tear escaped his eye and ran down his face.

Monique stood and proclaimed, "You're quite a man." She kissed him on the forehead, saying, "I have to go . . . I'll see you tomorrow night. Don't forget to see Lisse before you leave."

The door shut behind her. After remaining motionless for several minutes, Walker finally sat up and reached for a towel draped on a chair by the bed. He cleaned up, got dressed and then headed to reception and paid Lisse the full amount for all three sessions. Back in his room, he slept soundly until mid-morning.

Anticipation over his next session with Monique made it difficult to concentrate on points of interest Walker visited that day. Every few minutes she came into his thoughts, and he became aroused. He had triumphed in the first complete sexual experience of his journey and felt more alive because of it. His heightened sexuality attracted the women around him: he noticed friendlier smiles, longer eye contact and a brush on a crowded tram ride.

In the afternoon Walker visited the Schreierstoren or Weepers'

MONIQUE—A HANDS-ON SEX PROFESSIONAL

Tower, built in 1480 as place for women when their men were out at sea. It stood facing the harbor.

Walker watched the setting sun and thought about Henry Hudson setting sail from this very spot, in 1609, to the place that was now New York. Had a woman stood here, waiting for him to return? Walker stood at the base of the tower, wondering if a woman awaited his return. He wrote in his journal.

June 26

Weepers' Tower, Amsterdam

> Doctors, nurses, teachers, architects, lawyers, accountants, actuaries, engineers. These are all established professions made up of people who are well educated and trained in an area of expertise. They are recognized by society for their efforts and achievements.
>
> Professionals are expected to keep up to date with current practices in their fields so that they can understand their clients' needs and be providers of sound advice. They must be efficient as well as extremely competent in completing assignments, and must be able to solve problems creatively.
>
> As a reward for their efforts and abilities, professionals are compensated handsomely. And the better they are and the greater their reputation, the more they can charge for their services.
>
> Prostitution is often called the world's oldest profession. All the characteristics of a profession are present, and the factors determining success are the same.

At 8:25 Walker arrived at the agency. A younger woman who resembled Lisse—likely her daughter, he thought—ran the reception desk. Before he reached the counter or could say anything, the hostess held out a key and politely said, "Everything is ready, Mr. Fayt. You can go right up."

This demeanor impressed Walker and confirmed his choice in agencies. He followed the same route as the previous night, only this time he did not hesitate at the door. He unlocked it and stepped right in.

Monique sat on the bed in the same position as when he had arrived last time. Between her crossed legs, she held down a portion of her short, one-piece, navy-blue outfit. It fit tightly around her waist and flared out to a loose, pleated bottom. Shoulder straps connected the front and back and underneath it she wore an unbuttoned, short-sleeved white blouse showing enough cleavage to be innocently sexy. The whole look reminded him of a schoolgirl's uniform.

As before, the session began with them on the bed talking. Still taken by her accent, Walker asked her about it. More open than the previous night, Monique told him a little about her background.

Born and raised in Brussels, she had lived there with her parents until moving to Amsterdam. Her accent came from being a French-speaking Walloon—one of the two main ethnic groups in Belgium. The other was the Dutch-speaking Flemish. She could also speak Dutch.

Seductively, Monique pushed on Walker's chest until he lay flat on his back. Slowly, she undid his belt and pants button and moved him until his feet hung just over the edge of the bed.

With enchanting movements, she untied his shoes and removed them, as well as his socks. As she tugged on his pant legs, Walker arched his back and pushed up with his elbows, allowing her to remove his pants. He lay back, closed his eyes and heard her rubbing her hands quickly together. She touched his feet with incredibly hot hands.

The pressure Monique applied to his right foot with her thumb

MONIQUE—A HANDS-ON SEX PROFESSIONAL

hurt, and Walker flinched a little. She explained that the reflexes in the foot travel through ten zones of the body. Weaknesses in the body slow blood and nerve functions, creating deposits in the hands and feet.

Walker relaxed as she continued applying pressure to his feet. Monique resumed her explanation of the purpose of the treatment and he listened without any real interest in why or how it worked.

Breaking up the deposits restored both the nerve and blood supply to the affected areas. She told him that she would work all ten zones, but would concentrate on Zone 1, because it would indirectly stimulate his reproductive organs.

After forty-five minutes, Walker felt like gelatin. The pressure on his feet stopped and something warm, moist and pliable enveloped his big toe. Monique's tongue swirled and flicked while his toe remained in her mouth and she lightly tickled his feet and rubbed his calves.

Next she separated his legs by pressing on the inside of his ankles and then she kissed the inside of his right leg. Another kiss landed a little farther up on the left leg. She then kissed his right leg above the knee.

Each soft kiss ended with a gentle suck, and occasionally Monique flicked her tongue against Walker's leg. As she alternated between legs, she moved farther and farther up his body and he quivered and moaned involuntarily. His underwear restricted his hardened penis and she reached up and pulled them down.

Usually Walker's testicles were too sensitive to be sexually stimulated. Pain and fear of injury outweighed the reward of sexual contact. His caution vanished and he spread his legs wide, becoming completely vulnerable and exposed.

With the tip of her tongue, Monique caressed the underside of Walker's scrotum. He could barely stand the sensation and dug his fingers into the bed and rolled his head back and forth. His entire body tightened as she took one of his testicles into her mouth. When she released it, he uttered a sighed of relief, then violently retracted his breath as his other testicle entered her mouth. He thought that he was teetering between ecstasy and insanity.

Monique cradled Walker's testicles in one hand as her mouth moved to the tip of his throbbing penis. While flicking her tongue across its circumcised head, with her other hand she grabbed the shaft of his penis. Using both her mouth and hand, she rapidly increased the speed of the up-and-down motion on his penis and she gently squeezed with the other hand that still held his testicles.

After what seemed like a long time, Monique suddenly released Walker's balls, causing him to moan and shake uncontrollably. Just as he exploded, she removed her mouth from the head of his penis and watched him flow to physical ecstasy.

*

The next day moved forward with Walker just barely aware of it. In the morning he visited Rembrandt's house, but all the while his body ached for Monique's touch. In the afternoon, at the renowned Bloemenmarkt, he purchased a nice porcelain vase and an arrangement of fresh-cut lilies. The idea of buying beautiful things for Monique excited him. He arrived at the agency as if ready for an important first date. The young woman from the previous day cheerfully got some water and helped him arrange the flowers.

Walker knocked on the door and it clicked unlocked and swung open. Monique looked stunning. She was wearing a skin-tight, short black cocktail dress with spaghetti straps and black high-heeled shoes. Her physical beauty almost overwhelmed Walker and he found it hard to breathe.

"They're beautiful," she said as she came close, kissed him on the cheek, and accepted the vase and flowers.

The aroma of the lilies filled the room and Monique inhaled

MONIQUE—A HANDS-ON SEX PROFESSIONAL

deeply as she walked away from him to set them down. In her four-inch heels, her body swayed with enchanting femininity and Walker became aroused. Beside the lilies, an open bottle of champagne waited on ice. Monique poured two glasses and with the same charming motion walked back to Walker. With a smile, she handed him a glass and they toasted.

"Salut . . . compliments of Lisse," she toasted, as they both took a sip.

Monique pressed a button and slow dance music began to play. She set down her glass, then seductively took his away and put it beside hers. As they came together, their bodies touched in motion with the music. Walker kissed her hair several times and felt his hard penis rubbing against her rhythmically moving body. His desire for her pained him and his legs weakened with anticipation.

From the outside of his pants, Monique lightly ran her fingers along the length of his penis. In a voluptuous tone she said, "He's going to have to wait . . . tonight you are going to please me." She sauntered over to the bed, unzipped her dress, slid both straps off her shoulders and very slowly let it fall to the floor.

The sight of Monique in black high heels and tiny pink bra and panties increased Walker's desire. As she bent over and crawled onto the bed, she gave him an exquisite view of her cute behind. Then she went flat to her stomach, bent her legs at the knees and held them in the air with her high heels still on.

Walker moved to the bed and grabbed her by the ankles, spreading her legs. He didn't want to wait.

"No, no, big boy—I'm not ready yet. You can do anything you want once I'm ready. The massage oil is over on the shelf. It'll be worth the wait—trust me."

Before Walker poured the oil into his hands he rubbed them together briskly, creating heat with the friction. As he touched Monique on the upper back, she gave a sigh of pleasure. He didn't know what she expected and he tried remembering his own massage. As he attempted to duplicate some of her treatment, he realized from her sighs that she enjoyed receiving just as much as giving.

As Monique had done for him, Walker searched for the tight spots in her buttocks. He put his fingers underneath her panties and pulled them down her legs and over her shoes and she reached around and removed her bra. Arousal in her had moistened her panties and before tossing them to the floor, Walker brought them close to his nose to smell her excitement.

Monique's buttocks were soft, smooth and firm and she breathed deeply as Walker pressed hard, searching for tension spots. Finding none, he continued to massage her there because the motion of her body told him she enjoyed it.

She moaned, "Walker, I'm ready."

From underneath the pillow Monique pulled out a condom and handed it to him. She went to her hands and knees while Walker undressed. His excitement rose and he struggled opening the package and getting the condom over his pulsating member. She was still on her hands and knees, and he entered her from behind. Both their bodies rocked with pleasure, and the sensation was almost too powerful for Walker to contain.

Monique seemed to sense his approaching climax and pulled away. She rolled over, spread her legs, and lifted them into the air. The sight of her spread with high heels still on almost caused Walker to ejaculate, but he held on.

Gripping him by the penis, Monique guided its hardened head to her clitoris. She moaned, sighed and flailed her legs as she rubbed herself with the end of his penis. Her moaning found synchronicity with her body contractions, which became stronger and more frequent. Walker watched as her body shook with orgasm.

With a climactic sigh, she whispered, "Fuck me now."

With a slight thrust forward, Walker entered her again. He

pumped with vigorous abandon as she wrapped her legs tightly around him. The heels of her shoes scratched his back as he slid in and out in rapid succession. Sexual energy flowed between them and built into an inevitable crescendo. He stopped deep inside her and came with a loud groan.

Walker's softened self slid out of her as their sweaty and entangled bodies relaxed in exhaustion and pleasure. Monique quietly untangled herself and proclaimed, "I believe it's time to finish the champagne."

Their glasses touched softly in an unspoken toast and they finished their wine in silence. Monique got dressed, and the post-copulative glow made her even more attractive than before. Walker sat naked as she began to talk.

"The first night I used my hands, the second night I used my mouth and tonight I used my vagina. Do you know why we did not make love on the first night?"

After a long pause, Walker answered quietly, "Because you needed to gain my trust."

Monique smiled, nodded and then headed toward the door to leave.

"Wait!" he shouted.

She stopped and he continued. "I'm leaving by train for Brussels tomorrow at noon, and I'd like to see you before I leave." Monique left the room without a reply.

Several times the next day Walker imagined that he saw Monique or heard her calling to him. He took one last look around before boarding the train. With one foot on the ground and one on the first stair of the train, he felt a hand pull on his arm. He turned to see Monique. She looked stunning and sweet in a one-piece yellow sundress.

"Will you mail this letter for me in Brussels? It's to my parents. I haven't written them in a while."

commitment and fidelity that we call marriage.

The concept of fidelity, or faithfulness, began before recorded history and it is now doctrine in the major religions and is firmly entrenched as a social standard.

In societies throughout history, most of which have been male-dominated with women and children considered to be possessions, the notion of fidelity has helped connect children to the male power brokers of society. It has also reduced the number of unclaimed and therefore unwanted children.

In a viable way, fidelity has helped to preserve the species.

Walker arrived at Waterloo Station and, with a great deal of help from Londoners, found his way to Paddington Station. He would be leaving from there in the morning, so he checked into a small hotel nearby. That night he slept comfortably and dreamed of Monique. Her youthful beauty, her accent, her sexual treatments all blended together and touched him like a balmy breeze.

The train left early for Stratford-upon-Avon. Walker's cousin James had a son, Nigel, who was getting married there, and Walker had been invited to both the stag and the wedding. Walker enjoyed quietly watching the English countryside roll by. The pleasant scenery and the relaxing motion turned his thoughts to his British relatives.

Walker's mother's sister had married a Brit and moved to London before he was born. When Walker was ten years old, his aunt and her family visited them in New York. He remembered getting along best with his cousin James because they were the same age; his other two cousins were older.

James and his family were Walker's only near relatives outside America. Walker had contacted James while making travel plans and James had extended the invitation. This gave Walker an opportunity to connect with family that he really didn't know.

Walker's great-grandparents, on both sides of the family, were from England. This meant he did have distant relatives in England; however, he had no intention of searching for them as part of this trip.

Walker understood that issues get passed between generations. He thought that surely his mother and aunt shared common traits, and he considered whether the influences of his American grandparents were still at work in himself and James.

As the thought of generational influences went through Walker's mind, involuntarily he thought about his mother. The way she reacted to the world around her sometimes puzzled him. He relaxed his mind and thought deeply about his mother: an image of a frightened little girl, emotionally abandoned, formed.

Walker sensed that as a child his mother's source of love was also her source of pain. For reasons unknown to him, he believed that she had lost her mother's nurturing at a young age. His mother had buried the hurt deeply within her and carried it forward. This had had consequences.

Now when the ones that loved his mother most did not behave exactly as she wanted, her old feelings of abandonment immediately resurfaced, frightening her. As a means of protection, she reacted with emotional outbursts. He remembered her unbelievable tantrum when he and Marlene did not react as positively as she had expected to a minor dinner invitation. He now understood the source of that behavior.

Walker had arranged by telephone the night before to meet James at the train station. British and American cousins made a friendly reacquaintance. James had booked him a room at the Shakespeare Hotel, picked because of its proximity to downtown and the theaters. *Twelfth Night, The Merchant of Venice, The Tempest* and *Measure*

THE WORLDWIDE SEXUAL ADVENTURES OF WALKER FAYT

for Measure were playing, and Walker planned to see at least one comedy and one tragedy during his stay.

After Walker had checked in and freshened up, they drove to James' house, a modest but charming detached bungalow. James' wife, Linda, greeted Walker with a friendly handshake and apologized that Nigel's two older brothers and their families were crammed into the house and they couldn't possibly accommodate him as well. Warmly accepting her apology, Walker said he was quite pleased with the way the arrangements had worked out.

James introduced Walker to his two sons and their families: Thomas, his wife, Catherine, and their four-year-old daughter, Anne; Richard, his wife, Elizabeth, and their one-year-old son, James. Pride shone in James at the continuance of his name.

Nigel still lived in town, unlike his two older brothers, who had moved to London. James was also the youngest of three boys and Walker thought that perhaps the generational parallels strengthened the connection between James and Nigel. Could a strong bond with his father have kept him from moving away?

While thinking about Nigel, Walker inquired as to his whereabouts. It seemed that custom required that, on the day of the groom's stag, drinking with his mates start early in the day; by the time the stag began, Nigel should be drunk.

*

James, Thomas, Richard and Walker went to the stag together. Nigel, and many of his friends, arrived pumped-up and intoxicated, arms around each other and whooping and hollering. For Walker it brought back memories of his college days. James tried introductions, but it was not much use.

A few of the young men took an interest in Walker because he was an American. They engaged in ridiculous, drunken conversation. There were cheers to political allies, and to the success of the

PATRICIA—THE REMARKABLE STRIPPER

Gulf War. There were tales about beautiful Hollywood actresses. Arguments broke out over which actress would be the best in bed.

One story that Walker found particularly amusing had occurred at a stag a few years ago. The groom had had so much to drink that he passed out. His friends, some of whom were telling Walker the story, bought a one-way ticket to London, carried him onto the train and left him with no money and no identification.

The poor chump woke up in London not knowing where he was or how he had gotten there, and with no means to get back to Stratford in time for his wedding. He begged on the street and raised enough money to make a phone call to his father, who then drove to get him. He ended up being late for his wedding by two hours and was in very rough shape for the entire day.

As it turned out, the groom did not speak to his friends for an entire year after the wedding. Walker inquired about the bride. A moot point, they replied, because they hadn't been on speaking terms with her even before the wedding! The story got a big laugh, as did Walker's joke about taping a twenty-pound note to Nigel's ass.

After an hour of constant and heavy drinking, many of them staggered and slurred their words. Nigel had trouble being coherent. James didn't like it, but knew it was inevitable. James and Walker seemed to be the unofficial overseers and were not pressured to keep up with the pace of beer consumption.

The best man yelled for everyone to take a seat around a makeshift stage and went over to the stereo and put in a cassette. The music burst forth loud and heavy, with a steady bass backbeat. In the drunken atmosphere, only a few people noticed and took seats.

Into the roomful of intoxicated, rambunctious men strutted a girl in leather boots, hot pants and a halter top, all of it in white. She stepped with a lot of attitude, completely at ease with the crowd.

THE WORLDWIDE SEXUAL ADVENTURES OF WALKER FAYT

She jumped onto the stage and began to gyrate seductively. The guys yelled and whistled as they took seats around the raised platform. Walker and James stood back and watched.

The dancer moved with power and agility, and after the first song, yells and chants of "Take it off!" became constant. She smiled, unfazed by the taunts and the fists that pounded the stage.

During the second song, the woman's moves became increasingly unbelievable. They included getting her feet behind her neck; bending her legs backwards and touching her head with her feet while arching her back and rolling on her stomach; walking on her hands with her legs apart; balancing herself with one hand; and doing the complete splits hard into the floor. These moves captivated the men and the "Take it off!" yells ceased.

As the third song began to play, the dancer crawled to the edge of the stage. Keeping her knees on the stage, she leaned down and put her hands on either side of Thomas' chair and positioned her mouth directly over his crotch.

"She's blowing hot air on my dick!" Thomas yelled out.

At once almost everyone shouted a demand for the same treatment and she performed similar maneuvers on five others until the music stopped. When the next song started, she unzipped her pants and threw them to the back of the stage. Underneath she wore a tiny G-string.

For this dance, she kicked her leg high into the air and held it straight up with the help of her hands while balancing on one foot. Then she dropped to the floor and violently slammed her crotch repeatedly into the stage. The entire platform shook; it seemed that the whole building was about to topple. The power of this fake fucking sent the room into a frenzy and she continued this action until the song ended.

As the music started again, the young woman removed her top and pranced around the stage in boots and G-string. She tugged and

PATRICIA—THE REMARKABLE STRIPPER

pulled on her right nipple until it extended about an inch and a half from her breast. Then she did the same with her left nipple. She showcased her pointy, extended nipples by sticking out her chest and parading around the stage. Screams of appreciation rang out.

Next she took in a deep breath, stuck out her chest even more and slapped herself hard just under her left breast on the ribcage. The extended nipple shrank to its normal size. Then she slapped her other side in the same place and that nipple shrank too.

Heads shook in disbelief, as if no one in the room had ever seen anything like this before. The hired dancer repeated this oddity several more times, and each time was more amusing than the last. When the song ended, she asked for a lit cigarette. There were many offers and she accepted two of them.

The music resumed. Massaging her nipple, she pinched it, extended it and then pushed it inward. In the concave space of her inverted nipple, she placed the filtered end of the lit cigarette and held it there. Then she did the same with her other breast. With two smoking cigarettes sticking out from her breasts, she promenaded about the stage, proudly showing off her trick.

At the end of the song, she stood at the edge of the stage in front of the first cigarette donor. As before, she slapped her ribcage. This caused the nipple to pop back out and fling the cigarette into the air. It flew away from her and fell into the owner's hands; he put it back in his mouth.

Sauntering over to the second donor, she commanded, "Now it's your turn. Are you ready? Catch it—only this time in your mouth."

It seemed as if everything happened in slow motion. She slapped herself hard, the cigarette popped out of her breast, her nipple reappeared and the cigarette rotated through the air and landed in his mouth, lit end out. A boisterous standing ovation erupted.

A hard-edged tune broke the applause as she pushed her breasts together and domineeringly stood before the best man. She dropped to her knees, leaned forward over the edge of the stage, grabbed the back of his chair, and slapped his face with her breasts. Cheers and pleas were heard everywhere.

"Where's the groom?" she called out as she looked around.

All his mates pointed to Nigel. He had missed the entire performance because of an alcohol-induced stupor. His eyes were puffy and almost shut and he barely maintained consciousness.

The performer crawled over to him, bent over the stage, put her hands on either side of the chair and was about to blow hot air on his crotch. Then a huge smirk came over Nigel's face. He stood up slightly by bracing himself with one hand on his chair, leaned over top of the girl and touched her in the crotch area from behind with his extended middle finger. The crowd recognized the move as being incredibly deft for someone who could not walk and many cheered him on.

"Nobody touches my twat!" the performer yelled into Nigel's face. She quickly slapped him twice across the face and three times on the side of the head.

Nigel's head bobbed with the blows, but the smirk never left his face. "I just did . . . baby."

A few of Nigel's friends jumped in to stop any further physical abuses and the room filled with uncontrolled laughter.

Regaining her composure, the stripper continued with the show. To prove there were no hard feelings, she asked Nigel to come up on stage. He could not do so on his own, so with help from many friends he was seated on a chair on stage.

Undoing the top of his pants, the woman peeked in and held her fingers up to display a two-inch space and shook her head disappointingly. She indicated by waving her hands in front of his face that he needed to cool down. Next she picked up a glass full of ice and poured it down the inside of his pants.

Nigel didn't react in the slightest. She seemed at a loss as to what

PATRICIA—THE REMARKABLE STRIPPER

to do next, and stood back just looking at him. Nigel fell off the chair, hit the stage floor with a thud and lay there passed out with the same smirk still on his face. This ended the show.

The food arrived shortly thereafter and everyone ate to absorb the alcohol. While the stripper put on her street clothes, the best man invited her to stay for a bite to eat. Many of the young guys hung around trying to start up a conversation by saying, "Great show," "You're amazing," "It's unbelievable what you can do." She just smiled and acknowledged their praise.

In jeans and a sweatshirt, she looked like the unassuming girl next door—cute, nice brown eyes, five feet six inches tall, mousy-blond hair. She stood in an area that led out of the room and away from all the drunken activity. Her looks did not intimidate the young men, but her performance had and nobody approached her as she ate her food.

Walker went over to where she stood, leaned on the wall beside her, and said, "You're quite a talent. Do you have an agent?"

"Why, thank you. No." She smiled and looked him straight in the eyes and said in a tone indicating she joked as well, "Are you looking for clients?"

"No. I'm a relative here for Nigel's wedding. I have no doubt that they'll be talking about this evening for a long time."

"So you're not from Britain then?"

"Ah, the accent. No. I'm from the States."

"Do you think my act would be a smash over there—in America?"

"I don't go to places that offer your special kind of entertainment," Walker said, smiling. He paused and then added, "But I believe that you would be extremely popular. How could you not be? What you do is unique."

"I don't get much work. I'm sure if I went to London I could, but I won't go there. Actually, I've never been to London. Big cities scare me. I'm originally from Skegness, a small town on the coast," and she looked at him for a reaction.

"I can understand that. When I was a boy I lived in New York City and I know that big cities can be cold, scary and unforgiving places. It all depends on how you look at it. They can also be alive, exciting and ready to fulfill your dreams. It's just different sides of the same coin, and sometimes it's all in the luck of the toss."

In a formal tone that by its very nature also had a hint of light-heartedness, Walker stated, "I don't know London at all. However, it would be a pleasure and an honor if you would accompany me around London. We could discover the city, safely, together. Hi, I'm Walker Fayt. It's a pleasure to meet you."

The dancer extended her hand and they shook and as the greeting ended, in a tone that matched his, she said, "Hello, I'm Patricia." Then her speech became more hesitant as she continued. "I don't know. You seem nice enough and everything, but I did just meet you at a stag."

Walker looked into her eyes and saw an attraction to his words. He surmised that she understood that success from her act would only come in the big cities. He wanted to help her if he could.

Nodding his acceptance, he stated, "I understand." Then he asked, "What are your plans for later?"

"I need to make the trip worth my while, so I've agreed to do another show for the hotel. I'll be finished by about ten. Then it's the train back to Oxford. That's where I live now. I'd rather not travel by myself that late at night, but I have no choice."

Again in his formal, light-hearted tone, Walker said, "To prove I'm an honorable man, how about this: I'll meet you here after the show. We can go back to my hotel room and have a late dinner. I'll sleep on the floor and you on the bed. In the morning, we'll have breakfast together and I'll take you to the train station. It's not much time together, but it may be enough to consider my offer about London."

Walker changed his tone back to its normal manner and continued. "I'm staying here for two more days after the wedding, then taking the earliest train back to London. You could—"

Patricia finished his thought: "It goes through Oxford en route to London, and I could meet you on the train."

"Yes," he replied. "If you want to face your fear of big cities, you can meet me on the train. I'll try and make it safe and relaxed for you. Think about it. I'll give you my phone number at the hotel and you can call me with your decision—one way or the other.

"If I don't hear from you, I'll look for you to board in Oxford and if not, *c'est la vie*. Excuse me. I have to help my cousin get Nigel home. He's taking a vow of marriage tomorrow."

As Walker turned and headed back into the room, he heard her say, "All right then, I'll see you at ten."

chapter 6

I TRUST YOU—WILL YOU TRUST ME?
In Idyllic London, Love's Labors Heal a Painful Past

James and Walker got Nigel cleaned up, undressed and into bed. It had always been the plan for Nigel to spend the night at his parents' house. All of his friends liked Bridget, his fiancée, so an urgent call from London a few hours before the wedding was not likely to occur. Nevertheless, no chances were being taken.

Seeing her son in a drunken stupor displeased and distressed Linda. She worried about his condition for the next day, one of the most important days of his life. They were supposed to be looking out for Nigel. Why were his pants so wet, had he peed himself? Did he need a bath before being put to bed? Linda demanded to know.

Being the guest and a recent inductee into the family, Walker escaped the brunt of Linda's anger, but James did not. Walker took the lead in reassuring Linda that Nigel was fine. He explained that Nigel might have a slight headache in the morning, but otherwise he'd be all right. It looked worse than it was, and Nigel might even be up for a late dinner.

Catherine and Elizabeth wondered where their husbands were, if they were drunk, and if there had been any women at the party. Seeing Nigel's condition made them nervous. James and Walker

I TRUST YOU—WILL YOU TRUST ME?

downplayed the events of the afternoon; they explained that Thomas and Richard had been assigned the responsibility of wrapping things up and would be home soon. Walker told the wives, in a joking manner, that drunkenness was a relative state, one that they could assess for themselves when their husbands returned.

Catherine asked again, "Dad, Walker, were there any women there?"

James replied in a nonchalant way. "Just one. Nothing. Really."

"Why are men such pigs that they have to see other women naked?" Elizabeth blurted out. "What's so exciting?"

"It's disgusting," added Catherine.

Walker inquired, "Have you ever gone to a male strip show?"

"Yeah," said Catherine.

Elizabeth quickly interjected. "But just in good fun, for a few laughs."

"So was this," he responded, "and I don't believe for a minute that women are any more or less serious at these events than men."

Before the conversation could heat up any further, Anne ran into the room and stumbled with excitement, "Uncle Nigel sounds like a big animal."

Linda smiled and said as the others chuckled, "He's snoring." Anne giggled with the rest of them. This broke the tension nicely, and the previous topic did not resurface.

Still full from eating at the stag, Walker declined the late supper that Linda and her daughters-in-law were preparing. Nor did he want to be there when Thomas and Richard arrived to face their wives. He decided he would go to the theater.

Back at his hotel, Walker changed and arranged for dinner for two to be left in his room. The kitchen closed before the play ended and he wanted to be sure to keep his promise to Patricia. He ordered food that could be eaten cold, and a bottle of good red wine. Walker wrote in his journal before going out.

THE WORLDWIDE SEXUAL ADVENTURES OF WALKER FAYT

June 29

Shakespeare Hotel, Stratford-upon-Avon, England

Humans are at a point where mixed evolutionary messages are causing problems.

Our biological drive says to reproduce, reproduce, reproduce and this gets translated into sex, sex, sex. Most human males cannot control or direct their sexual interest in females. From a biological perspective, the drive is built-in and is indiscriminate, functioning at the reptilian level of our brain structure. Is this a social curse or biological salvation?

If you put any heterosexual male on a deserted island with any female, eventually he will want to have sex with her. However, in the socialized setting where fidelity rules, the human male must fight against the low-level, automatic instinct of attraction every second that he is around a female. It's very difficult because this attraction takes place on both a conscious and an unconscious level.

In general, women do not share men's instinctual desire for indiscriminate sex, and therefore do not understand or accept it. Reference to men as "pigs" when discussing their desires for sex is acceptable in our society. Most everyone wishes this situation were different; unfortunately, it is not. Men's sexual drive is also at odds with the religious and social custom of fidelity.

Now that technology can take care of reproduction, are we on an evolutionary road that will do away with the biological need for copulation and the desires that come with it? Imagine what could be achieved if our brains were released from the distraction of sex.

Or, are we on the road to the complete abandonment of sexual restrictions? Sexual repression has been the custom for a long time. This has affected the human psyche, producing an

I TRUST YOU—WILL YOU TRUST ME?

abundance of misunderstanding, misery and suffering. Collectively, we need solutions.

At the theater, pyrotechnics that would have been considered sorcery in Shakespeare's day made the opening storm scene of *The Tempest* memorable. After the show, Walker strolled over to the pub and waited outside for Patricia's performance to end.

Around ten o'clock, Walker heard whistles, claps and cheers coming from the pub. Shortly thereafter, Patricia came through the front door wearing the same jeans and sweatshirt as when he last saw her. He felt the energy charge from her performance flowing from her. Having witnessed her act first hand, he understood how it might take some time to come down. Her energy made her attractive and exciting to be around, and he tried not to let it show.

"How was it tonight?" Walker asked, feigning calmness.

"Oh, fine. I'm always amazed at the reaction I get," she said enthusiastically.

"You shouldn't be, but it's nice to see that you are. Try not to lose that." Walker didn't tell her where they were going as he headed toward his hotel.

"When did you get interested in this type of performing?" he asked.

It seemed to him that she debated with herself whether to tell the truth or whether to give a common, polite answer. After a long hesitation, she responded.

"I became sexually active at a young age. . . . My first experience happened when I was seven, the next at around ten."

"Patricia, you did not become sexually active at that age, you were molested. Do you remember who it was?"

"No, I don't really remember. I know it wasn't my dad or brothers. I don't think it was a relative, either; maybe a neighbor or friend of the family." She paused between phrases, trying to remember.

THE WORLDWIDE SEXUAL ADVENTURES OF WALKER FAYT

"Are you okay?" Walker asked tenderly, noticing her hesitancy, but not the cause. He thought it was due to the difficult subject matter.

"I'm fine with the discussion. It's just that I don't know where we're headed. Do you?"

When Walker mentioned the hotel, Patricia nodded and said, "Nice place. I've been in the hotel but never performed there. Perhaps it's too upscale for my type of show."

Walker wondered whether most strippers thought negatively about what they did, and whether it required low or high self-esteem to take one's clothes off in front of a room full of people. Not just anyone could do it. He concluded that the profession likely had people at both ends of the self-esteem spectrum.

After walking several minutes in silence, Patricia resumed the discussion.

"At this point in my life, I don't regret what happened. If anything, it has freed me from a lot of sexual hang-ups that I see other people struggling with. I have no doubt those early experiences are the reason that I'm able to dance and want to dance.

"At a young age, I touched my body for pleasure and experimentation to find out just what it could do. I may never have done that if somebody else had not done it first. I'm a dancer and very uninhibited sexually. Perhaps without those early experiences I would be a frigid secretary . . . I don't know."

"Your attitude is unbelievably positive. I'd like to string the bastard up who did those things to you. I have two daughters and if I thought that anything like that had happened to them . . . Your dancing and sexual freedom may be a defensive pattern you've developed to protect yourself from the pain of what happened."

"I don't believe that's true. I like where I'm at with myself and I feel good about it. All I need is to get over my fear of big cities and I'll be set. That's what this is about, right?" She took his arm in hers.

They were in front of the hotel and before they went inside, Walker perked up. "Absolutely, but first you have to trust me. . . . After you," he said as he held the door open for her.

A small, portable table on wheels and two chairs were visible in the dim light of the room. The wine had been left corked; a single, fresh-cut red rose adorned a small, clear vase on the table and silver lids covered the dinners. Thoughtful touches; he would leave the waiter a good tip.

Avoiding eye contact, Patricia spoke softly. "I appreciate your effort to make me feel special. It's very sweet. If this mood continues, I may hope that you go back on your word as a gentleman."

During dinner, Walker talked about his family and his life back in Appleton, as well as his revelations and his decision to follow them. More recent experiences, such as his failed attempt at sex in Rosse Buurt and his sessions with Monique, also emerged.

"I have a hard time believing that you have only been with two different women in your entire life," Patricia said. "You must have had many women trying to get you into bed. Why refuse?"

Walker did not understand all parts of himself or all the influences affecting his behavior. He wished that psychic communication were possible, so he could use it at this moment. Short of that, he knew he could not get her to understand him. He thought that perhaps it was not the successful explanation of self that was important, but the attempt to explain. With that in mind, he began exposing issues he had not thought of in years.

Strong Christian beliefs and values formed a part of his family's heritage. Both his parents, especially his mother, were active in their local church. Puritanical ideas that the human body was a place of evil and that pleasure was a temptation of the Devil were powerful concepts that still affected him, his family and his country.

Puritanism helped define the creation of America. As a historian, Walker understood the connection between the past and present, and the direct influences that such concepts had had on his life. But understanding did not make it easier to accept, and Walker wished he could be more liberal in his attitude toward sex, love, relationships and marriage.

They talked until one in the morning and then Walker made himself a place to sleep on the floor with a couple of blankets and a pillow. He washed up, brushed his teeth, stripped down to his underwear and a T-shirt and lay down in his makeshift bed. Patricia had a small travel bag with her and she took it into the bathroom. After a few minutes she came out and removed her jeans. Without taking off her sweatshirt she removed her bra and crawled into bed.

"Good night. Are you sure you'll be comfortable on the floor? I don't mind if—"

"I'll be fine. Good night," Walker said with a gruff tone of finality in his voice.

Shortly after eight in the morning, Walker woke up stiff and alone on the floor in the hotel room. Patricia had wanted to catch an early train home and must have boarded the 8:05 to Oxford. He took a shower, dressed and went to James and Linda's for breakfast. Excitement infused the household.

Stories of the stag and post-stag activities were retold in humorous snippets as Walker tried on James' best suit and shoes. The two men were close enough in size and the clothes fit. James would wear a rented tuxedo. The women looked lovely in pastel-colored dresses and the men handsome in black tuxedos. Anne looked angelic in a white lacy dress, white stockings, black patent-leather shoes and flower-bedecked hair. She felt proud to be both flower girl and ring bearer.

Throughout the rest of the day, the bride, the groom, the wedding party, family and guests all played their parts perfectly. Holy Trinity Church, along the Avon River, hosted the wedding, and the reception took place at a hall nearby. At about half past ten, the newlyweds left by limousine for London. They had an early morning flight to Spain, but for the rest, festivities continued well past midnight.

Over the next two days, Walker toured the town and attended the matinées of *Twelfth Night* and *The Merchant of Venice*. He spent some quiet time with Linda and James as their house emptied on Tuesday. They all got to know each other a little better. After their second evening together, Walker got out his journal to write.

July 2

Shakespeare Hotel, Stratford-upon-Avon, England

"All the world's a stage, and all the men and women merely players . . ."

The words are by William Shakespeare, from his play As You Like It. Individuality as mere nuance of a predetermined role may have been Shakespeare's truth about our existence and destiny, but I find the concept too confining.

For me the world is a mirror, and everything reflects back our inner selves, revealing what the world is to each of us. This includes our opinions and how we feel about everything that physically and mentally touches us.

Whether a person doesn't understand, doesn't care, dislikes or likes a painting, a sculpture, a book, a movie, a play, music, architecture, a dance or a television show is a reflection of the individual. It's not about the actual work of art. Art is nothing without our reaction to it, and yet our reaction to it means nothing about the work itself and everything about ourselves as the observer. Art and the individual form an interesting symbiotic relationship.

Critics of art fascinate me, because art cannot be discussed in the absolute. Critiques and reviews are really statements about *the critic's personality and not about the art. The same can be said of historians. Since history cannot be known in the absolute, its telling is always a reflection of the historian.*

Experience has taught me that every comment, every criticism, every judgment made about another person reveals volumes about the person making the statement and very little about the person to whom it's directed. This, too, is an interesting symbiotic relationship.

Listening to what people say about other people is one of the best ways to understand them. Listening to what I say about other people is one of the best ways I get to know myself. It's treasure hunting in an unexpected place.

For Walker's last night in Stratford, Linda and James treated him to dinner and a show. They saw *Measure for Measure*, and afterward said their goodbyes. In the morning, they were back to work and Walker was on the first train to London.

While trying to fall asleep, Walker thought of Patricia. She hadn't called or left a message. Fantasies kept him awake. Images of her flexible body and comments about uninhibited sexuality sent rushes up his spine to the back of his head. His hair seemed to tingle—a strange and delightful sensation. Eventually he fell asleep.

*

Thirty miles of anticipation had Walker edgy. Thoughts from the previous night remained and intensified. His breathing increased and his heart pounded and his palms became clammy. He remained unsettled as the train pulled into Oxford. A crowd waited on the platform for the train to stop. He searched through the faces to find Patricia. He had been so sure she'd be there, but now he felt doubt and disappointment. People filed into the car, but she was not among them.

Walker unzipped his daypack and took out the *Times*. He hoped

I TRUST YOU—WILL YOU TRUST ME?

his attempt to read would distract his conscious thoughts from sexual images of Patricia. He tried to read, but he did not comprehend the words.

Ten minutes out of Oxford, a ticket collector stopped at Walker's seat and handed him a small, feminine-looking, lavender envelope. Walker opened the seal and pulled out a matching sheet of paper. Delicately handwritten on it were these words:

> *I thought about our night together. You were thoughtful and considerate. It was very special for me.*
> *I know I can trust you to help me. Do you trust me to help you?*
> *If you do, then come to the car behind you.*
> *Otherwise, I will see you in London.*

Getting up, Walker tossed the newspaper onto the empty seat beside him, not thinking about what Patricia meant by trusting her to help him. Feelings of disappointment and rejection instantly switched to excitement and joy. Such a quick swing in emotions reminded him of being a child.

Patricia stood at the back of the car in a sheer, loose-fitting, pale-green, spaghetti-strap sundress that stopped about two inches above her knees. She wore white open shoes with a low heel. Dark-blond hair hung loosely to her shoulders and her fit, five-foot-six-inch body looked like a crackerjack ready to pop. Across the full length of the car, Walker saw the formation of her hardened nipples in the sheer material of the dress.

Upon seeing him, Patricia's expression changed to one of concern. She pointed sideways to a door, opened it and went in. Walker strode down the aisle without looking at anyone, his intent focused solely on Patricia. "Toilet" marked the door where she had gone in, and a latch bore the lit word "Vacant." He opened the latch and stepped into a freshly cleaned washroom. It had not been used, as that car had been reserved for passengers getting on in Oxford.

Walker began saying, "What's this all—" but before he could say the word "about," Patricia planted on him a hard, passionate, wet kiss and her fiery tongue slipped into his mouth.

Between kisses and breaths she managed to say, "You're going to help me get over my fear of cities. If I'm sexual and comfortable, my fear won't have a chance to take hold. Your sexual tension will make me nervous. We have to get rid of that. Despite your inhibitions, you may come to like it!"

Before Walker could respond, Patricia reached up, put her hands on his shoulders and pushed him to sit down on the closed lid of the toilet. She pulled the straps off her shoulders and let her dress fall to the floor. Except for her shoes, she stood naked before him. Then she pinched both her nipples at once, massaged them and made them erect. Immediately she dropped to her knees and blew hot air through his pants onto his penis.

Walker remained seated with knees spread as Patricia stood up between his legs. One of her legs went up on his shoulder and she inched forward, placing her pubic hair close to his face. She extended her leg straight up from his shoulder and held it in the air with her hands and then leaned forward slightly. Her soft, pink flesh pressed into his face. To give her more balance, he reached out and placed his hands around her hips. In the same instant, he lowered his head and slipped his tongue between her moist labia.

With the extra balance, Patricia thrust her pelvis forward and held the position of one leg on the ground and one leg pointing to the ceiling. Then she rocked her pelvis, as his tongue movements became quicker and deeper with each of her thrusts. Tasting her pleased Walker and he became hungrier for her sweetness as it covered his mouth, nose and chin.

Walker stopped her thrusts by pushing on Patricia's hips and then slowly, gently worked his flicking tongue up to her clitoris. When he lightly skimmed it, she moaned and her body shook, but she held her position. As he circled her clitoris with his tongue, her body pulsated and her breathing became short and quick. "Yes, yes, yes . . . ahhhh." Her leg dropped hard onto his shoulder. Juice and sweat dripped everywhere and he licked up as much as he could.

In a seductive voice she said, "Now it's your turn."

Patricia sat on the edge of the sink and watched while Walker slipped off his shoes, undid his belt, unzipped his fly and in one motion pulled his pants and underwear off. He went to her fully erect. She put a condom over his penis while she continued to sit on the edge of the sink. Then she wrapped both legs behind her head, which stretched open her vagina. Grabbing his penis with both hands, she guided him inside her.

Patricia's vagina felt hot, lubricated and tight. With his hands on the mirror behind the sink and his arms at either side of her, Walker inched ahead until she had it all. They moaned and gazed in each other's eyes with a stare too intimate and intense for first-time lovers to hold. Walker closed his eyes and began rocking in and out. The motion of the train set a natural rhythm until it became too slow to contain his wild thrusting. Walker's stimulation mounted toward the final few strokes before ejaculation. He backed out and then plunged back in, and on the way in she grabbed his head at the temples in both her hands.

"Walker, look at me!" Patricia shouted.

Walker opened his eyes and looked straight into her eyes and both their souls reflected back at one another while he came.

The businesswoman waiting for the washroom refused to look at either of them when they left. They had been about fifteen minutes, and Walker wondered why she hadn't gone to a washroom in another car. When he realized she had been listening, he blushed. Patricia collected her small carry-on bag and they headed for the seats in his car.

As they sat down, Patricia patted his arm and quietly said, "Now don't you feel better? I know I do. We'll be much more at ease when we arrive in London." Still blushing and recovering, he nodded his head in agreement.

Patricia felt safe on the train, but as it pulled into Euston Station, she tensed up. He took her hand and squeezed it, reassuring her. "I'm right here. I won't leave you. Everything is going to be fine."

They rounded up their baggage, took a taxi to their hotel close to Royal Albert Hall, checked in and unpacked.

Walker reasoned that if Patricia could connect with works of beauty, it might change her perspective of the city. He planned to start their tour of London with the National Gallery, which had a reputation as having one of the finest collections of art in the world.

Since Patricia felt apprehensive about leaving the hotel, getting her to the north end of Trafalgar Square, the busiest square in London, presented a challenge. On the taxi ride over, she put her head in Walker's lap while he stroked her hair. Often he brushed his hand over her ears to distract her from the loud sounds of the city. At one point, the cabbie indicated that just in case anyone needed to see a doctor, he knew of clinics close by. Walker thanked him for his concern and assured him that it wouldn't be necessary.

Once inside the National Gallery, it took about twenty minutes before Patricia stopped trembling and could view the paintings. They provided the perfect therapy. Paintings from the Italian Renaissance seemed to have the most profound effect on her. Works by Rembrandt, da Vinci, and Rubens also calmed her. They stayed until the 6 p.m. closing and the effect of the art carried her through the trip back to the hotel.

On the way up to the room, Walker read a notice on the hotel's bulletin board. Due to a change in the queen's schedule, Buckingham Place would be open for public tours for the next two weeks. Ordinarily, public tours were only available during August

I TRUST YOU—WILL YOU TRUST ME?

and September, but the first two weeks in July had been exchanged with the last two weeks in September. The fortuitous change elated both of them and they planned a visit for the following day.

*

Less pensive than the day before, Patricia asked Walker not to wear any underwear. He wondered with anticipation what she had planned for him and he complied with her request.

During the taxi ride, Patricia again rested her head in Walker's lap. They arrived at eight in the morning for the tour that began at half past nine. When the Palace is open for two months straight, during the touring hours a steady stream of visitors parades through. For this special circumstance, however, only thirty people at a time were permitted entry. Walker and Patricia were about twentieth in the queue, so they were assured of getting in.

They first visited ornate nineteenth-century staterooms used to entertain heads of state. There seemed to be an endless number of these rooms, varying in size. Some rooms could hold several hundred for dinner and others fewer than twenty. The guide informed the group of the many important people, both living and dead, who had attended dinners in each of the rooms. Various artifacts were singled out and their historical significance explained.

In one of the smaller rooms, as the rest of the tour filed out, Patricia pulled on the back of Walker's shirt so that he could not walk away. Once everyone had left, she closed the door and locked it. At the back of the room Walker observed doors on either side of the room—probably leading to service corridors.

"What are you up to?" he hesitantly asked.

Patricia responded by flicking off her shoes and removing her dress. On a beautiful oriental carpet, she danced completely nude. Massaging her nipples, she stretched them and made them completely erect. Walker looked nervously around the room and back at the doors several times; eventually he became mesmerized by her seductive dancing.

Patricia dropped, face down, onto the carpet, arched her back, grabbed her feet and rocked like a rocking chair. In a fluid transition she then moved to a sitting position with her legs behind her head, exposing her vagina to him. Unlocking her legs, she spread them as wide as possible and lifted herself off the ground, balancing only on her hands and then gracefully went to a handstand.

Letting her body fall face down to the floor, Patricia exhaled. "This feels so good!"

Lightly at first, then with terrific force, she slammed her pelvis into the carpet and moaned slightly. Her breathing became heavier and several times she paused and rubbed herself into the carpet. Arousal in her stirred similar desires in Walker.

Next Patricia climbed onto the nineteenth-century dining table. While kneeling on the table she grabbed her nipples, massaged them and pushed them inward. This peculiar ability fascinated Walker all over again. He pulled out a chair and sat down in front of her.

Breathing deeply, Patricia inhaled as much royal air as her lungs would hold. Imbibing the history of the English monarchy seemed to make her very hot. Sexual desire filled the room and she gazed into his eyes, and he into hers. They became transfixed.

Leaning over the edge of the table, Patricia put her inverted nipple close to Walker's mouth. Arching his head up, he kissed and licked her breast. Probing around the cusp of the inverted nipple with his tongue, he pushed its tip into the space. Gently, he poked in and out several times. Its soft tenderness felt strange and wonderful and her body shook with pleasure. She slapped herself hard on the ribcage and inside his mouth her nipple popped out to its regular shape. He sucked and bit the nipple with his lips and it became hard and erect.

I TRUST YOU—WILL YOU TRUST ME?

Patricia backed away and slapped herself on the other side, causing her other nipple to pop out. Using his thumb and index finger as a tool, she rubbed and pulled her nipple, making it enlarged and extended. With his other hand, he opened the zipper to his black jeans and let out his pulsating, hard penis.

Patricia crawled headfirst down his body, rubbing herself against his member. When her hands reached the floor, she stopped and whispered, "Fuck me now, Walker."

First Walker put on a condom; then he grabbed Patricia's thighs with his arms and lifted her torso as he stood. In a wheelbarrow position, he moved farther up her thighs and spread her legs. He pushed himself inside her as she tightly squeezed her legs around him. She walked forward face down on her arms as he walked with her, ensuring he stayed inside her vagina. Using her arms, she rocked her torso back and forth as he exaggerated the motion by jerking her legs back and forth. Sweat formed on his brow as the sexual and physical exertion continued. Moving about the room in the wheelbarrow position, they moaned and grunted.

The teeth of Walker's zipper grated against his penis as it thrust in and out. It hurt, but not enough to stop. An orgasmic shiver rippled through Patricia's body and she screamed out uncontrollably with pleasure. Walker, completely exhausted and gasping for air, pulled out, ripped off the condom and came forcefully onto her buttocks and up her back.

They had been away from the tour for about thirty minutes. When Walker and Patricia rejoined it, the guide did not lecture them, but she gave them a very stern look. At the first opportunity, she took them aside and explained that they should always stay with the tour. Walker elucidated that he desperately needed a restroom and didn't have time to ask permission to leave the tour. His dark pants hid the wet spots, but the smell of sex was still noticeable. Suspiciously, the guide nodded her head and did not push the matter further.

After the tour, the couple ate lunch at a small outdoor café and then went to the Houses of Parliament. Walker took pictures of Patricia in front of both Victoria Tower and St. Stephen's Tower, the home of Big Ben. They spent the final two hours of the afternoon at Westminster Abbey.

In the middle of a conversation, Patricia stopped and said, "I need to get back to the hotel room—and quickly."

Walker hailed a taxi. He held her tightly in his lap as she sobbed and shook uncontrollably all the way back to the hotel. After a hot bath and tea, Patricia lay in bed underneath the covers. He sat on top of the bed and they held hands.

"You should let it out. Tell me about it," Walker said.

"I think being exposed to my country's history has caused my personal history to surface. I know who did it. It's all come back." She sighed and took several deep breaths. "It was a friend of my father's. Twice our family visited his home. Both times his wife went out with my mother, father, and brothers while he stayed at home to watch his daughter and me. He followed me into the bathroom . . . ."

Patricia gasped for air; tears poured out of her eyes as she covered them with her hands. "The bloody bastard said if I told anybody I'd be taken from my family and would never be able to see them again . . . . He lived in London. It happened here in London."

Compassionately, Walker leaned over to hug her and give her reassurance.

"No . . . I'm sorry, I can't be touched right now," her voice quivered.

"I understand. It's okay to feel the way you do. There is no need to be sorry. I'm here if you need me. You're safe here."

Patricia cried herself into a restless sleep. Walker had difficulty respecting her wish not to be touched. He wanted to hold her and make it better.

I TRUST YOU—WILL YOU TRUST ME?

In the morning they lingered in bed and ordered room service. At about 10:30, Walker suggested that they spend the day in Kensington Gardens and Hyde Park. They made it just in time to see the queen's guard—the Household Cavalry—return in full regalia from their march though Rotten Row, Henry VIII's royal path that runs along the south side of the park. Once his private hunting grounds, the park now served as a peaceful, green oasis and they retreated there from the busy streets of London.

The wounds of Patricia's past were too close to heal with discussion, so they did not speak of them. Instead, they acted as any couple might on a first or second date and enjoyed a beautiful day in a lovely setting together. At the moment, the natural, tranquil environment served as therapy.

Patricia insisted that they swim in the Serpentine, a small S-shaped lake in Kensington Gardens. According to the story, Peter Pan lived on the small island in the lake. They waited until dark, then swam naked after hiding their clothes in bushes. After a sunny day in the park, the water refreshed them. In the darkness, on the very small island in the Serpentine, they made love. That too was part of her therapy.

With Patricia sleeping beside him, Walker thought of patterns begun in childhood that determine behavior for the rest of a person's life. Having sex in public places and in a way that mirrored her on-stage performance protected Patricia from having to become aware of her first sexual encounters, which were dirty and secret. Her fear of coming to London and eventually all big cities was an automatic defense against the tragedies of the past. Sexual liberation became her shield. In light of recent discoveries, Walker wondered if she would connect her painful past to her current behavioral patterns. Should he mention his thoughts to her?

Patricia was helping Walker stretch his mind as well. What defensive patterns and shields did he use? Before he met her, he would never have considered sex outside the bedroom. The idea of two people getting what they needed from each other without either person losing anything made him smile with appreciation.

In the remaining two days together, they visited many of London's tourist spots: Shakespeare's Globe, Tower Bridge, the Victoria and Albert Museum, St. Paul's Cathedral and the Tower of London. The Crown Jewels were housed in the Duke of Wellington's Barracks at the Tower of London. The largest cut diamond in the world, set in the Royal Scepter, and the three thousand precious stones set in the Imperial State Crown shone back at them. A moving belt ushered tourists past glass showcases housing the Crown Jewels and Patricia took numerous trips, trying to satisfy her visual desires. Walker noticed she looked flushed, as if her other needs required attention.

Patricia hurried them to the White Tower, the oldest and most distinct building in the Tower of London complex. Crossing into a roped-off stairway, she found the way to a room full of medieval armor. Among the metal-plated defenses of centuries past, she enacted her private/public performance. Before they left the room, both had achieved two orgasms.

After Walker's second climax, Patricia sighed, "I've been rescued in the Tower of London by a white knight."

On their last morning together, they went out for an early breakfast. Both of them admitted that they were sad to be leaving each other, but also that they were excited about the future. Patricia decided to leave the past where it was and, at least for now, would not seek justice. No longer fearful of big cities, she planned to find a booking agent and hoped her show would find broader and more lucrative audiences in London and perhaps other cities in Europe.

Patricia wrote her Oxford address on a napkin and handed it to Walker. Her train left at 10:30 that morning and his plane for

Stockholm at 11:15. With little time between his flight and her train departure, they could not see each other off and kissed goodbye outside the hotel. Walker smiled and watched a tear roll down Patricia's cheek as they parted.

chapter 7

FANTASY MEETS FANTASY
'If a Swedish Woman Likes You, She'll Go To Bed With You'

Thirty-four thousand feet over the North Sea, headed towards Scandinavia, Walker reminisced about his youth. For investment bankers like his father to land the top jobs, they needed contacts all over the world, a predisposition for international finance and a grasp of cultural differences. His father had accepted a transfer from New York City to Toronto, Canada.

Walker remembered objecting to the move and angrily informing his parents that in two years, when he was sixteen, he would move back to New York, back to "civilization." Since he had to start a new school regardless of the move, his parents didn't understand his reaction. Beforehand, they had been more concerned about Tracy. She had completed two years of high school and now had to switch. She didn't fuss at moving.

Strongly entrenched religious influences made Tracy conservative in her behavior. Peer pressure to partake in sex, drugs and drinking were prominent in her life. Walker had seen the interactions with her friends and knew that she felt uncomfortable among them. Every day her friends participated in activities she wanted no part of. Moving to Toronto and changing high schools provided an

FANTASY MEETS FANTASY

escape from the increasing ridicule and the increasing pressure on her. He kept that knowledge about her to himself.

After thoroughly researching Toronto-area high schools, Walker's parents had selected a Catholic boys' school and a Catholic girls' school. With their stricter discipline, uniforms, same-sex classmates and theology courses, these schools provided a better overall education, his parents believed. Before finalizing enrollment, therefore, his parents obtained signed documents excluding the children from Catholic ceremonies such as mass and confession. Family members were Christians but not Catholics, and that distinction remained important.

The choice of schools had made the move even more distasteful for Walker, but once school started, he quickly found new friends. The bonds of friendship that he developed there remained some of the strongest in his life. Most people that he knew did not retain strong friendships from high school, and he felt fortunate to have done so.

Timothy Cantrell and Walker Fayt met in homeroom on their first day of Grade 9. They became friends and had remained so ever since. They had not spoken much since university and had seen each other only twice in the last fifteen years, but neither time nor distance seemed to affect their friendship. Tim and his family lived in Stockholm.

As a university student, Tim traveled to Europe during his summers. He graduated as a structural engineer from Queens University in Kingston, Ontario, and obtained professional experience at a firm in Montreal. Specializing in international projects allowed him to travel extensively on business. It seemed that both as a student and in his career, Tim wanted to be somewhere else and date women who didn't speak English.

In his third year at the engineering firm, Tim met Teegan Larsson, an engineering student from Sweden. The firm employed her for the summer as part of an international exchange program to promote cooperation between Canada and Sweden. A torrid love affair began that lasted for the summer. Then she went home.

During subsequent telephone conversations, Tim pretended to be fine and continued dating other women. Walker knew that Tim hadn't gotten over her. Eventually love prevailed, and Tim quit his job in Montreal, moved to Sweden and married Teegan. They now had a ten-year-old boy and an eight-year-old girl.

Tim and Teegan's wedding coincided with the annual graduation ceremony at Appleton West, and after considerable internal debate, Walker decided to stay and see his students graduate. Now he relished the chance to pick up his friendship and to meet Tim's wife and two children, Markus and Nora. As the plane descended, he thought about the roots that he and Tim shared and hoped that they remained strong.

Finally the plane landed at Arlanda International Airport. Walker picked up his baggage, cleared customs and immigration, stepped through the doors to the arrival area, and found Tim waiting for him. All smiles, they embraced tightly and rocked back and forth as they hugged, laughed and called each other by nicknames that hadn't been used in over twenty years.

During the twenty-five-mile ride into the city, they discussed their younger days, and each had stories the other had forgotten. They talked about teachers, girls and stupid things the group of guys they hung out with had done.

"We were such immature assholes. I can't believe we all made it past twenty alive. We should have been dead from our stupidity—"

"Or from someone killing us," interrupted Walker.

This triggered a memory and Tim jumped back in. "Remember that ridiculous theology course on marriage, taught by that crazy math teacher?"

"Yeah, the whole theme of the course was not to have sex before

FANTASY MEETS FANTASY

marriage—and you yelled out, 'What if it's too late?' That got you a detention."

"Well, I wasn't as bad as you. Remember, you got three detentions for looking backwards and saying so the whole class could hear, 'Close your fly, I can smell your wife.'"

Walker tested Tim's memory: "Do you remember what prompted me?"

"Sure. Hayward told the story of his wedding night. He was so proud that he and his wife were both virgins. The point he wanted to make was that having no sexual history was the best way to begin a marriage."

"Right so far—I can't believe he told us this. Do you remember the rest of the story?" Walker asked.

"Are you kidding? I'll never forget it. Hayward says his wife came out of the washroom in her nightgown and knelt on top of the bed. Presumably, Hayward was under the covers waiting for her, although he never gave those details. She put her hands together, looked up to heaven and said, 'This is my body . . . this is my body . . . ,' a reference to the consecration of bread and wine at the Eucharist."

Tim began to gather steam as he recounted the story. "Just imagine it—the only way she could bring herself to fuck him was to think of her deflowering as the mystical conversion of bread into the body of Jesus Christ. Amazing. At this point the whole class had books in front of their faces trying to hide their suppressed laughter."

"I just said it to break the tension—and you're wrong; I got a week's worth of detentions," Walker corrected and they both laughed.

"How about the time we all went to the beach for the May two-four long weekend?" Walker said, starting a new story. This one had taken place on the May 24th holiday commemorating Queen

Victoria's birthday. "It rained the whole time and we were stuck in those tiny cabins with nothing to do but drink and smoke up. Every time Billy got the joint, he leaned over and flicked the ash down the back of a girl's pants. She didn't notice for the first five times, and even her friends were laughing."

Tim said with anticipation, "Yeah, yeah . . . I vaguely remember."

"When she finally noticed, she yelled, 'Fuck off, asshole,' and slapped him several times across the face. Billy deserved it. But remember, he got a sad and defensive look on his face and then in a crying tone of voice replied, 'What? What's wrong? I thought you were a hosebag.' Unbelievable."

"Oh man, we could go on for weeks just telling stories about the old days." Tim sang, "'Glory days they'll pass you by . . . glory days in the wink of a young man's eyes.' They were fun times, weren't they?"

"Yeah. Things change so quickly, and it's impossible to keep life that simple. They're good memories. But I don't want to go back and act that way; I could never recapture that feeling."

Tim replied, "Even if you wanted to and gave it your best try, at your age they'd lock you up." His tone changed now from joking to a more serious one. "But wait a minute, isn't that what you're doing now, trying to recapture your lost youth?"

Tim didn't let him respond. "I did my traveling in university; you haven't really traveled until now. When you called and told me you were getting divorced from Marlene and setting out to travel the world, I assumed it was to fulfill long-lost dreams. If I hadn't done it when I was younger, gotten it out of my system—"

"Tim, you still travel a lot."

"I do, but now it bugs me; I'd rather be home with my family. Besides, we were talking about you."

Hesitantly, Walker said, "There are very few people I have told this to and all have been women. Even though you're one of my best

FANTASY MEETS FANTASY

and oldest friends, I'm a little reluctant to tell my story to a chauvinistic engineer. You guys are the worst."

"Oh, fuck off. Give me a break," Tim replied and began a tirade. "What do you expect? I'm a Catholic—a religion where women can't be priests, and until I was six they had to wear hats in church to ensure that something was between them and God. There were no girls at high school, and in engineering, chauvinism is part of the curriculum."

"I can see you're a little sensitive about it. How have you adjusted to this land of social democrats?" Walker said sarcastically.

"I'm trying hard. So why don't you let me show off my newly developed, right-brain sensitive side and explain yourself."

As they pulled into the driveway of Tim's home, Walker finished telling his story. "I don't believe what I'm doing is about the past; it's about the present and the future."

Tim concluded the discussion by saying, "I've been inspired. Hell, at times I've been a creative genius in coming up with solutions, but I have never experienced the raw intensity of the things you've described. Here comes my sensitive side. Walker, my friend, I think you've come to the right place. In Sweden if the girls like you, they will fuck you. There's no sexual games, no bullshit."

It was late and Tim showed Walker to the spare bedroom in the basement. Next morning, not yet accustomed to the time difference from London, Walker awoke and got dressed. Light poured in from the above-ground windows, although the clock in his bedroom read 4:30 a.m. He sat on a comfortable couch in the family room outside his bedroom and read a book titled *The Missing Link: Egyptian Pharaohs to English Kings* for about two hours until he heard rumblings from above.

Fifteen minutes later, Tim came downstairs and commented, "I thought you'd be awake. Sleeping in the light takes some getting used to. It won't get dark the whole while you're here. I remember my first summer—I'd go and play tennis at three in the morning just because I could. . . . The coffee is made. Come sit on the back porch while Teegan and I get ready for work and make breakfast. The kids won't be up for a while."

The thermometer outside showed eighteen degrees Celsius. Time passed quickly as Walker read his book and drank coffee. Tim and Teegan stepped onto the back porch. Teegan's blond shoulder-length hair hung loose onto a smart dark-blue suit jacket with matching pants, which fit her slender five-foot-seven-inch frame just snug enough to show her womanly curves.

Walker stood up and shook her extended hand. "Hi, nice to meet you, it's nice to finally meet you . . . ah, forget this," he said, releasing the handshake and giving her a big hug.

Looking over to Tim and flashing a big, bright smile, Teegan said, "Your friend Walker is friendly . . . and you never told me he was so tall and handsome. I like him." Her English was very good through the Swedish accent.

Walker blushed from the compliment as Tim patted him on the back and put his arm around Teegan, saying, "Come on, you guys, not at this time of the morning. Let's go in for breakfast."

Although Tim had successfully mastered Swedish, both languages were spoken in the household and for Walker's sake they used English for most conversations. Nora and Markus seemed to actually enjoy practicing it.

Ordinarily the children attended state-funded childcare programs in the summer. But for the three days until the weekend, Walker insisted that he take the children any place they desired. He knew that going to places that children enjoyed would provide him with a good introduction to the city.

Before leaving for work, Teegan told the children to behave and to listen to Walker. She then said something in Swedish, and by the tone he understood she had said she loved them. Tim lightly gripped Walker's shoulder and wished them all a fun day, while Teegan kissed him on the cheek and handed him the keys to her late-model Volvo station wagon. She and Tim would drive to work together for the next few days.

Gröna Lund Tivoli, Stockholm's only amusement park, was the first day's destination. It had traditional rides and many attractions, and Walker enjoyed spending the full day there with Markus and Nora. It brought back many memories of when Petra and Amy were younger.

That night, after Markus and Nora went to bed, Walker told their parents what great kids they had been. He and Tim stayed up late, rejuvenating their friendship. In many ways, Tim would always be an outsider in his new homeland. Even to his daughters he would speak with an accent and be a foreigner. Connecting with Walker seemed to provide something that was missing for him.

Tim recalled the time in Grade 10, during swim class, when he and Walker had fooled around for the entire period. As the class filed into the change room at the end of period, Tim and Walker had jumped back into the pool. They hadn't seen Jensen, the phys-ed teacher, and thought he was elsewhere. They had been wrong.

After the class had taken showers, Jensen demanded that Tim and Walker take cold showers and come into the teachers' change room naked. He made them bend over and lean onto a bench with their butts in the air. Jensen took hold of a hard styrofoam flutter board, raised it over his head, and jumped into the air, smacking it onto Tim's bare ass. The crack of the impact rang throughout the locker room. Then the teacher hit him again. Tim didn't utter a sound.

As Tim retold the story, Walker recalled the anticipation of the moment. His turn was next and he braced himself, determined to be as macho as Tim and remain quiet. Walker took his two hits and began to walk away, and then Jensen called him back. In Jensen's opinion, he deserved another whack for being the instigator.

In the student change room, the rest of class joked and teased them. The echo of the impacts had been heard by all and both their asses were bright red. Both Tim and Walker played it down, saying, "It wasn't that bad," and, "It didn't hurt at all."

Everyone knew it had hurt, but in the pattern of male bonding, none of their classmates challenged any of their claims to the contrary. They had taken their punishment like men and earned the respect of their peers because of it. Due to the extra smack, Walker got a little more respect than Tim did.

"Can you imagine if that had happened today?" Walker asked.

Quickly Tim responded. "Jesus Christ! The fucking teacher would be fired and probably sent to jail."

"Yeah, I suppose there'd also be a multimillion-dollar lawsuit against the teacher, the school board and the minister of education."

Tim reflected, "Boy, have times changed. Do you think we're any worse off because of it, or the other shit that happened there?"

Walker thought about it for a while. "Nah . . . but times do change and that kind of crap isn't acceptable any more. Can you imagine our kids being treated like that? There's no fucking way."

"Fuck the legal route, I'd probably kill the bastard myself. But it does make for good stories." Tim smiled and laughed. Judging by the look on Tim's face, Walker speculated that Tim was remembering other tales from their youth.

The next day Walker and the children went to the Junibacken, a fairy-tale house based on the stories of Pippi Longstocking, an irrepressible character created by Swedish writer Astrid Lindgren. Markus and Nora especially liked this place. Expressions of joy lit up their faces as the trio traveled through the grounds in small, quaint carriages. That night, Walker had dinner with the family and after dinner he and Tim stayed up chatting.

FANTASY MEETS FANTASY

On their third day's outing, the threesome went to the Skansen. There they found displays of more than 150 full-sized, reconstructed traditional buildings from all over Sweden. There was also a zoo with native Scandinavian wildlife such as elk, wolves and lynxes.

At four o'clock they arrived back home. Teegan had arranged a baby-sitter for five, giving Walker time to shower and change before going to meet her and Tim downtown. On Friday evenings, people from Tim's firm met after work for drinks and snacks. Usually spouses and significant others joined the group, and Tim had invited Walker.

The gathering took place at Café Opera. Its location on the waterfront of the Kungsträdgården in the center of downtown made it popular with Stockholm's suit-and-tie crowd. Unsure of its exact location, Walker parked and asked for directions.

Walking, he passed people playing chess on giant boards with giant chess pieces and he joined the small crowd of onlookers. A bold or interesting move provoked open discussion. Walker's lack of understanding of both the game and the language excluded him from participating in the debate.

Upon entering the café, Walker immediately noticed the bar reputed to be the longest in Sweden. Scanning the crowd, he saw Teegan waving at him to come join them. Introductions were made in English.

Tim's popularity was high among his co-workers, and his profile within the firm meant he had to spend time socializing with his colleagues. This gave Walker and Teegan the opportunity to spend the first hour or so in exclusive conversation. They had a common bond in Tim and it made sense that they too should connect.

The talk centered on love, marriage, relationships and parenting. In Walker's experience, most people had difficulty discussing serious personal matters in a social setting, or when they didn't know someone that well; not so with Teegan. She discussed matters close to her heart in an easy, caring manner. He realized that Teegan lived his desire to be honest and direct in conversational exchanges.

Tim came up from behind them and put his arms around both of them. "I'm glad you two are getting along so well. I wasn't really worried, but sometimes you never know."

"Walker's a good listener and speaks from the heart, so of course we get along," Tim's wife said, smiling at her husband.

Tim squeezed Walker a little and said jokingly, "Boy, have you changed. I don't think I like you any more."

Teegan suggested, "No matter, I believe Janna likes him. She's been looking this way for the past hour and seems truly infatuated. I think introductions are in order."

Tim called out to a blond woman sitting with a group of his co-workers, "Janna, I'd like to introduce you to someone," and waved her over.

As Janna stood, Walker's pulse quickened. Ever since adolescence he had fantasized about being with a woman his height and size. When he and Marlene were together and a tall woman gave him a flirtatious glance, she'd say softly, "Settle down."

Confidently, Janna approached them. Her short hair set off her bright blue eyes and fair complexion. She wore a white long-sleeved blouse, trim medium-blue slacks and open blue shoes with a thick two-inch heel. Tim introduced them and in her heels Janna stood just a little taller than Walker. He thought that without her shoes she must be at least six-foot one; that made his heart skip a beat and it also put a lump in his throat.

Walker's excitement flowed out of him, and when he shook hands the electrical and sexual energy crackling between them became almost visible. They blushed at the embarrassment of having Tim and Teegan witness it.

To break the awkwardness of the moment, Tim cleared his throat

FANTASY MEETS FANTASY

and spoke up. "We're not going to leave you two alone just yet, so can I freshen up everyone's drinks?"

Tim took the drink orders and left Walker with the two women.

Teegan began the conversation. "Janna is an executive assistant in the firm; she works with Niklas, one of the senior partners." Walker nodded as Teegan continued. "She is also a member of our national volleyball team and has played in the Olympics. She is one of our most aggressive spikers."

"Oh yes, I'm feared around the world," Janna said sarcastically, but with also a hint of truth. Looking directly into his eyes, with the sparks still flying between them, she asked, "How do you know Tim?"

Dryness in his throat made Walker's voice crackle as he said, "We're old high-school buddies. We've known each other since we were fourteen." He drank the last sip of his mineral water, which helped his voice return to normal. "I'm traveling and wouldn't have missed coming to see Tim and Teegan, and I've had a few days of fun with the kids."

With all the power of Venus, Janna asked, "Can you stand to have some more fun?"

Walker's chest went tight with his next breath. Tim arrived with the drinks and handed them out. Then he fanned his face with his hand, acknowledging the flirtation going on.

Teegan interrupted this by saying, "Walker, tell us one of those amusing stories from high school. Tim has told us many, but we've heard them several times. I'm sure you must have some fresh ones."

Walker thought for a moment. "Have you ever heard the Father Ron recruitment story?" Teegan and Janna shook their heads, and a big grin came over Tim's face.

"Father Ron, the administrative clerk for the high school, considered it his job to try and recruit every student, in their senior year, into the priesthood. It must have been a thankless job, but it was one he considered necessary. Everyone knew the pitch would come and waited for their turn."

Tim added, "You were exempt, of course, since you weren't Catholic, but still I'm surprised he didn't try."

"Tim's turn came at the most inappropriate moment. We both played on the school basketball team and one Friday night after a game there was also a school dance. You can picture the scene: a local band, kids from many different schools looking for some fun and excitement."

Tim added, "You have to remember, back then we were young and foolish."

Teegan interjected, "Yes, we know. Things haven't changed much, except now you're older. Let him finish the story."

"Thank you, Teegan. We showered and changed, and then met some other friends who weren't on the team out in the parking lot. Our friend Matt had an old van, just two seats in the front and completely empty in the back. As usual, there were about twelve of us crammed into the thing. The beer and joints flowed. After half an hour of non-stop smoking and drinking, we returned to the dance. You can imagine our condition."

"We all reeked of pot and beer," blurted Tim.

"Yes, it wafted off us so thick you could almost see it—no, I think perhaps you could see it. As soon as we came through the door, we saw Father Ron. Silently, we all said at once, 'Oh shit.' He spoke in a very serious tone, 'Mr. Cantrell, may I speak with you a moment.' It wasn't a question, but a demand. What we couldn't understand is why Tim had been singled out. Obviously, we were all guilty."

Tim commented, "I was drunk and stoned, or 'droned' as we used to call it, and very paranoid. I could have been expelled."

Walker continued. "Father Ron put his arm around Tim's shoulder and directed him down a hallway, away from the rest of us. At that range, he must have been getting high from second-hand fumes.

FANTASY MEETS FANTASY

Tim looked back at us—his eyes were bloodshot and through the red we could see a look of panic. Tim, go ahead, please; it's always better to hear it first-hand. I can't believe you haven't told this one."

Tim picked up the story. "I don't remember exactly what he said, but it went something like this: 'Tim, as you know, the priesthood is always looking for fine, outstanding young men like yourself—men who set a good Christlike example for others to follow. You may never have considered it before, but I know you would make an exceptional priest.' He turned me around so that we were facing each other. He then said, 'Please, Tim, give it serious consideration, won't you?'"

Janna broke the silence. "I know it wasn't yes, but what did you say?"

"I had difficulty comprehending that this was 'The Talk.' I had been expecting to be in deep trouble. I felt relieved and confused at the same time. As seriously as I could muster, I said to him, 'You know, father, my mother used to pray every night for one of her sons to become a priest.' He then patted me on the back and said, 'My son, make your mother's prayers come true—join the priesthood. Now, go on back to your dance."

Walker said to Tim, "You bastard, I never heard that part of the story. For all these years, you held back the good bits." Then he looked at the women and said, "Tim ran back into the dance and found us. Immediately, we wanted to know what was up; the questions flew fast and furious. Did he smell it on us? Did he know we were high? How much trouble was Tim in? Did Father Ron want to talk to anyone else? Tim, smiling like the Cheshire Cat, said, 'I just got "The Talk,"' and we all burst into laughter."

After the story, Tim and Teegan excused themselves to go mingle. Once left alone, there were no barriers to contain the natural sexual attraction between Walker and Janna; it bubbled over into their conversation, body language and eye contact.

Walker learned that Janna had worked with the engineering firm for eight years. Her leaves of absence for Olympic training and travel were accepted both because she was good at her job, and because a nationally known athlete brought the firm prestige.

At twenty-nine, she was the oldest member of Sweden's national women's volleyball team and near the end of her competitive playing career. Her maturity, aggressive play and personal confidence made her the natural team leader. She confided to Walker that when she decided to retire from play, the coaching job awaited her. It would mean less earnings and she'd miss the people and the social aspects of her current job. However, she could stay involved in the sport she knew and loved.

Janna explained that coaching also had a potential financial upside. If the team did well internationally, promotional deals could be in the offing. No Swedish volleyball player had ever signed such a deal; however, it was becoming more common with athletes of other sports. Janna's good looks and confidence were traits sought after in spokespersons. She knew that usually the star players got those kinds of deals and not the coaches, but she thought she still had a chance.

Walker advised her that she should follow her heart and the financial issues would work themselves out.

"I've been struggling to reach a decision for some time now," Janna responded. "I have discussed it with no one. Even my parents and close friends—"

"Don't worry. I understand . . . it's confidential. I won't mention it to anyone. If you do decide to coach, the firm will be sorry to lose you, but they'll understand. You'll have their support."

A flirtatious look returned to the Swedish woman's eyes as she gazed directly into Walker's and said, "I feel so much better now. It was good to talk to someone about my problems." She looked down and continued. "Not that they are really problems. I should be more

FANTASY MEETS FANTASY

positive about my opportunities," and returned to the eye contact. "I feel that you have helped me, and that I can trust you completely. Can I trust you completely?"

In the moment it took for Walker to answer, many thoughts swirled together in his mind. He had never been asked that question by anyone. To be asked it by a new acquaintance seemed strange, but to be asked it by the embodiment of a long-standing unfulfilled sexual fantasy, put it way over the top. As well, Tim's remark of a few days ago, "If they like you, they will fuck you," rang loudly in his head. Could he even trust himself to answer honestly? He broke their gaze and looked away.

The American once more established eye contact and replied, "Yes, you can trust me."

"Then I'm taking you out for dinner. Not here, though—we wouldn't get the privacy I want. Sweden invented smorgasbord and I know of a great place not far from here."

They said their goodbyes to everyone. Teegan and Tim were on their way out as well and offered him the car for as long as he needed it. Tim made a crack about not waiting up, but leaving the lights on.

The expensive restaurant was located in the elegant Opera House. They dined on the veranda, since the main dining room was closed for the month of July. It appeared to Walker that many of the businesses in Sweden were on vacation. With the good weather, in a pristine environment where even in the downtown areas the water was clean enough to swim in and to eat the fish from, it seemed natural to take time off to enjoy it.

The food, the conversation and the atmosphere made for an enchanting evening, although Walker felt that these were just surface stimulants and that something much deeper had a grasp of both of them. A strong, pure, basic desire for one another eliminated their need for elegant verbal communication. This feeling continued throughout dinner and remained with them on the drive to her house.

Admiring the peacefulness of the late evening as they stood on the patio at the back of her apartment, Janna took his arm. Birds flitted and chirped in the faint light. She closed her eyes, breathed deeply and squeezed his arm a little tighter. While exhaling, her body quivered slightly, as a body does when someone is nervous before a performance. Her confident, take-charge manner seemed to evaporate into the evening twilight and Walker's sexual fantasy of being dominated faded with the change in her.

Leaving his side, Janna opened the unlocked patio door and stepped inside. Walker turned to see where she had gone, and their eyes met. Vulnerability, total and absolute exposure, and a need to be fucked aggressively projected out of her eyes and into him. He had never understood a look as completely as he did that one.

Walker strode toward her with a singular drive and purpose, and then he picked her up. She grabbed his head and they French-kissed with mutual passion. He carried her into the bedroom, flicking on the light switch inside the door with one hand as he passed it; he wanted to see everything clearly.

After throwing her onto the bed, Walker put his hands on the inside of her blouse at the collar, ripped it open, and heard each button popping off in quick succession. Then he slid his hands underneath her bra and tore apart the thin piece of lacy material that held the two cups together. Janna's bare chest heaved with excitement. She did not stop him when he forcefully pinched her nipples. Although Walker was ordinarily a very thoughtful partner, his self-control and physical awareness were now being replaced by animal instinct.

Walker tore the remnants of her blouse and bra off her shoulders and arms and let her fall back down. He brought his face to her chest and sucked her nipples and licked her breasts, covering them in his saliva. He then kicked off his shoes, pulled off his socks, undid his pants and dragged them off, along with his underwear. His shirt-tail covered his hard and completely erect penis.

With one hand Walker forced her head forward, and with the other he arranged pillows that put her into a tilted position. He ripped off his shirt, his last piece of clothing, and straddled her head. Her tongue and lips were fiery instruments of pleasure and her mouth felt like an inferno. He pulled his throbbing appendage from deep inside her throat and held it in one hand over her face. Using her spittle as lubrication, he began to masturbate and she held her mouth open, waiting to accept anything he had to offer.

Walker stopped and removed a condom from the wallet in his pants. She had not moved and continued with deep, rapid breaths. On the way back to the bed, he grabbed the torn blouse and proceeded to rip it into smaller strips. He tied one piece of the shredded sleeve tightly around her right wrist.

Janna's eyes widened as he undid her slacks. She lay back as he yanked at her pants to pull them off. With her thumbs, she pushed down on the inside of her white panties to ensure they slipped off with her slacks.

Walker rolled her tall, athletic body over to her stomach and tied the sleeve remnant attached to her wrist to the brass bedpost. He used another piece of the blouse to secure her left wrist to the other bedpost. He then slid the safe over his throbbing dick.

Janna lay face down on the bed with both arms stretched and the bindings taut. With each deep breath, her back and ribcage expanded and contracted. Walker could smell her excitement. Lifting her up by the abdomen and spreading her legs, he rammed an unforgiving cock inside her. Her juices flowed so freely that he easily slid in. With long, hard, thunderous strokes he slammed and smashed his pelvis against her firm buttocks.

Like a crazed genie released out of a bottle after a thousand years,

THE WORLDWIDE SEXUAL ADVENTURES OF WALKER FAYT

Walker continued his relentless assault. He had never inflicted such a savage sexual explosion. A less powerful woman could not have endured such brutal treatment, he thought.

Walker pulled out of her and in the light of the room saw her vaginal lubrication glistening off the condom. Over on the dresser sat a bottle of skin moisturizer and he left her to go get it. In the few seconds that elapsed, Janna raised her buttocks toward the ceiling and panted loudly, gasping for air with each lunge upward.

Walker squeezed the bulk of the bottle's contents onto her lower back and butt cheeks. Vigorously, he rubbed the lotion on her ass; her body shook with excitement as his fingers entered her anus. Circling around with one finger at first, he then primed and sensitized her for his ultimate act of domination.

Raucous moans rumbled from Janna like thunder before lightning. Walker maneuvered the tip of his penis to her backdoor entrance and knocked by applying a little pressure without actually going inside. She pushed back, forcing him inside her. With a few strokes in and out, lightning struck and her body spasmed with the release of an orgasm that had been caged for too long.

No longer able to contain his ejaculation, Walker pulled back, yanked off the condom and came in several large spurts over her buttocks and lower back. He groaned as he stroked his penis, letting the final few drops fall onto the quiescent body below him. Then he untied her and they kissed, holding each other, until they fell asleep.

*

Walker awoke alone and tried to make sense of the night before. Other than in high-school sports, he had never used his size to get his way. Marlene was five-foot six and of slight build, and could not match him physically.

One of her favorite forms of foreplay had involved jumping into his strong arms and being carried into the bedroom. He had enjoyed

FANTASY MEETS FANTASY

it, but deep down in a private place, he wished that he didn't always have to be the strong one. He had always thought that his desire to be sexually dominated prompted his attraction to tall, physical women.

Walker now realized a different truth. It shocked him to believe that such violence existed within him and that his deepest desire was a longing to unleash his sexual aggression to the fullest extent. Fear of injuring his partner had always stopped him from doing so. Jumbled somewhere in all that mess, he still held consideration for his sexual partner and that made him feel good.

Physically and mentally, Walker thought, Janna would threaten most men and those drawn to her likely wished to be dominated. In school, she must have been bigger and stronger than the boys, and later, the men she met who were physically bigger may not have possessed an equivalent strength of character.

Questions formed in his mind. "Did last night constitute a perfect union? Could two people connect at an unconscious level and give each other exactly what they needed, without knowing that they were doing so?"

Noise came from somewhere in the apartment, and soon after, Janna walked into the bedroom. She wore shorts and a T-shirt.

"Good morning." She bent over and gave Walker a warm kiss on the lips. "I'd like you to come upstairs for breakfast . . . and meet my parents."

Stunned, Walker replied, "What are your parents doing here?"

She laughed. "Oh, I guess I never mentioned that this is their house."

"No! What about last night?"

"Don't worry—they didn't hear anything. Extra soundproofing," she said as she pointed to the ceiling.

Not convinced, Walker asked, "Then what about my shirt? It has no buttons."

"You can use one of mine. It might be a little tight, but I'm sure it will fit. No more debate. Get dressed—they're waiting to meet you."

Walker put on his clothes and found a T-shirt that fit. He used the washroom, found a brush and gave his hair a few strokes, squeezed some toothpaste onto his finger and finger-brushed his teeth.

Janna led him from the downstairs apartment to the main floor and into the kitchen, where her parents sat drinking coffee. They both stood for the introductions. Her father, a man in his mid-fifties with a powerful build, towered over Walker; he must have been six-foot seven. Her mother, about five-foot ten, had a healthy, trim body and looked him over through big blue eyes.

"Walker, this is Tyke and Rigel Svensson, my mother and father. Mom, Dad, this is Walker Fayt—a friend." Walker uneasily shook both their hands.

Tyke began in a bold, straightforward manner. "So, how is sex with my daughter?"

After a few seconds, when Walker did not reply, Tyke added, "Look at her—she is glowing. Something has been released from her and I do not think it was caused by conversation. You Americans shy away from this kind of talk like it was a poison. Your prudishness can result in much trouble."

Walker tried to hide his intimidation and replied, "In my country, men brag to be macho or they are chivalrous and say nothing."

"Ah, I have made you defensive. I like that," Tyke said.

"Dad, stop it. Sometimes there are things that go beyond sex."

Rigel quickly added, "And sometimes it's best to mind your own business."

Tyke turned to Janna. "I only want to see you happy, and you seem very happy." He looked at Walker.

"I'm sorry if I've offended you. Whether it's sex, love or something else, if Janna is happy with you, then I'm happy with you. Let us start our breakfast."

FANTASY MEETS FANTASY

*

Plans had been made for Walker to travel with Tim's family for the weekend to Tällberg and Nusnäs. Both were small villages northwest of Stockholm on Lake Siljan, rich in Swedish folklore. Walker favored spending time with his old friend and his family as well as seeing other parts of Sweden. He knew that Teegan and Tim wouldn't mind Janna's company, and he asked her to join them.

Janna declined. Starting in a couple of hours was a volleyball camp to decide the fall roster for the national team. She couldn't miss it.

Walker knew that they would likely never see each other again. In their final kiss and hug, he felt the gift they had received from one another, a gift that had allowed two people to go deep within themselves and get what they wanted and needed from the other. Fate would ensure that the experience would not be muddied with other, lesser, moments.

Janna waved goodbye as the Volvo backed out of her lane and onto the street. Walker drove away, saluting her with his own wave of farewell.

That morning, before heading off for the weekend with Tim, Teegan and the children, Walker wrote in his journal.

July 15

Tim's place, Stockholm, Sweden

> *Fantasies, sexual fantasies in particular—what are they? Where do they come from? What do they tell about an individual?*
>
> *Certain fantasies of mine are so private that I hide them from everyone—at times even myself. I wonder if it's shame or embarrassment that propagates such behavior. Or, perhaps there's something in my human nature that does not want anyone to know me too intimately, so I instinctively protect the true nature of my being.*

THE WORLDWIDE SEXUAL ADVENTURES OF WALKER FAYT

I'm sure that having sexual fantasies is a requirement of human existence—but creating new ones to replace the old after they are enacted might eventually become mentally unhealthy and physically dangerous.

I have discovered that fulfilling a sexual fantasy can open pathways to a deeper understanding of myself—so I have decided that occasionally I should enact one.

chapter 8

SELENA—THE WOMAN WHO IS EVERYTHING
Heaven & Hell in a Picturesque French Vineyard

At mid-August, exactly one month had passed since Tim had dropped Walker off at the bus station in Stockholm. A lifetime of sightseeing had transpired since then, and Walker's body ached to settle into one place, if just for a while.

Zipping out of Paris aboard the Trains à Grande Vitesse (TGV) at speeds up to 190 mph toward Dijon, Walker felt somewhat disappointed. Three days ago when he had arrived in Paris, he had felt promise in the air and had expected something to happen. Passion and romance are said to abound in the city, yet none had come his way.

In the last month, he had met many interesting people and lots of women, but nothing had clicked romantically or sexually. Walker thought about some of the spectacular places he'd seen and the things he'd done. He remembered crossing from Sweden to Helsingør, Denmark, on the ferry and witnessing the construction of the three-billion-dollar bridge that would link the two countries. In Helsingør he toured Kronborg Castle, the setting of Shakespeare's *Hamlet*.

Walker thought about the major cities he had visited—

THE WORLDWIDE SEXUAL ADVENTURES OF WALKER FAYT

Copenhagen, Berlin, Prague, Nürnburg, Munich, Innsbruck, Venice, Florence, Rome, Geneva, Paris—and all the countryside in between. His knowledge of history blended with his own experience, giving him new perspectives about Europe and its influences on America and himself. If he ever taught history again, these personal encounters would be woven into the lessons.

Less than a week ago, on his way to Paris from Geneva, Walker had been close to where he was now headed. At the time, stopping at one of the most prestigious wine regions in the world held no appeal. Now it seemed to be calling to him with a sense of urgency, and its pull caused him to select the fastest and most expensive means of getting there.

The Chapeau Rouge Hotel near the thirteenth-century Notre-Dame church in Dijon had a cancellation and Walker booked himself into it. A quiet, tasteful room with a shower would be his home for the next twenty-four hours. At the time he checked in, he did not know that the hotel's restaurant had a reputation for serving the finest regional cuisine. Dinner that night consisted of an escargot appetizer and, for the main course, veal with a pommeroy glaze. He drank a delightful glass of red wine to accompany the meal.

During a dessert of fruit ice, Walker overheard two American couples talking at the table next to him. They complained about the attitude of the French toward tourists and concurred that Americans were snubbed more than other nationalities. These people were in their early sixties and, judging from their remarks, quite set in their ways. Walker thought, "If they want it to be like the States, why travel?" Complaints filled their entire conversation and the negativity became irritating.

"Sorry to barge in on your conversation, but perhaps I can be of some help."

The American group all stopped talking and waited for Walker to continue.

"I find that if you try even a little bit of French, it makes all the difference in the world. Like *bonjour* for hello, or *merci* for thank you."

The most vocal male of the group spoke up. "Well, if you can teach me French in the next two minutes, I'd be grateful. I've always felt that we're the paying customers and they should cater to us in English. They should try and make us feel at home and welcome."

The other husband said, "Besides, we've tried that *bon . . . bon voyage* and that . . . *merry say* stuff, and it just doesn't make any difference."

"Do you speak the language here?" one of the wives asked.

"Yes—I learned French in high school. I'm quite rusty but I've been practicing it with varying degrees of success. People seem to genuinely appreciate the attempt."

The woman with the fewest complaints brightened. "Tomorrow afternoon we're going to that castle made by the monks; you know the one—now it's that famous wine center."

Walker pronounced the name for her. "Yes, it's the Chateau du Clos de Vougeot."

"Yes, yes, that's it. Well, like I said, we're going there tomorrow afternoon. We have a rented van and you are more than welcome to join us." The others all nodded in agreement. "If you would be kind enough to translate for us, I'm sure we'd be treated better, and we'd have a better time. Then we wouldn't have to be such miserable old coots."

Walker consented to the arrangement, and they agreed to meet at the restaurant at half past twelve for lunch and to head out afterward. He had himself planned a trip to Clos du Vougeot for the next afternoon, and now he had transportation.

The next morning, clouds covered the sky and a light rain fell. Bad weather had no effect on Walker's sightseeing today. He visited both the Notre-Dame, with its centuries-old stained glass, choice stonework and elegant towers, and Cathédral St.-Bénigne, the city's oldest church. Being a non-Catholic did not detract from his interest in Catholic churches or any site where rituals of faith were practiced. Religious beliefs and their fundamental impact on human history drew him to these holy places.

Walker arrived at the restaurant a little late and the two couples sat enjoying a bottle of white wine. During lunch they exchanged information about themselves. Both couples had retired early, moved to Scottsdale, Arizona, and now lived a few doors away from each other in a new, gated subdivision. Frank and Louise were originally from Baltimore, where Frank had been an insurance salesman and Louise a homemaker. Dennis and Tammy had lived in Dayton, Ohio, where they had owned and operated a small printing business before selling out and retiring.

After lunch, a premonition told Walker to check out of the hotel and to take his baggage with him. Their destination was only fifteen or so miles away and coming back would not have been any great trouble; however, he did not believe he would be coming back to Dijon. His traveling companions were surprised to see his luggage.

Light and good-natured conversation complemented a leisurely drive south along Route D122. Walker tried teaching them some French words and phrases. They were terrible at pronunciation, but took it with a sense of humor and teased each other's inadequacies. Louise offered some details on their destination from a guidebook.

The Cistercian monks started construction of the castle in the twelfth century; it was not completed until the Renaissance. It now served as a center for the Burgundy region's wine enthusiasts. Each November, the Confrérie des Chevaliers du Tastevin met at the castle for an annual three-day festival. Louise pronounced the French names poorly, but surprised them by her attempts. Walker congratulated her and suggested she keep practicing.

In the rain, they walked quickly from the parking lot to the castle. Well-maintained grounds and beautifully restored stonework could not be dulled by the darkness of the day. A hostess greeted them at the front entrance. Walker translated her instructions and the many questions the Americans had for her. Young, patient and sweet, she treated them well, a fact they attributed to his speaking the language.

A sense of history and awe at the effort needed to create and maintain such a place engulfed Walker. He felt calm and relaxed. However, the people from Arizona were impatient to find a place where they could do some wine tasting. After half an hour, Frank and Dennis were already bored and wished to continue on to Beaune, where for the price of admission they could taste as many wines as they wished. It appeared they desired quantity, not quality. The wives wanted to stay longer, but gave in to the restlessness of their husbands and agreed to go.

Convinced that his translating had led to their good treatment, they all pleaded for Walker to go with them. They were even willing to wait for him. When he told them of his intention to spend the rest of the afternoon there, they decided to carry on without him. Walker collected his bags, said goodbye and went back inside.

The hostess showed him a small room where he could safely store his luggage. He wanted to slow down his pace, let the aroma of fine wine fill his senses and carry him away to an earlier time, a long-forgotten time when anything seemed possible. Leisurely Walker strolled around the castle and its grounds. While outside in a small vineyard, without warning lightning flashed, thunder clapped and a downpour immediately began. By the time Walker could get back inside, the rain had soaked him.

Leaving small puddles on the stone floor with each footstep, he made his way back to a room that had large sinks and counters. He saw no one around and decided to use the room to dry off. Leaning over a sink, Walker wrung as much water from his shirt as he could without taking it off. Then he hung his head over the sink and rubbed the excess water from his hair.

A glass carboy on a shelf above wobbled and began to fall. Out of the corner of his eye, Walker caught a glimpse of it. With quick reflexes, he snared the large bottle before it could crash into the sink and break into a thousand pieces. He wondered what had caused the big glass jug to fall in his direction. He hadn't knocked against anything to cause it to topple.

Now a second carboy moved. Walker quickly set down the one he had in hand and prepared to catch the next one. It fell from the shelf and he caught it easily. Before he could set it down, another carboy moved to the edge of the shelf and fell. He caught it with an outstretched arm, let it roll down and trapped it with his chest. He quickly set the two jugs down.

Walker looked up at the space on the shelf from where the carboys had fallen. Suddenly something pounced in his direction. Instinctively he protected his face from the impending collision. The creature bounced off his forearms and landed on his right shoulder and crawled onto his back as he hunched over.

The next moment, Walker heard a loud purring and felt his hair being licked. A cat had caused all the commotion! He reached up and removed the animal from his shoulder and held it in his cradled arms like a baby. Still purring loudly, its big greenish eyes looked at him and its mouth opened in a sweet little "meow." He laughed and rubbed its belly as it rolled around in his arms.

Walker had never had an affinity for cats, but this one seemed different. This feline had unusual and beautiful markings: a ginger-orange patch around one eye and a black patch around the other, otherwise a pure white face except for its little orange nose. Its stomach and the bottom of its four legs and paws were also white, while the rest of the body and tail were spotted with the ginger-orange, black and white in a truly gorgeous pattern.

SELENA—THE WOMAN WHO IS EVERYTHING

The cat's appearance and personality instantly captured Walker's heart. He had never made such a fuss over an animal before; with this creature he just couldn't help himself.

The cat rolled around in Walker's arms and stretched out its body. It then crawled up close to his face and rubbed its head against his cheek and licked his nose several times. The action of the rough tongue made him grin.

"Stop that! Cut it out, that tickles! No, actually it kind of hurts." The cat continued to lick him.

A powerful feeling of being watched suddenly overtook Walker. As he moved the cat away from his face, he saw a woman standing in the room. Being caught in an intimate moment with a cat made him blush. He felt heat burning his ears and knew they were beet red.

"Ah, you have found Zara! What mischief has she been up to now?"

Walker remained too flustered to say anything and just glanced from the shelf above to the carboys on the floor. The woman followed his look.

"Yes, I can see. Thank you, *Monsieur*. You have probably saved Zara from having her last life taken. If she would have broken all these bottles and made a great mess, it would have been the last straw; the maintenance people would have had her skinned. She has been in trouble here before. Zara is my baby and in my eyes she can do no wrong. I take her everywhere and spoil her rotten."

Just as she spoke her last word, the cat leaped from Walker's arms and sauntered over to her. "Oh Zara, come to your *maman*," she said, and leaned over to pick up the cat.

Walker watched intently. As the Frenchwoman bent over, the rounded neck of her smock hung open, giving him a full view underneath. A sheer white bikini bra held firm, tanned breasts.

Mesmerized, he could not look away. With cat in hand, she glanced up and caught him staring at her cleavage. She balanced Zara in one arm and moved her hand over the loose-fitting neckline. Now she blushed.

"Thank you for saving Zara—I'm grateful," and she extended her slender arm for a handshake. "I'm Selena."

For the first time, Walker noticed her lovely French accent. In the touch of their handshake, he felt years of wisdom and experience. "You're welcome. *De rien*, it was my pleasure." Holding her hand longer than was custom, he then said, "I'm Walker Fayt. It is very nice to meet Selena . . . and Zara."

The cat rested against her breast, purring. As he reached out and scratched behind the ear that wasn't touching her chest, Walker noticed that Selena's pupils became larger. By his quickened pulse, he sensed that his own pupils had enlarged, trying to capture as much of her light as possible.

Selena held up her hand, revealing the water he had left behind from their handshake. She wiped it on the side of her dress to dry it off.

"I'm sorry. I didn't mean to get you wet," Walker said apologetically. "I got caught in the rain and came in here to dry off when Zara started her mischief."

"You're soaked right through. For all the trouble Zara's caused you, I insist that that you come to my place and dry off and join me for dinner."

Feeling quite uncomfortable in wet clothes and being without any immediate plans, Walker had two reasons to accept her invitation. He would have broken other plans regardless. Was this love at first sight? Was it Selena that had caused him to be drawn here? It did not matter to him that she might be ten to twelve years his senior. She ignited a spark within him.

Walker collected his backpacks, dropped them into the trunk of

SELENA—THE WOMAN WHO IS EVERYTHING

Selena's Peugeot and they drove south toward Beaune with Zara sleeping comfortably on his lap. The lovely countryside became brighter when the sun broke through the clouds. She told him that she lived about ten minutes from Beaune on the way toward Sully.

Selena's bright white smile and alluring, dark hazel eyes enchanted him. Her shoulder-length black hair, parted in the center, bounced and shone when the sunlight hit it. A smattering of gray added to her mature and mystical appeal. Soft and delicate skin highlighted her olive complexion. Voluptuous, firm breasts, a small waist with shapely rounded hips and a flat tummy gave her a classic 1950s pinup girl figure. At about five-foot ten, she stood somewhat taller and thinner than the average sex symbol of that era.

A strange mixture of sophistication and a breezy, devil-may-care attitude added personality to Selena's physical beauty. She gave a running commentary on the wineries and their owners as each one of them passed by. Walker watched her closely, consuming her spirit deep within him. It became sustenance to his soul. Walker had just met this woman and in less than an hour, he never wanted to leave her.

The sun shone brightly and it became very warm in the car. In mid-sentence she interrupted herself and asked, "My feet are getting so hot. Do you mind if I take off my shoes?"

Walker glanced down at her feet and said, "No, I don't mind at all." Then he smiled and asked, "Should I roll down the window?"

She laughed. "It's your choice."

"I think I will. It's a bit warm in here. It's not your feet—really."

Selena and the fresh French country air filled Walker's lungs as they drove. With the windows down, the wind blew her gorgeous hair around her face and behind her head. He stared admiringly.

Selena suddenly quipped, "I'm thinking of cutting it short. What do you think?"

"No, no, don't do that," Walker urged. A strand of hair had

wrapped around her sunglasses and he reached over and removed it and said, "It suits you just the way it is."

Selena smiled lovingly and turned the car off the main road, onto a quaint country lane lined on both sides by mature vineyards. "We are here. This is home."

"You live on an estate winery?" Walker asked, somewhat surprised. His enchantment had precluded any thoughts about where she lived.

"*Oui*, yes, it's only about two hundred acres, but I believe it produces the best wine in France. It is such a glorious way to make a living."

The immaculately manicured grounds around the villa were spotless. A garage door opened and Selena drove into the empty space. A four-wheel-drive Mercedes and a BMW sports car filled the other spots. Zara jumped off Walker's lap and out the window and Selena popped the trunk. He tried to hide his surprise at her wealth as he got his bags.

"Come. Let's get you into some dry clothes and ready for dinner. It'll be served in about an hour."

An older gentleman, who appeared to be a butler, greeted them at the door. Walker felt uneasy about letting a less able-bodied man carry his things. After some debate in French between the butler and Selena that Walker didn't fully understand, they decided that Pierre would carry the smaller of the two bags.

Selena waved him to follow Pierre as the Frenchman walked away with his bag. "See you in a short while." Then he heard her call out in French, "Pierre, tell Pascale there will be a guest for dinner."

"*Oui, Madame,*" he replied.

Pierre led Walker upstairs to an airy, bright and spacious room with big windows and views of the vineyards. Antique furniture created elegance; a four-poster bed, complete with overhead canopy, formed the centerpiece. The room, with en suite bath, exuded affluence.

Walker shed his wet clothes and let the warm water of the shower soothe his body. He washed his hair, shaved and put on the new black Levi's jeans that he had been saving for a special occasion. As he put on his black T-shirt, he spotted a black sports jacket hanging in the open closet. He hadn't seen it there before the shower.

Walker surmised that the household followed a tradition of wearing jackets to dinner, and selections of them were available to guests who arrived jacketless. As a resourceful butler, Pierre must have guessed his size and left the jacket while he showered.

A knock on the door was followed by, "*Monsieur*, it is time for dinner," in a thick French accent. Walker opened the door and Pierre looked him up and down. "The jacket it fits, *très bien*."

"Yes, Pierre, it fits," Walker replied in a friendly tone, "but how did you know the color would match?" Pierre did not seem to find the question relevant and ignored it.

More beautiful antique furniture filled the dining room. A finely crafted table that could accommodate twelve dominated the room. The legs were ornately carved in fascinating designs of ghouls and angels. High-back chairs cushioned with black leather completed the set. Zara slept in front of a fire that burned heartily.

Selena greeted him with the customary light kiss on either cheek. A skintight gold dress showed off her womanly curves, and an understated rhinestone necklace fit perfectly in the V-neck and rested on her partially exposed breasts. She wore her hair up, revealing a shapely neck that was set off by dangling rhinestone earrings. Outlines of a garter belt and stocking tops formed in the tight, thin material of the dress. Her black silk sheer stockings carried a seam along the back.

Elegance, grace and style combined with her outrageous attire gave Selena the aura of a high-class hooker. It was certainly not what Walker had expected, given her simple fashionableness of earlier in the day. Her new image struck a very provocative note, as if she were deliberately trying to tempt and possess him.

Shortly after sitting down to dinner, Walker noticed a slight separation in the side seam of Selena's dress, under her arm and near her breast. The gap, due to the tight fit, revealed a tiny bit of olive-colored skin. Time and time again he glanced at the tear along the seam. Looking at that little bit of prohibited skin became a fixation. With certain movements, more of it would show, and he felt he had no control, he had to look.

Although the tight dress prominently displayed her breasts, waist, hips and legs, and her arms, neck and much of her cleavage were bare, that one tiny spot of exposed skin had Walker transfixed. The forbidden held him captive.

The meal began with roasted eggplant soup and the best dry red wine Walker had ever tasted. The main course consisted of veal steaks accompanied by small roasted potatoes and steamed asparagus. Crème au caramel completed the repast.

During dinner, Walker discovered that Selena had inherited the winery from her husband, who had passed away more than twenty years ago. She had married at twenty-five a man three decades her senior. Since his death, she had run the winery on her own.

On several occasions during the conversation, Selena hinted that it would be nice to have a man around to help during this year's harvest season. As in other years, she hired many Moroccans to do the vineyard work. She found that they were thankful to have jobs, they were trustworthy and would work for less than Europeans.

Rivals accused Selena of exploitation. She found this ridiculous, since without the seasonal work the North Africans would have no work at all and would be impoverished. Loopholes in immigration remained open to her, due to the influence of a European dignitary. Walker wondered what influence she held over this person.

Selena commented that Walker looked tired, and that he might be better off to stay put for a while. The good food and wine, the luxurious accommodation and her words focused attention on his travel weariness. Walker had no reason to say no to her when she made him the offer, but many reasons to say yes. He agreed to stay for the harvest.

After dessert, Pascale, the resident chef, came to the table with espresso. She spoke only French and with Selena translating the parts he didn't understand, Walker did his best to follow the conversation. She wanted to know if he had enjoyed the dinner and, with his stay being extended, wished to know his preferences in cuisine.

Walker expressed his fondness for meat and potatoes—thus today's dinner had been perfect. He added that, in an effort to expand his culinary horizons, he was willing to try other dishes.

The evening ended with coffee and apéritifs, and afterwards they stood to leave the table. While Selena rose, the seam tear stretched to its widest point and Walker's eyes widened with it. This time Selena noticed his stare and lifted her arm to search for the spot where he was looking. When she found it, she covered it with her hand.

"Ah, merde!" she cursed and looked Walker directly in the eyes, blushing. "I am so embarrassed. Has that been there all evening? You should have said something—I would have changed. Walker, if you are going to be the man around here, you must look out for me."

Walker reddened like a twelve-year-old boy caught with a girlie magazine. "I'm sorry, I didn't know what to say. I was hoping it would go unnoticed. . . . Next time I'll say something."

"What's done is done. Good night, sweet dreams." Selena leaned toward him and they kissed on each cheek.

*

THE WORLDWIDE SEXUAL ADVENTURES OF WALKER FAYT

During the days, Walker acted as Selena's personal assistant. For the next couple of weeks they were together almost constantly. Everything about her enchanted him: her speech, her smell, her dress, her hair, her body and her passion for her work. She often asked him to do tasks that were beyond her strength. Completing these gave him a huge rush.

Other employees did not understand Walker's status around the vineyard and rumors abounded. The Moroccans hotly debated whether Madame Selena and the American were lovers. The villa staff knew the truth, but nothing they said could dispel the gossip. Word quickly spread in the small community of Selena's tall, handsome foreigner. Not so coincidentally, neighbors and friends dropped by the vineyard to see if they could help with anything or if she needed something picked up in town. Occasionally Selena played along to be polite and graciously accepted.

It amused Walker to be the center of so much speculation and attention. He ignored it as best he could and concentrated on the work. Work for him had always been only an intellectual endeavor and he immensely enjoyed the physical aspect of his duties. Most of the tasks were done outdoors and he enjoyed that part as well. His compensation consisted of free room and board, and he believed he had gotten the better of the exchange.

Selena knew every task intimately, but could not be everywhere at once. Her attention to detail and her demand for perfection ensured the fine quality of the wine.

After busy and hectic days, in the evening they would dine together and the pattern remained similar to that first night. Selena would dress in a vampish style, they would converse throughout the meal, he would get glimpses of other forbidden places of her body, Pascale would check on the meal, Selena would wish him sweet dreams and they would kiss each other on both cheeks. They usually dined alone or sometimes with an invited friend or a business associate of Selena's.

SELENA—THE WOMAN WHO IS EVERYTHING

Two weeks after Walker arrived, a serious accident befell a young Moroccan child. The seven-year-old was thrown from the flatbed truck as it drove through the vineyard. In his inexperience, Abd had stood to move position, and just as he did the truck carrying workers hit a large pothole and threw him off. He was the son of a couple who had been working at the vineyard for the last ten seasons. Eight years prior they had fallen in love here and had been married in a ceremony hosted by Selena. The father, Moulay, believed his son should learn a trade, so he accompanied his parents for this season's work.

When the unconscious boy arrived at the villa, he was breathing irregularly. Selena barked out orders with authority and compassion. "Walker, get the four-wheel drive. Pierre, telephone the doctor. Pascale, fill a towel with ice. Someone get Abd's parents."

Moulay and Jamai arrived, panic-stricken. Selena reassured them that all would be fine. Moulay sat in the front as Walker drove; Jamai helped Selena attend to her son in the back seat. The ten-minute drive to the doctor's clinic seemed to take an eternity. As they pulled up to the clinic, Abd regained consciousness. Jamai wailed in praise to Allah and Moulay clasped his hands together and bowed his head several times, chanting in Moroccan.

A series of tests showed that Abd had suffered a concussion. He sported a rather large bump on his head. The doctor released him after about an hour. On the way back to the villa, Selena held Abd in her arms and stroked his hair as the rest of his body lay across Jamai's lap. Selena insisted that Abd stay in the villa for the next few days and that Jamai be released from her duties to help care for her son. She arranged for an extra bed to be set up in the room so that Moulay could stay the nights if he wished. The parents protested the special treatment, but Selena held firm.

The events of the day solidified Walker's feelings for Selena. The accident became the catalyst that allowed him to focus on what had been building ever since he first saw her. Lying in bed that night, unable to sleep, he surrendered and finally admitted to himself that he loved her deeply—beyond anything he had ever known.

In fact, Walker loved her with a devotion so profound, it was taking him over completely. His love mirrored the universe before time began, with all possibilities about to explode in a big bang, soon to become everything. At this moment it was a singularity within his heart, compressed; its forces unleashed would be the event horizon of his soul—a harmony so almighty that all the angels in heaven sang its melody and all the devils in hell danced to its rhythm: angels and devils, good and evil, all singing and crying the same tunes. One—one pure emotion that cannot be compromised or divided. A one-sided divinity did not have the power of this love.

This was a love that could not be changed—it just existed. In all its purpose, serenity and focus, it created a state of living hell. Beyond control, it continued without end or justice or fairness—spirit, thought, mind and body bound by consuming love. Ageless, timeless, relentless it continued. He wondered: could this be God's creative gift?

This love for Selena was a miracle, planned before the beginning. It became greater than his soul; it acted as a personal guide, taking him to Forever. It held the secrets of eternity and it whispered light where darkness once was in him. This light drew him with a force as powerful as a universe contracted.

Walker felt he now had an unfaltering destiny that was committed to his complete surrender. He could give his life for her, without question. And how could all these things, these opposites, be true? He knew not. He only knew they were—these truths so pure, so deep, so private he could not let her know them. Her knowing them would destroy him.

Sweet mysteries of the universe filled Walker beyond his capacity to accept them. He became the one chosen to channel the vibrations of love into physical form. All of this because of her, her spirit, her essence, her body close to his in divine harmony. Why? Not a question to be asked, for no explanation existed. The only option—acceptance. He had to live it, breathe it, feel it and lose himself in the abyss.

Walker thought that his human body could not maintain this pure force of love. The body's weak and feeble construction rendered it hopelessly insignificant. Love's manufacture was greater, even greater than all the goodness that had ever been or ever would be. Existing from before time, it had awaited this moment to break through into reality—in him.

It was the opposites of matter and anti-matter colliding, eliminating everything known everywhere. All things were now possible, everywhere. Past, present and future merged at the point of creative contact in him. Nothing else was meant to be, and nothing else mattered!

Where could he go to hide from love's fury, Walker wondered, from its torment and its completeness? He knew no such place existed. When would he be released from his sacrifice as bearer of this unadulterated love? Never, was the only word he heard.

As all things meant to be, it was good, and Walker rejoiced and treasured the gift of love harbored inside him. Outlets for this treasure presented themselves constantly, he realized. Every touch, every glance, every word spoken to her came from that place. Human experience muted the powerful, absolute and constant feelings in his heart and soul.

At the same time, Walker knew he could never project the honesty of his heart and soul in a human touch. Touch was too base an incarnation for the emotions he felt. Desire for touch nevertheless burned in him like the fiery furnaces of hell, a crude reminder of his divine attachment to her, an attachment he would completely abandon just to know that she loved him.

THE WORLDWIDE SEXUAL ADVENTURES OF WALKER FAYT

All of Walker's senses resonated at the primary frequency of life: love. All sounds, smells, tastes, sights and touches filtered through his love for Selena. He loved her, and the universe evolved because of it. Without it there would be nothing, all terms of reference destroyed; an empty, hollow blackness that his human soul could not bear. He had to love her; it was the only possibility.

Walker knew that his love for Selena left him exposed, vulnerable and open to ruin—but it could not be contained. Every molecule, every atom, every subatomic particle of his body pulsated to her name. He prayed for the redemption of his love. He sold his soul for the release of his love. It had no effect, and he loved her still.

At times, pain besieged the pleasure of his love—pain so great it felt as though a horrible eternal torture had been inflicted on him, perhaps from the manuscript of a gruesome and cruel satanic ritual. Raw open wounds of pained love covered him. He was stabbed and burned. It would not end; it could not end. At these times, death would have been welcomed as a friend.

Then the delicious sweetness returned. All the glory of God cried out in the ecstasy of his love. She consisted of the air in his lungs, the blood in his veins and the nourishment of his soul. He would not trade the power in a hundred billion galaxies for one microsecond of his love for her. All of this was Walker's truth, his unique, lived experience of the universe.

At times Walker imagined easily channeling this love into the world, creating a circular flow of energy, as the universe intended: whatever he sent out returned many times over. There were other times when the projection had nowhere to go and reflected the love back into his soul in an intense, blinding brilliance that completely surrounded him. These times were frightening and claustrophobic.

Walker wished he could reach out to the past, present and future and give Selena everything. He wanted to fulfill every wish, satisfy all her fantasies, heal every wound, dry all her tears, fix all her problems, kill all her enemies, make her completely happy. Then, maybe then, she would love him as he loved her.

The desire to dig his hands into the flesh of his chest and tear open his body to find the love within him inundated Walker's mind. Inside, there would be tangible proof of love's existence. Once found, love could be waved in the air, like a flag on Independence Day. However, he was not independent, for he depended on her to be the object of his unwavering love, his only purpose.

Walker could not believe in anything more fundamental than his love for Selena. He could not imagine loving anybody more than he loved her. He could not want anything more than for his love to be returned.

The window to Walker's soul expressed all of this in a teardrop that fell to the pillow. Then he slept.

In the morning, Walker woke later than usual. Upon opening his eyes, he noticed that a bouquet of bright red roses in a beautiful red vase sat on the table beside his bed. Filled with inspiration, Walker got out his journal.

September 14
Looking out at the vineyard, Beaune, France

> THE ELEMENTS OF LOVE
> Earth, Air, Fire and Water
> —the elements of old;
> They're whispering your name to me
> incessantly and bold.
>
> Animal, Vegetable and Mineral
> do beautify the earth;

THE WORLDWIDE SEXUAL ADVENTURES OF WALKER FAYT

And broadcast the wholeness of your name
  —I've known it since my birth.

Air, Land and Sea
  comprise this planet so rare;
They're echoing your name to me
  powerfully, with care.

Good and Evil, Heaven and Hell
  are stories that seem real;
They incarnate your name to me.
  —you've taught me how to feel.

The Universe and Time,
  are everything, I'm told;
The name "Selena" radiates
  from all that I behold.

At breakfast, Pascale informed him that Madame Selena had left very early; she had gone out of town for business, and would be away until the next day at noon. Walker found this odd. For the last several weeks he had arranged all her movements, particularly all appointments and meetings. Pascale's red apron caught his attention as she walked back to the kitchen.

Walker longed to see Selena. He knew that if she looked into his eyes she would see the universe that was moving, alive, in his heart. Of all days, why this day to be away? Agitation grew with each second he did not see her. He drove the tractor that day. Frustration rumbled inside him like the engine of the red tractor, heating up, spitting out exhaust, burning fuel at a highly inefficient level and shaking with a constant racket. Where was she?

Anyone who came in contact with Walker felt his irritation. Word spread quickly among the workers to steer clear of the American. Exasperated, with every breath he wanted to retreat from the world until he could see her. He asked several villa staff if they were free for dinner; none accepted his invitation. It seemed they all had other plans and could not break them on such short notice. In his misery, he suspected they didn't want to be near him.

Dinner consisted of beet soup, sirloin steak prepared very rare and cherry cheesecake for dessert. On this night Pascale did not appear to inquire about the meal. She too had plans, and left before the meal was finished. Back in his room, Walker continued to fume. His entire day had been consumed with thoughts of Selena. Why wasn't she here?

Fresh red roses replaced the ones Walker had woken up to. Fury erupted and he knocked the flowers and vase to the floor. It smashed into hundreds of small red shards. He turned out the lights and fell into a restless sleep.

In the very early hours of the morning, Walker opened his eyes. Nervousness rippled through his body as the stillness of the night took on an eerie closeness. The room, the villa seemed to be alive, breathing, then holding its breath as if it knew of some event about to happen. His pulse quickened and his heart pounded.

Walker sensed someone outside his room and felt their power over him. Too frightened to move or scream, he remained paralyzed as slowly the brass doorknob to his room turned and the door inched inward. In the darkness, a shadowy figure entered the room and the door shut behind it.

Terror ripped through Walker's body and blinded him of perception as the figure drifted toward him. He blacked out momentarily.

When he next regained his senses, his arms and legs were tightly bound to the four posts of the canopy.

As Walker lay on his back, a transparent material brushed over his body. At first it covered his face; then, as if floating on air, it moved along his chest, down his stomach and stopped at his abdomen. Gentler than the lightest breeze, it swayed backward and forward across his penis as it lay secured in his briefs. Astonishingly, the sensuous touch produced his arousal.

The ravishing arms of a woman appeared from the darkness beyond Walker's vision and freed his erection from the confine of his underwear. Her hands caressed his penis without any visible means of touch, then retracted.

Drifting into view from the darkness, the naked back of a voluptuous woman appeared. Rhythmic movements of her back, hips and shoulders provoked a terrifying lustfulness in Walker. She moved forward into the blackness so that only her buttocks remained visible. Hypnotic movements of her body intensified the eroticism. Gradually she came closer and then lowered herself onto his erection. With only the use of her vaginal muscles, she squeezed and pulsated his penis.

It felt to Walker as though his semen spilled into her body by involuntary extraction rather than its usual forceful ejaculation. As soon as he reached orgasm, she slipped away into the darkness. Crying out in disgust and horror, he turned his head and glimpsed flowing, shoulder-length black hair and a long, red, sheer negligée exit the room.

Walker awoke restless and edgy, remembering the nightmare. The bright morning light evaporated the lingering memories and emotions of the dream. He rolled over to get out of bed and choked for air when he noticed the clean floor. No spilled roses, no broken vase, no trace of his anger. With trepidation, he flung the duvet aside. On the outside of his dark blue underwear were white crusty stains of dried semen.

SELENA—THE WOMAN WHO IS EVERYTHING

Showering did little to change Walker's mood. Misery from the day before had turned into ugliness. He tried changing his mood, but it got worse. Lewd, unthinkable thoughts filled his mind, especially if a woman, any woman, came near him. Such a condition had never possessed him this strongly before. After a couple of hours of dealing with his dark encumbrance, he retreated to his room, claiming to be ill. His erratic behavior had upset productivity and he sensed that the staff welcomed his absence.

Rather than inflict his abuse on the hard-working people around him, Walker maintained his self-imposed quarantine. He declined Pierre's call to lunch. Like a trapped, wounded animal instinctively ready to release its fear, anger and viciousness, he paced the room. By mid-afternoon, rot and decay from inside had left him cold, while frustration and anger had made him hot. Escape, release, fulfillment—he needed it all now to avoid insanity. A knock came on the door. He stopped his pacing and exploded by shouting, "What?"

The brass knob turned and the door opened. Selena stepped into the room wearing a smartly tailored red business suit. "I heard you were ill; is everything all right?"

Walker locked his eyes with hers and said, "Lovesickness, I suppose. Where were you? I need to be with you. You know I love you."

Selena stood motionless, staring at him with her big hazel eyes twinkling with anticipation. Silence reigned for what seemed like an eternity, with neither of them moving. They searched for soul truth in the blackness of each other's pupils. Unable to contain his fervor any longer, Walker stepped toward her. Her widened pupils signaled him to proceed. . . .

Lovemaking entangled them for the rest of the afternoon. Expressed as a series of orgasmic peaks, deep-rooted passion came to life in an explosion of beauty, care and tenderness. Sensual and sexual bliss that he wished would continue forever filled Walker's awareness.

THE WORLDWIDE SEXUAL ADVENTURES OF WALKER FAYT

An expression of insecurity crossed his face as Selena left him to get ready for dinner. She read Walker's emotions perfectly and kissed him tenderly on the lips. She touched his face and in all sincerity said, "Walker, you gave me the most emotional fuck I've ever had."

Sex remained intense in the days after their first consummation. They spent each night together. Most times Walker smuggled himself into her room and sneaked back just before sunrise. At other times, Selena came to him. She wished to keep their rendezvous a secret, at least as a pretense. They didn't know if they fooled anyone, but their discretion kept the villa staff from talking openly about their encounters.

Mirrors hung everywhere in Selena's bedroom, including one inside the canopy of her bed. At first, all the reflections made Walker uncomfortable, but he came to enjoy it. No matter where he looked, he could see several reflections of Selena and depending where he chose to look, he could see almost any part of her body.

One of Selena's rituals involved masturbating in front of him. Waves of pleasure rippled through her body as she drew herself closer and closer to climax. Pulsating contractions reflected back to Walker from numerous mirror angles, creating an erotic capsule. Sometimes during the excitement he masturbated as well. At other times he waited in a heightened state of desire and entered her just after she had climaxed. Either way, seconds after reaching her orgasm, as she descended from the height of her sexual release, she insisted that he repeat several times, "Selena, I love you."

After several nights of such activity, a rebirth began in Walker. Everything in the world appeared differently: colors were brighter, food tasted better, birds sang sweeter, the sun shone more, the rain refreshed him and his orgasms were stronger.

Selena and Walker filled their days with joyous work in the vineyard and their nights with sexual rapture. After an especially hard day, Walker would massage Selena's naked body. In the third week of September, it dawned on Walker that school classes had been back for a couple of weeks and he hadn't thought about it until now. This was a sure sign of how different and exceptional his life had become.

Other memories of home drifted into his consciousness. He wanted Marlene to be happy without him in her life. Several months of not seeing Amy and Petra left him sad. His parents had retired to Appleton to be close to him and the family, and he regretted not calling them more often. He tried to shake these thoughts as he left his room for an important dinner meeting.

Jean Bonnefoy, majority owner of the largest winery in the Bordeaux region, had expressed an interest in Selena's operations and wished to meet over dinner. She knew the man from industry functions and certainly by reputation. His many business and political connections meant he usually got his way.

The doorbell rang exactly on time, but when Pierre escorted Monsieur Bonnefoy into the room with a gorgeous young woman on his arm, it surprised both Walker and Selena. They had expected only him.

At sixty-eight, Jean made the woman on his arm appear younger than her age. He wore a dark blue, double-breasted business suit with a white shirt and a striped blue, white and red tie. Her pink-and-white, polka-dot designer dress smartly showed off her figure. Auburn hair hung loose onto her bare shoulders and her large breasts held up the dress, which showed a generous amount of cleavage. Big, brown twinkling eyes, a bright smile, tanned skin and shapely hips and legs made her stunning. Despite him being a man of power, all the focus went to her.

"*Bonjour, Monsieur Bonnefoy.* It's a pleasure to see you again," Selena said in English. "This is my friend Walker. He has been helping me with this year's harvest." She turned and looked directly at the woman. "I'm not usually caught by surprises. Who is this unexpected beauty?"

Jean spoke in English as well. "This is my youngest daughter, Chantel. I hope you do not mind that I have asked her to join us. I know I am being a bit bold—"

"No, it is our pleasure," Selena reassured them. "I'm sure that Pierre has seen to it already. Jean, Chantel, please come in and sit down."

Before dinner, conversation consisted mostly of pleasantries. They told the story of how Walker and Selena met, as Zara rubbed against Jean and purred. Walker spoke French along with them, being more fluent now than ever before.

At the dinner table, Selena sat at the head of the table, with Chantel and Jean to either side of her. Walker sat beside Chantel, the farthest away from Selena. He hid his irritation at the seating arrangement. Walker resented being that far from his lover after eating at her side for over a month. Childhood memories of business coming before his wishes involuntarily resurfaced.

Walker realized that Jean must have learned of Selena's involvement with a younger man, and as a premeditated move to pair up the conversation, brought along Chantel. Jean and Selena discussed business one on one, while Chantel monopolized Walker's attention. Rebuffing her seemingly genuine interest in the United States and her endless questions would have been socially unacceptable to the point of being rude. If Jean indeed had planned the social arrangements, Chantel worked them to perfection.

Walker played the role of gracious host and conversed with Chantel while eavesdropping on the other conversation whenever possible. However, technical French terms and lowered voices assured that he didn't get much. He learned that Chantel had been significantly involved in the family business, but for now her duties centered on raising her preschool son and daughter. Her husband, who had political and business connections, had joined the winery after they married. His expertise in securing export licenses and contracts was turning out to be an invaluable asset to the winery.

After dinner, Jean lavishly complimented Pascale on her preparation and presentation of an exquisite meal of quail, his favorite dish. To accompany the after-dinner liqueurs, she offered Jean another of his favorite indulgences, Cuban cigars. He accepted and filled the dining room with strong-smelling blue smoke.

At the end of the evening, as Walker shook Jean's hand goodbye, it struck him that Jean intended to use something he knew against Walker. He let the thought go as nonsense. He and Chantel kissed on both cheeks, as did Selena with both Chantel and Jean.

As soon as the guests were gone, Selena asked him, "When you came down for dinner you seemed a bit blue and just now something troubled you. What is it?"

"Earlier tonight I thought about the people who care for me and I wondered how they were doing. And the other, it was nothing."

In a pampering tone, she whispered, "Now, now, I care for you . . . . I'll come to your room tonight."

Before they made love that night, Selena presented Walker with a two-carat aquamarine stone. It hung from a gold box-link necklace and she put it around his neck, saying, "Keep this next to your skin; it represents courage and it will help you in times of turmoil."

"I don't know what to say. Thank you. I love you." Walker rubbed the stone on his chest. "Yes, I think I feel its power." He smiled at her and kissed her softly on the lips. "I'll wear it always. If you're giving this to me, then I know it's important."

After a glorious rampage of lovemaking, they lay in bed, and in that passage between consciousness and sleep Walker asked her, "Selena, are you a witch?"

Her reply, barely audible, was, "If you would have asked me that twenty years ago, I would have said yes. Now I don't believe that such labels serve any purpose. I am not. We are who we are, and we do what we do."

*

Harvest season reached its chaotic crescendo. It seemed that everything needed to be done at the same time, and there weren't enough people available to do it. In the midst of this pandemonium, a driver had taken ill and Walker had to fill in to pull a flatbed full of picked grapes with the tractor. Heat rising up from the lane bent the light and blurred his vision. Out of this mirage walked Selena. She had left for the day on business, so how could this be her? Confusion set in and Walker stopped the tractor and focused on the image before him.

The woman moved closer and Walker felt dizzy and out of sorts. Standing there in front of the tractor, Selena appeared many years younger than when she had left. She shouted to be heard over the noise of the tractor, "Walker, you look like you've seen a ghost!"

Walker jumped out of his seat, landed on the ground and stumbled, regained his balance and stood before her, examining her from about two feet away. She seemed to understand his despair.

"I'm Selena's daughter. Is she here?"

"Her daughter?"

"Yes, I'm Cosma. It's nice to finally meet you. Mother told me about your fortuitous arrival and about the big help you've been to her. She said you were tall and handsome—she always did have a way with understatements."

"It was nice of Selena to mention me, but she never mentioned you. Your resemblance is phenomenal, so please excuse my shock. I thought she had returned twenty years younger."

"Seventeen to be exact," Cosma corrected him in her eloquent French accent.

Quickly Walker did the math and said, "So that means—"

SELENA—THE WOMAN WHO IS EVERYTHING

"I was born several years before she married, yes. René raised me as his daughter from the time I was eight until his death. He was the only father I knew. My biological father . . ." Her voice faded away and she shrugged her shoulders.

Out of empathy, Walker changed the subject. "Selena isn't here right now; she's away on business and not expected back until late tonight."

Cosma laughed. "Yes, I imagine things are quite insane around here. Can you believe it? It's just like mother to cause a stir and get married right in the middle of harvest. Jean Bonnefoy is just as crazy."

No words in the universe could have had a more devastating effect on Walker. It must be a hoax, he thought, a bad joke done in poor taste. It could not be true. He became light-headed, felt he was about to faint. No words entered his thoughts; words were well beyond his ability at this moment. Blood drained from his face and his eyes glassed over.

"I'm sorry. I thought everyone knew. I guess I was wrong," she said in apology.

Walker realized in an instant that Cosma was almost as perceptive as her mother, and that she saw the catastrophic pain wreaking havoc on his soul, and that she suddenly understood that he loved her mother deeply.

"Oh, I am sorry! If I had known . . . I would never have said it like that. She should have been the one to tell you. I'm so sorry." Cosma shook her head and said, *"Merde!"*

Too shaken to drive, Walker began pacing back to the villa.

"Will you be all right? I will walk with you if you wish."

Walker acknowledged that he had heard her by shaking his head and waving his hand requesting that she keep her distance.

Who knew? Was there a conspiracy against him? How long had they been engaged? He quickly spun out of control. The weather was warm and sunny and he wondered how such a terrible thing could happen on such a fine day. Nothing made sense. Chaos theory applicable in every way bumped the universe out of harmony. Inside his shirt, Walker rubbed the stone against his chest and then he stopped, paralyzed. From a different perspective, everything did make sense.

Instantly a different reality bolted through Walker's awareness. He was filled with Selena's thoughts and motivations. She quested for power and influence, not love or happiness. Wealth, recognition and prestige acquired in her first marriage had been craftily built upon to take her to this point. She now positioned herself to move to the next level.

Jean Bonnefoy may have been a billionaire, but the exact tally mattered little. His sphere of political influence stretched beyond France to Europe and the international scene. Selena could wind herself into the fabric of that power and influence, feed off it, get stronger and then use her skills to gain even more.

Other, more sinister, connections became clear. The powerful European diplomat who granted the winery immigration favors was Cosma's father. Getting Selena pregnant when she was seventeen would have ended his budding political career. Instead it remained a secret with the understanding that future benefit would be derived. It wasn't the secret daughter that currently held his influence, but the fact that he had allowed himself to be blackmailed all these years.

Cheap labor, guaranteed and protected by political influence, could make Jean Bonnefoy's winery the biggest in the world. Walker wondered what type of deal Selena had secured for herself after Jean's death. He suspected she'd get control of his winery.

Had Walker been a pawn from the very beginning, used to make Jean jealous, and force him to speed up his marriage plans? That depended on different truths, some of which Walker could not believe, such as Selena possessing the power and ability to summon him to Chateau du Clos de Vougeot. That had been fate and the rest was now history. Walker's love for her remained the only sure truth. The instinct to flee overwhelmingly defeated his instinct to fight.

Back in his room, wishing to capture the intensity of the moment, Walker wrote in his travel journal.

September 21

The vineyard at Beaune, France

> *Today is the autumn equinox. I know I must leave without saying goodbye—it is the only way. So strong are the emotions holding me here, if I don't go now I fear that I may never depart. An aquamarine stone on a gold neck chain lies against my body, a gift from the one I have loved so dearly. I was told it represents courage. Does it betray me?*
>
> *What is more courageous, to never let her eyes see the poem that expresses my heart, or to leave behind the poem for her to see after I have left? The choice truly haunts me.*

On the opposite page, the poem he had written the week before for Selena reflected back at him. He reread it, then stared down at the words, not knowing what to do next. Then he tore the page with the poem on it from his journal and gently placed it on the dresser. He packed all his belongings and started for the door. Hesitantly, he returned to the dresser, crumpled up the poem, threw it on the floor and departed the room for the last time.

Walker knew he hadn't the power to refuse Selena's requests to stay, so he hitched a ride to Dijon before Selena arrived home. He had to get away, far away from the haunting pull of Selena's stealthy dominion. He needed to escape from her mystical influence over him, her entangling webs of entrapment.

THE WORLDWIDE SEXUAL ADVENTURES OF WALKER FAYT

Yet at the same time Walker felt he was leaving a woman he truly loved. A strange mixture of triumph and defeat, of salvation and damnation clouded his thoughts and followed him on the train to Paris. Walker buried his love for Selena deeply alongside his other treasures, and in doing so created his own heart of darkness.

chapter 9

HAVOC IN THE AFRICAN JUNGLE
Gentle Gorillas & Wild Women

In the early afternoon, Walker arrived at Charles de Gaulle Airport. At the information center, he obtained the names of several airlines that flew to Africa. After a couple of frustrating hours, he finally purchased tickets from Sabena, the Belgian national airline. He bought a one-way ticket to Cairo and an open round-trip ticket from Cairo to Kampala, Uganda. No discount fares existed in and out of Uganda, so the flights were quite expensive. However, the cost of remaining in France was much higher.

Fate knew his lot and smiled on him that day and he boarded the plane less than three hours after his arrival at the airport. Walker slept during the flight, and in the early hours of the morning the plane touched down in Egypt. Customs and immigration hassled him for arriving without an entry visa—all tourists from non-Arab countries needed one to get in. Just beside immigration, the Banque Misr had a desk that sold entry visas and he was sent back there.

The attendant could not be found. After forty minutes, the young man returned to his post. Politely he apologized. He had not expected anyone to arrive at this early hour without a visa. More delays ensued while the man tried to figure out the type of visa Walker required.

THE WORLDWIDE SEXUAL ADVENTURES OF WALKER FAYT

Once through immigration, Walker entered customs, where he was asked a few questions and then sent on. Given the delays, his next flight was less than four hours away. He proceeded to the departure gate. The place was deserted. Using his carry-on backpack as a pillow, he lay down on the floor and went to sleep.

Walker woke up to a bustle of activity. The liveliness and motion of the waiting passengers filtered through his grogginess. Usually so much noise would have awakened him much earlier. He attributed his weariness to a lingering emotional hangover.

Western travelers bound for a safari adventure bubbled with anticipation. Ugandans seemed anxious to get back home. He observed the contrast in the people. Did anyone see his pain and the reason he had fled to Africa?

Instinct had sent Walker away to heal from his relationship with Selena. He needed to do that in a completely foreign environment—a place where all his truths were irrelevant, where a concentrated focus on his surroundings blocked everything else out. He believed that seeing wild gorillas in their natural habitat would provide sufficient distraction from his inner turmoil, so he had chosen Uganda.

The three-hour flight from Cairo went almost due south, through Egypt, across Sudan, over Uganda to the north shore of Lake Victoria. Uganda's international airport is in Entebbe, 21 miles southwest of the capital. For $2 U.S. he hired a public taxi to transport him to Kampala. There he found a very clean place to stay with a private bathroom for $10 per night.

Walker knew about Uganda mostly because of its infamous army leader, Idi Amin. After reading a guidebook for an hour, he knew a little more. He read that an estimated 300,000 Ugandans had been killed in horrific ways during Amin's reign of terror that started with a military coup in 1969 and lasted until 1979. Walker remembered hearing reports that claimed Amin liked the taste of human flesh.

The war Amin started with Tanzania ended with his troops being defeated and him fleeing to Libya. In 1994 and 1996, non-party elections re-established political stability in the country.

Mystery, intrigue and the possibility of endless discoveries sent Walker into the streets of Kampala. He observed a capital city in transformation. Construction and rehabilitation of restaurants, nightclubs and casinos provided evidence that foreign investment had returned. It surprised him that he could walk safely around any part of the city, day or night, without fear of being mugged or threatened. The dangers of some American cities, in contrast with this African one, twisted his perspective on civilization.

The next day, after visiting the Kasubi Tombs and the shining white Kibuli Mosque, Walker went to the Uganda tourist office. A young Ugandan provided information about the seven national parks and their abundance of wildlife. He told Walker that during the war, many animals were slaughtered for meat to feed the soldiers, but since then wildlife populations had returned. His pride showed as he explained that the best places to view animals were in his country because there were far fewer people than in the crowded parks of Kenya or Tanzania.

Of all the descriptions and possibilities of safaris, mountain hiking and tribal-village visits, seeing the mountain gorillas still fascinated Walker the most. Two of Uganda's national parks permitted close encounters with gorillas in their natural habitat. He recognized it as the chance of a lifetime, because at the rate they were currently disappearing, in less than a generation the mountain gorillas would be extinct.

It was more than just the threat of extinction that captured Walker's interest. When he had seen gorillas in zoos, he had always felt connected to them in some way. Genetically, they were close cousins to humans and it intrigued him to watch their behavior. They were powerful wild animals living in harmony with their environment and each other. Why did the beast in them not get converted into wars, prejudice, manipulation, and destruction? He thought that paying them a visit might provide insights into his questions.

The young man suggested that Walker check with the Uganda Wildlife Authority office. They made the bookings to see the gorillas in either Bwindi Impenetrable Forest National Park or Mgahinga Gorilla National Park. He took a taxi to the office.

The Wildlife Authority explained that 640 animals were left. Half lived in Bwindi and the other half in the Virunga Mountains in parks that involved three countries. Protecting the world's remaining mountain gorillas was a responsibility they took very seriously.

Due to the heavy demand, there were no vacancies for months. The spokesman delivered the same disappointing information to several other tourists as well. After about an hour, when the office emptied of tourists, Walker was told that for each of the two groups of gorillas tracked in Bwindi, a standby position remained open to walk-ins. If he traveled to the area and waited a few days on standby, he might get on a tracking group. No guarantees were offered and he was requested to keep this information secret.

The rest of the day Walker spent collecting things such as dried fruit and nuts, bottled water and high-speed film so he could take pictures in the forest. For dinner he ate at a cheap Indian restaurant; that night he slept little because of the anticipation.

The twelve-hour bus ride, which began in Kampala at six o'clock, seemed to take three days along the narrow muddy mountain roads. He overheard other tourists referring to Uganda as the pearl of the British Empire in East Africa, but light, misty rainclouds hid much of the beauty. Rain fell the entire day, giving the eerie feeling that the bus traveled in its own closed-in universe, and was drifting into an even darker and deeper unknown place.

HAVOC IN THE AFRICAN JUNGLE

Walker had until now always been satisfied reading or watching documentaries about rainforests. It thrilled him to actually experience one. He felt disconnected from people and did not socialize with other travelers. Most of the passengers were Westerners, who, judging from their conversations, seemed to be anxiously moving deeper into a wet, dark forest that held the promise to reunite them with a lost world. The few Ugandan passengers were let out in what appeared to be the middle of the jungle.

Little daylight remained as the bus pulled into the Butogota drop-off. The tourist office had warned Walker that there was no public transport beyond Butogota. He had left believing that some enterprising person would drive tourists the remaining ten miles to the park headquarters at Buhoma. He was wrong.

Drizzle fell and darkness set in as Walker contemplated what to do next. Constantly scrambling to make arrangements had kept his thoughts busy and away from the vineyard. It seemed the only option was to stay the night and walk or hitch a ride to the park the next day. That plan evaporated because all rooms were booked at Butogota's only inn. They did offer him the uninviting chair in the lobby and he secured the spot by leaving his bags in it.

Walker donned his raingear and went and stood outside. Looking up at the darkening sky, he let the rain mix with his tears to began to wash away the pain. He stayed there until all light left the sky.

A sudden flood of lights blinded Walker, interrupting his healing process. A Toyota Land Cruiser stopped alongside him and three people stepped out and onto the muddied dirt road. A tall, good-looking man drove and appeared to be the guide.

The man nodded his head at Walker and said, "Nice night for walkabout, isn't it? Watch out for the lions, mate; they're hungry this time of day."

Walker appreciated the man's sense of humor. A couple hurried in out of the rain and left the guide to attend to the luggage. Walker assisted by hauling a large knapsack from the car. By the time he and the guide got to the lobby, the couple had left for their room.

The guide said, "If you insist on being a porter, there is still some more stuff in the car."

"Sure. I've got nothing to do and no place to go until morning. I couldn't get a room. It's completely booked," Walker said in an annoyed tone of voice.

"Yeah, I know. I booked the last room for my clients. They've come all the way from New York to see the gorillas, but can't because they're sick. They've come down with something. We've refunded their money and guaranteed a spot for them when they're better. Still, it's bloody hell to see their disappointment; but the gorillas are susceptible to human disease and they come first."

Back outside in the rain, Walker asked, "I don't want to appear as a vulture, but is there any possibility that—?"

"Ya know, mate, I like ya. It looks like you can duke it out pretty good, but the rules are real sticky."

They picked up the remaining luggage from the back of the 4x4, and its driver said, "It's a bit dodgy—but I might be able to get away with something."

"I'm Walker Fayt. Good to meet you—anything you can do would be greatly appreciated," and he extended his free hand to shake.

The man's grip was firm and his handshake was strong. "Nice to meet you, mate. I'm Clarke Fox, originally from Tasmania. I came to Africa twenty years ago, fell in love with it, and made it my home."

They unloaded the last of the luggage and Clarke checked with registration to ensure that his clients were settled in to their accommodation. He waited until porters came and picked up the remaining baggage before heading back outside.

On the way out, Clarke pointed to Walker's knapsacks. "Is that your gear, mate?" Walker nodded and Clarke went over and picked up the larger of the two bags, leaving the smaller one for Walker.

Once they were outside and away from everyone, Clarke said, "Here's the deal. The owners don't know that the sick city folk have shipped out. It only happened an hour ago. They had the room booked for four nights and it hasn't officially been canceled."

"Sounds perfect so far, but I have a feeling that there are some big 'BUTS' coming."

"I think you're going to be my best new mate. You're right. There are several big 'BUTS.' First is the price. It's an upscale, Class B, luxury camp. It's a permanent facility and each room has an en suite hot shower—we call them bush showers—and a long-drop toilet. They had it booked for five hundred U.S. a night for the two of them. That includes room, food, drinks and transportation to the park. To get that space, you'd usually have to book it at least eight months in advance."

"I'm sure I won't be disappointed. What's your offer?"

"Right to the point, no bullshit. I like that." The open hatch cast a dim light and he could see Clarke smiling. "My employers think the room is rented to two people and they'll be expecting two thousand for the four nights. Since you're only one person, that means less food and if you promise to only use one bed. . . . I could settle for four-fifty a night, for a total of eighteen hundred."

Immediately Walker snapped his counter offer. "Fourteen hundred dollars!"

"Make it eighteen and as part of the deal, I'll bribe your way onto their three-day gorilla-tracking permit," Clarke shot back.

"I know I'll have to pay the hundred and fifty U.S. a day for the tracking permit, plus park admission. I thought our arrangement included getting me on a tracking permit," Walker said, continuing the negotiations.

"No, that's another of the 'BUTS.' It's very tightly regulated and it's going to be quite tricky to get you on their permit. I'm best buds with the rangers and trackers, so I'm sure for the right price I can get them to mess up the paperwork."

Walker made another offer. "Okay, sixteen hundred for the room and a hundred-dollar bribe to get a three-day tracking permit with my name on it. And of course I will still need to pay four-fifty to the park for the permit. Is it a deal?"

"Deal!" and with that Clarke threw the bag in the back of the sport utility, as did Walker.

As they bounced along the mud road, Clarke said, "Well, mate, room price and permits weren't the only big 'BUTS.' There's one more."

"Nice negotiating tactic, at night, in the middle of the jungle, and in the pouring rain. It must be a doozy."

Clarke laughed loudly, "You're a clever guy, mate; I like that. I don't know how to say it, so I'll just come right out with it. There's a real looker in camp. The best I've ever seen here. On top of that, she's a mean bitchy piece of work. I can't get her out of my mind. By the way she looks at me, I know that she'd like to give it a go. They say where there's smoke, there's fire. Hell, she's all flame. It's been a long time and I can barely keep it in my pants."

"How does this involve me and affect our arrangement?"

"I'm up here in the forest most of the time and don't get a crack at many women and certainly none of her caliber. I'm a straight guy, so don't take this the wrong way. You're a tall, good-looking fellow, in good shape and you might catch her eye. So I'm askin' ya as one of my mates: give me the courtesy of taking the first shot. If it doesn't work out, then it's open season."

Clarke did not understand the tone of misery in Walker's reply. "Don't worry, I'm not in the least bit interested."

"No offense, mate, but you're not gay, are ya?"

"No, I'm not gay. I'm just not interested. What's this woman's story?"

"Ah, what a woman! She arrived two days ago from London. She and her whole entourage. She's like a queen bee. The workers and drones buzz around, attending to her every instruction. It's quite incredible to watch."

"It sounds comical. Do you know what she does?"

In a serious tone, Clarke said, "Believe me, it's no joke. This woman is a self-centered, no-nonsense, demanding dynamo. She'll slice ya to pieces with her verbal barbs just for the fun of seeing you squirm." He shook his body as if remembering being on the losing end of recent exchanges, and continued talking.

"She works in the movies or TV or something; there are always cameras and microphones around. To tell ya the truth, it's a goddamn nuisance. She's here for two weeks and paying top dollar, so I can't complain. Besides, I love having her around; it makes me so horny. Ya know, mate—I think I can trust ya on this one."

Clarke negotiated the vehicle along the muddy road with skill and determination. They discussed Walker's background, then Clarke's. The son of sheep farmers, he was born and raised in Tasmania. After high school he left home to travel and never moved back. He spent a year traveling to Southeast Asia, India and Europe and then came to Africa. Here he felt the most connected to everything else; this was the place where he felt the most at home. Eleven years ago, out of an unexplained desire to save the gorillas from extinction, he had settled in Central East Africa.

"I've just started mid-life and the only thing my life lacks is the love of a good woman." Clarke clapped his hands together, and as the car almost steered off the road, yelled, "And mate, things are looking up!"

Clarke pointed into the darkness, indicating the way to the park entrance. He then turned the wheel and made a sliding turn into a smaller mud lane. In the headlights, through the rain Walker saw the tents of the safari camp.

"Welcome, mate, this is home. It's way past dinner, but I'm sure the kitchen staff saved me something." Clarke turned off the engine, opened the door, stepped out into the rain, then leaned back inside and quipped, "Come along, mate; I'm sure there's enough to keep ya from starving."

Walker followed him through the flaps of a very large tent. A green tarp atop wooden planks made the floor. A bright, warm and cozy atmosphere filled the tent. The kitchen staff had left a place setting for Clarke.

"Mister Clarke, you have returned with a guest. Is everything all right?"

"Everything is fine, James. This is Walker Fayt. He'll be staying in place of the Starkmans. Please set another place for dinner."

James said in an English Ugandan accent, "Yes, Mister Clarke, right away. Welcome, Mister Fayt. Enjoy your stay," and he turned to walk away.

Walker nodded in acknowledgment of his courteous manner and said, "Thank you, James, it's a pleasure to meet you."

Walker sat on a comfortable wooden fold-up chair with a canvas seat and back. There were six of these chairs around a wooden table covered with a white tablecloth. On top of it were lit candles and a flower arrangement. At the side, in a large bucket, soft drinks, bottled water, wine and beer chilled on ice. Another table of similar size had been cleared and washed.

Clarke went over to the beverages, removed two beers, set one in front of Walker, opened his, took a long swig, and said, "So mate, is it what you expected?"

"I didn't have any expectations of the place," responded Walker. "I came here to look into a gorilla's eyes and find a truth about my past—our past."

"That's a strange thing, mate. I'll give ya some advice: if it's a silverback, don't bother looking into his eyes. He might take it as a challenge to his authority and charge you. I kid around a lot, but that's no joke."

They talked mostly about the gorillas while they ate their chicken and pasta. Clarke told of encountering a mother gorilla teaching her young baby how to peel a piece of fruit. For several hours he observed the mother's patience and the child's steady progress. Then he told the story of the time he found several slaughtered adult gorillas. Poachers had killed them in an attempt to capture a baby. That story put a knot in Walker's stomach.

Impassioned, Clarke explained how Uganda had turned the corner from the horrors of its past. Political and economic stability had returned. Opportunities for its people were better now than they had been for decades. Despite recent history, its people were among the friendliest on the continent.

"The lure of quick, easy money for a few has the potential of ruining it for everyone—everyone in the world. Poachers either don't understand or don't care that a healthy gorilla population is a huge potential revenue source for Uganda. If they're eliminated, what's really left? Disgust and disgrace."

"I heard that in some places, it's legal for the park rangers to shoot poachers," Walker commented.

"In Uganda, it's not officially legal. When I shoot at poachers, it's overlooked and the rangers actually encourage it. If I actually shot one, and they lived, I know it'd be deemed an accident. If I killed a poacher that would be a lot more serious. If a park ranger did it, they'd get off. Want another beer?"

"Would you really shoot a poacher?" Walker questioned.

"Damn right, mate!"

Clarke explained that the poachers' main aim is to capture a baby gorilla. To do that they generally need to kill the mother and many other guardians. The dead bodies weren't completely worthless and if there was time, they'd cut off hands and feet and try to sell them as souvenirs. Some people used them as ashtrays. Other body parts were sometimes cut out and sold for medicinal purposes. In rare cases, heads were severed and sold as mantel trophies.

Walker thought about how a human child would be affected by witnessing the savage murder of its mother and extended family. It would be traumatized and emotionally disturbed forever. So too for the baby gorillas. Walker became tremendously upset.

"Why? Why the fuck does this happen?"

"Some rich people want to have a gorilla in their private collection. A disreputable zoo can attract many paying customers with a baby gorilla. That's the demand. A supplier can easily make the equivalent of several years' pay if they fill it."

Walker slammed his hand on the table in an explosion that had been building since France. "It's a sick fucking world we live in." Clarke glared back, surprised at the intensity of Walker's reaction.

The tent flap opened and in strolled what looked like Hollywood's version of a woman on safari. "The Tasmanian Devil hero has returned from his mission," were her first words. "Along the way he has found a beleaguered man who is angry at the world. Oh, what joy."

Walker ignored her comments, waiting to take his cue from Clarke. Even through his rage, the woman's attributes were hard to overlook. Clarke seemed spellbound and became speechless.

The woman stood about five-foot nine. Wavy, shoulder-length blond hair hung loose behind her ears and away from her face. She wore bright red lipstick on her thick, sensuous lips and showed a little tongue as she spoke. Staring out were cold, piercing, blue eyes.

She was squeezed into a tight-fitting, tan, short-sleeved shirt. Her breasts were so round and large that the pockets sat above them, almost parallel to the ground. She wore the bottom buttons undone and the shirt tied in a knot under her breasts, exposing a firm abdomen and a flat stomach. Tan hip-huggers, made of stretchy material, formed to her shapely hips, butt and legs. A thick, black, double-notch belt cinched her thin waist. Black leather riding boots completed the outfit.

Walker and Clarke sat across from each other at one of the tables. The woman sat down at the other end, put her elbows on the table, formed fists and rested her chin on her hands. Glancing back and forth between them, she put on a fake pout.

"What wrong, fellas? Can't a girl join in on your heated discussion?" A long silent pause hung in the air.

"Clarke, you're so rude. You haven't introduced to me to your angry—" she licked her lips slightly, "good-looking hitchhiker."

As she spoke, Walker studied her face, particularly her eyes. He sensed no deception at work. She was a straight-ahead, completely in-your-face, cocky woman in her early thirties.

Clarke stood up. "Sorry, Taylor—I don't think clearly when you're around. Okay . . . um . . . then . . . ah . . . Taylor Sinclair, this is Walker Fayt. Walker Fayt, this is Taylor Sinclair."

"So, Walk, what brings you to the jungle?" she asked in an uncaring way.

"I prefer Walker, and I came to the rainforest to escape the callousness of human behavior, only to find further examples."

"Has Clarke been spreading false stories about me again?"

Skipping her attempt at disruption, Walker continued. "I thought the gorillas would give me a glimpse of humanity's early beginnings. After hearing some of Clarke's experiences, I expect humans have far more to learn from the gorillas."

Taylor placed both hands on the table and leaned forward as she stood up. This gave both men a nice view of her chest. "Well, boys, this talk is way too deep for me. I'll leave you two alone to argue over who's going to be my companion. It's awfully lonely in that big tent of mine." She waved as she exited. "Nighty-night."

Walker raised his eyebrows and shook his head from side to side.

Clarke said, "See what I mean, mate; she's a solid ten that just doesn't let up."

"You're right, my friend, but tonight the last laugh is on her." He waited a moment for Clarke to think about it. "She's going to bed tonight believing that she's laid groundwork that will get us dueling for her affections. Not a chance. Go for it."

Clarke slapped him on the back. "Let's get ya bunked in. I've got something planned for tomorrow that I think you'll enjoy."

In Walker's tent there were two single beds, two dressers with mirrors and a vanity between the toilet and the shower. A handcrafted carpet lay on top of a clean floor of polished wood. Several gas lanterns illuminated the interior. The center of the tent stood at least eight feet tall and each side about five feet where the beds were. Flaps on the sides could be unzipped, exposing a mesh window to let in air. His accommodations pleasantly surprised him. They were better than many of the European hotel rooms he had stayed in. Walker got out his journal and began to write.

September 24

Safari camp, Butogota, Uganda

> Billions of years before our sun goes supernova, destroying our entire solar system, mankind will be extinct. Earth will be fine after our sojourn here, as it was before our arrival.
>
> From the planet's perspective, mankind is like a malignant tumor feeding on its host until this host is spent and lifeless. Unlike a human body attacked by terminal cancer, Mother Earth will survive us. We will kill ourselves through either greed (consumption), stupidity (overpopulation and pollution) or hatred (Armageddon)—or nature will tire of our arrogance and ignorance and eliminate us by its own methods.
>
> "Survival of the fittest," "master of the beasts," "created in the

likeness of God"—these are the concepts that help justify man's eradication of other species, an undertaking performed with such vicious aptitude that countless numbers of species have disappeared since man's arrival. Is this all part of the world's natural evolution?

Approximately 99.5 percent of a gorilla's DNA matches human DNA. It's the 0.5 percent that's different that gives humans the ability to completely eliminate gorillas from existence. Does it give us the right? With each act of xenocide, we get one step closer to our own extinction.

In the likeness of God, insects are patiently waiting to assume their dominant role.

The following morning, Walker surfaced from his tent at about 8:15 and ate some of the food he had brought. Clarke took him behind the dining tent into the kitchen area, and made sure he got something more substantial. He explained the normal routine on a day of tracking. They served breakfast from 6:30 to 7:30 and by about 8:00 the guests left for the park. At 8:30, the park staff checked permits and if they found everything in order, tracking began.

After eating enough eggs, ham and toast to keep him satisfied until lunch, Walker got in the Land Cruiser and they headed up the mountain road toward the park. A light rain fell in the cool morning mist. Walker could not see through the thick vegetation that hugged the road or the low ceiling of cloud that surrounded them. These conditions made him feel caged.

When they arrived at the park gate, a ranger looked in the car, smiled and waved them through without checking anything. They traveled up a small mud road for about twenty minutes and then turned onto a path. The car barely fit, and after another thirty minutes the undergrowth closed in so tightly they could go no farther.

It seemed like they were parked on the edge of the world. Looking out, above and below they saw only a white mist. Behind them a thick mass of jungle climbed into the mist. Walker inhaled deeply, admiring the rich, clean air.

Clarke popped open the hatchback and took out a rifle. He leaned it against the back of the car and retrieved another. "Hey mate, catch." He tossed a gun at Walker.

Walker caught it with both hands, looked it over, shaking his head, and said, "What the fuck is this for?"

"We're tracking today, too, but we're tracking poachers. After our talk last night, I thought ya might be up for it."

"I've never fired a gun in my life and I'm not about to start now."

Clarke got a smirk on his face. "Don't worry, mate, it's not loaded. It's only for show. Just in case we run into anybody, it looks like we have more fire power."

Walker pointed the gun into the jungle and squeezed the trigger. Nothing happened.

Clarke laughed and then said, "Don't trust me. I like that. The safety is on. Release that lever on the right-hand side by pulling it back and down, then try again."

Walker did as instructed. When he aimed and pulled the trigger, again it clicked. The rifle wasn't loaded.

"Good man. Ya should always inspect your weapon and never rely on somebody else. Otherwise people get killed."

With an expression of concern, Walker said, "This is great; now I'm a target without even being a threat. This is just plain stupid."

"I'll put bullets in it if you want," Clarke suggested, but Walker shook his head.

As Clarke led the way up the steep mountain trail, he said, "There've been reports of poachers in this area. I volunteered to check it out. It's great to have some company. Usually I go alone."

A multitude of unfamiliar sounds and smells filled Walker's senses.

Much of the jungle's distinctiveness remained hidden to his untrained eye. Being on a private tour of a mountain rainforest was a rare and wonderful opportunity. Carrying an empty gun over his shoulder only detracted mildly from his pleasure.

Walker passed by a small cave and Clarke called him back. It made for a good place to get out of the rain and eat lunch. His raingear and hiking boots were waterproof. However, the morning's arduous ascent produced enough perspiration to soak him.

Clarke poked a stick around in some ashes. He seemed a bit uneasy when he told Walker that someone had been there within the last day or two. After lunch he planned to head back down and take an indistinguishable trail away from the ridge to a thicker part of the forest. They ate lunch and were on their way.

Slowly they maneuvered along an overgrown trail. Suddenly a thunderous grunt echoed throughout the forest. Instinctively Walker fell to the ground; he hit it with a thud. Clarke stood over him with one finger over his mouth for silence and pointed off into the forest with the other finger. Quickly stumbling to his feet, Walker followed Clarke into the thicket.

Clarke stopped. Walker stood behind him and held his breath while his heart pounded. In a partial clearing, about twenty yards away, were three big gorillas. The two men watched for a few incredible minutes and then Clarke pointed backward.

They eased back about fifty yards and Clarke whispered, "This is not one of the groups that is tracked. We'll have to be cautious. If ya see the silverback, immediately sit on the ground, put your head down and pretend to eat out of your hand. I reckon that this group has fifteen to twenty individuals. This is a rare event, even for me, so let's do it right."

Clarke flashed a big white smile and raised his eyebrows. "We can get closer if we circle around and approach from the other direction—it's downwind. They probably know we're here, but if we don't get too close and don't do anything threatening, I don't think they'll care."

Adrenaline released into Walker's system, causing his heart to pump faster, and he heard pounding on the inside of his ears. They reached the spot Clarke had intended and not more than twelve yards away, in clear view, were a dozen or more gorillas.

Clarke and Walker watched as several females built nests. The older and larger ones built on the ground, the smaller, more agile ones in the trees. They wrapped the vines and stringy plants around their bodies, weaving them in and out to form a loose frame. Once the framework was strong enough, the gorillas lined the bottom with leaves. The older females constructed their nests in about five minutes.

A baby, in an obvious display of theatrics, tried to copy its mother. It broke and bent stems and twigs and dropped them into its lap, then stuffed a few leaves on top, stood up, turned around and quickly sat on top of the pile. Walker saw the look on the baby's face and knew it believed that the best nest in the world had just been constructed. He almost laughed out loud. They had watched the group for about twenty minutes.

Walker knelt side by side with Clarke, who tapped him on the shoulder and pointed. The silverback came into view. BANG! A shot ricocheted off a tree just above the head of a female that held a baby.

Complete chaos followed the shot. Gorillas screamed. The silverback roared and ran into the forest. More shots banged, and then hissed as they bounced off trees. Clarke ran like a madman straight to where the animals had been. The sound of breaking tree branches and cracking bamboo echoed through the woods. Not five yards away, a man carrying a rifle ran past Walker.

Walker pursued him. His earlier adrenaline rush was only a trickle compared to the geyser that now flowed. Darting through the forest, he quickly gained on his prey. In a small clearing the man turned and raised his weapon. In his terror he fumbled with the gun, and before he could regain his coordination Walker collided with him at full speed.

It was a classic shoulder tackle that Walker had executed a thousand times before in football practice. With his size and speed, the effect devastated his target. The poacher's gun dropped on impact and the momentum carried the two of them six feet through wild celery, with the poacher taking the brunt of it from both the front and the back.

The man lay unconscious beneath Walker, who was scratched and scraped but otherwise unharmed. He climbed to his feet, retrieved the dropped rifle, walked back to where the man was still lying and nudged him in the ribs with his boot while aiming the gun at the man's chest.

Slowly the man came to, and as he realized his predicament, he began to whine and plead for his life. Wanting to keep the upper hand and stay in complete control of the situation, Walker addressed him in a tone that made it clear he meant business.

"Shut the fuck up or I'll shoot you right now! I'm tempted to blow your head off anyway. You would have shot me just to get away, you sonovabitch! Get up, keep your hands in the air, and walk slowly back the way we came."

The man obeyed. As they got closer to where they had started, Walker looked around for his own dropped rifle. The other man spotted it before he did. Walker's voice kept its steely edge.

"Don't even think about it! One step toward that weapon and you're a dead man."

Again the man obeyed, much to Walker's relief. Shooting someone was the last thing he wanted to do.

Walker's adrenal glands kept him pumped and unaware of how shaken he really was. He stooped down and picked up the unloaded rifle, then demanded that they proceed to the nesting area where the action began. There Walker sat the man against a tree while he sat against another a few feet away. For now his only plan was to wait for Clarke.

All kinds of thoughts raced through Walker's head. Had Clarke fared as well? How many more poachers were there—none or ten? How many weapons did they have? Was Clarke even alive? If not, how would Walker get back to camp? He attempted to put a stop to his obsessive questioning by addressing his captive.

"Hey, asshole—how many in your group?"

The man remained silent. Walker raised the gun and pointed it at his head.

"Three, there were three of us." The man looked away.

Walker kept his aim. "Did all of you have guns?"

"We all had guns," the man replied. "All of them like that one you're pointing at me."

Noise came from the woods beyond. Walker realized that he might have to surprise his adversaries by shooting them before they shot him. As the sounds of footsteps got closer, the tension increased. Walker put his finger to his lips, signaling his captive to keep quiet. Then he slid his finger across his throat, letting the man know that if he didn't comply he was dead.

Out of the forest and into view walked two Ugandan men with their hands in the air. Walker stood and called out, "Over here!"

Clarke stood behind them, his rifle pointed at the Ugandans; two more long guns were slung over his shoulders. When he saw Walker and his quarry, he flashed a grin of relief mixed with humor. "Didn't I tell ya that you'd like tracking poachers? Well done, mate! Not bad for your first time out."

They walked the men at gunpoint back to the car. While Walker stood guard, Clarke tied their hands and feet and loaded them into the back seat. Clarke drove down and Walker held the loaded gun in case there was trouble. The experience gave him a whole new meaning for the term "riding shotgun."

Clarke radioed ahead and when they reached the park gate, local law-enforcement authorities were waiting to collect the poachers. Clarke and Walker gave sworn statements to be used as evidence. Attempted murder would be added to the charges against the man who had pointed the gun at Walker. Poaching was a serious crime in Uganda, and all the men faced stiff sentences if convicted.

Clarke and Walker were given accolades befitting heroes by the authorities and the park rangers. The capture was big news, and two-way radios, walkie-talkies, telephones and word of mouth ensured that it traveled quickly. What made the story even better was that none of the gorillas had been hit by the gunfire.

It was well after dinner by the time Clarke and Walker arrived back at camp. All was quiet until they opened the flap of the dining tent, when they were greeted with shouts of "Surprise!" and a chorus of "For they are jolly good fellows."

The party came complete with a cake that crudely resembled a gorilla. The tent was crowded with camp guests and staff, park rangers and other park employees, town officials and even guests of other camps who wanted to congratulate the heroes and be part of the celebration.

The festivities continued well past the customary turning-in time. Everyone wanted to have a drink or toast with Walker; he got a bit drunk. As the party wound down, he said goodnight to the hangers-on.

Clarke stayed, impaired and in full celebratory mood. As it turned out, it was his first capture of poachers. He had exchanged gunfire before, but nothing more. Clarke and Walker gave each other a big hug and slapped each other on the back. Whoops and hollers followed Walker as he left.

Walker opened the flap to his own tent. It was dark. Usually the camp staff left a lantern burning.

"What took you so long, Walk? I've been waiting."

It was Taylor. She lit a match, started the lantern and placed it on one of the dressers.

"I saw gorillas today, too, but I'd rather have been with you." She waited for him to respond. When he didn't, she persisted.

"Walk, you avoided me all night. Is there a reason for that?"

"Yes. And I don't wish to discuss it. Please leave." His tone was curt and dismissive.

Low light cast mysterious shadows across the tent walls and ceiling. Taylor came very close to him and her voice sweetened. "I'm not the girl you think I am. I'm tough and brash on the outside, but on the inside I'm a pussycat. You should get to know me from the inside."

The alcohol had relaxed his resolve, but not enough to break his word. "I'm sure you're sweet, but I'm not biting."

"Oh shit. You're gay."

Walker found Taylor's reaction consistent with her personality. If a man refused her, he must be gay. He let it go, saying only, "It's not that."

"Are you married?" Her tone indicated annoyance.

"No—divorced," he said softly.

"Then what's the problem, Walk? I really want to know," she said, running her hand along his chest.

"I don't think you do. I think you're here for a quick fix, or to cause shit or for some other game." He snatched her wrist and removed her hand from his chest.

"Your honesty is refreshing," Taylor replied, "but you've misread me. I want to know your problem. I really do. It's fine with me if we just talk all night. Trust me."

Intoxication had lowered Walker's resolve and memories of

Selena flooded his emotions. He reasoned that talking about it might help him heal. Taylor's words seemed sincere. What harm could come by telling her? He reached out and held her soft, strong hand and led her over to the bed. He sat down and she beside him.

"This may take a while and I want you to promise that you'll speak to no one about it."

Tenderly, she said, "Walker, I promise."

Taylor provided the perfect shoulder to cry on, and once Walker started, he vented for the next thirty minutes. His bewitched love for Selena poured into his words like honey from a jar—slow, thick and sweet. Taylor sat and mostly just listened.

When Walker had finished talking, she hugged him and gave him a small kiss on the cheek. She tenderly encouraged him to talk about other matters in his life. Eventually he told his whole story. Taylor sympathized and questioned him inquisitively about the women he had been with, but she made no attempt to seduce him. This made it easier for him to stay true to his pact with Clarke.

Walker had come to Uganda as an escape and felt fortunate for the healing he had just undergone. Taylor intuitively picked up on his renewal.

"I know it can't work between you and me. You've made that quite clear and I think I understand why."

Taylor gently touched him on the arm, saying, "How about somebody else? You know; it's kind of like learning to ride a bicycle. Once you've fallen off, you should get right back on."

Walker spoke softly and slowly. "What are you getting at?"

"Following your desires is great and I want to help, that's all. Should I continue?" He nodded yes.

"My local personal assistant, Beatrice, has an incredible crush on you. We've had several girlie talks about it. It's like she's a schoolgirl and you're the teacher. Well, you *are* a teacher—you know what I mean. It's very sweet."

"So-o?" he said, stretching out the word. Taylor continued.

"It would be such a thrill for her; something she'd remember for the rest of her life; probably tell her grandchildren about it. If you're really good, you might be remembered for years to come in her village's folklore. That's a joke, of course. You're not laughing. Oh, come on, it would be good for her and good for you too—another experience with no commitment and no complications. It's a way to get you going again. In case you haven't noticed, she's a vibrant young woman."

"Your sales pitch is too much. What's in it for you?" he asked. Taylor put her hand on her heart.

"Walker, after what we've been through tonight, I'm crushed. Let's just say, if you did this, I wouldn't have to tip her; she'd want to tip me. Jokes aside, I like to help people. I truly believe it would be very good for both of you."

"Even if you convinced me, I wouldn't risk it. AIDS and HIV are extremely common in Uganda." He said it in a tone that suggested the subject was closed.

"Beatrice and I have talked extensively. She's twenty-five and has worked for the camp for four years. She hasn't had sex since she was twenty, and then only twice. Before coming to Africa, I had all the places I'm staying in checked thoroughly. This is the only one I know of that requires medical check-ups for its staff. They say they test for AIDS. Besides, you can practice safe sex."

Something about this circumstance triggered a distant memory in Walker. He was fourteen. School had finished for the summer and his days in New York were numbered. He hung around with his friends as much as possible, stayed out late and broke curfew. Five days before the move to Toronto, he heard a rumor that Patty McKnight had a massive crush on him. She was one grade below him in school and he had never really noticed her.

Flattered by her interest in him, he decided to check her out more closely. He talked to friends of friends, seeking more details about her. The reconnaissance revealed that she scored two out of three: a great personality and nice large breasts. She was just average looking.

Walker went to the neighborhood where Patty lived and found her house by asking around. At her door, she seemed elated to see him. As they chatted, she beamed with joy. He explained to her that in a few days he would be moving away with his family. Awkwardly, he suggested that although it couldn't be for a long, if it was okay with her, he'd like to ask her out. At that time it meant to go steady. Patty fainted on the spot.

Once she revived, Walker had to convince her that he meant his proposal. To consummate such a relationship, custom dictated a rendezvous at the local park. They arranged one for the next day at 7 p.m. After an hour of hugging and kissing behind some bushes, they walked arm-in-arm, passing many mutual friends and acquaintances along the way. Embarrassment kept them from saying hello to any of them.

Walker's intentions had been quite honorable; he had felt no desire to exploit her in any way. He just wanted to give Patty a bit of a thrill. He saw her again, on the afternoon before he moved, and officially broke up with her.

Walker looked into Taylor's cold blue eyes. "Okay, I'll consider it—but it must be discreet. Her reputation can't be tarnished."

In the dim light, Taylor's eyes twinkled. "Tomorrow afternoon the entire camp is going on a bird-watching hike. Find an excuse to stay back. I have a tent to myself—you know which one it is. Go to it. Beatrice will be waiting for you. I know neither one of you will be disappointed. What changed your mind?"

"A buried treasure," he replied softly, as if still far off in thought.

Taylor shrugged her shoulders, signaling to him that she didn't understand his comment nor did she care to. As she stretched to kiss him on the cheek, her breasts pressed against his chest and she whispered in his ear: "I had a brilliant time tonight. I'll see you tomorrow. Good night."

At breakfast, Taylor received rock-star treatment from her staff. Walker couldn't determine what everyone did for her, but they all managed to constantly look busy. Two bodyguards, one local and one from England, stood close by at all times. Taylor spent most of her time talking with the cameraman. Two personal assistants were there to do whatever she asked. Beatrice was one and the other was a big homely girl from England. The equipment handler and a technical gofer ranked at the bottom of the pecking order. Taylor's staff paid constant attention toward her. It symbolized her importance.

A few times during breakfast, Walker caught Beatrice checking him out. She tried not to notice when he covertly looked at her. They played an innocent game of peek-a-boo, attempting to satisfy their sexual curiosity in one another with very short glances. Although Taylor appeared preoccupied with the imperative details of her day, Walker noticed her watching the interaction between them.

After breakfast, Taylor requested that Beatrice inform "Mr. Fayt" that she wished to speak with him. Beatrice slowly approached him and Walker could see the excitement in her building. By the time she reached him, her face beamed. She looked down at him, her big brown eyes sparkling and a bright smile stretched from ear to ear.

"Miss Sinclair says she would like a word with you, Mr. Fayt." She turned, and before walking away, added, "And from me, thank you for saving our gorillas." Walker smiled back, accepting her praises.

Before going over to Taylor's table, Walker sat and finished his coffee. Taylor staged introductions with her staff as a pretense to introduce Beatrice and Walker prior to their rendezvous. At the conclusion of their introduction, as he had done with the others, he put out his hand to shake with Beatrice. She was embarrassed and refused to shake his hand. She looked away, hid her face in her hands, laughed and put her hand over her mouth. Her dark skin hid the blushing, but not her manner.

On the ride to the park, Walker and Taylor sat beside each other in the back seat. Two of her staff also squeezed in. Clarke drove and he frequently glared back at them. Outside the car, at the park's front gate, Clarke was curt with Walker, but didn't openly say anything. He paid attention to the other guests. Despite being upset, Clarke ensured that Walker's tracking permit cleared the checkpoint.

In less than an hour, the park tracker found a gorilla group approved for observation. Getting close to them was another matter. The trek to the gorillas required a difficult climb down into a wet, cold gully, then a grueling assent up a steep hill. They pulled themselves up by grabbing hold of bamboo and vines.

Taylor lost her grip on the slippery bamboo and quickly slid back down toward Walker, clutching and grabbing for anything that might break her fall. In the instant before she crashed into him, he braced himself with one arm, reached up and stopped her fall by jamming his straightened arm into her descending buttocks. He pushed her back up, pressing deeply into the fleshiness of her ass and vagina. She regained her hold.

When she made it to the top, her staff fussed and pampered her. Walker climbed onto the ridge and Taylor gave him a hand up. "Thanks, you really saved my ass."

A warm and moist sensation lingered on his fingers and hand.

The remaining fifty yards to the gorillas was flat. The group maintained silence while the guide made low grunting noises, alerting the gorillas to human presence. Familiarity with the guide's style of communicating did not eliminate the gorillas' cautiousness. He attempted to put them at ease by continuing to grunt and imitating their feeding behavior by picking leaves and chewing on them.

As the human and animal groups interacted, they seemed to share the same emotional response—fascination. The gorillas watched the humans as intently as the humans watched them, Walker thought. The humans were treated with respect and were warmly accepted by their hosts.

Adult females stayed about eight to ten feet away and tenderly allowed their children to get as close as they wished to their guests. They even seemed to encourage close encounters. Did they know that their survival depended on these daily visits?

Sometimes the babies came within one foot of a person and appeared ready to jump onto them. The guides stopped them from doing so by waving their hands or branches. Humans could transmit diseases to gorillas, so they prohibited contact.

The silverback controlled the encounter. He displayed his dominance in a powerful, elegant and sophisticated way. He observed every movement. His silence and stillness meant approval; any noise or motion from him caused reaction in both the human and gorilla groups.

For just a fraction of a second, Walker looked into the eyes of the silverback. In that instant he felt the sadness and pain of a great leader who had seen his followers defeated by an enemy he could not understand. The giant gorilla harbored neither hatred nor ill will, only regret. If threatened, instinct would allow him to kill; otherwise he sought peace, reconciliation and refuge. The qualities he possessed would have been a compliment to any human leader.

Daily contact could not exceed sixty minutes and soon the group was on its way back to camp. Taylor discreetly informed Walker that the arrangements were set for the afternoon. She had discovered that Beatrice had never touched a white man, and this had been the cause of her reaction earlier that day. Walker misunderstood the context of the remark and reminded her that he had never been with a black woman. Taylor explained that in Beatrice's case, touch meant nothing more than simply touch.

On the ride back to camp, Walker sat in the front seat and Taylor sat in the back. This seemed to put Clarke more at ease.

After lunch, one of the camp porters came to Walker's door and informed him that the bird-watching trek was to begin in a few minutes. Walker declined, saying that after the excitement of the last few days and the late party of the night before, he wasn't up to it. The man persisted by telling him that Uganda had more than a thousand species of birds and that many would be seen on the walk. Again Walker politely declined.

Walker showered and shaved off several days' growth. Secretly he made his way over to Taylor's tent. Pausing outside the flap entrance, he deeply inhaled the clean, moist Ugandan air. His feelings were similar to those he had experienced when he had stood on Patty McKnight's front porch. At least this time he didn't have to go behind the bushes. Walker stepped inside the tent.

He didn't see anyone and softly called out. "Hello, is anybody home?"

Beatrice appeared from the shower area toweling her wet hair. When she saw him, she placed the towel in front of her face and mumbled into it.

"I feel so strange. I don't have a word for it. This is just weird," she giggled. "I don't want to look at you."

Walker had never experienced sex as a teenager and imagined its antics and emotional exchange would have been much like this—both people wanting to physically participate, but feeling somewhat naughty and unsure of how to make the first move.

"All right, Beatrice, we'll do it your way and never look at each other ever again." He sensed her big bright smile behind the towel.

When Walker touched her hand, she gasped in surprise. He caressed her by softly sliding his fingers over hers. In the palm of her hand he drew circles with his fingers and then blew light bursts of air onto them. After he kissed each one of her fingers, he slipped her index finger into his mouth and began lightly sucking it. Beatrice's breathing became heavier.

Walker slipped her finger from his mouth and planted a wet kiss on the inside of her wrist. She dropped the towel from her face to the floor. They were no longer children experimenting with their sexuality, but adults full of sexual cravings. Instinct drove them to kiss passionately.

As they feverishly kissed, Walker slipped his tongue past her warm, luscious lips and into her mouth. Immediately she pulled away and gave him a look of surprise. Quickly Beatrice resumed kissing him and experimented with the lesson just learned and slipped her tongue into his mouth. Her large, soft breasts pressed against his body and the heat between them increased.

Still in a playful mood, Walker lifted her long, loose skirt and ducked inside it. He kissed her calf, then her knee, then behind her knee. Chuckling, she asked him to come out. He continued kissing up the back of her leg and worked his away around to the front of her leg halfway up her thigh. The body he was kissing trembled.

The eroticism seemed to put Beatrice off balance. Walker steadied her by wrapping his arms around her legs. With her balance secure, he spread her legs. Tilting his head up, he ran his tongue the full length of her moist labia. Then he thrust his tongue farther into her vagina and quickly moved it in and out. Beatrice's sweet, youthful excitement ran down his face.

Walker took a firm hold of her legs and stood up, lifting her into the air. Beatrice steadied herself by hanging onto his shoulders. Unable to see from beneath her dress, he continued to lick and suck, balancing her on his face. He ventured in the direction of where he thought the bed should be. When his legs touched it, he dropped her onto the mattress. With his hands now free and Beatrice lying on her back, he flipped up her skirt, and then spread her labia.

The contrast between her dark brown skin and the bright pink of her vagina was erotically beautiful. Beatrice sat up and removed her one-piece dress, exposing dark, gorgeous breasts with massive black nipples. Pointing to his clothing, she signaled to him to get naked as well. As he removed his pants, he retrieved a prophylactic from his pocket. She gently took it from him and examined it.

"You don't need this. I'm not fertile at this time and I'm free from disease."

"I am too, but you don't have proof of that and you shouldn't trust anyone who says they are."

Beatrice gave him a big smile. "If you insist on wearing it, then I'll put it on you."

Walker did not interfere with her attempts to get the condom over his hard penis. Once she got it in place, she pulled him on top of her, rekindling some of the lost intensity. Like a guided missile, his penis easily found its wet, warm target.

Beatrice's body vibrated as she wrapped her legs firmly around his back. He held her arms down and ground his pelvis into hers with each riveting stroke. Squeezing him tightly with her legs, she jolted her abdomen in the air and cried with pleasure. He jammed himself in as far as he could and exploded into the sheath deep inside her tight, warm, lubricated vulva. She released her leg grip and he fell limp on her dark, sweaty body.

Walker and Beatrice lay still and silent for a long while. Humidity and their sexual exertion caused sweat to pour from their bodies, and eventually he slipped right off her. They both laughed and the impish mood of adolescence returned. In a giddy foolishness, they nicknamed his penis "Moby Dick" and her breasts "Kilimanjaros." Pomp and ceremony preceded the dropping of the used condom down the toilet. The uneasy silliness continued for about fifteen minutes. Both mentioned that they wished for their encounter to remain a secret as the time came to leave Taylor's tent.

THE WORLDWIDE SEXUAL ADVENTURES OF WALKER FAYT

Walker left first and through his caution, thought he had avoided detection on the way back to his tent. Twenty minutes later, Beatrice left and resumed her scheduled duties for Taylor.

For the rest of the afternoon, Walker slept in his tent. His nap came to an abrupt end by a voice yelling, "Come out here, ya bastard, and face me like a man!"

Clarke had been in Kabale for the day receiving official honors from the Uganda Wildlife Authority. It did not seem real that he was now outside the tent, screaming. Through his grogginess, Walker thought that perhaps he was dreaming and would wake up at any moment. In a hazy state of consciousness, he stepped out of his tent and into the sunshine of the late afternoon.

"We had a deal, ya bastard!"

Walker heard the cursing and then the crack of his jaw being struck. Dazed and lying in the dirt, he did not know what was happening, but the pain in his jaw told him it was no dream.

A commotion quickly formed as witnesses rushed toward the action. Camp employees held Clarke back while he challenged Walker to get up. Word spread like a brush fire through the camp and reached the returning hikers as they approached. Taylor ran to the scene and stood between Clarke and Walker, who had now gotten to his knees and was about to stand. Taylor tore into Clarke.

"What the fuck is this all about?"

Clarke yelled right back, "I heard from a reliable source that he was seen leaving your tent this afternoon, and I assumed—"

"And like the Tasmanian Devil you created a whirlwind! In the first place, it's none of your damn business." Taylor's anger intensified as she continued. "And in the second place, you assumed wrong. I was on the hike all afternoon. Walker asked if he could borrow some high-speed film and I told him where to find it."

Webs of different truths had spun together, tightly entangled.

Walker deduced that a camp employee must have seen him leaving

Taylor's tent. Being loyal to Clarke and understanding his feelings for her, they had reported it to him. Believing that he had been betrayed, Clarke had displaced his anger with a macho show of chivalry. When Walker had exited from the tent, Clarke had interpreted this as an acceptance of his challenge.

Walker understood Clarke's reaction and did not hold it against him. He viewed Taylor's fabrication as a means to defuse the violence, put Clarke in his place and protect Beatrice's honor within the camp. Walker also knew that Clarke's actions jeopardized the job he loved so much. No excuse existed for hitting a client. The next few moments were critical to his future. Clarke needed to make amends quickly.

Taylor played the situation to her benefit. She shook her head at Clarke in disgust. Then she tenderly fussed over Walker's sore jaw.

Clarke made the first gesture of reconciliation. "Hey, mate, I fucked up big time. You were straight and I'm an idiot. No hard feelings," he said and he put out his hand to shake. "I knew from the first that you could duke it out. I wouldn't have gotten up after a hit like that. Let me buy the drinks tonight."

Walker grabbed his hand. "No hard feelings. I know where you're coming from. Now if only this sexy Brit would accept it, everybody could be happy." Puzzled, Taylor looked at Walker, then at Clarke, and her expression turned to innocent charm.

"Why, Clarke, all you had to do was ask." As she strutted away, she turned her head and gave Clarke a sultry stare that melted him on the spot. She smiled and said, "I'll see you tonight at dinner and *I'll* buy the drinks."

At dinner, jokes flew around and Clarke got teased over his mistake. Taylor sat next to Clarke and refrained from her usual viperous attacks on him. Every so often she would give Walker a wink and an expression of amusement.

In this atmosphere of camaraderie, Walker sensed an uneasy

tension. A false discord resonated just beneath civility's thin veneer. During dinner, he ignored the troubling dynamic and stayed friendly and sincere, but shortly afterward, he excused himself and went back to his tent.

*

Walker was relieved by Taylor's absence on his last two days of gorilla tracking. If the rumors around camp were true, then Taylor and Clarke were an item. Walker did not want Clarke's jealousy to be unleashed by another misunderstanding.

On Walker's last night at camp, Beatrice came to his tent full of womanly desires and wishing to satisfy him as a man. In the dim light of the lantern, their naked bodies entangled, becoming as alive as the jungle.

Beatrice excitedly experimented with sexual maneuvers she hadn't tried in their previous tryst. Her oral pleasuring made his penis stiff and hard. When Walker got out a condom, she did not allow him to put it on. Instead she guided him between her breasts, which completely engulfed his throbbing erection. He stroked his penis over her hardened nipples. She pressed her large, soft, dark breasts together until her nipples touched and he rubbed his purple, circumcised head across both of them.

Their sexual frenzy quickened and Walker stroked between her tits. With each thrust he slid closer to her face until he touched her under the chin with each lunge forward. Tilting her head forward, she flicked her tongue over the head of his approaching penis. He pulled back and aimed, then squirted his pearl-white come all over her dark breasts. The sight so excited him that he wished he could immediately come again, but that was impossible. They French-kissed and held each other tightly. Eventually they fell asleep in each other's arms.

Walker's travel alarm rang at five o'clock in the morning. He and

Beatrice reluctantly peeled themselves away from each other and said their goodbyes with long passionate kisses.

Ten minutes before breakfast, Walker tramped though camp to load his gear onto a departing supply truck headed for Kabale. Taylor's "gofer" stopped him to relay a message: Taylor wanted to talk with him privately before he left.

At breakfast, Clarke presented Walker with a fake medal in recognition of his contribution to the poacher arrests. As he handed it to Walker, Clarke leaned over and whispered in his ear, "Thanks, mate. In more ways than one," and winked at him.

Walker shook everyone's hand, and again Beatrice shyly refused to shake. With sufficient cajoling from staff and guests, she pretended to break down and they shook hands. He squeezed tightly and she squeezed back. In the hubbub, no one noticed that their eyes twinkled from a special treasure they shared.

Taylor joined Walker as he headed toward his ride. He had never seen her looking so stern.

"I don't know why, but I'm going to come clean. That crap you fed me the other night about your revelations is bullshit. You're a middle-aged man who just wants to get fucked, and you'll justify it any way you can.

"Walk, you and all men like you disgust me. You cut your wives loose after twenty years of marriage—and for what? Just to get your dicks wet in another woman. Do you really think you could give Beatrice any pleasure? She is circumcised, for Christ's sake. Not that you would notice, you selfish prick."

The words struck a nerve in Walker; they hit harder than any physical punch.

"Not only are you an asshole," Taylor continued, "you're a stupid asshole. I'm not doing a TV show about gorillas, but about sex—it's called *Sex on Safari*. You've provided me with more material than I can possibly use for three of my tabloid spots.

"Our little talk is on audiotape and your night with Beatrice—let's just say Moby Dick won't get away this time. Your tussle with Clarke, with the right editing, will be brilliant. I had someone tell him about your visit to my tent."

Walker's brain could not register the words he was hearing. Everything had been a setup, and he was leaving a place again, having been a pawn in someone else's game!

"Clarke knew about this? Beatrice was in on your sick trap?"

"Hell, no. They are as naïve as you are. They were the bait to get what I needed—the story that will captivate my viewers for fifteen minutes. They say that people will kill for fifteen minutes of fame. Well, Walk, you've got it. It's too bad my show doesn't air in the States—then you could be famous at home too. The pleasure has been all mine. Bye!"

The circumstances had stretched beyond Walker's comprehension. Thoughts rushed through his head: her actions were unethical, likely illegal; her words painted her as a loose cannon. Stunned into motionlessness, he was unable to find words to respond. As the Kabale-bound truck began rolling, Walker realized he had to move, and he vaulted into the back. His shock gradually gave way to a fit of anger that stayed with him all the way to Kabale.

chapter 10

TANYA—THE COLORS OF PLEASURE
In Jordan's Deserts, Surrender to Sexual Gratification

Walker stared at the wake behind the ferryboat and thought about Moses cutting a path through these waters so that his people could flee Egypt. Walker visualized the parted waters of the Red Sea and a road to freedom. These thoughts turned his mind to memories of his month in Egypt.

Walker had arrived in Cairo from Kampala, Uganda, and cleared Egyptian customs and immigration without incident. He found the people, the monuments and the geography to be far beyond his preconceived notions of Egypt.

Warnings of terrorist attacks against tourists in Egypt were still being published by Western embassies after the incident several years before when many Western tourists had been killed by machine-gun fire while traveling by bus. Egyptian authorities had countered with prominently displayed posters and advertisements depicting the country as safe and secure.

Walker wondered, by comparison, how many foreign visitors were killed while traveling in the U.S. and whether embassies issued travel advisories on the dangers of U.S. travel. He believed that his comprehension of world politics and the use of the media to form public opinion had improved because of his travels in Egypt. He understood that embassies everywhere covered their political behinds by issuing warnings in case an unfortunate incident should happen. It was their job to do so.

History had shown Walker that America needed an enemy. Islamic fundamentalists served that purpose well. From Walker's perspective, media reports had created a narrow view of the Middle East by promoting the dangers of its extremists. This strategy ensured that Westerners understood why some people in this part of the world were America's enemy.

In reality, Walker had encountered frequent acts of hospitality and genuine friendliness by Egyptian people. Yet, in the back of his mind, he had stayed on constant alert in case of ambush.

Walker had toured the Great Pyramids of Giza and the Sphinx, standing monuments to humanity's accomplishments from forty-six centuries ago. Each night at the Sphinx, a spectacular sound-and-light show blended together ancient and modern technologies. The entire concept was so bizarre that he went twice.

Often while touring Cairo, Walker had felt that Egypt's entire population of 62 million had crammed into its hot streets. Bullock carts, Mercedes-Benzes, trucks, sheep, motorbikes, chickens, beggars in dirty rags, businessmen in suits, and flies—more flies than he had ever seen—all traveled together. Cairo was a huge sea of diversity constantly in motion and Walker had immersed himself in its foreignness.

The Islamic section of the city, once called Babylon, had hardly changed in the last few centuries. St. Sergius Church, in the old part of the city, marked the spot where the Holy Trinity rested as they fled King Herod's tyranny. Walker had stood in the same place where the Son of God had been!

Next he remembered the attractive Nile city of Aswan. It had made an excellent base from which to explore the High Dam, Lake

Nasser, the Coptic Christian monastery and the incredible temples at Abu Simbel. At that site, in the 1960s, a UNESCO project costing $40 million U.S. moved the Ramses II temples and saved these treasures from being submerged after the dam's completion.

Floating down the Nile on a felucca had been a highlight for Walker. The traditional sailing vessel accommodated six guests on the trip from Aswan to Edfu: Walker, a young German couple, two twenty-something Australian men, and a middle-aged man from South Africa. The captain also acted as cook and engaged his guests to help with the food preparation when necessary.

From Edfu, Walker had bused it north to Luxor and stayed in the village for a week while he visited the temples of Karnak and Luxor, the Valley of the Kings, the Valley of the Queens, the Tomb of Nefertari and the Deir al-Bahri, or Temple of Hatshepsut. He had discovered that the town of Luxor was built on the ancient city of Thebes, which dates back more than 4,000 years.

Walker's historical reference points were wiped clean by dates going that far back. In his mind, even the time of Christ had always seemed "biblical" and not very real. He had now touched humanity's creations that were twice as old. It represented a history that could not be explained or understood. The experience had left him with a sense of human momentum flowing forward into a mystical creation of what would be.

At the resort town of Hurghada on the west coast of the Red Sea, Walker had learned to snorkel. He had spent two glorious days in the sun and sparkling waters swimming among colorful fish.

From Hurghada Walker had caught the ferry to Sharm el-Sheikh on the Sinai Peninsula, a territory wedged between Africa and Asia that had been fought over for centuries. While heading north along the Gulf of Aqaba, he had passed Mount Sinai. On this clear, cloudless day he had looked out at the place where Moses had received the Ten Commandments.

THE WORLDWIDE SEXUAL ADVENTURES OF WALKER FAYT

Walker had gone to Egypt to see humanity's ancient and mysterious treasures, and as Nuweiba, his departure point from the Sinai Peninsula, faded away in the distance he contemplated his good fortune at having had a chance to experience those treasures.

Ahead of Walker lay Jordan, the country that had provided the name of his daughter, Petra. The name meant "rock" in Greek, and Petra represented strength and beauty in his life. Walker had known somehow that someday he would get to the ancient and unique town of Petra. It saddened him that the same actions that led him there had also estranged his daughter whom he loved so much.

Passengers aboard the crowded ferry suddenly became excited and they pointed in several directions at once. Walker inquired about the cause of the commotion. A young Arab man who spoke English patiently told him that four countries could be seen at a glance: Egypt, Jordan, Saudi Arabia and Israel. Thirty minutes later the ship docked at Aqaba, Jordan.

A popular tourist destination, Aqaba offered a variety of Western-style hotels, restaurants and stores. During his walk along the shoreline, Walker found many upscale hotels that specialized in diving and snorkeling trips for tourists. He checked into one that had a lovely pool and outdoor café; it overlooked the gulf to Eilat, Israel. While touring the area, he came across a Western-style bakery, an ice-cream shop, a liquor store, a T-shirt outlet and many small shops offering crafts.

In front of one store, a young man carefully poured colored sand into a clear glass bottle. Walker watched for a while as the artist dropped purple sand down a thin funnel into the bottle, layering it on top of beige sand. Below were various colors that appeared to be in a pattern. Looking in the window, Walker noticed other bottles ready for sale. Within them were scenes of camels walking across the desert and cacti growing in colorful landscapes. They were capped with pieces of tissue to seal the sand inside.

TANYA—THE COLORS OF PLEASURE

The artist appeared to randomly weave the colored sand together. Watching the process to fruition made Walker think that life cannot truly be judged until it is finished and the complete picture is revealed.

After a dinner of roasted chicken and potatoes, Walker returned to his room and from his balcony watched the sun set over the Gulf of Aqaba. Once the burning ball of flame had disappeared behind the parched brown ridges high above Eilat, he went to his comfortable bed and fell asleep anticipating an active day of snorkeling.

In the morning, Walker ate a typical Middle Eastern tourist's breakfast: two pieces of pita bread, one hard-boiled egg, olives and a slice of white processed cheese that came individually wrapped in foil. He arrived at the dive shop at half past eight for the nine-o'clock departure; the extra half hour gave him time to equip himself with a mask, snorkel and fins.

Naguib, the stocky Arab dive master, had a confident manner. Graciously he informed Walker that the water temperature was about 21 degrees Celsius. The divers would be down for about an hour, and with a wet suit Walker would be comfortable in the water for the entire time. Otherwise, he'd be blue-lipped and shivering in about twenty minutes. The buoyancy of the wet suit could be countered with a weight belt that allowed him to dive and stay below the surface.

Walker accepted Naguib's recommendation and found the largest wet suit in the shop. For the next fifteen minutes, he struggled to get into it. Exhausted and totally frustrated, he finally decided that the suit was just too small for him and gave up fighting with the neoprene.

A woman carrying fins, regulator, buoyancy compensation device and air tank, and with a wet suit draped over her shoulder and a mask and snorkel on her head, walked past him. As she went by, she said pleasantly, "Try getting it wet; your body will then slide into it."

THE WORLDWIDE SEXUAL ADVENTURES OF WALKER FAYT

Before Walker could thank her, she went outside and headed toward the boat. Long sinks with freshwater taps ran along one side of the dive shop, and he went there and doused his suit with water. Once wetted, it slipped on with only a minor struggle. He gathered his mask, snorkel and fins and boarded the boat with about twenty other divers and snorkelers.

Before heading out, the captain explained the routine. It would take about fifteen minutes to get to the dive site. Once anchored, the divers would be first in the water and once they were away from the boat, the snorkellers could go in. At eleven o'clock a bell would ring, indicating that everyone should return to the boat.

Walker wished to learn more about diving and asked Naguib for a few details. Naguib explained that divers with more experience were usually more comfortable in the water and could make their air last much longer than beginners. But because of the possibility of errors in gauge readings and other unforeseen events, all divers were trained to be back to the surface with a quarter tank of air left in reserve. Since all the divers on the trip today were equipped with single tanks, they would be back at the boat well before the designated departure time.

The morning sun shone softly and reflected off the blue waters of the gulf. The woman who had given Walker the tip leaned back on her arms, tilted her head toward the sun and, with her eyes closed, let her long hair blow in the breeze of the moving boat. Her one-piece Body Glove bathing suit fit as the name suggested and its peachy-pink color accentuated her well-tanned, shapely figure. Walker didn't want to break her solitude by thanking her for the tip about the wet suit. Instead he watched her.

She was turned away from him slightly so he could not see her entire face. Based on what Walker saw, she encapsulated his image of a "California girl." He had never been to California, but Walker carried a mental stereotype created out of television, movies and music videos. Her youthful air, physically fit body, sun-bleached blond hair and tanned skin all fit the bill. He would have bet his teacher's pension that she also had blue eyes and perfect white teeth.

Walker thought about people from southern California being better-looking, on average, than people from other places. For the last few generations, good-looking people have flocked to Hollywood with the hopes of being discovered. Those that were, and many of those that were not, continued to make the area their home. Good-looking people attracted other good-looking people, resulting in better-looking people.

While Walker contemplated the theoretical genetic dynamics of southern California, the young woman shook her head and let her long, straight hair blow free. She slipped a sparkling elastic tie from her wrist and with it put her hair into a ponytail in preparation for the dive. He moved to the seat across from her and waited for her to look at him before he spoke.

"Thanks for the tip; it worked like a charm," he said as he pointed to his donned wet suit.

She looked directly at him and smiled. Her eyes sparkled like the crystal-blue waters of the Caribbean and her teeth were a vision of a toothpaste ad. He smiled, confirming that his pension had been securely wagered.

"No problem. You learn from experience. Awesome day, isn't it? I feel so free out on the water. It's great. Are you diving or snorkeling?"

"Just snorkeling. I did it for the first time a few days ago in Egypt and loved it. I had to give it another try." He waited a few seconds and then asked, "What brings you to Jordan?"

"I'm a nurse working in Saudi Arabia on a two-year contract. I get six weeks' vacation, but I can only take them in two-week intervals. I'm from California—Huntington Beach area. With the traveling time, it's not worth going back home for only two weeks, so, instead I go to places that are closer."

Walker beamed with big grin as he soaked up her youthful beauty and gloated just a little at guessing her heritage. She interrupted his internal celebration.

"Did I say something funny?"

"No, not at all. It's just that before you told me, I'd have bet the farm that you were from California. Believe me, it's a compliment. I'm from Wisconsin. It's a pleasure to meet you. I'm Walker Fayt."

Walker held out his hand to shake. She delicately extended her hand and they shook. Her hand was yielding yet strong to the touch. After she released his hand, she looked him in the eyes and spoke.

"Hi, Walker, I'm Tanya. It's great to meet somebody from home. Is there any news? I get almost nothing in Saudi. When my co-workers travel outside the country, they try and smuggle in newspapers and magazines from the States. They get passed around, but by the time I get them they're usually outdated."

"I've been traveling since June and haven't kept up on current events. I've actually tried to avoid them."

"Oh, why is that?" she asked.

"While I've been away, I've come to realize that all the information in the daily news, whatever it may be—politics, social development or reform, economics, crime or weather—is presented as being critical knowledge we need to have. But, from a historical perspective, these are just slow-moving patterns headed in a direction that cannot be understood while in the midst of them. I now take the attitude that if a current event is not having a direct and immediate effect on me, then it's not really that important because it's beyond my control."

Tanya looked toward the sea and said, "I suppose I miss news from home so much because of the censorship in Saudi. I just don't understand their restrictive attitudes."

The engine cut out, indicating they had reached the dive site.

TANYA—THE COLORS OF PLEASURE

This ended their chat. Tanya had drenched her wet suit before leaving and she slid into it easily. Walker tried not to stare as she bent over and attached her regulator to the BCD and scuba tank.

Tanya had been partnered with a woman from Germany and they performed the equipment safety checks. Walker pretended to be fascinated with the routine rather than in Tanya. On her turn to enter the water, she stepped off the side of the boat, holding her mask in place with one hand and the regulator to her mouth with the other. Gravity submerged her and the buoyancy of the BCD and wet suit returned her to the surface. She breached, giving the okay signal with her hand. Before diving under, she waved goodbye to Walker.

The water clarity, pristine conditions and the lack of divers reportedly made the Red Sea one of the best places in the world to dive. Locations in Jordan and Saudi Arabia were best, but since Saudi Arabia did not issue tourist visas, Jordan became the accessible option for most travelers.

In less than fifteen minutes, Walker saw the people without wet suits head back to the boat. There they stretched out, trying to warm up in the sun. When Walker heard the bell it surprised him. He had become so engrossed by the brilliant coral and the countless species of fish, it seemed like only a few minutes had passed.

Divers resurfaced around the boat and came aboard full of exuberance and with tales to tell. Tanya and her dive buddy were the next to last group to come aboard. Tanya sat down beside Walker.

As they warmed themselves in the sun, Freda, Tanya's diving partner, engaged them in conversation. She was a beginner and had dived with Hans, her husband, five times in the last three days. Hans was a dive master and had been getting anxious for a challenge. He and Naguib had teamed up for a deep dive—about 120 feet. For Walker's sake, she explained why they weren't yet aboard.

"At that depth, even with a short bottom time, they will have to spend five minutes at ten feet below the surface before they can safely come aboard. The equalization time will allow the pressurized nitrogen to be released from their blood."

Walker listened to her words but understood little of their meaning. He nodded his acceptance, not wanting to complicate the discussion with his ignorance.

Once Hans and Naguib were back aboard, the captain started the engines and headed the boat back to Aqaba. Hans and Naguib conversed in their common language, English. After a few minutes, Naguib left to attend to his duties and Hans and Freda talked in German about their dives, which left Walker and Tanya together.

Tanya pulled down the front zipper of her wet suit and unsnapped the clasp between her legs that held the jacket in place. She removed it and doffed the pant part of the suit as well. She told him that he would warm up much quicker with the suit off. Again he followed her tip. She stored her gear under a bench, undid her hair, put on a pair of trendy sunglasses and sat beside him.

"So, are you traveling with family, or—" He did not let her imagination wander for too long.

"No, I'm traveling alone. My divorce was finalized just before I left."

"I'm sorry to hear that." Pausing a moment, Tanya looked at him and chuckled. Then she touched his arm ever so lighty and said, "Well, not that sorry. At least I'll have someone to dine with me tonight. You're free, aren't you?"

Her forwardness caught Walker by surprise. He let out a laugh as he declared, "Yes, I'm free."

Tanya patted his arm a few times and said, "Good, it's a date. I've heard that Naguib and the other divers meet at the English Pub at six-thirty for drinks. We can meet there. It usually lasts an hour or so. After that we can go for dinner. All right with you?"

Walker flashed his most charming smile and said, "Perfect. I'm looking forward to it already."

TANYA—THE COLORS OF PLEASURE

Walker, genuinely interested in Saudi Arabian culture, wished to get her viewpoint on the subject. As their boat cruised home, he allowed her to do most of the talking while he gently questioned her.

Tanya had completed eighteen months of a two-year contract. She planned to spend the remaining two weeks of her vacation time in Paris over Christmas. Her parents and younger sister would join her there. It disappointed her that her older brother, sister-in-law and nephew could not make it. However, the possibility of seeing her first snowfall for Christmas thrilled her.

Coming from the openness of southern California, Tanya was shocked by the closed culture of Saudi Arabia. Details from the recruiting agent and all the materials provided to her hadn't given a clear picture. Restrictive laws and attitudes were foreign to her realm of beliefs. Her body language suggested that she did not agree with Saudi culture, but her carefully chosen words did not criticize it either. She told her stories as objectively as she knew how.

Shortly after arriving in Saudi Arabia, Tanya had planned to bake a cake for a co-worker's birthday and needed some almond extract. She discovered that due to the alcohol content and the fact that artificial extract could be a way of smuggling in the real stuff, both were banned substances in Saudi Arabia.

Most foreign workers lived in compounds provided by their employers. She and her co-workers had no proof that they were under surveillance, yet most of the time when a covert party took place, it got raided without warning. If illegal substances such as alcohol were found, the goods were confiscated and the foreigners quietly deported. The official sentence if caught with illegal drugs was the death penalty. Given the authority's success rate at finding alcohol, she had not heard of any foreigners willing to risk possession of illegal drugs.

Tanya went on to explain that if the police caught a woman alone with a man other than her husband, father, grandfather or brother, she could be jailed. A powerful religious police force called the Matawwa enforced all such laws, including the law requiring women to cover all parts of their body except for hands, feet and eyes. Saudi women had to wear a one-piece cloak called a chador to ensure compliance.

Western women were not required to follow the rules; however, they had to dress conservatively. Tanya had heard of Western women having their legs spray-painted by the Matawwa because, in their opinion, too much leg showed.

A few Saudi women had befriended Tanya, and although such cross-cultural friendships among women were frowned upon, the authorities tolerated it. She related a story told to her by one of her Saudi friends.

The woman's male cousin drove the car while she sat in the back seat, as the law required. They were shopping for a gift for her father, his uncle. The Matawwa stopped them and the officers asked for her photo ID. She pretended to be her cousin, the sister of the driver, and carried her cousin's ID as proof. Sensing uneasiness, the officers requested that she remove her facial veil so they could match her face with the ID. Since the police were of no relation to her, she refused and insisted that under the law they had no right to see her face. She and her cousin were let go.

Two months after Tanya's arrival, the director of the hospital invited some nurses to a party for government officials and businessmen. Since it was to take place after hours and at a private residence, they were offered $1,000 U.S. as encouragement to attend. Tanya and five other nurses decided to go. They were single and thought it would be fun to meet Saudi men in a social setting. At worst, it would be an easy thousand dollars. They had been told to dress up and that a limousine would transport them to and from the function.

When they arrived at eight o'clock, the six nurses were the only women in a room of more than one hundred men. An exploding bomb could not have triggered a bigger impact. All eyes turned toward them and she recalled the rising excitement in the room. Shortly after their arrival, four other women joined the party. Tanya found the ten-to-one ratio exhilarating.

At first they were just ogled, but as the evening proceeded, the men became more frenzied and agitated, almost like sharks in bloody water. The smell of alcohol projected strongly off the breaths of some men. Indiscreet verbal badgering began and shortly after that, pinches and gropes. The women soon realized that they were not guests, rather the entertainment, and had made a mistake by accepting the invitation.

Next each woman was offered $3,000 extra to walk around in her underwear. The women became sure that the ante would be upped and that even larger sums would be offered to walk around naked. They all firmly refused to remove any clothing. Soon thereafter they were taken back to the compound without a hassle.

Although they had been targets of verbal and sexual harassment, Tanya did not believe they were ever in physical danger. She revealed to Walker that many of her bathing suits showed more skin than her underwear and she had no problem freely exposing her body in most circumstances. In that particular setting, however, the offer of so much money made her feel like a prostitute and gave her the creeps.

The Arab men were certainly disappointed at their refusals and, in retrospect, she realized that the men were also truly confused. They had somehow come to believe that removing clothing for money was perfectly acceptable and normal behavior for single Western women. Again, Walker saw the effect of media misinformation working, this time in the other direction.

The boat docked and the captain shouted that anyone going out again in the afternoon could leave their gear on board. Walker carried Tanya's scuba tank and BCD back to the dive shop. As she thanked him, she rubbed her hand along the back of his arm. He still held the tank and his triceps was flexed. Her light touch against his firm arm felt provocative and he anticipated their evening together. They parted company for the afternoon.

Walker ate an enjoyable lunch at the café by the pool and afterward sat under the shade of an umbrella with a cold beer in the hot Jordanian sun. The afternoon trip began at half past one with fewer people than in the morning. The site offered even more spectacular snorkeling. The divers surfaced elated, but they didn't seem as enthused with the dive as the morning group had been.

Hans and Freda conversed with Walker on the way back to Aqaba. Hans and Naguib had done another deep dive. Freda confided that she preferred Tanya as a partner and wished that the California woman had been along on the afternoon dive. When they finished talking, Walker turned his sights to the rugged beauty of the landscape around the gulf.

In the soft light of the late afternoon, the barren mountains migrated in color between ivory and dark chocolate. Heading toward Aqaba, at once he could see both the Israeli and Jordanian sides of the gulf. He thought about the people on either side of that invisible line sharing the same topography, but little else.

Back at his hotel, Walker showered, changed and then headed for the pub. The place sported many couches and booths and had stools by the bar. There were dart boards, a pool table and a few outdated video games. Its décor made foreigners like himself feel comfortable and must have contributed to its success. Still, it seemed out of place for the Middle East.

Naguib and most of the people from the dive trips were already there. Walker scanned the room looking for Tanya, but did not see her. The drinks flowed and people relaxed. Brian, the Australian dive assistant, challenged Walker to a game of pool. He accepted.

During the game they chatted about themselves. Brian was twenty-three and had been working at the dive shop for three months. He had been traveling just over a year and needed to earn some money before continuing on. Thus far he had been to Southeast Asia and India and planned to go to Europe and North America before returning home. He expected to be away about three years in total.

Brian told stories about his travels. Tales of Bangkok's legendary sex trade held no appeal for Walker, whereas stories about trekking through remote villages in Thailand struck a chord and he fancied that experience.

Neither of them was a good pool player and it required thirty minutes of play before Brian finally sank the eightball and claimed victory. That gave him the right to play Hans, the next challenger. Moments after the game ended, Tanya walked into the bar.

Walker sat beside Tanya and they listened to the divers tell their stories from the day's outings. A teenage boy came into the bar and delivered an envelope of freshly developed photographs to Naguib. Brian had taken underwater pictures and Naguib offered them for sale: three dollars each or two for five dollars. Everyone purchased at least one picture of themselves next to multicolored fish or resplendent coral. Each person acquired a special treasure from under the Red Sea.

Suddenly Freda came into the bar crying. Her father had just passed away in Germany, she lamented through her tears. Hans consoled her as best he could. Of course she wanted to leave immediately for home.

Naguib and Brian had the unfortunate responsibility of telling them it would be dangerously unsafe for them to fly so soon after diving. Freda had never been below sixty feet and would be fine to fly in the morning. The bigger concern was the two deep dives that Hans had done.

The jovial mood vanished as the rest of group learned of the predicament. Ordinarily Hans could have done the calculations, but he said, under the stress of the moment, he did not trust himself to do so. Brian, who had consumed several beers, adjusted quickly to the serious situation. He said he needed statistics from Hans's dive log, such as bottom times, surface times, depths and equalization times of recent dives, in order to calculate when it would be safe for Hans to fly. This ended the party and the group dispersed.

Tanya and Walker went to dinner. At first they discussed the situation of Freda and Hans. Tanya explained some of the technical issues of depth and dive times and the seriousness of not following the rules.

"Decompression sickness or the bends has to be avoided; it results in extreme pain and in the worst case, death. If contracted, there are only two ways to correct it. One way is to take the diver back down and have them equalize properly. In most cases this is impossible because of its crippling effects. The only other alternative is to get them into a decompression chamber. I'd be very surprised if there's one nearby."

Walker told her that in Egypt he saw signs for a decompression chamber at Sharm el Sheikh, at the tip of the Sinai Peninsula. It amazed her that such a facility existed in Egypt. Regardless of where the nearest one was, it wouldn't do Hans much good if he chose to fly out of Aqaba too soon.

Once the ice had been broken between them, the talk turned more intimate. Tanya described herself as a free and uninhibited person. She attributed this to her childhood and the openness of her upbringing. Her parents were not ashamed of their bodies and most of the swimming and all of the hot-tubbing had been done naked. Her parents were open about their lovemaking. From a young age, the children understood that their parents needed some private time together. Sexual intimacy was not something to hide, rather something to be cherished.

In Tanya's home, sexuality and sex were discussed as naturally and

TANYA—THE COLORS OF PLEASURE

as frequently as any other topic. As each child went through the various stages of curiosity, discovery, maturity and experimentation, her parents' approach changed to accommodate the particular circumstance.

Tanya admitted that she had become the most sexually liberated of her siblings and that she unabashedly sought sexual gratification without remorse, guilt or any sense of wrongdoing. To her it seemed as natural and as necessary as breathing. She confided that living in an excessively conservative country, where conveying such ideals was dangerous and probably illegal, had taken its toll on her sanity.

Tanya's home in Saudi Arabia was a dormitory where only other unwed women lived. On both a social and professional basis, the rules restricted interaction between the sexes. To be alone with someone of the opposite sex became a spy-versus-spy game. For some, it added to the excitement, but for Tanya it just added to the frustration. In college she had experimented with lesbianism and, given her current isolation from men, she had contemplated returning to it. She held back from pursuing such relationships because all the women in the dormitory were also co-workers.

Over the last eighteen months she had resorted to masturbating frequently, and had become bored with it. Tanya finished the last of her fish, took the last sip of her wine, then tilted her head and looked directly into his eyes.

"So, Walker, have I scared you off? You seem like the type who is a little uptight about sex. Being from the Midwest, you probably had a strong moral Christian upbringing." Raising her voice a notch and almost in a mocking tone, she said, "Deep down, sex is bad; something to be ashamed of because pleasure is indulgent."

"No, I'm not scared off and I don't think sex is bad; I rather enjoy it," he said, a bit perturbed now that she had stereotyped him, as he had done with her earlier in the day.

"I'm glad to hear that, because I like to know that my partner can enjoy sex, and the sensations that come with it. So you'd be willing to let me take you to orgasm?"

Walker felt his body temperature rise. Dryness overtook his throat, and in a raspy voice he said, "Of course."

Tanya licked her lips and raised her eyebrows. "Right now!"

Walker's body temperature rose a few more degrees and he pulled at the collar of his shirt to let out some heat. "Are you crazy? We'd be thrown in jail."

"There's a tablecloth—no one can see underneath." Tanya smiled a mischievous smile. He read her eyes and knew that she wasn't serious and was only testing his limits.

"Why don't I get the bill and we can find a nice beach to walk along," he said.

"That sounds great, except for one thing—we'll split the bill."

If Walker had been in New York, London or Paris, he would have abandoned his conservative ways and passionately kissed Tanya in the middle of the busy street. Arab culture excluded such actions in public. It went as far as not accepting a touch between a man and woman in public places. Neither of them wanted to upset the local culture.

They walked barefoot along the beach and stopped at a dark, secluded spot near his hotel. Spotlights from the Israeli side of the gulf shone across the water into the sky and onto the mountainous hills above Eilat. Walker spoke softly as he brushed her cheek with the back of his hand and moved her hair away from her face: "See, I told you it was dangerous. They're looking for us already."

In a tone that let him know it was time to kiss her, she said, "Let them find us."

Delicately their lips came together. As the pressure increased, she pressed her body against his. Walker felt the sexual tension inside her and knew it needed emancipation. Tanya put her leg behind his and pushed. He could have easily maintained his balance, but chose not to and fell to the sand with her on top of him. She lifted up his shirt, exposing his abdomen and chest. He squirmed and resisted as she sucked his nipples. Finally she stopped and whispered in his ear.

"Come on, Walker, let yourself go."

Tanya was right. For reasons unknown to Walker, he could not allow himself to accept this particular pleasurable sensation. Perhaps he had never fully accepted the fact that his body contained zones of sensual stimulation. To counter being pleasured, he fixated on a woman's needs in order not to have to concentrate on the regalement of his own body. Tanya stopped kissing his chest and held his head in her hands and spoke while staring into his eyes.

"Relax, Walker, we'll both come. Just let it be."

Walker lay back in the sand, arms to his side, and surrendered completely as Tanya resumed licking and sucking his nipples. The bodily sensations began to release denied pleasure trapped deep within the caverns of his unconsciousness, and he moaned with delight.

As Tanya undid his belt buckle, a kaleidoscope of colors burst into creation behind Walker's closed eyelids. As she enveloped the head of his penis with burning hot lips, purples mixed with white and aqua shot through his consciousness. He faintly realized he did not recall the sensation of his pants or underwear being removed . . . FLASH! . . . the colors resumed, like meteors crashing against Jupiter.

Walker became an array of colors; he felt nothing and he saw nothing other than the purity of the colors that changed in rapid succession. They were the colors of pleasure's purity and he became pure pleasure. At the speed of light, all the colors of the universe streaked into his head and imploded into a blinding blackness. Painfully, sensation returned to his body and he felt the end of his penis touching the back of Tanya's throat. His sperm had mixed with her saliva. She slipped her lips off his erection.

Slowly, Tanya kissed her way up his body until she reached his chin. Then she passionately French-kissed him, wrapping her tongue around his. Traces of sperm remained in her mouth. He had smelled his sperm many times, but this was his first taste of it. She released her kiss, ending the strange culinary experience, and sighed between heavy breaths, "Okay, Walker, I'm ready; now it's my turn."

Tanya rolled sideways until she slid off his chest and onto her back. Then she removed all her clothing except her cotton panties. Sitting on top of her shirt and pants, she put her thumbs on the inside of her briefs, making ready to pull them off. Walker stopped her from doing so, then slid his hands along the inside of her thighs until they reached her pubic area. Curving his fingers to the inside of the crotch, he touched her hot wetness with the backs of his fingers. She arched her back to allow him to pull off her moistened underwear.

Walker recalled that Tanya had not touched a man for a long time; pleasuring him had probably acted as foreplay. Vaginal fluid oozed out of her lips and down her legs. Every part of her body rippled with anticipation. She pinched her nipples and rocked her pelvis up and down. He placed his hands on her knees and separated her legs. Her pubic hair was short, fine and so a light a golden color that it seemed there was almost none. He wondered whether she shaved or if it was naturally so.

Starlight twinkled off Tanya's naked body and Walker hungered to unleash her sexual ecstasy into the universe. He plunged his mouth down on her steaming mound. Nectar of wild mountain flowers could not have tasted sweeter, and the lack of hair allowed his tongue to explore every minute area of her joyous tract—inside, outside, around and over; faster, slower, harder, softer. Tanya's body retracted as she acquiesced closer and closer to climax.

Tanya released her nipples and reached down to spread herself open and give him unencumbered access to her clitoris. Walker flicked his tongue rapidly across it for a few seconds and then slipped two fingers into her extremely wet vagina. While continuing the rapid tongue strokes, he thrust his fingers in and out of her. Vaginal fluid gushed out of her body and splashed against his face. Her body shook as the effects of orgasm flowed down her legs and soaked through her shirt to the sand beneath it. The volume of her bodily reaction startled him and he thought he had injured her.

"All you all right?"

"Oooooooh! I'm just fine, thank you."

With the juices of her pleasure covering his face, Tanya sat up and French-kissed him passionately, tasting the purity of her orgasm. They went back to Walker's hotel and slept soundly in each other's arms; Walker dreamt only of vivid colors.

Twilight brightened as the day began. Tanya stood on the balcony, letting the cool desert air tingle her naked body. Off in the distance, a faint, almost inaudible chanting echoed. A call to prayer was being broadcast from a loudspeaker at a mosque in town. It would be the first of five for the day and she closed her eyes and listened while inhaling deeply through her nostrils. Walker came up from behind and wrapped his arms around her, holding her tight.

"Oh, you're so warm, it feels nice," Tanya said, and snuggled against him. She kissed his chest and ran her hand along it. "I want to feel you inside me. I've missed being touched for so long."

Walker gave her a slow, lingering kiss on the lips and then said, "Wait here."

He returned with a blanket and surrounded her with it. "Wait here again." He went to his luggage and retrieved a condom.

Tanya allowed him no place to hide and demanded that pleasure beam from every pore of his masculine body. A light cool breeze of sea and desert air played with their intensely hot, entwined bodies. As the sky changed from dark navy to a lighter blue, they lay together, filling each other with pure rapture.

*

Sitting outside at the hotel's restaurant having breakfast, Walker and Tanya joked about the previous night on the beach. "I should have had one of those with me last night," Tanya said with a chuckle, pointing to a red flag with a single white diagonal line running from corner to corner. "It's the 'divers down' flag." Walker smiled.

"Yes, and I was going to offer you a beer but was afraid you'd get sand in your Schlitz."

Once more on the boat, cruising toward the dive site, they made plans to travel together. In the remaining four days of her vacation, Tanya wanted to see some of Jordan's above-sea attractions. Both of them desired to see Petra. They planned to rent a car and make the four-hour drive after the afternoon's dive.

The mention of Petra drew others into the conversation. Some had been there a few days before and offered advice about what to see and when. Over the loud hum of the engine, Naguib's ears perked up when he heard Walker talking about going to Petra that evening.

"Tanya, aren't you diving this afternoon?" Naguib asked in a matter-of-fact way.

She raised her voice so she could be heard over the engine noise. "Yes, I was planning on it. Is there a problem?"

In the same tone and style, Naguib replied. "There is if you're planning to go to Petra tonight. It's a few thousand feet above sea level. You can't go that high after a dive. It'll have to be one or the other. An afternoon dive and stay in Aqaba tonight or no dive and Petra." He waited so the details and the importance of what he had just said registered.

"If you dive this morning, I suggest you don't go below fifty feet and wait until about 4:30 this afternoon before leaving."

Walker sensed Tanya's internal struggle and asked Naguib, "Where are you planning to dive this afternoon?"

"At the wreck. It's my favorite site." Naguib shrugged his shoulders as he said it and then added, "About ten years ago the Prince of Jordan arranged for a large vessel to be sunk. Now it's an artificial reef that provides another destination for sport divers."

"How about Wadi Rum?" Walker inquired. "Would it be safe to go there this evening after the dive?"

Naguib smiled, appreciating Walker's cleverness. "As long as Tanya doesn't climb the high cliffs, she should be okay."

After the morning outing, Walker and Tanya ate lunch and then checked out of their hotels. Naguib agreed to let them keep their luggage at the dive shop for the afternoon.

While Tanya went to see the sunken vessel, Walker prepared for their trip to Wadi Rum. He rented a small Suzuki four-wheel drive, loaded up on water and food, and found a shop that sold inexpensive rings. He didn't purchase them, believing it would be more romantic to wait and buy them together. To eliminate the expense of two hotel rooms and the inconvenience of sneaking between them, they had decided to travel under the pretense of being married.

It had been Tanya's best dive. When she met Walker, she still buzzed from it. Quickly she changed and they said their goodbyes and thanked both Brian and Naguib for their incredible diving and snorkeling adventures. They packed their gear, bought the rings and set off on the Desert Highway, heading north from Aqaba.

Wadi Rum was a place of legend and natural beauty. Both the real-life Lawrence of Arabia and his movie counterpart, Peter O'Toole, had inhabited this spectacular desert setting. It thrilled Walker to be going there and it also intimidated him somewhat.

For such a famous place, the road signs were pathetic—tiny little wooden markers with most of the paint peeled and the letters barely legible. Fortunately a guidebook that Tanya had purchased when she first arrived was helpful. Its descriptions of distinguishing landmarks, distances and turn-offs guided them to their destination.

They arrived to find not much there. A small restaurant acted as a tourist center and desert police station, and that was about it. Still, the scenery captured their breaths as they stood and looked out over the expanse of desert.

Jutting upward, 3000-foot rock cliffs grew out of the desert sand. These ancient, majestic giants varied in shades from reddish brown to a light gold. Their daunting radiance propelled Walker and Tanya to venture deeper into the barrenness of desert. They asked several locals the best way to go and everyone just pointed in the same direction. There were no roads, paths or trails, only burnished sand leading nowhere except to more spectacular views of vivid, towering monoliths.

Without much success, they both tried maneuvering the standard-shift four-wheel drive through the sand. Tanya drove in other tracks until they disappeared, then Walker plowed through the sand in a low gear.

As the sun lowered toward the horizon, they knew it would be dark within the hour. Their survival wasn't in question; they just hadn't gone very far. Upon setting out, they had hoped for a better experience. Cursing the car's inability to handle the desert sand, they made a U-turn and headed back to the settlement.

Shortly after turning around, they were hailed by a young Bedouin lad of about fifteen in a battered pickup truck. His English was quite good, and he offered to drive their vehicle and be their guide. This included an overnight stay in the desert and a tour of local points of interest in the morning. He would charge $30 U.S., but as part of the deal he would share their food and water. This would save him having to go back to his village, and would give them more time in the desert. They agreed to his proposal.

The boy's pickup easily drove through the sand to a secluded outcropping in the rock about a minute away. It took Walker five minutes to get there. On the way over, he suggested to Tanya that it might be best to take the truck and offer the boy more money to do so. She agreed. The boy did not lock the truck but he did remove the keys from the ignition and a woolen blanket from the back. Obviously he intended to leave his truck there until the next day. Walker leaned out the window and spoke slowly.

"So you want to take this one, huh? It's not very good."

The boy patted the roof of their rental car. "No. This is very good. I drive many times—yesterday last time. Hello, my name is Gamal."

Walker got out of the driver's seat, Tanya moved to the back and Walker took the passenger's side as the Bedouin got behind the wheel. He took the vehicle out of four-wheel drive and tore off quickly through the desert sand with no difficulty at all. The trick, they saw, was to drive fast and handle the steering wheel ever so lightly.

They stopped and Gamal pointed at some rocks above, suggesting they climb up if they wished to get a good view of the sunset. They made the easy climb of about 100 feet. When they reached a large ledge near the top they sat in silence, appreciating the gorgeous vastness. The ever-changing colors of the landscape and the setting sun awed them. A snippet of fiery red disappeared behind the jutting edifices a few miles to the west.

Walker heard nothing, not a single sound. He could not remember a time in his life when the silence deafened him so. Usually he heard something—birds, crickets or background noise such as traffic, electric lights, a refrigerator or furnace—but not here. He even quieted his breathing so that it was inaudible. He glanced over at Tanya and knew by her complete stillness that she absorbed the same pleasures.

Ten minutes after sunset, a sharp whistle shattered the extraordinary tranquility. Gamal waved that they should come down. The last bit of waning light vanished just as they reached the bottom and they were swallowed by the blackness of the desert night.

Gamal drove in darkness as effortlessly as he did in light. Periodically he'd look up at the stars and the ominous outlines of the skyscraping rocks that were distinguishable from the black sky only because they blocked out the stars.

After twenty minutes of driving in the blackness, Gamal arrived at the spot where they would camp for the night. With the use of the car headlights, they all gathered prickly dried scrub. Tough to pull out of the sand, it would fuel the night's fire. When they had piled it as high as Walker, Gamal indicated they could stop collecting. Walker found a few more bunches close by and he pulled them out of the ground and tossed them on the heap.

Gamal untangled a few bushes from the pile, stomped on them to crush them, then took out a lighter and set them ablaze. The fire took readily. While he did this, Walker carried the food, still in bags from the store, over to the campfire. He had purchased things that required no cooking: a head of lettuce, tomatoes, cucumber, carrots, apples, pears, a piece of cheese, a bag of chips and some cookies. It was the best he could find with the little time he had in Aqaba.

Walker had purchased more than enough water, and he and Tanya used the contents of one of the bottles to wash the vegetables. They laid out one of his T-shirts as a tablecloth and set the food on it. In keeping with his culture, Gamal asked very personal questions. He wanted to know if they were married, where they were from, how long they had been in Jordan, where they were going next, how many children they had, if they both worked, how much money they made. They answered truthfully.

Only Walker had eaten any lettuce and he broke off his fourth leaf and ate it. Gamal motioned that he wanted some as well and Walker handed the head over to him. Gamal peeled the leaves back and asked for a flashlight. Tanya gave him hers and he shone the light into the inner part of the lettuce. Gamal went to Walker and showed him a large black bug crawling around on the leaves. It was too late; if Walker had eaten one, he hadn't noticed.

Walker resented Gamal a little bit. Why did he wait until Walker's fourth leaf to check for bugs? Perhaps it was an intentional lesson. Even if it wasn't, Walker would not forget it.

Near the end of the meal, Gamal requested some bread. They hadn't brought any. Pita bread was a staple in the Middle East and it shocked Gamal that they had none. He explained that in his language, bread and life were the same word. He shook his head in disbelief that anybody, of their own free doing, would come into the desert to spend the night without bread. As a sorry substitute they offered him potato chips. Gamal graciously accepted some.

With dinner cleaned up, they turned their attention to settling in for the night. Gamal laid out his blanket by the fire and Walker retrieved his sleeping bag from the car. They had come to Wadi Rum to sleep under the stars, curled up together in his lightweight sleeping bag. Dramatic romantic notions crackled along with the fire.

Walker suddenly heard "tick, tick, tick." Then he heard the faint sound again and this time it seemed closer. After the third time he asked Gamal what he had heard.

Gamal made an excellent facsimile with his mouth. "Did it sound like that?"

Walker nodded yes.

Gamal said, "Scorpion—tick, tick, tick . . . tick, tick, tick."

"Aren't you frightened you'll get stung during the night?" Tanya asked in a surprised tone.

"It is true, scorpion like heat and like to get next to you. I no scared. Bedouin mother feed baby scorpion poison. No hurt me."

"Oh, they give it to you as a baby until you are immune," Tanya said.

"Yes, immune. I am immune," Gamal replied, practicing an unfamiliar English word.

Touching Tanya's arm, Walker announced, "I'm sleeping on the rock."

"Yeah," she concurred.

After a few minutes, it became all too apparent where the saying "as hard as rock" came from. Worse still, the rock angled slightly. They decided to give up on sleeping. Walker put a few bushes on the fire and noticed there was not a stir coming from Gamal.

With sleeping bag in hand, the couple moved away from their campsite to a more open part of the desert. The moon shone brightly overhead, making a flashlight unnecessary and allowing them to see for miles. The silence of the desert again overtook them. They were about to disturb it.

During their wilderness lovemaking, Walker and Tanya engaged their imaginations to create delightful positions. While on his back with her buttocks on his abdomen, he pumped his penis in and out of her vagina. In a cosmic display they took to mean that their pleasuring of each other had been accepted, as he exploded into the rubber deep within her volcanic vulva, a shooting star streaked across the heavens and burned out overhead.

They collapsed onto the sleeping bag fully aware and appreciative of the events just awarded them. By the time they had finished, Tanya had sprayed her orgasmic juices several times onto the thirsty sands of Wadi Rum. Even their highly euphoric state did not ease their fear of scorpions, however, and they returned to the car to sleep.

Walker and Tanya awoke before sunrise and watched the day begin. From their vantage point they could not see the sun, only the desert getting lighter and waking up. When Gamal rose, they ate the remaining food. In the light of morning Walker carefully checked the lettuce; he found a couple more bugs and picked them out.

Walker peered out into the desert as he ate. The dry white scrub that burned so routinely, that he had mistaken for being dead, glistened with a light green hue. Life-giving water droplets clung to the plants and sparkled in the soft morning light. He had spent his adulthood studying the long cycles of history: movement through centuries. The cycle of the desert seemed to last only one day—birth, life, death and renewal every day into forever.

Gamal drove them to the spots that most tourists wanted to see. They went to the bridge rock and the ruins of Lawrence of Arabia's fortress. The small lump of rubble could have been anything. After that they went to a massive sand dune several hundred feet high. Gamal called it "the place of moving sand."

Walker and Tanya returned to Gamal's truck a few minutes before one o'clock and paid him what they had agreed upon, plus a small tip. Visibly pleased, Gamal asked with a boyish grin if they wanted to see his camel. They agreed and he led the way in his truck. Walker used the freshly made tire tracks from Gamal's truck for traction and followed easily in the rental car.

They had gone only a short distance when they came upon a truck with a tire removed. Two Arab men wearing head scarves and long robes spoke in Arabic with Gamal. By their hand gestures and looks of concern, Walker knew they were not locals. According to Bedouin tradition, anyone in the desert requiring assistance received it.

The men loaded the tire in the back of Gamal's truck. One man stayed with the stranded vehicle while the other got in with Gamal. Fifteen minutes later all arrived in the village. Gamal dropped off the man and the tire at the home of someone who could fix it. He then drove to his house with Walker and Tanya following.

Smoke filled the air inside the small brick building. In the center of the room, a fire burned from a hearth built into the dirt floor. From the soot and grime covering the ceiling and walls, it appeared that it burned constantly. Gamal's mother had made lunch and invited them to stay. They politely declined, indicating they had to be on their way.

Gamal guided them outside to the back of the house to meet his camel. Petting the dusty, dirty animal left a pungent smell on Walker's hand. Saying the creature appeared nasty, Tanya refused to touch it. Gamal laughed at her hesitation as he hugged its neck, proclaiming its friendliness.

In curious fascination, Gamal's young brother and sister had followed them out of the house. They giggled as they witnessed a Westerner's reaction to the camel. After a few minutes, Tanya and Walker said goodbye to Gamal and his family and thanked him again.

Walker drove and Tanya read from the guidebook as they began the three-hour drive to Petra. They learned something of Petra's setting and history.

"'It's protected in all directions by sheer and rugged sandstone cliffs that rise out of Wadi Araba. The easiest, and really the only way to get to the inner city, is through the Siq. What's a Siq, you ask? Well, it's a passage created by a tectonic breakage of rock. The walls of the Siq vary between 30 feet and 600 feet in height and at times appear to touch overhead. It runs for two miles.

"'A nomadic western Arabic tribe called the Nabataeans came to the area around the sixth century BC. At first they raided the rich caravans passing through their lands and when they became more settled, they got richer by levying a toll for safe passage. As their territory expanded and more caravan routes came under their control, their influence over the region grew. They defended themselves and prospered for many centuries. In 63 BC, while other settlements fell to the Roman forces, the Nabataeans maintained their independence with payoffs.

"'Their demise came from siding with the Parthians in a war

against the Romans. When the Parthians were defeated, Rome required Petra to pay tribute. Herod the Great attacked the city twice to enforce payment and finally in 106 AD, the Romans took the city as their own and transformed it to the standards of the day.

"'Excluding the Roman structures, such as the colonnaded street, there are very few freestanding structures in Petra. The Nabataeans carved their buildings right out of the rock cliff. One of the masterpieces is an 8,000-seat amphitheater carved out of solid rock. They built it around the time of Christ.'"

As Tanya continued to read, it became apparent that two days at Petra would be insufficient. They would have to choose what to see and what to leave out. Walker stopped the car at an unimpressive small building with three white domes. They were a few miles from Wadi Musa, the village around Petra, and Tanya shrugged her shoulders.

"Why stop here?"

"It's Ain Musa. It means Moses' Spring," replied Walker. "As it is described in the Bible, his people were thirsty and at this very spot Moses struck the rock and water poured out." Walker got out of the car and stood before the domed structure, fascinated.

Blending religion and history together in a tight weave of reality allowed Walker to linger at the spot. Tanya's spirit lived more in the present than in the past and she jumped behind the wheel and drove away very slowly. He ran to catch up and climbed in the open passenger door while the car moved. Tanya drove the curvy road down into the village.

They found a small hotel within walking distance of the entrance to Petra, checked in, left their bags in the car and headed off for the park on foot. Since the park closed within the hour, Walker inquired with the two men working the entrance whether they could stay in the site longer. They told him no, but Walker's travel experience led him to believe that one of the men said yes with his eyes.

Walker took the man aside and inquired about a special permit or fee that might be obtained to stay after hours. None were available. Then he suggested a willingness to pay a private guide for a tour of the park that included an overnight stay in some private place.

At that, the man smiled. He and his partner, a desert police officer, just happened to provide such a tour. Walker and his "wife" each needed to purchase two-day tickets that evening. After the park closed, the man would take them to a Nabataean home carved from the rock. They could not venture out and would have to spend the night there. In the morning, they were to remain secluded until thirty minutes after the park opened; then they could roam freely. The private tour cost $50 U.S. Walker agreed and they arranged to meet in front of their hotel at 8:30 that evening.

Walker and Tanya bought the required tickets and headed off down the road for Petra. The excitement built in Walker as he held Tanya's hand and walked toward the entrance of the Siq. Although Petra meant "rock," for Walker it meant so much more—a place, a name, his daughter; a deep, protected, spiritual cavern encapsulating the beauty and solidarity of all his memories of the young woman Petra. She should be the one at his side.

A wave of guilty apprehension welled up. Walker wanted his daughter to know and understand what she meant to him. These thoughts disappeared as Tanya interjected, "You know they used Petra in the filming of *Indiana Jones & the Last Crusade?*"

At the opening of the Siq, thirty or more Bedouin with horses appeared to be packing up for the day. Others arrived with tourists coming back from Petra. Hoping for one last sale, they swarmed Walker with offers for a ride. Without transport, much of the hour before closing would be spent walking through the Siq. It meant only minutes at the most spectacular Nabataean building, the Khazneh, or Treasury. Walker negotiated a round trip on a horse and cart for the one-way rate.

Despite the waning light, an array of colors swirled together in the rock walls of the Siq. It reminded Walker of pleasures colliding. Earth-tone purples, rusts, yellows, greys, pinks and browns in layered patterns expressed a colorful history dating back far longer than human memory.

In the cool, noisy narrows of the Siq, a steady flow of people, horses and carts headed in the opposite direction. Both Tanya and Walker were silent as they bounced along, comforted only by a thin woolen blanket between their behinds and the hard wooden seat of the cart.

After a time the driver turned slightly to the left, then to the right. A narrow glimpse of the Treasury framed by the crooked walls of the Siq and the sand of the desert floor came into view. It was a sight so incredible that it branded into Walker's memory like hot iron on flesh. Walker involuntarily whispered the famous words from Dean Burgen's poem about Petra: "The rose-red city half as old as time."

The 120-foot-high building, carved out of solid rock, glowed an orangish pink. Exquisitely shaped and amazingly preserved columns, moldings and ornamental sculptures on ornate pedestals, along with perfectly-angled roofs crowned with chalice-like pinnacles left them speechless as the architecture came into full view. Colors changed moment by moment on stone arches and porticoes as the sun slowly set. They quietly let the magnificence fill their senses and watched until it was time to leave. On the way back, they could not find words to express what they had just seen and felt.

Back at their room, Walker and Tanya showered, packed and prepared for a night in Petra. They ate a hearty helping of shawarma—lamb, onions and tomatoes wrapped in pita bread—that they bought from a street vendor. At a small market in the village they purchased food and drink to last them until morning. Everything was in order, and now they awaited their guide.

With an air of secrecy, the man waved at them from across the street. In these types of arrangements, Walker knew that a scam could be at play. After some deliberations, he gave the man twenty-five dollars and agreed to pay the balance in the morning on the way out.

The guide accepted the arrangement, took the money and had them follow him to the locked gates at the visitor center. He pulled a key from his pocket and used it to open a side door. Walker followed him inside, with Tanya close behind. They were led through the building and out a door on the other side of the heavy gate.

The man spoke in Arabic to the two desert policemen guarding the padlocked gate. There didn't seem to be a problem and they were allowed to proceed. Walker hoped that on this night he and Tanya were the only ones who had bribed their way in.

In broken English, the man told them that up until fifteen years ago the Bedouin people lived in much of the city and used the many carved-out caves as their homes. When the government decided that Petra could be a major tourist attraction, the Bedouin were relocated to a new village built just for them. Most were not happy with the arrangement, but not much could be done.

Their guide seemed to sense this information caused them tension and assured them that villagers no longer had a reason to come to the park at night. Desert police patrols ensured that this was so. They would have no contact with other people that night.

The Siq was dark and silent, a spooky contrast from the afternoon's activity; the two-mile walk seemed to take forever. Once at the Treasury, they were again captured by its towering presence above them.

At the bottom of the twenty-five-foot-high entrance portico, small orange glows from lit cigarettes held by two desert policemen moved against the darkness. Their bodies were made invisible by the blackness surrounding them. As he went past, Walker made sure not to shine his flashlight in their direction. Again there seemed to be no problem, and they proceeded.

The threesome headed farther into Petra. In the dim moonlight, Walker could distinguish the architecture of the amphitheater. It occurred to him that after all these centuries, the basic design of such places had not changed.

Walker held Tanya's hand tightly as they walked along in silence. Occasionally their guide spoke and pointed off into the darkness, indicating a place of importance. In unfamiliar surroundings and under the cover of night, their long walk seemed that much longer.

After a long while, their guide finally said something in Arabic and pointed at a steep rock facing. Many places on the rock wall appeared darker than the rest of the surface. When Tanya shone her flashlight on these spots, the light disappeared. Walker added the beam from his flashlight to hers. The combined light still did not illuminate the cavernous dormitory. Entrances to the cave homes of ancient Nabataean families spread out before them along the rock facing.

Pointing to a relatively accessible black spot, the man suggested they use that one for this night's stay. Walker thanked him for his assistance and the man bid them farewell. They stood alone holding hands in the faint blue hue of Petra's night.

Inhaling large breaths of fresh air, Walker and Tanya listened to nothing but the wind blowing lightly around the sleeping rocks of Petra. Tanya broke the spell when she lifted his hand to her mouth and gave it a gentle kiss. Then she worked her way over to his fingers and slipped his index finger into her mouth. Her hot tongue twirled around it and she sucked it deeper into her mouth. The sensation began his arousal.

Looking into Tanya's face in the dark, Walker sensed a sparkle in her eyes that indicated sleep held no interest for her. They unrolled their sleeping bags right there on the hard, parched ground and disturbed the silence around them with lovemaking.

Tanya's body rippled with minor convulsions and Walker felt her orgasm rise to the verge of a crescendo. Then she moved slightly, decreasing the intensity of the sensation. Sexual pleasure sent him to the brink of no return. Then she let him cool down just a bit by easing her thrusts. Each kiss and sensual touch made him cry for a final release. The physical and mental strains of going to the brink of orgasm several times pushed their pleasure into the stratosphere. Their bodies perspired in newfound peaks of sexual intensification.

Walker's body, mind and spirit spun together in the colorful pattern of a gigantic galaxy beginning. Stopping its creation and release into the universe was not imaginable. Yet he did stop it, and then confusion settled into his awareness. When he opened his eyes, he witnessed Tanya's naked body climbing up the rocks, carrying a knapsack. The image induced a surreal state of consciousness in him. In this state of mind, he saw her enter the ancient Nabataean home and disappear into its darkness.

Walker's body craved a release and he grabbed hold of his condom-covered penis, still dripping wet from being inside her, and began stroking himself. But Tanya had created this heightened state of arousal and he wanted her to participate in its conclusion. He stood up, looked around to ensure no one was about and headed toward the rock face.

Sensitive to the touch, he feared the friction of putting his pants on would evoke a premature ejaculation. As Walker packed food and clothing into his knapsack, the gentle desert wind massaged his hardened penis. Intense sexual arousal maintained his erection during the climb to the cave. Trying to avoid scraping himself on the rocks made the ascent difficult.

Halfway up, Walker noticed a glow emanating from the entrance to the cave. A soft, enchanting flicker melted away the blackness and brought life to the colors of the rock. He climbed faster, protecting himself with one hand, gripping little craggy ledges with the other.

Once inside, Walker beheld twenty or more little tea candles burning. They created a stunning effect. The rise and fall of brightness and dimness connected to his frequency of sexual stimulation. The candlelight made the colors of the rock swirl together, reminding him of mystical pleasures past.

Lying on her back in the soft dirt, Tanya rubbed herself gently and moaned ever so quietly. Without opening her eyes, she began to speak: "Oh Walker, take me . . . take me beyond. . . . "

Walker tossed away his gear, put his hands on her knees, spread her legs and drove his face into her hot pink flesh. His resourceful tongue strokes soon created an orgasmic explosion. Her vaginal juice gushed like lava from a volcanic eruption, spraying his face and saturating the ground beneath her. Tanya's body shook and convulsed as if shocked by a powerful electric current.

The tinted walls in the cave reflected the severity of its history and added brilliance to the moment. The cool stillness of the dirt that held Walker's sweaty, naked skin contrasted with Tanya's hot body that quivered to his touch. Her sweet taste and smell stuck to his face. In a tempest of sensory overload he exploded a long forgotten sense of self into the Nabataean air. Their pleasures mingled together in the dust of time.

Lying naked in the dirt, Tanya and Walker slept until the waning obscurity of night gave way to the dawn of a new day. They dressed, ate and discussed plans for their last full day together. Just after seven o'clock they decided they could safely leave their den of delectation and return to the main gate.

As they passed the Treasury, Walker could not decide whether its beauty was more spectacular in the morning or afternoon light. Walker and Tanya could not just walk past, and halted to gaze for a few moments. They noticed that the hues of the Treasury changed in response to the varied lighting of the day, and that each moment here was breathtaking. Soon they left.

The light of early morning made the walk through the Siq feel much shorter than the night before. At the entrance, the man who had shown them the way in waited for them and smiled. He greeted them good morning in his own language.

"*Sabah al-khayr.* A night in Petra is good, no?"

Tanya nodded and smiled, while Walker said, "Better than I imagined," and then thanked the Jordanian man, "*Shukran.*" Walker paid what they owed and again thanked their guide warmly for his hospitality.

Back at their hotel, Walker and Tanya showered, ate breakfast and then headed back to Petra, where they joined other tourists for a more typical site visit. The couple debated whether to tackle the six-hour hike to Aaron's Tomb at the top of Mount Hor. From there, sensational views reportedly gave a true sense of the rugged impenetrability of the entire area.

Such a trip would take the rest of the day, however, and they'd miss seeing other parts of Petra. They decided that, rather than make the climb to Mount Hor and visit the monument to Moses' brother Aaron, they would tour Petra and view the peak from the site.

After spending another fifteen minutes admiring the Treasury, Walker and Tanya moved on. In the light of mid-morning, the amphitheater assumed a purplish shade. They strolled past a few of the Roman columns that had been re-erected; during the Roman occupation, a traditional colonnaded street had been constructed here. They watched in fascination as an American team of archeologists restored what many believed to be the oldest Byzantine mosaic ever discovered.

The Temple of the Winged Lions, named for the carved lions that topped the capitals of the columns, caught their attention for awhile. An ancient rock-cut path led the way to the Monastery, two hours away. Streams of tourists headed in both directions on the path, but, quicker than most, Walker and Tanya maneuvered their way past other sightseers. Beautiful and peculiar patterns of color adorned the sandstone along much of the path. The pair stopped several times to photograph them.

The sight of the Monastery erased the fatigue from the two-hour hike to get there. Standing 140 feet high and 150 feet wide, it too had been completely carved from the rock cliff. Walker and Tanya gazed in amazement at the building's elegant columns and archways, evidence of the craftsmanship and determination of the Nabataeans.

On a rock outcropping across from the Monastery, they sat and ate lunch. From that vantage point, they had a panoramic view of the entire rock setting from which the Monastery had been carved. Standing in the forty-foot columned doorway, people looked the size of mice, as did those who climbed the staircase to access the rim of the urn on top of the Monastery.

Walker and Tanya lingered as long as they could, soaking up the magnificence before them. Sooner than they would have liked, it was time to leave. Going back down took them far less time than going up and they arrived at the Treasury in late afternoon. Walker approached a huge carved column and laid both hands on it, wanting to absorb its strength, beauty and timelessness.

Weary from the long day's walk and the previous night's release, the two lovers welcomed the sight of Bedouin and their horses. Walker helped Tanya into the saddle and then made arrangements with the handler to pay the non-discounted rate for the ride out of the Siq. Keeping the horses side by side, the satiated American visitors rode slowly and glanced at each other often; they were in no hurry to leave Petra.

After an early dinner, Walker and Tanya retired to their hotel room. No one had questioned their marital status, and on their last night together they felt truly coupled. They tenderly cuddled, caressed and kissed, overcome by a blissful, divine connection. Over the last few days their loins had surpassed the known physical boundaries of satisfaction. Their erogenous zones ached from the memory of pure gratification, from their honest expressions of self, unleashed from matter to spirit. A higher connection freed them from making love on their last night together.

In the early morning hours, Walker and Tanya drove south on the Desert Highway toward Aqaba. Soon the bright, scorching sun would parch the land, part of the daily cycle of renewal and death. In a few hours, Tanya would be on a SAPTCO bus destined for Riyadh.

They spoke of her completing her tour of duty in Saudi Arabia. After that, she had no immediate plans except for hanging out in southern California and reacquainting herself with family and friends. When finished with that, she would likely try to find a nursing job somewhere in the U.S.

Tanya wished to stay in contact and gave Walker her address in Riyadh. She also wrote down her parents' address and phone number. They would always know where she was.

An unnerving reality hit Walker—he did not have an address to give her. If she wanted to get a message to him, it could be done through American Express Travel Services. Whenever Walker visited a major center, he sought out the AMEX office and checked for personal messages. Otherwise she could write to him in care of his parents' in Appleton and he would get the message whenever he returned. He gave her their address.

Walker and Tanya spent their last few hours together intimately discussing themselves, their beliefs and their fears. Tanya dreaded the last six months of her contract. Anticipating Christmas with her family in Paris made it all bearable. Walker praised her outlook on life and expressed his good fortune at having met her.

TANYA—THE COLORS OF PLEASURE

In an array of inner colors, Walker told her, he had released his deep-rooted fear of pleasure. Until this had happened, he hadn't known this fear's hold on him. Tanya's free-spiritedness and enthusiasm had produced a change within him, and for that he was grateful, he said.

Tanya replied that, although she did not fully understand all that he was saying, she valued his honesty and the courage he demonstrated by sharing his truths with her.

Breaking all the rules, they kissed passionately at the bus platform. In the moistness of her lips, Walker felt Tanya's tension. Returning to a restrictive environment troubled her. He hugged her tightly and whispered in her ear: "Everything is going to be fine. Take care."

With Tanya aboard, the bus pulled out of the terminal bound for Riyadh. As it drove away, through the dark-tinted glass of the window, they waved goodbye. Neither of them knew if it was forever. All Walker could think about was how colorless life would be with her gone.

When he got back to his hotel room, Walker wrote in his journal.

November 11

Aqaba, Jordan

Pleasure—and more specifically, sexual pleasure—can exist only in the absence of guilt. Sexual pleasure should be as free-spirited as the wind blowing through the leaves. Have I now shed all my restrictive childhood training toward sexual pleasure?

Although I have previously wanted to move on and leave my old attitudes behind, they have been like a rusted-tight emergency-brake mechanism on a car. The values and beliefs of my parents, church and community kept me firmly stuck in position. No matter how much I pulled and tried to release the hold, it would not budge. If I had forced myself to unlock, something might have snapped, causing more damage than if I'd left this whole subject alone.

After the wind has rustled, tossed and fluttered the leaves, there is little residual effect. Movement only lasts for the moment, then it's gone. Life continues, waiting for the next breeze to blow. I want to accept sex as freely as the leaves accept the wind—no expectations, no promises; only a passing touch enjoyed in the moment, and when finished only anticipation of the next airy exchange.

Living by such ideals would release me from the burden of guilt and allow passage to the spiritual side of sex, a place where only the purity of pleasure exists. That place is free of control dramas, performance anxiety and personal or cultural domination games. It is a divine union of two people surrendering themselves to only one goal: total sexual gratification.

I know such a place exists because I have experienced it in someone else.

Many other Middle Eastern cities and ancient historic and holy sites held an appeal for Walker, and he could easily have spent many more months in the region exploring them. But without Tanya at his side, he needed to add lushness to his surroundings, to replace the barrenness of sand and rock with greenery. He decided further desert treasures could wait. Longing to breathe moist, rich air and walk through thick vegetation, Walker made plans to leave the Middle East.

chapter 11

ANCIENT VILLAGE RHYTHMS
Full-moon Rites with a Thai Tribal Girl

Walker cleared his thoughts and then drove to the dive shop to find Brian. By chance, Brian was working at the store while Naguib led the dives that day. After a leisurely hour and a half hearing about exciting spots that Brian had visited, Walker knew he must travel to Thailand and other parts of Southeast Asia. From Brian's descriptions, Thailand seemed to offer the lushness that he sought.

The route Walker plotted was rather indirect. It included taking a bus from Aqaba to Amman, Jordan, then flying to either London or Paris and from there on to Bangkok.

For most of the five-hour ride to Amman, Walker slept. The big, air-conditioned bus gave him the luxury of doing so. From the bus station he hired a taxi to take him the twenty miles to Amman's Queen Alia International Airport. After a half hour of checking fares and schedules, he found that for about the same price, a flight for Paris left early the next morning and a flight to London left the next evening.

Initially Walker planned to save a day and take the flight to Paris. While waiting in line to purchase the ticket, though, strange ideas and emotions filtered through his consciousness; he stepped out of line to examine his indecision.

Flights from London to anywhere were usually cheaper than from Paris, and he could save money if he waited a day in Amman. Whichever city he flew into, it meant a stopover of a few days.

If Walker stayed in Paris, however, Selena would only be a few hundred miles away. The thought of being that close to her unsettled him. Even from Amman he felt the pull of her dark hazel eyes and could hear her breath, see her bright white smile, smell her alluring perfume and taste her womanliness. She haunted him and he pushed back the panic that tormented him.

"She knows you are coming close," a voice teased. "Go to her. You ache to do it, you long to do it; do not deny yourself. Don't worry whether you will have the strength to run away, to part from her. Fly to Paris."

It did not matter that Selena was married and would likely use him to make her husband or another lover jealous; Walker craved to see her again. He snapped out of the trance by focusing on Tanya and her free-spiritedness and the purity of its intent. His memory of the colors of pleasure inspired by her touch protected him. He knew it would not be so if he were closer to Selena.

Remembering Tanya's essence became his salvation, and he purchased a ticket to London.

*

Walker's time-zone hopping from Amman to London to Bangkok had completely confused his body and he spent most of the first two days in Thailand sleeping. When he felt rested enough to travel again, he booked an overnight journey by rail. The 450-mile trip from Bangkok to the city of Chiang Mai on an express train started just after seven in the evening and was due to end at eight in the morning.

ANCIENT VILLAGE RHYTHMS

The berths were converted to beds at around ten. As the train headed farther north, the constant click-clack of the wheels against the rail joints, along with distant whistle blows and the gentle rocking motion, prevented Walker from falling into a deep sleep.

He spent the first two days in Chiang Mai walking and cycling around the city. The noise, the congestion, the heat, the pollution and the hustlers of Bangkok had been left far behind; Chiang Mai seemed like a haven in comparison. With cooler temperatures and more than 300 temples in a city of fewer than 200,000 people, Chiang Mai was comfortable as well as visually pleasing.

One afternoon Walker hired a tuk-tuk—a noisy, three-wheeled taxi—to drive him the ten miles up Doi Suthep, a mountain northwest of Chiang Mai. Along the road near the summit, 300 steps rose to a temple. He admired the carved nagas that lined both sides of the entire staircase. The heads of these multi-headed dragon serpents were at the bottom; their colorfully painted, snake-like bodies rose with the staircase.

Many vendors displayed birds in wicker cages. One seller explained in halted English phrases that good luck would come if the birds were released in the main square of the temple. Walker did not understand the Buddhist symbolism in releasing birds from a cage. However, he did feel sorry for the small birds trapped in the tiny cages and for a small fee took two of them. As the birds anxiously flapped their wings, he started up the stairs

On the clear day, Walker enjoyed fabulous views from high above the city. Visiting young monks dressed in bright orange robes took pictures with their disposable cameras. The five-story golden chedi in the center of the temple compound reflected the sunlight. The outer temple buildings contained ornate carvings, and Walker took time to admire the detailed workmanship. A vast, polished black marble floor surrounding the chedi mirrored the white clouds and blue sky.

Shoes were prohibited on temple grounds; in his bare feet Walker found a quiet spot away from other people. He opened the little wicker doors and the birds fluttered their wings and bolted for freedom.

At the bottom, Walker begrudgingly returned the cages and then hired another tuk-tuk to go three miles farther to the royal family's winter palace. While strolling in the well-maintained gardens, he wondered whether royalty was a life of privilege or of bondage.

The people of Thailand truly loved their royal family. They had not turned royalty into a media circus or a tourist trap, as the British had. Although the King of Thailand had no governmental powers, he held the love and respect of the people. That unto itself was a political force.

After four days in Chiang Mai, Walker headed north and slightly east to the town of Chiang Rai. He went there to begin a trip to the Golden Triangle. Fifteen years prior, tourists who visited the area risked their lives. If they didn't work for an army general or an opium baron, they had no business being there. For decades such men operated with impunity and became very wealthy, thus the term "Golden." "Triangle" came from the fact that the three countries of Thailand, Burma and Laos met there.

Walker knew little about opium and spent some time reading and investigating its history and importance to the region.

Opium use went back as far as the early Greeks. In the time of Kublai Khan, the late thirteenth century, Arab traders introduced it to China. The hills of China and Southeast Asia had soil ideal for the cultivation of poppies. Opium as well as heroin made from the poppies became a cash product for the poor and nomadic hill tribes and provided them a way to pay taxes to their political masters. Persecution in China and Burma forced many hill tribes to seek refuge in Thailand and Laos. As they migrated, their most valuable crop came with them.

The opium and heroin trade expanded significantly during the

ANCIENT VILLAGE RHYTHMS

Vietnam War. An American presence in the area gave the drugs increased exposure and opened up worldwide channels of distribution. Everyone wanted a piece of the lucrative action. Success meant a huge accumulation of personal wealth and sufficient resources to finance political power and influence.

The national armies of China, Burma, Thailand, Vietnam, Laos and Cambodia needed funds to purchase military hardware, so they became involved, as did the separatist rebel armies of the Shan, a hill-tribe people. Walker found it incredible to learn that the CIA also became a major player, transporting the drugs on U.S. aircraft to Vietnam and other destinations. It became a way of raising additional funds without the required congressional approval. Covert funds could be used for covert operations.

Such large-scale distribution networks made heroin more available around the world. Availability raised demand as well as profits. The people of the hill tribes grew the poppies, but were at the bottom of the chain and the poorest link. They became more and more dependent on opium production for their existence. The power brokers became more violent as they vied for control of the drug trade, and wars within wars raged.

The CIA ceased to be a significant player when the U.S. pulled out of the region in 1975. Around the same time, a local drug lord, Khum Sa, who had been operating in Southeast Asia for various factions since the Fifties, consolidated his power by becoming the head of the Shan United Army.

For the next seven years very little was done to stop Khum Sa. In the early Eighties, the Thai army initiated a full-scale assault and forced him to flee to Burma. Then in 1985, the U.S. Drug Enforcement Agency paid the Thai army to destroy poppy fields and heroin refineries. For a mere $800,000, they eliminated twenty-five square miles of poppy production.

In 1959 the Thai government had started a program to subsidize the hill-tribe farmers for their loss of income if they replaced the poppy crop with a food crop such as tea, coffee, fruit or corn. It had little success. In 1980 they revived the program and called it "A King's Project." Under its new name, the project had flourished.

By the time Walker arrived, the opium and heroin trade had been, for the most part, eliminated or at least controlled. In the heart of the Golden Triangle, on the banks of Sop Ruak and Maekhong Rivers, first-class tourist hotels now served cocktails on the terraces. Rooms boasting excellent views of the intersection of the three countries had replaced the secret landing strips and their machine-gun guardians.

After a few days in the Golden Triangle area, Walker bused it back to Chiang Mai and investigated various options for a trek to visit hill-tribe people. He reached a decision based on the small group size and the background of the guide, who had been educated with funds provided by a Canadian adventure-tour operator.

Marching into a remote village with a large number of tourists did not appeal to Walker. He knew that very little interaction would take place under those conditions. The trek he booked for the following day had only two other people on it.

In the morning, Walker waited at the designated area outside one of the hotels. The package included a four-day, three-night tour and the operators guaranteed that no other tourists would be seen. Hill-tribe trekking had become so popular in northern Thailand that achieving a sense of remoteness had become difficult.

Hill-tribe people lived primarily in remote, mountainous areas of Southeast Asia, with the largest populations being in China. Many of them migrated to Thailand after World War II to escape persecution in China and Burma, while other tribes had been long established in Thailand.

There were dozens of different tribes that branched off into subgroups, each with its own dialect and culture. Walker read estimates that suggested a quarter of a million hill-tribe people lived in the northern regions of Thailand and that in all of Southeast Asia, including China, Vietnam, Laos, Burma and Thailand, there were 13 million.

Shortly after eight o'clock, a couple in their late twenties arrived. During the introductions, Walker learned that Don and Rachel were professionals from Vancouver, Canada. She worked in marketing and he in advertising. They had visited her brother, who had been living and working in Bangkok for several years. After a week in Bangkok, they were looking forward to seeing a completely different part of the country and culture.

A small pickup truck pulled up, its back lined with wooden benches. A Thai driver in his late thirties smiled at his waiting customers. On the passenger side sat a young Thai man of about twenty. He smiled as he opened the door and hopped out. He seemed very personable. Through a heavy Thai accent, he said his name. None of them understood it.

Rachel inquired, "How do you pronounce your name?"

"MANLY. You know—" and he held his arms up and flexed his biceps, "like man . . . lee."

It wasn't a Thai name and Walker concluded that the fellow had coined it himself. Walker chuckled inwardly at the thought of it, because Manly stood only about five-foot five and was not very muscular. He had an outgoing, confident manner and held a steady job, so from that perspective Walker thought perhaps he carried the title well.

Manly sat with the driver in the comfort of the cab, while the farang bounced around in the back. After two hours of driving, they stopped in a Palong village north of Chiang Mai. Manly explained that the Palong tribe had its roots in the Mon-Khemer family. The people who had migrated to Thailand had adopted a rural Thai lifestyle and in the process had lost most of their original culture and language.

THE WORLDWIDE SEXUAL ADVENTURES OF WALKER FAYT

After a much-needed washroom break and the purchase of wrapped candy and bottled water, the tour continued. As they drove out of the village, Walker noticed a large group of villagers watching a soap opera on a television set. It disappointed him; he hoped for better things to come.

Early in the afternoon they stopped for lunch in a Mong tribe village, where they had noodle soup with the villagers. Shortly after leaving the village, the tourists were informed that the truck ride would conclude and an elephant ride would begin. As a marketing angle, many of the tour operators included an elephant ride and river rafting. These were offered more as a novelty rather than out of necessity.

Two elephants were hired to transport the group. Manly and Walker rode on one and Rachel and Don on the other. Each elephant had a boy keeper who acted as a guide. The guide sat in the nape of the elephant's neck and gave it instructions. Walker learned that a special bond formed between the elephants and the young boys who rode them.

The guests sat atop the elephants in wooden-framed carriers lined with thin blankets. Holding the carriers in place were ropes extending around the belly and the underside of the tail. The formidable shift the elephants made with each stride of their huge legs required a paralyzing grip on the carrier's safety rails and made the ride quite uncomfortable. The terrain did not help matters; the paths were quite narrow and very steep and tree branches constantly knocked the passengers about.

On the muddy, narrow paths, the elephants often stood on three legs trying to find a footing that would keep them from slipping. If an elephant was to fall off the path and down the sheer side of the mountain, the chances of survival for those aboard would be slight.

Despite the danger, it fascinated Walker to watch as the elephant ahead blindly felt for the pothole into which to place its next step.

ANCIENT VILLAGE RHYTHMS

His own manly pride stopped him from getting off and walking. Trusting the skills of a giant working animal created a strange feeling of fatalism within him.

After about forty-five minutes, Rachel asked to get down; she had decided walking was a better way to go. Now on foot, Rachel became the group's photographer. Walker gave her his camera for a posed shot of himself and Manly waving from their perched carrier.

The elephant trek ended none too soon for Walker. What seemed like many hours had been only one and a half, and he welcomed the chance to walk. He petted the elephant, tipped the boy keeper and followed Manly along a path into the forest.

In late afternoon, on a high hillside clearing surrounded by jungle-covered peaks, the four of them walked into a Mong tribe village. There were no adults about, only children. It seemed the day's outdoor work had been done and people were preparing for the evening meal. Their arrival had been expected and custom required that guests be shown to the headman's residence. Intrigued by the foreigners, a few curious children cautiously kept their distance as they led the way.

The two branches of Mong tribe included the Green Mongs and White Hmongs. Manly explained that they could distinguish this as a White Hmong village because of the two doors to the residences. One opening was for guests and the other for family; guests used the lower of the two doors. Green Mong homes had only one door.

At the headman's hut, the visitors and villagers sat around a fireplace and tried to converse despite the language limitations. The people did not speak Thai but Manly's White Hmong was better than Walker expected.

Dinner consisted of a simple vegetable broth with a plate of rice. The villagers were hospitable, yet rather shy, and the guests turned in for an early night. The foreigners slept in their sleeping bags in the guest section of the hut, separated by bamboo dividers from the headman and his family.

Before heading out for the day's trek to the next village, all three of the Westerners sat in the hut and applied sunscreen. An old woman with dark, wrinkled skin sat across from them and watched. Her eyes twinkled as she smiled and giggled, exposing bad teeth. She simulated the application of the lotion and pointed to the container of sunscreen. Her amusement grew to the point of being an embarrassment to the guests.

Manly returned from outside and Rachel asked him why the old woman found the sunscreen so interesting. He said a few words but the woman didn't reply and just continued to point and smile. The headman's wife said a few words to Manly and he began to laugh.

"What is it? What's so funny?" Rachel's voice sounded a bit perturbed. Manly managed to speak through his embarrassed sputtered laughs.

"She thinks that you are going into the bushes."

Still annoyed, Rachel said, "What's so funny? We *are* going into the forest."

"No, no, you misunderstand. They only put cream on when they go into the bushes for . . . sex."

Rachel suddenly caught the significance. "She thinks . . . that we're—" and Rachel looked around, realizing that the two men and her had all applied the lotion. "Oh no! No, no, no, no," and she shook her head from side to side, facing the old woman, and with hand signals and broken phrases tried to explain that the lotion protected them from the sun.

The crone seemed to understand little of it. She continued to giggle, point and nod her head with a look of nostalgic appreciation.

Unfamiliar with the territory and villages on the second day's route, Manly hired a local guide for assistance. Some trails involved steep up-and-down paths, while other parts wandered beside flat, cultivated fields of crops. During the hike, Walker did not see or hear any wildlife. There were no birds, no squirrels, nothing but insects. He postulated that either the animals were very elusive or everything had been hunted to extinction. He hoped for the first.

They stopped for lunch at a small Lisu village. The meal consisted of a broth, and a side plate of rice served with finely chopped hot green peppers. Each individual decided the amount of peppers to take. It became an exercise in measuring masculinity.

Rachel avoided them altogether. Walker and Don both claimed their appreciation for hot spicy food and took about the same amount. To make sure they were not being outdone by the foreigners, Manly, the local guide and the headman all took a double helping.

Shortly after lunch, Walker found Manly and the local guide slumped against the wall, sweating profusely. They made excuses to stay a little longer before moving on, but no one mentioned the peppers as the reason for the extended rest. The older, and on this occasion, wiser farangs had gotten the better of the younger locals. Wisdom also dictated that it would have been impolite to say so. It took Manly and the local guide about fifteen minutes to recover.

Two hours after lunch they were on the edge of another small Lisu village. The villagers must have been quite accustomed to receiving travelers because the children ran to them and gathered around. Young girls crowded around Rachel and the young boys actively jostled with Walker and Don.

Again the children led them to the headman's home. Like others in the village, it had been constructed out of bamboo. The twenty-by-ten-foot rectangular structure stood on posts; the floor was five feet off the ground. Part of the roof was thatched and the rest made of corrugated metal. Entry doors, along with the porch, were on the downhill part of the house.

The two guides and three Westerners were warmly welcomed

into the headman's home and seated around a fire. The man's eyes sparkled with friendliness and his salesmanship gleamed as he placed two bottles of water and a bottle of Mekong whiskey in front of them. They accepted the water; the offer of whiskey surprised the foreigners. Rachel and Don looked at Walker and they all shrugged their shoulders. Finally Rachel spoke up: "Oh, why not!"

Don reached out and cracked the top. As he opened the bottle, the headman's wife brought out plastic cups. Walker had seen the Mekong brand of rice whiskey all over Thailand and hadn't been tempted to try any. The 150 baht the headman wanted for the large bottle was about double what it would have cost in Bangkok. Split three ways, it meant that Walker's share came to about $2 U.S.

Everyone drank and toasted their arrival. The whiskey tasted good to Walker, a bit sweet with a mild, burning finish. Over drinks they conveyed very basic information: where they were from, if they had any children and how many, how long they were going to be in the country. The headman advised that the village had thirty families and had been in that location for six years.

When they had finished the bottle, the headman vigorously set out another. The man had style and the effects of the alcohol made the gesture somewhat comical to his visitors. They laughed as they declined his latest offer. With no more whiskey to drink, and work waiting for him, the headman excused himself and invited his guests to explore the village on their own. They would eat and sleep in his home and were to return there in a couple of hours for dinner.

Word of their arrival spread quickly throughout the village and most, if not all of the young children, waited outside for them to reappear. The girls were sweet as they held hands and politely showed the visitors to the washrooms and the place in the stream where the females bathed and the different spot in the stream for the males.

The boys ran up and pinched and lightly struck the three visitors.

ANCIENT VILLAGE RHYTHMS

In keeping with their defined roles, the girls tried to prevent the boys from getting too close. Walker assumed the boys behaved that way to prove their boldness and bravery. Regardless of their motivation, they were a nuisance—much worse than the mosquitoes. Finally it became too much. Walker pretended to be angrier than he really was and shooed the boys away. It would only be temporary.

During this interval of peace, however, the three wandered throughout the village. Walker observed the people and their living conditions; the contrast with Appleton was profound. Faces, hands, feet, torsos were all dirty, as were the clothes that the villagers wore. The boys had on ratty, dirty, Western-style clothes and girls wore wraparound patterned skirts that were in better condition but just as dirty. Many of the younger children, both boys and girls, went bare-chested.

On their stroll they came upon a group of older boys, about eleven to fourteen years old, playing a game with a hard wicker ball about ten inches in diameter. They watched for a while, then were invited to play. Walker and Don joined in, while Rachel continued to watch.

The skills required were a cross between soccer and hackysack. As such, the game did not permit the use of hands. Each person displayed their best stuff for a time, then kicked the ball to whomever they wished. Etiquette dictated that it should be someone who hadn't had a turn lately.

Since Walker and Don were guests, the youths gave the ball to them more often than to their fellow players. They did this partly out of politeness and partly because they were curious to see what the foreigners could do. Judging by their enthusiasm at their guests' participation, Walker guessed that outsiders didn't play with them that often.

The Lisu boys seemed surprised that both foreigners were quite good. Out of the twelve players, they certainly weren't the worst.

THE WORLDWIDE SEXUAL ADVENTURES OF WALKER FAYT

After about a half hour, Rachel indicated that they should return for dinner. On the way back, Don and Walker complimented one another on their play. Both men admitted that they had played a little hackysack in their day. Walker commented that he found it interesting that a minor leisure activity from his teenage days had come back to help him connect with hill-tribe people in Thailand.

The soup at dinner had more substance—little bits of chicken, carrots, corn and onion floated in it. Afterwards, the Westerners went to bed early while Manly stayed up and chatted with the local guide and headman.

In the morning, all were awakened by a squealing noise of deafening proportions. Walker went outside to confirm his suspicions. Directly underneath them, a pig had just been slaughtered. Walker guessed that tradition or maybe just the invoking of good luck dictated that such an important undertaking take place at the headman's house. Dogs from all over the village gathered to lick up the rare treat that stained the ground in little red pools. The butcher swatted them back, not letting them come too close to the freshly killed pig.

Walker went back inside to find a horrified look on Rachel's face. In a barely audible voice, she hoped her suspicious weren't true.

"Is it what I think it is?"

Without saying a word, Walker nodded. He picked up the empty bottle of whiskey from the day before, put it close to his nose and took a big long whiff. In his best Robert Duvall impression, he uttered the line from the movie *Apocalypse Now*, substituting for the word "napalm":

"I l-o-o-ve the smell of Mekong in the morning."

The humor helped relieve the stark reality of what had occurred only feet from where they slept. However, being so close to the life and death of a village had perturbed the Westerners and eliminated their appetite for a village breakfast. They drank tea and ate granola

ANCIENT VILLAGE RHYTHMS

bars, said goodbye, and waited outside for Manly to finish business and pleasantries with the headman.

Having been in the mountainous setting and interacting with various hill-tribe people for two days, Walker now began to see and appreciate some of their distinctiveness. Up until this point he had noticed only the dirt and grime of the people and their clothing and hadn't looked past that.

The personable headman was not indicative of the adult Lisus that lived in the village. They were reserved and shy and for the most part avoided foreign guests. The children were just the opposite and reflected a shift in attitude between generations. Perhaps as they got older, they too would become more reserved; perhaps not.

Walker's mind linked the past, the present and the future and he thought that eventually all people of the tribe would become accustomed to foreign visitors. Their customs and beliefs would hang in the balance. Could they hold on to their language and traditions, or were they destined to lose their culture, like the Palong tribe?

On this cool morning, as the heat of the sun lifted the mist to higher elevations, Walker covertly watched a mother and her young son. The mother held something, perhaps sugar cane or bamboo, and sliced it with a small ax. Her son helped by steadying the stock at its base. He was about four or five and, as with all the males of the village, wore Western-style clothing. His light blue T-shirt and tan cotton pants were filthy. Except for a small puff of thick hair at his forehead, the rest of his head had been shaved very short.

The mother, like most hill-tribe women, wore clothing according to her tradition. It appeared to be clean and neat. As she crouched to get a better angle with the ax, Walker closely observed her colorful mix of apparel.

A black skirt hung to her ankles. A two-tone sleeveless smock with a slit up the side to allow for walking and bending hung outside the skirt. The back of it was bright yellow and the front sky blue.

Beneath it she wore a bright-red long-sleeved shirt. Accessories included a belt around the waist that tapered the outer garment, many distinctive bracelets adorning both wrists, and a headband with brightly colored stripes that accentuated her jet-black hair, which she wore tied back into a ponytail.

When she finished cutting the stock, the mother tenderly handed the shaved treat to her son and he immediately began to lick and suck on it. Walker suspected that if this Lisu mother had known he was watching her, she would have moved out of view. He considered himself fortunate for having witnessed such a private moment between a mother and her son. Then the rest of the traveling group appeared, ready to depart.

During the hike, Manly pointed out the rare remaining teak trees in the forest. He explained that about twenty years ago Thailand had completely banned the harvesting of forests. It required political courage to go against local and multinational interests. But without the ban, all of Thailand's forests, along with their ecosystems, would have been eliminated. Even with the ban, significant poaching occurred, especially for the finer woods such as teak and mahogany.

The foreigners reveled for a moment at seeing a live teak tree growing in its natural setting, a survivor of logging and poaching. While looking at the tree, Walker remembered all the fine antique teak furniture in his parents' home. He had never given any thought to where it came from or the environmental cost of owning such beautiful things.

They broke for lunch at a farm growing crops under the King's Project. During lunch, Manly told them that their last night would be spent in a Lahu village. His heritage was part Lahu and although he didn't know the people of the village, his common tribal roots would ensure a warm welcome for them all.

More than once during the walk, Manly mentioned that "free

sex" existed in the next village. He didn't explain the term and the trekkers understood it to mean that the culture of the tribe accepted premarital sex. Manly knew the route from the farm to the next village and no longer needed the local guide. It didn't surprise Walker that the guide decided to come along anyway. On one of the rest stops, Manly mentioned the free sex again and this time Rachel reacted to the comment.

"Do you know how dangerous that is? If AIDS were to get into one of these villages, it would wipe it out. In no time at all, the entire region of northern Thailand could be infected and thousands of people would die. Manly, if you're going to do anything, tonight or in the future, I certainly hope you do it with protection."

Rachel's stern warning seemed to affect Manly. He avoided any further discussion of the matter, as if he was taking what she had said to heart. Rachel had mentioned the possibility that his people could be eliminated as easily as the teak trees. Walker wondered if Manly contemplated the vulnerability and innocence of the hill-tribe people and the significance of not only his actions, but the actions of his clients as well.

The Lahu village, of Shehleh heritage, warmly welcomed Manly. His roots were Red Lahu, but that didn't seem to make a difference. The headman knew some relative of Manly's and that made him even more accepted. As in the other villages, there were many children who were just as friendly and just as dirty. The adults were also very friendly and did not shy away from the guests. They actually sought them out and attempted interaction.

Following hill-tribe custom, the visitors were taken to the headman's house for introductions, and in this case, tea. The headman explained, through Manly's interpretation, that the village was putting on a dance this very evening; he would be honored by their presence. They would be his guests for dinner and the festivities would begin afterwards. The headman also explained that the village had built a separate hut for guests; that would be their lodgings during their stay.

After dinner, and before the show started, Rachel, Don and Walker strolled about the village. A tremendous energy, like loose electricity, filled the air. Children ran around with excitement; young teenage girls dressed in fancy wrap skirts and white blouses walked about, their adult eyes twinkling.

With so much activity and anticipation, Walker initially missed some of the detail. The teenage girls had covered their faces in a white blush made from limestone. They all wore wide silver bracelets and thin silver necklaces, as well as brightly colored hair bands that pulled their clean, shoulder-length black hair behind their ears.

The atmosphere seemed to be that of a first prom. The girls displayed an attitude of innocent confidence that came from dressing up and feeling mature and it mixed with a self-consciousness of not knowing if they were doing it properly. Patiently they stood outside their homes. The Westerners discussed the significance of their dress and decided it related to the evening's dance. Inwardly Walker suspected it was something else.

The white-faced teenage girls and their families encouraged their guests to take pictures of them. It felt more and more like prom night. Walker and Rachel photographed the five girls with this special facial distinction. Walker's subconscious searched for the character trait that they all shared, but it eluded him. He shot pictures freely: solo shots, group shots with family and shots with two girls arm-in-arm.

Using the protection of his lens to shield his curiosity, Walker studied their eyes. They all told the same story, but he couldn't read it. Eyes of other villagers showed excitement, but the white-faced teenagers were different. Their dark eyes were silent, intent,

ANCIENT VILLAGE RHYTHMS

mysterious, piercing his soul with every glance. They seemed to have a hunter's intensity in their stare.

The outdoor dance began. Very young girls and boys still wearing their soiled clothes participated hesitantly. Girls from about eight to eleven wearing colorful clothing in the tradition of their village led the singing and dancing.

The village shaman, dressed in a clean white shirt and a light blue pleated skirt that went to his ankles, focused everyone's attention toward the center of a loosely formed circle of people. By pounding a drum and blowing into a wind instrument, he created a rhythm that the children followed. His hair, longer than that of the other men of the village, hung loose below his ears and around his collar.

Outside the dancing circle of children, the younger women of the village cradled their babies in slings around their chests. They openly breast-fed and some kept a breast permanently exposed so their babies could feed at will. They had not changed for the performance and wore what they did every day. The mix of styles and material led Walker to believe that tradition had been abandoned for whatever clothing they could get.

Farther outside the circle stood the men, teenage boys and the older women. It made for quite a gathering. The shaman marched in the center around a makeshift lantern as the children sang and clapped their hands to his beat. Soon the guests, including Manly, were encouraged to participate. They all joined in by holding hands and forming a human circle that paraded around the light and the shaman. Rhythm united the group, and in synchronized motion they first turned their bodies toward the middle of the circle and then outward again.

After dancing had continued in this way for some time, the headman quieted the crowd and gathered the girls in costume and the younger children to the center of the circle. With accompanying foot and hand movements, they performed two different songs.

THE WORLDWIDE SEXUAL ADVENTURES OF WALKER FAYT

The older girls carried the tune and steps while the younger ones tried to imitate them. Walker found it very sweet to watch.

When the songs and dances finished, the villagers prompted the Westerners to perform for them. After a moment's thought, Rachel suggested "Ring Around A Rosey." Joining hands and skipping while moving in a circle, the threesome sang, "Ring around a rosey, a pocket full of posies; ashes, ashes, we all fall down!" and then they fell to the earth.

Children and adults in unison laughed and clapped. The next time the visitors did it, some children joined in and by the third time about ten kids followed the routine. Outside the main group, Walker noticed other little children holding hands, going around in circles, singing and falling to the ground.

The villagers had performed two songs and since the Westerners' first song and dance had been a hit, the villagers wanted another one. The three of them racked their brains for something they could do. Then Walker remembered the "Chicken Dance."

Don and Rachel both knew the dance and so the three of them started to hum the tune, "Dute do-do doo-doo-doo-doo", as they moved their fingers and thumbs together like a clucking beak. "Dute do-do doo-doo-doo-doo" they sang again, this time flapping their arms like wings. "Dute do-do doo-doo-doo-doo" they sang once more, this time with their hands on their hips as they flailed their elbows and shook their behinds. "Dute do-do doo-doo-doo-doo" they continued, now repeating the previous actions only lower to the ground, in a near-crouch. They stood up and started the sequence again only quicker, and then performed it a third time quicker yet.

Everyone laughed and clapped and wanted to learn how to do it. Don leaned over to Walker as they were going over the movements yet another time. "You know, you've corrupted these people forever."

ANCIENT VILLAGE RHYTHMS

"Yes—I have these terrible visions of people coming into the village a few years from now and getting 'Chicken Dance' as the village performance number."

When the Westerners tired of their song-and-dance routine, the festivities returned to the traditional circle dance around a fire. This style of dance carried on for a long time and various people joined in and left as the activity heated up. Walker noticed the headman's wife enjoying herself as she joined the group, clapping her hands and chanting. Two of the white-faced girls came to the inner circle and joined hands with other participants. Manly, while in the inner group, often mimicked the moves of the shaman. A looser, freer movement replaced the form and style of the earlier dance.

Walker readied his camera and flash. In the dark, the auto-focus did not adjust properly and he reverted to manual. Still he could not ensure a focused image, but pressed the shutter button regardless. FLASH! The intense bolt of extreme light startled the crowd and many people screamed in surprise. They weren't frightened or offended, just surprised. As Walker snapped more pictures, they became accustomed to the shocking effect and the yells became less frequent.

In the dark, Walker could not attain great composition and just hoped to capture the lively mood of the gathering. One image that remained vivid to him was a village woman inhaling deeply on a cigarette while her baby sucked heavily at her bare breast.

Villagers began to gather around Walker, interested in the source of the flash. A curious boy desired to look into the viewfinder, likely hoping to recreate the mysterious burst of light. After peering into the little window he shouted, bounced around and then scurried off, explaining the mystery he had learned to anyone who would listen. Soon almost everyone at the gathering wanted to look through the viewfinder, and a long line formed as people waited their turn. The foreign visitors had added their own magic to the evening.

THE WORLDWIDE SEXUAL ADVENTURES OF WALKER FAYT

At the end of a night's performance, it was customary for the guests to make a small monetary donation to the village and to hand out candy. The intensity of the dance, the flash, the novelty of seeing people in a camera and now the anticipation of eating a sweet whipped the villagers into frenzy and they crowded around the foreigners.

Manly gave the little individually wrapped candies to Walker, Rachel and Don and they distributed them as evenly as possible. Pushy and aggressive, the children clamored to get as much of the treasured loot as possible. Adults wanted the candy just as badly, but they were more reserved in coming forward to get it.

When the candy ran out, the villagers began to disperse. For those that remained, the fervor still lingered and many children darted and jostled among the adults. The noise of the crowd faded, and as it did, a rumbling echoed off the mountain peaks that surrounded the village. Rachel and Walker stopped their conversation to listen. It had a pattern. They looked in the direction of the sound. It came from off in the distance, uphill from the village.

Rachel asked no one in particular, "What's going on?"

Walker answered her, "I don't know, but it's very spooky. Look at the full moon shining through the mist."

Just as he finished his words, a white-faced girl ran past pulling Don by the hand. She led him toward the pulsating beat. Wide-eyed and confused, he had the oddest expression on his face. He helplessly stared at his wife as they went past. By then, Rachel had an equally odd but different expression on her face.

"I don't think I like the idea of a childless, unwed teenage girl, dressed for some sort of fertility ritual, dragging my husband into the hills under a full moon to the beat of a drum. I don't care about village protocol, I'm going after him."

Rachel walked away quickly, keeping her distance, but at the

ANCIENT VILLAGE RHYTHMS

same time not letting them out of her sight. Soon she was out of view, having disappeared into the misty darkness.

That was it, Walker thought—Rachel had solved what he could not. His hunch about something more to the evening than just dancing for the guests had been true. On a full moon, the mood of the village intensifies and anticipation builds. Childless, unwed girls paint their faces white, symbolizing their availability and attractiveness, and seek out potential mates.

Immediately upon having this revelation, Walker felt a warm hand join with his and tug his arm. It caused him to step in the direction of the pulsating sound. Dryness in his throat increased as the white-faced girl pulled his arm harder and motioned with her other hand for him to hurry and follow her. She let go of Walker's hand, ran faster for about ten yards, and then waved at him and waited for him to catch up. When he reached her, she took hold of his hand again and moved quickly up the hill toward the drumming. This time Walker moved with her.

The beating grew louder with each uphill stride. Distinct thoughts raced by so quickly in Walker's mind that they became impossible to capture. Each beat pulled him deeper into the consciousness of the village; each step carried him closer to the pulse of their reality.

A circular fence made of upright bamboo stalks surrounded a sizeable hut. As the girl urged him toward a small, door-like opening in the fence, she squeezed on Walker's hand. Upon entering, he noticed that the temperature seemed to rise. He wondered whether his imagination or physics made this so. Lunar light beamed through the misty night, illuminating his immediate surroundings. He could almost see the sounds pouring into the moonlight from the open door of the hut.

Walker glanced up and saw the bright full moon emerge partially from behind the clouds. The silvery outline of the clouds against the moon made him remember his childhood game of looking for images in the formations. What did he see on this night? Before anything came to mind, a tug on his arm drew him into the hut.

As Walker passed from light to darkness, from coolness to heat, from his own reality to some other one, his senses were suspended, captured and then dissolved by the fluidal pulse of the room. It seemed like forever before he could distinguish a visual reality. While anticipating the return of his senses, he felt her hand in his, leading him farther into her realm of magic.

Slowly Walker's eyes and body adjusted to the confined space and to the ceremony, seemingly a dance undertaken to celebrate the full moon, fertility and the abundance of life. This was not the dance of children for the entertainment of tourists. It had purpose and he saw its importance in the faces of the people and felt its meaning in the movement of their bodies.

They required no costumes for this gathering. Spirits danced to the beat of the drum and were incarnated in the smoke of opium that circulated thick and rich in the air. Walker let it fill his lungs as he swayed back and forth in a circle of human celebration.

For an instant Walker's mind held a single notion. It was that of Manly telling the Westerners that his tour company prohibited the villagers from selling or using opium around its clients. They maintained this policy out of respect for government initiatives to rid the country of the drug trade. Then he realized that the moment he passed through the fence, he became a participant and not a guest. Protocol was outweighed by tribal tradition and his immersion was complete.

As part of the tribe, Walker did not refuse the headman's offer of friendship. They smoked a mixture of tobacco and opium rolled together in cigarette form. Waves of strange stimuli transfigured his awareness and pushed his mind and body to the edge of control.

ANCIENT VILLAGE RHYTHMS

The drug swept across his being with the fury of desert winds.

For moments he was himself, sentient as Walker Fayt with all of his history and experience intact. Then, like the swell of a tsunami, a feeling would build from the pit of his stomach and wash away his civilization in a giant wall of destruction. Community and individuality were buried by the immense power of Mother Nature. Drum rhythms replaced his heartbeat as he connected to all things with a clarity too intense to escape.

For a moment, Walker felt his body submerge into the dirt floor. In the next moment, it soared outside the hut and he saw the moon shining brightly in the sky. The next moment he was back to the reality of holding hands and dancing in a circular motion, twisting and turning.

As the drug surged through Walker's body, waves of alternating realities continued to flood his consciousness. When they ceased, he exhaled air from his lungs in a sigh of relief. He was grateful for the moments spent as himself. They provided him the chance to recover and reflect on ideas that had never before struck him. Yet he welcomed the next rise to insight, where thought and universal vibration were visible and understandable.

Time seemed to stand still as truths around Walker were revealed. Realities returned that were abandoned long ago by man's ancient ancestors as they crawled out of the jungle and fought for survival on various planes of conscious and unconscious existence. They shed unnecessary realities and accepted others. The discarded truths waited in the ethers, ready to be rediscovered.

Accepting the Shehleh tribal traditions, Walker now moved to the cadence of their ancient reality and beliefs. Up and down in opium waves of self and universality, he followed the white-faced girl along a path to a cave in the hills above the ceremonial hut. The lunar gods sent their loving light as a blessing to show them the way. Each drumbeat from the hut traveled to the confines of the cave and echoed a vibrating, instinctive message to each cell of his material body—the message to mate.

Nothing could be seen in the blackness of the cave. Without a visual point of reference, the effects of the drug migrated into their bodies. Thought became action; their thoughts became one, rising and falling like powerful waves swelling up and crashing onto the rocks. Clothing fell away like dust in the wind and their naked bodies mingled with the cool dirt of the cave floor.

In one of his sentient moments, Walker found his money belt and put on a condom he had stored there. He touched small breasts, subtle and soft, not yet as large as the women of the village who had borne children. That was the last he remembered of himself.

The teenager's skin radiated intense heat and emitted sexual energy in perfect rhythm with the beat of the drum. Boom! Her body heaved against his and in his heightened connectivity he could smell her joy and feel it running down her leg onto his. Boom! He lay on his back with her vagina enveloping his hard penis. Boom! He thrust in and out of her as she lay on her back. Boom! Him on top, her on top, from behind, legs up, legs down. Each beat of the drum flashed a different sexual image not remembered from one beat to the next—just like the light bursting from his camera snatched successive snapshots of reality.

Walker easily lifted her small frame while staying inside her. As he stood, she wrapped her legs around him and they fucked with her completely off the ground. Drumbeats, waves of the drug and orgasmic pulses came together with the speed of creation and then fell apart in a fear of Armageddon. In the blackness of the cave, he rocked her against his body, his penis enjoying the full power of gravity. She clung firmly with her legs, not wanting him to stop.

In a moment of suspended animation between swell and crash, between high and low, between truth and lie, between good and evil, between reality and void, Walker came. His squirts, groans and breathing followed the beat of the drum and with the ejection of sperm he became himself once again. Aware of his individual existence and circumstances, he lowered himself onto his back and lay in the dirt. The girl still clung to him and she fell asleep lying on his chest.

Walker knew that she hoped for conception and he also knew that she had no understanding that it would not be possible. He did not wish to father any more children, whether he knew about them or not, and was grateful he had used protection. Rachel's warning to Manly rang clearly in his ears as well.

Walker's body shook slightly as he came down from his orgasm and the opium. Cold air dried his sweat, making him shiver in the stillness of the cave. The girl awoke, and in the darkness they found their clothing and went outside the cave to dress in the moonlight.

Although she was childless, he doubted she was a virgin. In a village that allowed premarital sex and encouraged the propagation of children, she had probably been trying to get pregnant since shortly after she became fertile, likely several years before.

Moonlight danced off the Lahu girl's naked body, revealing how tiny she really was. She probably weighed about 100 pounds. Her small hips curved slightly without much formation and there was no roundness to her buttocks. Her pubic hair was black and silky and not very thick; her nipples small and dark. When both of them were dressed, she took Walker's hands and pulled him tenderly so that they could kiss. It was a little, fragile kiss on the lips, without any promise of passion or commitment.

The girl led him down the path to the village. On the way down, Walker suddenly noticed that the drums had stopped. The sound link between people and nature had served its purpose. Although the drums had been silent for some time, Walker hadn't noticed until that moment. Except for the occasional barking dog, all was quiet in the village.

As the Lahu girl pointed the way to his hut, in sign language

THE WORLDWIDE SEXUAL ADVENTURES OF WALKER FAYT

Walker offered to walk her home, but she refused. As she bowed to him, he noticed that some of the white on her face had smeared off. Upon rising from the bow, she pointed to the moon. It hid behind a hillside peak, with light streaking out from all sides. She rubbed her belly, smiling. Walker remained expressionless.

Back at the guest hut, Walker saw Manly sleeping underneath blankets provided by the village. Walker concluded that he must have taken Rachel's advice and declined the free sex. The local guide slept there too. Don and Rachel looked cozy in their sleeping bags. A flashback of the ceremony suggested all of them had been there, but he hadn't realized it until now. Had they smoked opium too? He could not recall.

In the morning, no one spoke of the adult celebration. An undeclared awareness made it taboo. Topics centered on the day's activities and the village's tourist performance. They ate breakfast at the headman's house and left the settlement with relatively little contact with the villagers.

To complete their trip, the Westerners hiked for a few hours, floated on bamboo rafts down a river and then drove back to Chiang Mai. At the end of the hike, they thanked Manly and gave him a generous tip. Don and Rachel wrote out their address so that Walker could mail them copies of the pictures he had taken.

That evening, Walker sat calmly by Wat Suan Dawk, a temple containing a 500-year-old bronze Buddha image. In the stillness, he made plans for the next few weeks. His full-moon baptism into Lahu culture remained in his thoughts. In every way—physically, mentally, emotionally, spiritually—he felt a long, long way from Appleton.

Walker got out his journal and began to write.

ANCIENT VILLAGE RHYTHMS

December 1

Wat Suan Dawk, Chiang Mai, Thailand

The various cultures on Earth have evolved very differently. Why are we so fearful and intolerant of others' notions of civilization?

Last night I did some things that would be considered criminal back home. Committed in the U.S., these acts would cause outrage. If found out, I would be at risk of losing everything and would face a possible jail term. Here these actions are acceptable and seem to be in the natural course of things.

I do not feel like a criminal. Actually, I feel fortunate to have experienced immersion into a culture completely different from my own. When I get back home, however, I know these are some of the things of which I must not speak.

chapter 12

HUMBLED IN BANGKOK
Money Can Buy Anything, Including a Breast Massage

The day after the hill-tribes trek ended, Walker flew from Chiang Mai to Bangkok. The early afternoon train from Bangkok to Kanchanaburi had departed before his arrival, so he purchased a ticket for the next morning and booked into a cheap hotel near the Bangkok Noi Train Station.

As he didn't feel ready to face the chaos of Bangkok for any extended period of time, leaving in the morning suited Walker fine. However, he did have one night to spend there. This notion triggered a song from years ago, a melody buried in him that waited to be played: *"One night in Bangkok makes a hard man humble . . . Bangkok, Oriental setting . . ."* Walker wondered at the human mind's ability to store such trivia and then reproduce it at the strangest times.

Wandering along narrow, dark, noisy streets, Walker found an available tuk-tuk. He headed for Patpong Road, the world-renowned red-light area of Bangkok. His first impression of the area conflicted with the song; it didn't appear to *"make a hard man humble."* It all actually seemed very tame, more of an open street market.

Vendors hawked a wide variety of wares. Walker passed by a display of knock-off designer watches. After an idle inspection, he casually commented to a vendor with a large inventory, "No Rolexes?"

"Please, sir, wait here," the man replied and fled into the crowd. After two or three minutes he returned and handed Walker a Rolex wholesaler's catalogue, showcasing every Rolex watch made. It listed perhaps a hundred or more.

Slightly confused, Walker asked, "So which one do you have?"

"You pick," the man said and smiled.

Walker flipped through a few pages, and without looking very closely, pointed to one. The man took the catalogue from him and again ran off into the crowd. Unsure of what he should do next, Walker waited. In less than five minutes the man returned and handed him the selected Rolex.

"How much?" Walker quipped.

"One hundred U.S. dollars."

The opening price suggested counterfeit merchandise and not stolen property. The watch appeared real, right down to the small identification number stuck on the back of the casing. The lightweight texture of the fake gold, however, gave away its true nature, but all in all it was a great replica. Walker drove a hard bargain and reluctantly the man sold it to him for twenty-five dollars. With no desire to tempt fate by getting mugged over a fake, Walker hid the watch in his pocket.

After observing the market merchants and the sex-trade workers, Walker thought of Thailand as the Wild West of capitalism—a place where anything he wanted to purchase, anything he wanted done, anything he wanted to see, was all available for money. He just had to offer an acceptable price and it would be so.

As he wandered the streets, Walker got bombarded by young men propositioning him to come into a club or see a show. Since they received a commission on every customer they brought in, they hit heavily on foreigners, aggressively promising the unimaginable.

THE WORLDWIDE SEXUAL ADVENTURES OF WALKER FAYT

Often Walker had three or four young men simultaneously trying to convince him that their club offered the best show. He subtly used his height and size advantage to intimidate the smaller Thai men and rebuff their sales pitches. He knew they would have been much more forceful without that advantage.

A polite, enterprising young man who spoke English relatively well approached Walker. Away from the crowds and other salesmen, he produced a two-inch-square homemade booklet. On the inside were hand-drawn pictures of stick people performing all the acts available in his club. He quietly explained the entertainment.

"Boy-girl make love show." The picture showed a stick man on top of a stick woman, the woman distinguished by her long hair.

Walker shook his head no and the young Thai man turned the page. Stick people were in similar positions as on the first page except long hair had been drawn on both figures.

"Girl-girl make love show—lesbian act," and he nodded, waiting for Walker's reaction.

Walker smiled at the unique sales pitch but still indicated he wasn't interested, so the man flipped to the centerfold and moved it closer for Walker to see the pictures drawn on these two pages.

"Pussy eat banana show."

Walker looked more closely. One page showed a hand-drawn, partially peeled banana and the other page showed a stick woman with her legs apart and an abundance of curly pubic hairs drawn in at the appropriate place. With less assurance than before, Walker shook his head no.

The last page showed a stick woman with her legs apart and between them a big round circle had been drawn. Fascinated at the possibilities, Walker lifted his shoulders in a shrug.

"What is this?"

"Pussy blow up balloon show." He read Walker's curious expression and added, "My favorite—very good for you."

HUMBLED IN BANGKOK

Walker laughed at both the sales routine and his own amusement and then said, "Okay, resistance is futile; you've got me. Where do I go?"

Inside, the maître d' took Walker to a table three back from the stage and waited. Walker understood that such a prime location garnered a generous tip and he gave the man five American dollars. The host bowed graciously and left. At the same table sat two middle-aged Oriental men, their stares glued to the stage.

Walker glanced toward the platform and saw a young Oriental man entering a woman. Accompanied by sound, light and music, live sex was occurring on stage. Strategically placed microphones picked up all the grunts and groans, which bellowed from loudspeakers. A video camera captured the action and displayed it on TV screens around the club. The weird atmosphere was a blend of bar, strip club, whorehouse and circus freak show.

Less than two minutes after Walker had been seated, a waitress placed two drinks on the table in front of him. He believed that she had delivered them by mistake and tried to convince her to take them away. Dressed in the tiniest halter top and shorts and balancing on five-inch heels, she flaunted her exposed body and spoke only in Thai. He suspected she understood English but had conveniently forgotten it.

The men at the table also tried to explain; however, Walker understood little of what they said. Walker ordered a beer and the waitress immediately understood that and brought him one. The fancy red drinks, with little umbrellas on top, remained on the table.

The three men tried conversing, but without success. Walker did learn that they were from Malaysia. Groaning from the stage intensified and focused their attention there. They turned just in time to see the man pull out of the woman and come onto her stomach. The crowd cheered. From the back of the room, Walker heard a drunken man with an Australian accent yell out: "Pullin' out ain't manly. Next time leave it in, mate, and get the job done right!"

As the performers quickly exited behind a curtain at the back of the stage, Walker noticed that the man hadn't worn a condom.

Loud music pounded from the speakers while a young man changed the stage for the next show. He laid out a rug and arranged some pillows. The deafening music made it impossible to carry on a conversation and that suited Walker fine. He was in no mood to wade painstakingly through non-existent English and hand signals just to learn how much the Malaysians enjoyed the strange entertainment.

Two nude women made their way on stage. They started by licking each other's breasts and sucking nipples. As they performed oral sex in the sixty-nine position, he wondered if these Oriental teenagers were actually lesbians.

When the girls were sufficiently stimulated, they inserted a long, black, double-headed dildo into each of their vaginas. With one girl lying on top of the other, they slammed their pelvises together. On the upward motion, the connecting black dildo shimmered from their inner wetness. They fucked at a frantic pace.

Only the performers knew whether they faked it or actually achieved climax. Walker suspected that it was a very convincing act—a better fake than the watch he had just bought. Deception, greed, money, sex, forbidden voyeurism, fascination surrounded him. The waitress put an unordered beer down on the table and left before he could argue.

Rather than sexually stimulating, Walker found the show sickly fascinating, like a train wreck. He had watched the interaction between the performers and the crowd. Why was all this necessary? The performers did it for money, but why? The patrons paid to see it, but why? And what came first, the need to do it for money or the demand to see it done? It was all too weird for him, and yet he stayed.

HUMBLED IN BANGKOK

A young Thai woman came on stage and lubricated a banana with some type of gel and used it as a vibrator. During the act, via hand signals, the Malaysian guys wondered if he wanted the two cocktails still untouched and sitting on the table. They obviously needed more alcohol to maintain their high and enjoy the show. He let them have the drinks.

Just about the time the routine became boring, she peeled the banana and gently reinserted it into her vagina. With delicate movements, she slid the meat of the fruit in and out several times. Even if the fruit wasn't totally ripe, it required care not to break it off inside her. Walker thought that she must practice a lot to be so skilled at it. She slipped the banana out of her vagina and into her mouth and took a bite. The next bite she offered to the audience. Of course there were more hungry mouths than banana to go around.

Before the next show began, the Malaysians left and two Germans were seated in their place. As had happened with Walker, two drinks each were put in front of them. The same commotion ensued with the same result; the drinks were left on the table with no explanation. Another unordered beer came for Walker.

An attractive woman emerged from behind the curtain and began to dance. At around thirty, she was older and not as thin as the other performers. Walker thought about why that would be the case. He concluded that her ability to blow up a balloon by forcing air out of her vagina must be rare. To ensure longevity of their revenue stream, the club owners likely treated her as a valuable asset, sparing her from the harsher forms of abuse inflicted on the girls. The young ones were expendable because any young woman could serve the same purpose. The whole idea made Walker quite uncomfortable. Still he did not leave.

The woman performed as any stripper would, removing more clothing with each passing song. Her special ability spared her from

241

having to be a good dancer as well. After three songs, she stood completely naked. Jeers from hecklers competed with the sound system.

"Blow it up, baby!" and "Let's see the big bang!" rang out, as well as other calls in languages that Walker did not understand.

The performer moved a chair from the corner of the stage to front and center, then straddled it. A white spotlight shone between her legs and a drum roll blasted from the speakers. The crowd cheered louder and louder as a bright red balloon filled with the air being expelled by her vagina. It was no trick and the crowd didn't care how she did it, only that she could. She blew it up, the stage lights went out and immediately Walker needed to get out of there.

He nodded goodbye to the Germans and left the table. On the way to the door, he signaled the waitress for the bill. She gave it to the maître d', who examined it, nodded his approval for her to leave and in a heavy Thai accent itemized it for Walker.

"One entrance fee, two mandatory cocktails, three beers and four floor shows—that totals ninety-six U.S. dollars."

Walker yelled, "What? Yeah, right!"

The man handed him the bill. It added correctly: twenty-five for the entrance fee, ten dollars per floor show, eight dollars each for the two cocktails and five dollars for each beer. Walker shook his head.

"No! No way! Nobody said anything about a cover fee or mandatory drinks or a price per floor show. I'm not paying this."

A loss of temper meant a loss of face and the man politely said, "I am sorry if these things were not explained to you, sir, but this is what you owe."

Other men gathered round and Walker assessed whether they worked for the club as bouncers and collection agents or whether they were customers interested in the building ruckus. Regardless, his adrenaline began to flow and an old brain instinct kicked in: fight or flight.

Walker reached into his pocket and pulled out a wad of both

HUMBLED IN BANGKOK

American and Thai bills totaling around thirty U.S. dollars. In his money belt there was two hundred more. He held out the crumpled bills for the maître d' to accept.

"This is all I have—take it or leave it."

"We will take it, of course. You can put the balance on Visa, MasterCard or American Express—your choice; for me, same same."

The air seemed to thin as the tension mounted and the crowd closed in tighter. Another round of shows started. The "boy-girl make love show" featured a different couple than before. Walker assumed that if he stayed much longer, he'd owe another ten dollars. He stalled for time, thinking of a way out. He handed the maître d' the money, forcing him to take it. Walker yelled over the music accompanying the live fuck on stage, "The rest on credit card—what do I owe?"

The man straightened, sorted and began to count the crumpled bills just handed him. The crowd eased just a bit and the door opened to let in more unsuspecting farang.

Opportunity knocked and Walker plowed for the door like a linebacker fighting through an offensive line to sack the opposing quarterback. Men tried to stop him but were no match for his height and strength as he barged his way out the door, down the stairs and onto the street. Once outside, he darted though the crowd and mingled with people in the street market.

After walking for about ten minutes, Walker's heart rate slowed and his breathing returned to near normal. He strolled along Silom Road, one street over from Patpong. Many street vendors and people crowded the street, but in a less aggressive manner than on Patpong. With a determined look, a young Thai man approached Walker.

"Mister, you owe the club money; please pay it."

Something wasn't right. Walker recognized him, or more accurately, his bright Hawaiian-style shirt. He had been a customer in the club and had sat two tables over from Walker during the last two shows. It was another attempted shakedown of a farang.

"Get lost!" Walker barked.

"Mister, I can find out where you stay. There could be much trouble for you."

All of Walker's travel experience came into focus. If this had happened at the beginning of the trip, he probably would have buckled at the club and certainly now at this demand.

"I don't think anything is going to happen, and you don't need to follow me. I'm staying at the Royal Orchid Sheraton, Room 314. Come and see me; I'll buy you a beer," he lied boldly.

Boldly, but not stupidly. Walker had no intention of letting a hustler find out where he stayed. To save face, the man played along.

"I will come by tomorrow around four o'clock. See you then." He left in the opposite direction.

*

History had enticed Walker to Kanchanaburi Province. After the heat and pollution of Bangkok, its cool, moist jungle air came as welcome relief. Halfway between the bridge in the north and the town center in the south, Walker found accommodations. It was a raft house floating on the Khwae Yai River. For eight dollars per night, he got a bed, a mosquito net and a bathroom with toilet and sink. For an extra charge he could shower, but it had to be done outside his room. In a rustic, jungle kind of way, it charmed him.

On leaving the raft, about ten minutes away from his lodging Walker stopped for lunch at a crowded restaurant. The crowd was a good sign in Thailand. The only spot available was across from a Western man in his late twenties. Walker asked to join him.

Walker liked listening to stories from other travelers; it was a way of filling in the gaps on places and events missed. Even second-hand tales added to the overall experience of the region visited.

During lunch, Walker learned that John lived in Toronto and had been vacationing with his wife for three weeks throughout Thailand. Unfortunately John's wife was suffering from traveler's diarrhea and didn't feel like venturing too far from their room, and most certainly didn't feel like eating anything. They had spent their first week in the south of Thailand relaxing on the white-sand beaches, eating fresh fish and unwinding from their demanding jobs. Both of them were chartered accountants. Walker remained open-minded, not holding that occupation against them. How boring could they be if they had decided to rough it in Thailand?

John told of their visit thus far to Kanchanaburi, while Walker mentioned that he had been at school in Toronto. John inquired, "Have you ever been to Wasaga Beach on a May long weekend?"

A story Walker had told Tim many months ago in Sweden had taken place at Wasaga Beach and thinking of it now brought a huge grin to Walker's face.

"Yeah, I have. It brings back a lot of fond memories."

John continued. "During this week, you'll get the same kind of atmosphere here. Crowds of young people flock from the city to drink, eat, party, shop, relax and basically just enjoy themselves. I don't know if you know it, but December fifth was the king's birthday and the people are very festive in honor of that national holiday. Here the celebration lasts several days.

"Each night they commemorate their history on the River Khwae with a spectacular sound and light show, simulating the attack in 1945 that destroyed the bridge. The movie about it, *The Bridge on the River Kwai*, was never as good as this display—it's amazing. You'll have to check it out tonight. It comes complete with missile firings and other fabulous pyrotechnics. Some shots just miss the bridge and splash into the water, while others hit the bridge and explode. For the finale, one shot fires from across the river, hits the bridge, and a piece of the railroad track falls into the river."

THE WORLDWIDE SEXUAL ADVENTURES OF WALKER FAYT

Walker raised his eyebrows. "It sounds bizarre. I'll definitely check it out. Does it really feel like the bridge is being attacked?"

"The simulation is quite good, but lasts only about ten minutes and it comes at the very end of the show. The first forty-five minutes doesn't make sense if you don't speak the language. As best I could determine, they try to recreate the Japanese treatment of the POWs and forced Asian laborers. A lot of screaming in several Asian languages bellows out of the loudspeakers, and occasionally floodlights come on, giving a brief illumination of a concentration camp across the river."

"Really!" Walker said, bubbling with anticipation.

"Before it all starts, it's quite amusing. As it gets dark, thousands upon thousands of people, most of them Thais, fill every available nearby position. Music is played over the sound system. Being a history teacher, you probably know the event is in memory of the Allied bombing of the bridge. The bridge was part of a system called the 'Death Railway' because 16,000 POWs and 100,000 Thais, Chinese, Burmese, Malaysians and Indonesians died building the link through the mountain passes into Burma.

"On one of the nights, a Phil Collins song, 'Groovy Kind of Love', blasted out. I had to laugh; it was more than a little ironic given what the show represents. Not to mention that ninety-five percent of the people couldn't understand the words and those who did, knew how inappropriate it was. Oh well, this is Thailand."

They left the restaurant together and continued talking. On the way back to the river, John recounted an event that had occurred on the king's birthday.

Beneath a large tent in town, many vendors sold jewelry and raw gems. People milled about looking; buyers and wholesalers from around the world were among the customers. For John's wife, Susan, this meant there were deals to be had. By John's own admission, she was smarter than he was and a very able negotiator. However, in this instance he came up with a strategy that allowed both of them to get the most out of the afternoon.

John suggested that she shop for stones, and when she found the ones she wanted and hit the lowest price possible, she was to come and find him. He held the money. While she shopped, he would blend in with the crowd and watch the Thai people and take candid photographs.

"It gave me the opportunity to observe the Thai people in a festive mood. It was great. Many of the people here seem affluent by Thai standards. I assumed they were Bangkok's middle class on holiday. I watched for a while and concluded that Thais are very much like us and do what we do.

"Mothers watched small children. Young couples with puppy-dog eyes for each other, oblivious to the rest of the world, hung out. Teenage boys girl-watched, while the girls pretended not to notice. Street vendors jockeyed for the best spot to ensure a good day's business. Except for the language and a few Buddha images, it was very much like observing any town fair back in Canada."

Walker asked, "How did Susan make out?"

"Perfectly. It went according to plan. For the first half hour she shopped. She found several sapphires, rubies and one yellow sapphire to her liking. For the next forty minutes she negotiated her best price. When she hit bottom, she came and found me."

"So you paid, and everyone was happy with the day?"

"Oh no! We played into the Thai custom of males being dominant and used it against them. I walked up with my camera gear dangling everywhere looking real macho. Susan showed me the stones and told me the prices. I immediately came out with a resounding 'No—the price is too high!' and walked away.

"We let the atmosphere cool for about five minutes and she dragged me back and I began the negotiations in earnest. At first I didn't realize the stones belonged to two different vendors who were side by side, so I opened with one price for them all. Once she and the vendors explained it was two separate purchases, the divide-and-conquer strategy kicked in. I played the two vendors off each other, driving the price lower. We pretended to be more interested in the gems of one vendor than the other and then vice versa.

"In keeping with our strategy, Susan kept out of the direct bargaining process. Several times we walked away so the merchants couldn't hear us. This allowed us to discuss price between us and at the same time lead the vendors to believe I had refused her the purchase. She pretended to plead with me. It worked like a charm. I waited patiently until one of the vendors agreed to my price and it took less than a second for the other vendor to agree as well. We bought both sets of stones."

Walker polished him up. "Sounds like you're a real wheeler-dealer."

"Yeah, well, I probably still got taken. It'll be interesting to get them appraised back home."

They stood at the lane to John's guesthouse. Walker said, "I'm sure it didn't cost you too much. You made a great day of it and now you have the stories too. I hope Susan is feeling better. I'm sorry I didn't get a chance to meet her."

Walker waved goodbye and returned to his raft house, where he collected his camera, mosquito repellent and sunscreen and set off for the afternoon, now a bit more familiar with the Kanchanaburi scene. On the main road up from the river, Walker hired a songthaew—a small pickup truck with two rows of bench seats down each side in the back—to transport him to the Kanchanaburi War Cemetery, then to the Japanese War Memorial and north to the Bridge on the River Khwae.

For the average person there really wasn't much to see, but for a history buff like Walker, it was memorable. Original sections of the bridge remained in use and he took a picture of the steam-propelled tourist train rolling along the narrow-gauge tracks and over the bridge. Afterward he visited the rail museum in front of the bridge.

In 1942, Japanese engineers estimated that it would take five years to complete the mountainous 250-mile rail link between Thailand and Burma. With a total disregard for the cost in human lives, the Japanese army completed it in sixteen months. During World War II, the Bridge over the River Khwae was an important supply link connecting Thailand and Burma. The Japanese used it for over a year and a half before the Allied forces bombed it and broke passage.

During the day, Walker had met several Western tourists and many told him he would enjoy a visit to the JEATH War Museum, if not for the exhibits then to meet the monk who devoted his time to the upkeep and promotion of the museum. The name JEATH stood for an ill-fated meeting between Japan, England, Australia, America, Thailand and Holland that took place in the region during World War II. The museum's location in the south part of town along the banks of the Mae Klong River made for a decent walk through town.

Strolling along the street, Walker passed a small middle-class home. At the front of the house, a father and his daughter worked in the yard. The girl, around twelve years old, stopped working and watched Walker as he approached. As he came closer, they seemed to connect telepathically. He read her mind and felt her emotions.

Walker "saw" that he represented excitement, mystery and all the notions a young girl thinks about when alone with her fantasies. As he got closer, he noticed that time seemed to pass more slowly, and when he reached the front of the house, time, motion and thought merged in a frozen waltz. He noticed that her father had stopped working and had begun watching his daughter watching Walker.

In the same super-slow motion, Walker sensed the father's troubled emotions. Telepathically Walker saw that he represented a threat to the father's and daughter's way of life—their traditions, customs and beliefs. The daughter must have felt her father's stare and she slowly looked away from Walker and toward her father. She knew that he had watched her gazing at Walker and that he had read her thoughts as well. She took a half glance back at Walker and then broke the spell between them when she hung her head in shame.

Walker and the father locked eyes. Walker saw no hatred in the other man, only concern and hopelessness at a world changing faster than he could understand and control. How could he stop the outside world from destroying her from the inside? With his eyes, he begged Walker, and others like him, to stay away so that he might keep the daughter that he loved dearly safe and secure, out of harm's way.

The entire sequence only lasted a few seconds. After it had ended, Walker desperately desired to tell the girl that no matter what she felt, or what promises were made to her, or whatever she thought she was missing out on, her dreams and desires could not be fulfilled by going to Patpong Road. Walker wished he too could protect her.

Back at his accommodations, Walker wrote in his travel journal.

December 4

River raft house, Kanchanaburi, Thailand

> *How do we protect our children? The dangers are many: violence, pollution, sexually transmitted diseases, unemployment, natural and financial upheaval, political scandals, split families, drugs, weapons and a general loss in values. As a parent, I am horrified at what our children face.*
>
> *Parents must make children understand the dangers of the world—without scaring them into a paranoid state of immobility. It is a difficult balancing act. If richness and texture are exchanged for security and safety, children are robbed of a fullness.*

Burdened with so many stresses, how do children cope? They were born into this chaos; they accept it as normal, not believing that anything can or should be different. Being a parent is even worse, because I've experienced within myself a gentler, more compassionate world, and know how things could be. Feeling the anxiety in my children and watching them harbor it as an accepted fact of life causes me great pain. I want the world to be a better place so that they can live a fuller potential.

Each generation cannot stop its eventual replacement. Like waves crashing on the beach, new generations come along and with them comes change. Our beliefs and passions, our artistic and musical tastes reflect who we are, binding minds to the notion that we are as youthful as we ever were. As powerful as that notion is, it does not stop our replacement and the flow of human history into what will be.

When children reach the age of reason and do not behave in accordance with our wishes, or when they embrace actions or ideas that are incomprehensible to us, we get annoyed. I see this as the signs of progress—a barometer indicating movement toward a new future. When technology, social behavior, art, politics or any other human invention scares me, I know I'm experiencing "generational replacement."

It's our responsibility to protect our children by explaining the dangers and teaching them to swim. We must ensure that at the right time—which is usually before we think it is—they have the confidence to go into the water alone. As parents, the only certainty is that we cannot keep our children out of the water—after all, they are the next wave.

Walker headed for town to witness the celebration and the

recreation of the Allied bombing of the Bridge over the River Khwae. Thousands of people nestled into every nook and cranny along the riverbanks, waiting for the festivities to begin. He didn't hold out much hope of securing a good spot and searched the area carefully.

By a railing overlooking the river and bridge, Walker noticed a very slight space between a Thai family and a Western woman. John had been right, the crowd consisted mostly of locals, and so this seemed his best opportunity to secure a spot. He approached and stood a step behind the Westerner in the crowd of people.

"Excuse me—do you mind if I squeeze in there?"

The woman turned and in a melodic voice said, "D'ye think I've been standin' here fer an hour holdin' this wee place just fer ye? Ah, well, maybe I have. Squeeze in."

The Irish accent made it seem as though angels danced on her tongue. Maread Flannery was her name and, pressed together with Walker as part of the waiting crowd, she began a conversation.

Maread, like Walker, had been traveling for many months. Her husband had died of colon cancer a year ago and she had decided to use travel as part of her healing process.

The Irish woman's curly dark hair, soft, pale skin, large blue eyes and petite body combined for an attractive appearance. A feisty temperament gave her real character. Beyond all that, he noticed a sense of muted vulnerability and attributed it to her recent loss.

The show followed John's description, with much of the beginning part in Thai and perhaps some Japanese. During this part of the presentation, Walker and Maread chatted about their travels and other personal matters. Right off, they were comfortable with each other and conversation came easily.

The simulated bridge bombing lived up to its billing. Afterward, they left together along with hordes of Thais. Maread's guesthouse was in the same area as Walker's and they walked together, continuing

HUMBLED IN BANGKOK

their fine rapport. At the junction to her lodging, he offered to walk her there.

"D'ye think I'm an eejit; a helpless woman flailin' about? I'll have ye know that I've traveled to places a lot rougher than this and I'm still standing here talkin' to ye—aren't I? But, if it'll make ye feel better, I won't object to ye seein' me back."

Walker believed that her strength of will, sharp tongue and hot temper would squash any trouble before it started and that she'd be fine on her own. Despite those beliefs, he said, "I'd be honored."

Along the way, Maread asked him if he would like to join her in the morning for a trip to Erawan Falls. A bus left at eight o'clock and they'd likely be gone all day. Walker had planned to go there at some point during his stay, so he agreed to join her.

The two-hour trip cost less than a dollar each way and provided them with a pleasant ride through the countryside. At the park, they changed into their bathing suits. Underneath a thick forest canopy, they swam in the shallow pools along the stream and let the water from small waterfalls cascade over their bodies.

They also ventured to the top of the seven levels of waterfalls, seven being a symbolic number for the Buddhist faith. At the top, water poured out from an elephant's head carved from the rock.

They caught the last bus back to Kanchanaburi and arrived in town by six o'clock. At dinner, rejuvenated from their outing together, they watched the setting sun cast a lovely orange and red hue over the river, silhouetting men with long sticks slowly propelling boats past them.

*

Maread and Walker spent the next ten days traveling together to some of Thailand's lesser-known tourist destinations. Highlights included the famous bronze flame-dragon Buddha in Phitsanulok, commissioned in 1357, and a tour of the impressively restored ruins at Ayuthaya—Thailand's former capital city.

As accommodation in Thailand was relatively inexpensive, they always stayed in separate rooms. It had been several weeks since Walker had ejaculated and this was making him sexually edgy. After about a week of traveling together, in one of the moments where his need to come overpowered his rational side, out of the blue he said to Maread: "I have such an SRH."

Maread responded with a puzzled expression on her face. "An SRH—what might that be?"

Sheepishly Walker replied, "A sperm retention headache."

Nonchalantly Maread reached into her handbag, pulled out a tissue and dropped it into his lap. "This might be of some use to ye then."

It was a joke, but not a joke too. Neither of them wanted to ruin their friendship with a sexual encounter. In many ways, they were kindred spirits. Both of them were middle-aged, traveling on their own, searching or waiting for something without knowing what it might be, only hoping to recognize it when it occurred.

They spent two days visiting some of Bangkok's treasures. The Grand Palace and the Temple of the Emerald Buddha were too awesome for words and in photographs they tried to capture the intricate and distinct carvings and the fine craftsmanship of the buildings. Walker guessed that it would have taken millions of man-hours to create the beauty that filled the Palace grounds no matter where his eyes wandered.

A sense of mystery surrounded the Emerald Buddha. A guidebook stated that the origins of the most revered Buddha image in Thailand were unknown and that its recorded history began in the fifteenth century. According to legend, the Emerald Buddha was found inside a larger Buddha image of plaster and gold leaf located in Chiang Rai. The temple that housed the plaster Buddha had been ruined by a storm and during transport, the plaster Buddha dropped, revealing the Emerald Buddha inside. Since its discovery, it had been moved many times by different conquering armies, finally coming to rest in Bangkok in the twentieth century.

Carved from jade, the twenty-eight-inch statue sat in a glass casing inside Wat Phra Kaew. Photography inside the Wat was illegal and it disappointed them not to have a picture of the Emerald Buddha. As a second choice they bought postcards.

Walker and Maread stayed at the Riverview Guest House in Bangkok's Chinatown area. Located close to the train station and water-taxi stands, it made many of the city's tourist spots easily accessible.

The first few days in the area were unsettling for Walker. From his perspective it looked like an urban ghetto, and in such an environment in the U.S., his life would have been in danger. Tiny, narrow streets were cluttered with old rusted equipment: machinery, wire, iron bars and oil barrels. Sweatshops opened onto the street and in them older boys and young men with blackened, greasy hands pounded old car parts with hammers. Small, discreet brothels catering to local customers, not tourists, lined several alleys.

Eventually Walker acclimatized to the visuals and discovered the area to be completely safe. In other parts of Bangkok, foreigners were like magnets attracting con men, pimps and vendors wishing to sell anything and everything—as he had discovered on his first visit. In Chinatown he felt invisible. The locals ignored him and he found it rather refreshing. Only after several days did he reveal these observations to Maread. It turned out that she had never been concerned about walking through the squalor in this part of the city.

On their second day of touring Bangkok, from their hotel they walked to Wat Traimit, the Temple of the Golden Buddha. Inside the old Wat stood a nine-foot-high, five-and-a-half-ton, solid-gold statue of Buddha. Both of them stared at the gleaming image for a long time before either moved or spoke.

They read that the discovery of the Golden Buddha resembled the finding of the Emerald Buddha. Approximately forty years earlier, while it was being moved, a crane cable snapped and the stucco statue dropped to the ground. When it hit, the exterior cracked and fell away, exposing the Golden Buddha inside. Experts speculated that it had been covered over several hundred years ago to protect it from raiding Burmese armies. As an artifact it was priceless. Maread calculated its value in gold bars at $53 million—not quite priceless, but getting there.

"I wonder why there's no security around," Walker said to himself, but Maread heard him.

"Are ye an eejit? How do ye suppose a thief would move it?" she responded.

Other stops that day and evening included the Temple of the Dawn, the National Theater and a snake farm. Demonstrating how viciously his snakes could attack, one of the handlers prompted a snake to pounce at him and it hung by its fangs from the fabric of his shirt. Shortly thereafter, several snakes were allowed to slither free from their handlers, causing instant panic among the audience. The snake handlers further enhanced the terror by dropping the back end of a python onto a woman's lap.

The pretense of letting deadly snakes escape into the crowd amused Maread and Walker. They may have felt differently had they not been seated in the back row. Walker thought that if the same snake show existed in the U.S., the lawsuits would be staggering.

Later that evening they attended a Thai classical dance drama at the National Theater. Preadolescent girls in full makeup and costume performed the age-old tradition elegantly. The contrast between that performance and the snake farm captured the extreme diversity of Thailand.

Maread's flight left in the morning. She wanted to be home for Christmas with a few days to spare. They decided to make her last night in Bangkok a relaxing one and dined at the restaurant on the roof of their hotel. The sun set over the Chao Phraya River and the heavy traffic of every shape, size and description, faded into lovely crimson silhouettes. The setting softened the mood and their conversation turned intimate.

Being a Catholic from Dublin, Maread explained, she had been close with many Catholics, and they had given their support after her husband's premature death. Although grateful for their concern, she found that their beliefs came up short, and that she now needed to find something else. Maread confessed that she had searched everywhere for an explanation.

"Fer almost a year after Sean's death, I searched fer truth. I wanted to know the meanin' of it all, somethin' I could point to and say, 'now I understand.' Eventually I gave up the search fer truth, because I sensed it was drivin' me toward insanity. During my quest, I realized that truth is much too difficult to understand because it doesn't exist in the absolute. There's no absolute truth. I know there're mathematical rules and laws of physics, but these are facts or principles to be applied within the universe, not a definition of truth. If truth does exist at all, then its source is from a relative perspective.

"Just look around and ye'll see there are an infinite number of perspectives, all happenin' at the same time—what each person believes to be true, what each animal believes to be true, what each atom believes to be true, what each pulse of energy believes to be true. All these truths exist concurrently and are equally valid—so absolute truth does not exist. I've given up my search fer truth and now seek an inner peace and tranquility—happiness fer myself. When I'm happy, the universe is happy!"

Walker reached across the table and delicately squeezed her hand.

THE WORLDWIDE SEXUAL ADVENTURES OF WALKER FAYT

"Thank you for sharing that with me. Have a wonderful Christmas with your family."

*

It had been a week since Maread had left and Walker missed the companionship. He meandered through the night streets with no real destination, lost in thought about nothing in particular. He happened to notice a clock in a store window. It read fifteen minutes past midnight. It was Christmas in Bangkok! Deep-rooted connections sparked conscious memories linking him to the people he loved. At eleven hours behind Bangkok time, his family would at this very moment be preparing for Christmas Eve. In past years, by this time in the day, the aroma of pine needles and baking filled the house, along with love and anticipation.

Homesickness resonated in every cell of Walker's body—the strongest he had ever experienced. He stopped and sat on some steps. As sad emotions flooded over him, involuntary tears streaked down his cheeks. Temporarily immobilized in loneliness, disabled with memories of Christmases past, he sat there remembering.

In a few hours, all his family would be gathered at his parents' house. He hoped the tradition continued in his absence and it pained him to think otherwise. Viewing the scene in his head, he saw the muted happiness in the family. Without him there, the circle remained open and incomplete.

Walker thought about Christmas in terms of any other human invention. The holiday acted as a double-edged sword: joy and happiness when swung one way and loved ones were together; sadness and sorrow when swung the other way and they were apart. He wanted to think of something else—anything to release him from the consequences of following his epiphany.

A deeper understanding formed in Walker's thoughts. He loved his family—his emotional and physical reaction measured that.

Rather than ignoring the reaction by attempting to concentrate on other things, he embraced his emotions. They were a part of him—the part that connected him to his real self and to powers greater than himself. He acquiesced to the spirit of Christmas present. As he did so, tears flowed freely and fell upon the dusty concrete below. He had no idea how long he had sat there crying when someone called to him.

"Hey, mister, I take you—cheer you up. I take you to massage."

Walker lifted his head from between his knees. A well-dressed young Thai man stood two steps down from him. As Walker's head rose to look, the man continued speaking.

"It is very, very good. Make you better. Follow me, not far. Please come with me—make you happy."

Walker thought, "My sexual adventure began with a massage. Perhaps it's time for a revisit—a Christmas gift to myself." He could not and did not want to alleviate the pain. But adding a little physical pleasure to the mix could be the right ingredient.

"Okay, sir, lead the way."

Instantaneously the man flashed a big smile and became struck with an urgent sense of mission. He became Walker's best friend. Did Walker need anything to drink or eat? What type of massage would he prefer?

Walker knew that traditional Thai massage had evolved over thousands of years and was widely available in Bangkok and throughout Thailand. Connoisseurs of the trade professed that the blind delivered it the best. The red-light area massages were much more infamous and Walker believed that the man represented one of those places. He anticipated some sort of reaction.

"Do you offer traditional massage?"

The response was unexpected. "Yes, sure, anything you wish, sir. We also offer more if you desire. Whatever you wish, I can do."

Walker said, "Yes, good. I would like to start with a traditional massage, then we'll see."

"Yes, very good, sir. I can tell you wish to relax. With traditional massage there is a one-and-a-half-hour minimum; for you I recommend two hours minimum—best relaxation. Once you are completely relaxed . . ." the man smiled and slowly ran his hands parallel to the ground, "I suggest the best for you—breast message."

"A breast massage?" Walker asked in a puzzled tone.

"Yes, yes, very nice for you; very relaxing."

They stopped outside a dark doorway and Walker asked again, "What's a breast massage?"

"How many you wish—one, two, three, four young beautiful girls massage you with their breasts . . .very nice. Best I recommend four, you like very much. This is the back door. I take you inside for two-hour traditional massage and one-hour breast massage with four beautiful women."

The images entering Walker's mind made it harder to resist the offer. "How much?"

"For you, Christmas special: two hundred U.S. dollars."

After ten minutes of negotiating, they settled on a price of $100 and went inside. Walker followed the man down a narrow, dimly lit hallway until they arrived at what appeared to be the front desk, with an attendant sitting at it. The two Thai men spoke quietly in their native language, not wanting him to overhear. With the conference complete, the host smiled and faced him.

"Welcome. We can take care of you. Usually not much ask for traditional massage at this time of night. We can do, no problem. Come this way."

Before Walker left the foyer, he nodded goodbye to the young man who had delivered him. The Thai man acknowledged Walker by saying, "Merry Christmas, mister, Merry Christmas. You get good present."

HUMBLED IN BANGKOK

Around the corner from the front desk, a stairway led to upper floors. Walker accompanied the man up two flights of stairs to the second floor. The man took a bundle of keys from his pocket and searched for the right one; on finding it, he unlocked the door in front of him. As he went inside the dark room he hit a switch. A dull red glow suddenly filled the space. Walker's eyes required a few seconds to adjust to the lighting and when they did, he scoped out the room. A few mats and rugs lay on the floor. There were no windows, and on the left-hand side of the room, he noticed a closed door.

The man said, "Room is ten dollars extra—good price for three hours."

Walker didn't intend to argue. He knew the price agreed upon had included everything. He paid the tip the man sought.

"Washroom in there," the host said, and pointed to the door Walker had just looked at. "I go now, massage begin soon. Thank you, the best for you, sir," and the man bowed to him before leaving.

In a few minutes, a girl came into the room. She wore a T-shirt and loose-fitting sweat pants. To Walker, she didn't look older than fifteen, but he had a difficult time determining people's ages in Thailand.

He said, "Hello."

She smiled and returned, *"Sawat-dii, pen yangai?"*

Walker commented in a low voice, "If you didn't understand 'hello' then obviously we aren't going to be talking much."

The girl motioned for him to lie down on the mat and he did so. She removed his shoes and nothing more. For the first hour she worked just his legs. Using ancient techniques perfected over the millennia involving various forms of leveraged stretching, she exaggerated the movement by entangling their limbs. Bending, twisting, folding and squeezing, she forced out stiffness and stored tension in his muscles, tendons and ligaments.

In the next hour, she worked his arms, back, neck and shoulders. Walker relaxed so completely that he fell asleep while she tended to his back. The two hours quickly evaporated into the end of the treatment. She rolled him onto his back and closed his eyelids with her fingers. Gently, she pressed down on his chest with both her hands and he correctly understood this to mean, "Wait here."

Again Walker slipped into a relaxed sleep, or it may have been a tranquil state of meditation induced by released chi. In that condition, minutes or perhaps hours passed; time became irrelevant to him. Dreams, imagination and a blurred sense of a far-off reality converged into a slow-motion image of large, warm raindrops pelting into the desert sand. As reality became less removed, the images migrated to his awakened consciousness, transporting him into the moment. He remembered his surroundings. Opening his eyes just a crack, he could not make sense of things. Slowly the sensations took form.

Warm, soft nipples touched his head and face. Without his knowing it, the breast massage had begun. Four women fluttered around him, touching him incessantly with their nipples. Giggling and whirling, they hovered and then gently landed all over his body. He felt as though he had been swarmed by a band of beautiful butterflies.

When they realized Walker had awakened, they tenderly undressed him down to his underwear and continued with their pattering of skin on skin. He closed his eyes; the sensation felt more loving than erotic. Occasionally he opened his eyes and observed young breasts and dark hair dangling, tickling his naked flesh. At these times the experience became more sensual.

The four young women coordinated their technique. While two pressed their chests firmly against Walker's body, the other two applied caresses with their nipples. Frequently they squeezed their nipples, making them firmer and more pointed, and then they rubbed them across him. They also used a land-and-drag technique whereby they touched him with only the tips of the nipples. They teased him by applying this method across his lips, daring him to open his mouth and expose his tongue. Overpowered with temptation, he slid his tongue across the nipples that delicately brushed his lips.

"Oooh, yes," softly echoed in his ears.

When Walker closed his eyes he found it easier to control himself; while they were open, not so. It required tremendous self-control for him not to become a raging copulating lunatic. They rolled him onto his stomach, making it easier for him to keep his eyes closed and enjoy the sensation of butterflies landing on his back, shoulders, buttocks, legs and feet. In this position, they slid off his briefs. Shortly thereafter, breasts were pressed into his butt crack and rubbed along the back of his scrotum. The rest of his body continued to be fondled by young, nubile breasts as well.

Walker's legs were spread farther apart. This exposure allowed them to plant their breasts onto his hanging testicles. His arousal began by having soft, subtle breasts pressed and sensitively rubbed against his balls. When they turned him onto his back, he stuck straight up like a flagpole and his erection became the focal point of attention. Bears to honey, fish to water, nipples to penis—to him, at this point, they all seemed natural.

Three of the girls concentrated on his penis while one girl went to Walker's lips. She encouraged him to lick, kiss and tenderly bite her hardened nipples. He opened his eyes to the overwhelmingly erotic scene. One of the girls held another girl's breasts and squeezed his cock in-between them. The motion built up friction and chafed slightly. One of girls spit to apply lubrication. It landed perfectly, allowing him to slide up and back without much resistance. He Hawaiian-muscle-fucked his way to orgasm and released two large gushes and two smaller ones between the breasts of his masseuse. The girls laughed and cheered.

Coming had not been part of the arrangement and he knew that the girls provoked it to secure a good tip. One of them spoke and understood a little English and she conversed with him while he dressed. They put their tops back on too.

Walker asked how old they were. They were all eighteen or nineteen except for the oldest, who was twenty-three. He now recognized her as his traditional Thai masseuse. He found them all to be incredibly young-looking for their ages. He then inquired about whether they were being forced to work. It took a few seconds for them to understand his intent. The girls spoke Thai among themselves, trying to determine the intent of his question.

After a few seconds of discussion, one girl spoke in broken English, "No must stay here. We can go. Other places, girls must work. Here no same same."

Walker wasn't sure he believed the reply, though he wanted to. He gave them each twenty dollars and they were sincerely grateful. They openly expressed their appreciation with many bows. Repeatedly the young women said, "Thank you, thank you."

On the way out, Walker paid the man at reception. He was having the farthest thing from a traditional Christmas morning that he could imagine—but one that he would distinctly remember. Thoughts of his early morning encounter remained as he walked back to his hotel under a clear, warm night sky that was beginning to give way to daylight.

Despite Walker's treatment session, images of his family gathered together for Christmas resurfaced. So strong were his memories that he tasted rum and eggnog and his mother's special stuffing and spice cake. The aroma of cooked turkey and ham filled his nostrils. He listened to carols playing in the background and the laughter and stories of Christmases past. The warmth of family love touched him from the other side of the world. Then suddenly all of this vanished, leaving him only with visions of disappointment on the faces of the people he loved.

HUMBLED IN BANGKOK

Although he had been up all night, the overwhelming presence of Christmas in Appleton kept Walker wide awake. Rather than toss and turn trying to force sleep in the dusty heat of just another day in Bangkok, he decided to start his day and went to the hotel café for breakfast.

Eating a standard breakfast of greasy eggs and bacon—in Thailand much of the food was prepared in oil—Walker was thankful for his "iron gut," a reference to his high-school ability to drink copious amounts of alcohol in short periods of time, and not vomit. His strong stomach had served him well in his travels so far, and certainly during this breakfast spent in emotional turmoil. After breakfast, he headed to the markets of Bangkok to go Christmas shopping.

Marlene had a taste for unusual things of beauty. After searching many markets and shops, near the end of the day Walker finally found something that seemed appropriate. He bought an exquisitely detailed traditional dancer hand-painted onto fine Thai silk. He had not seen anything like it in his travels and he knew Marlene would love it.

As Walker made out the shipping documentation, he was filled with doubt. He had not spoken to Marlene in five months and had not even mailed her a letter or postcard. Would this act of love be taken the wrong way? Rather than bringing her joy as a thing of beauty and a representation of his love, it might also remind her of the husband who had left her to travel the world and boff other women. He did not wish to cause her any more pain. What words could he send along with the gift that would bridge the gap? "Thinking of you on Christmas, thought you would like this. Love, Walker." It seemed empty, shallow and heartless.

Out of consideration for Marlene, rather than his own guilty conscience, Walker ripped up the shipping document with Marlene's new address and rewrote it with his parents' address. At the right time, he would deliver the gift in person.

THE WORLDWIDE SEXUAL ADVENTURES OF WALKER FAYT

Christmas Night was not an important time in this part of the world. A sad strip of lights had been strung along the railing of the outside balcony of the restaurant at his hotel. A miniature, fake Christmas tree, about a foot tall with lights and tiny plastic presents underneath, sat on the bar. Walker glanced at it several times during dinner and in his somber mood it appeared to him as a discarded reject from the discount bin at a dollar store.

Dwelling on the day got to be too much for Walker. He decided to jolt himself into forgetting the sentimental feelings singing inside him like carolers on a snowy winter's eve. If the blanket of eighty-degree heat, the thousands of people worshiping Buddha, and his meal of chicken, rice and peanut sauce wouldn't do it, what would? He quieted his mind of all thought. Out of the depths of stillness, one word filled his consciousness: "Cambodia."

chapter 13

INDEARA—A PhD IN LOVEMAKING
The Kamasutra as Pathway to Fulfillment

Very few airlines service Cambodia's capital of Phnom Penh. Walker found it necessary to first fly to Vientiane, the capital of Laos, then on to Phnom Penh. The flights were with two different carriers. He knew that transferring would be a hassle, so he decided beforehand to spend one day in Vientiane rather than have to rush to change planes.

Southeast Asia's most powerful communist government, ruling in Vietnam, dictated policy to the less powerful communist governments of Laos and Cambodia. Its directives did not permit private leisure travel within Cambodia, so Walker had to purchase a state-controlled tour package from a tour operator in Bangkok. The prices of the packages were extremely inflated compared to the cost of free-market travel. Governments of the region desperately needed foreign currency, so travelers wishing to go there had to pay the premium.

As with many communist regimes, the concept of increasing demand by lowering the price did not compute in their economic equations. Walker had little choice but to accept an expensive tour with many added services such as meals, a guide and a car with driver. Also, it seemed strange to be calling it a tour package since he was the only person on it.

Walker understood that, from the government's perspective, state-controlled packages had the added benefit of ensuring that foreigners did not spend too much time alone with the general populace. That could lead to the spread of non-communist ideals and the polluting of the minds of its people with capitalist propaganda. The tour-package system allowed the authorities to know the whereabouts of all foreign tourists at all times.

A woman in her thirties met Walker at Wattay Airport on the outskirts of Vientiane, Laos. She held a white sheet of paper with his last name written on it in black magic marker. After Walker settled in at the hotel, they began a one-day sweep of as many sites as possible.

The first stop was Wat Si Saket, the oldest temple in Vientiane and one of the few to escape destruction by the Siamese in 1828. In niches and cubbyholes in its interior walls, the temple contained more than 2,000 Buddha images made of silver and ceramics.

Wat Pha Keo, only a hundred yards away from Wat Si Saket, was no longer a temple but a museum. According to legend, in 1565 the Lao monarchy claimed sole right to this temple, which housed the Emerald Buddha before its recovery in 1779 by the Siamese. Walker's guide explained that the Laotian people believed the revered statue belonged in their homeland.

Their next stop was Wat Si Musang. There the faithful asked a Buddha image to grant them wishes or to answer troubling questions. For a small monetary offering, they lit incense and received a small slip of paper giving advice. Both Walker and his guide made a donation and asked their question.

Walker asked if the purpose of his travels would soon be revealed to him. His guide roughly translated the Laotian script. Through her spotty English, Walker determined that the message said,

INDEARA—A PhD IN LOVEMAKING

"Important matters are close by." A rather generic answer, he thought—perhaps something had gotten lost in the translation.

The guide's own question and answer she kept private. However, she explained that if the advice was useful or the question was answered correctly, according to custom she would return to the temple with an offering of two bananas and two coconuts. Mounds of fruit nearby indicated much success.

The Great Sacred Stupa, or the Pha That Luang, was the most important religious and national monument in Laos. Legend suggested that in the third century BC, monks from India enclosed a breastbone of Buddha at this location. No historical or physical evidence existed to support the claim. It required faith, and many people believed.

Walker and his guide also visited the Pratuxai Monument and the Unknown Soldiers Memorial, both somewhat interesting, but definitely on the tour because of governmental persuasion.

When touring ended for the day, Walker's guide drove him back to the hotel for dinner. A gracious and courteous waiter catered to him exclusively. As the only patron, it did not surprise Walker when the meal of roast chicken looked old. He dared not eat it and instead went out to a street vendor for the staple rice and noodle soup.

Walker's Lao Aviation flight for Phnom Penh left at seven in the morning and he had arranged for his guide to pick him up at 5:30 a.m. At 5:50 he flagged the only cab he saw. The driver's rate to the airport was $10 U.S., three times what it should be, but both he and Walker knew the situation. Walker paid the fee.

The guide arrived at the airport shortly after him and explained that she had been at his hotel shortly before six and when she didn't find him, had come directly to the airport. She apologized for being late and excused herself so that she could obtain his boarding pass. Upon her return, she appeared worried. Apparently the flight had been overbooked and Walker had no seat.

THE WORLDWIDE SEXUAL ADVENTURES OF WALKER FAYT

Saving face would help him, demonstrating his anger would not, so Walker hid his annoyance from her. He had experienced similar situations in his travels and suspected that a tip or a bribe would secure his seat on the plane. It wasn't the amount of money that bothered him, but the idea of being taken. He held firm to his position that pre-booking had guaranteed him a seat on the flight.

Walker could not determine exactly what was going on and decided to hold off on suggesting a tip. His steadfastness worked, and in a few minutes his guide told him a mistake had been made and that he could board. Suspicious, he thanked her and gave her a $5 tip for her services.

Instead of landing in Phnom Penh as scheduled, the plane flew past it to the southeast and landed in Saigon (Ho Chi Minh City), Vietnam. No explanations were given. Walker didn't care; at least now he could claim a visit to Vietnam. "When you travel, shit happens," he thought. Despite his cavalier attitude, he wondered what had taken them so far off course.

Americans traveling with Wings Around the World, an upscale tour operator that offered exotic trips, occupied most of the plane seats. All of the passengers were required to leave the plane, but they did not need to show passports to anyone. The passengers were led to an open room with washrooms and drinking water and told not to leave the designated area.

Frustration and anger rose among the detained and the boisterous group demanded an explanation. Finally a local airline official told them the delay would be about an hour, but no reason for the stopover was given.

Walker found it no small coincidence that the room where they were held also contained the airport's gift shop. Booths conveniently opened shortly after their arrival. Gorgeous young Vietnamese women dressed in elegant silk outfits just happened to be on hand to act as sales clerks. Walker suddenly realized that rich Americans

INDEARA—A PhD IN LOVEMAKING

with time to kill and hard currency in their wallets had just been kidnapped! The reason for the diversion to Vietnam and their detention became more apparent to Walker with each passing sale. He smiled at the ingenuity of the perfectly planned heist.

After forty minutes, Walker wanted to stand up and yell, "Stop buying things and we'll be out of here lickety-split." He held his tongue and decided to look around—not at the merchandise, but at the young Vietnamese women that had caught his attention. They were so lovely he could smell and taste their freshness.

On one display shelf sat a clear-glass carafe full of small gutted snakes in a greenish-yellow liquid. Walker inquired about its contents and became completely smitten with the sales clerk. Her gentle, feminine demureness captured his heart, while her eyes taunted the sexually aggressive beast inside him with elusive flashes that seemed to say to him, "I'm really a dirty-minded whore and I want you to savagely take me in every orifice."

The beautiful young Vietnamese clerk embodied for Walker the two polarities of a woman, and the greater the opposites, the stronger the electrical current. He had never been as physically close to a woman with such a natural force as this. Was it her or was it him? Or was it something in both of them pulling them together like a high-powered magnet? No matter the explanation, he could not be in the same room with her without being consumed by thoughts of stripping her naked, bending her over the counter and taking her from behind.

When the clerk explained that in Vietnam men drink the snake juice to make them more virile, Walker almost lost control. At the moment, if he became any more virile, he'd be tossed in jail for attempted rape. To avoid suffering an immediate sexual breakdown that would include a trip to the washroom to masturbate, Walker decided to immerse himself in something non-sexual. He thought that reading James Michener's *The Source*, or having a talk with an elderly American traveler would help to defuse his sexual charge.

Walker sat down beside a man who looked to be in his mid-seventies. They chatted for a bit and shortly into the conversation the man confessed with a whisper, "Have you noticed the women here? If I were twenty years younger, well . . ." Walker excused himself to read his book.

*

At the international airport in Phnom Penh, a Soviet passenger jet with a bombed-out tail sat lame on the tarmac. It was the first thing that Walker noticed while looking out the window after his aircraft had landed. Pointing to the other plane, he said to the older man beside him, "Some welcoming symbol. What are we getting into?"

The airport appeared to be about thirteen minutes away from chaos. United Nations military equipment, white with distinctly painted black "UN" markings, was everywhere. Men in army fatigues, armed with weapons, stood ready in full force. Hordes of people pushed and shouted on the other side of a chain-link fence that separated the runways from a small, badly damaged, one-story concrete building that functioned as the airport terminal.

Walker waited on the tarmac with the other passengers for his luggage to be unloaded from the belly of the plane. The heat and humidity of Cambodia soaked into his pores along with the frenetic activity around him. His plane's jet engines still roared, blocking out every other sound. Some of the passengers tried to communicate by yelling directly into the ear of the other person. A two-man crew unloaded the luggage and left it on the pavement.

It didn't seem real. Walker felt as though he was watching a movie mocking what landing in Cambodia must be like. But then a movie could never do it justice. He collected his baggage and waited for the others to do the same.

The guide from the expensive tour company led his group to the terminal. Walker followed them. The plane's engines were cut, but the ringing in his ears continued. Along a fenced-in pathway leading to the airport, Walker heard a voice shouting, "Mister Fayt, Mister Fayt, Mister Fayt!" It came from a man in the crowd pinned against the fence. The cries continued.

An expression of relief ran across the shouting man's face when Walker waved. The man pointed to the terminal, indicating he would meet Walker inside. Then he pushed his way against the crowd and disappeared from view.

A Cambodian soldier acted as immigration official and he inspected the stamped entry visa in Walker's passport. The man who had been calling Walker's name pushed his way past several people and stood beside the immigration officer. He said a few words in Cambodian and the official stamped Walker's passport.

Walker's guide picked up both of the American's bags and introduced himself as Haing. He spoke slowly in English. Walker could see his mind working as it selected and translated the proper English phrases.

Haing led Walker outside the airport to a new white Honda Civic. The driver wore the clothing of a lower-middle-class Westerner—dress slacks, shirt and leather shoes. He wore glasses and what appeared to be a fairly expensive wristwatch. Haing did not introduce the driver to Walker. Judging by their attire, it appeared to Walker that the driver was much better off financially than Haing.

The road from the airport into the city bustled with activity. Many of the countries involved in the United Nations Transitional Authority in Cambodia (UNTAC) initiative had bases along this route. Haing pointed to the lookalike army encampments of the

Dutch, the Canadians, the Indians and the Ugandans. He indicated that many other countries had camps as well.

Haing had been waiting all morning for the plane to arrive and Walker briefly discussed the detour to Saigon. It was almost noon, and Haing asked Walker if he wished to stop for lunch before checking into the hotel. They decided on lunch first.

In Phnom Penh's crowded streets, masses of people were all going somewhere. Cars, bicycles, trucks, ox carts, motor scooters and pedestrians all seemed in perpetual motion. The dusty streets, crumbled buildings and raggedy people blended together to create a savage memory. The ravages of war visibly loomed around Walker. Suffering, misery and survival flowed through the routines of daily life. Both sorrow and joy were layered as one expression on the faces of the Cambodian people. The driver stopped outside a busy café.

The restaurant catered to foreigners; only the elite of Cambodian society could afford to eat here. Haing introduced Walker to the owner, an elderly Cambodian gentleman who spoke French. Many of the country's older people spoke this language, a reminder of French rule over Indochina (Vietnam, Cambodia and Laos) from 1860 until after World War II.

Conversing with Walker in French, the owner personally served a five-course meal of traditional Cambodian dishes, including soup, fish, beef, vegetables and rice. Walker did not even eat a quarter of the offering and Haing refused to have any, despite a look that suggested he wanted to. He did drink tea while watching Walker. Walker surmised that Cambodian guides had strict orders not to accept invitations to eat with the tourists.

At first Walker felt guilty, eating like a king with so many unfortunate people everywhere. He wanted to take the unfinished food into the streets and feed the hungry. Then it dawned on him that it probably happened anyway. The perfectly good food would not be tossed in the garbage; it would find its way to people who needed it.

Some of the realities of the country came into focus. Walker had prepaid an inflated price for an amount of food that he could not possibly eat. The government took its cut, the tour guide took his cut, the restaurateur took his cut and peasants got their cut as leftovers. The system worked, in a contorted sort of way.

At the end of the meal, the owner bowed with both hands in front of his chest and said, *"Merci, au revoir."* Walker replied in kind.

Outside the restaurant, the driver leaned against the car smoking a cigarette. When he saw the two men coming, he butted it out, put the remaining portion of the cigarette in his shirt pocket and then opened Walker's door. On the way to the hotel, Walker sensed that the driver actually owned the car and provided his service to earn money. Walker never verified these assumptions. The only information Haing ever revealed about the driver was that he was Chinese.

While in Phnom Penh, Walker stayed at the Hotel Samaki, a four-story building designed in the French colonial style, painted yellow with white shutters and bearing a red tile roof. Until 1975, most foreign journalists while in Phnom Penh stayed at this hotel. On April 17, 1975, all that stopped. On that fateful day the Khmer Rouge won their final conquest, the Cambodian capital of Phnom Penh.

Five days earlier, on April 12, 1975, U.S. Marines had airlifted to safety the last of the Americans wishing to leave the city. From a heavily armed compound surrounding the U.S. embassy, ambassador John Gunther Dean symbolically carried the embassy's U.S. flag under his arm, jumped in the chopper and flew to a waiting ship in the Gulf of Thailand. Like Pontius Pilate in the Bible, the U.S. washed the blood from its hands, turned its back and indifferently allowed history to take its course.

The next morning Walker relived the tragic events that reigned from 1975 to 1979. The cruelties inflicted by human beings exceeded his comprehension. A thousand hells could not have been meaner in intent and crueler in application. A tour of Security Prison 21 and the extermination camp at Choeung Ek felt like looking down a gun barrel and staring into the darkest part of man's soul.

Security Prison 21, or S-21, a school turned into a torture chamber by Pol Pot, the Khmer Rouge leader, had been the detention point for as many as 20,000 Cambodians before they were sent to Choeung Ek, the Killing Fields. The last fourteen torture victims lay buried in a nearby courtyard. Their decomposing bodies had been found by the Vietnamese Army, which liberated Phnom Penh in early 1979. Other than for the burial of these bodies, very little about the prison had changed. It stood as a gruesome reminder of the legacy of the Khmer Rouge.

As he toured S-21, Walker asked Haing questions. Refusing to answer would have been impolite and unprofessional, so Haing replied, but Walker noticed the anxiety in his eyes before he answered each one. Haing lowered his voice to a whisper and looked over both shoulders, ensuring no one other than Walker could hear. Even though Haing could safely discuss these matters, he could not escape his personal horrific memories of the Khmer Rouge. Reliving the tales of torture pained him.

Walker thought it likely that many of Haing's family and friends had seen the inside of this prison. Thousands of photographs of numbered men, women and children adorned the walls throughout S-21. The Khmer Rouge took these pictures as a means of record-keeping. Haing did not look at them.

Walker thought about the sick twist of fate that required his guide to conduct tours in a place where many of the people he knew and loved had been exterminated. Compassion prompted him to suggest that Haing wait outside until he finished looking around. Haing understood his intentions and politely declined to leave his responsibilities.

Walker thought there could be no place worse than S-21. Then, a short way down the road, they arrived at the Killing Fields. Nine miles from downtown Phnom Penh lay 129 mass graves entombing thousands of people. Many of the graves remained untouched and a distinctly pungent odor still drifted in the air. The place encapsulated the reign of the Khmer Rouge.

The Killing Fields were a necessary part of the Chinese-designed plan to transform all of Cambodia into an agrarian cooperative. Its purist form required only simple peasants to farm the land. Anyone who was educated, spoke a foreign language or wore glasses was exterminated. Even under duress, those traits could be safely hidden for extended periods of time. However, any opposition, complaints or uncooperative behavior, no matter how slight, also meant a tortured execution.

The Chinese supported the experiment by providing the Khmer Rouge with advice and financial aid. In the four years that the Khmer Rouge held power, over two million Cambodians are said to have died as a result of its policies.

The area of the Killing Fields had its own guide and it pleased Walker that Haing remained in the car. Walker thought that the bits of cloth and shards of bone that had risen up from the graves littering the ground were a call from those below to never forget what had happened in Cambodia.

Small paths separated the pits that had once been mass graves. As Walker paced them, he read the signs in Cambodian script and in English placed at some of the exhumed communal graves. They read like nightmares dreamt in hell. "MASS GRAVE OF 166 VICTIMS WITHOUT HEADS." "Mass grave of more than 100 victims children and woman whose majority were naked." "MASS GRAVE OF 450 VICTIMS."

The guide explained how the Khmer Rouge killed its victims. They did not waste bullets, but employed gruesome methods such as bludgeoning, suffocation, bayoneting, smashing children's heads against trees and cutting off heads with a sharp, corrugated jungle plant.

The fact that all of the most horrific acts were carried out by boys between the ages of twelve and seventeen terrified Walker. He thought about the Khmer Rouge leaders understanding the predisposition of boys to follow orders without conscience or consequence. Exploiting the inherent need of boys for a strong bond of acceptance and the right to hold unconditional power, the Khmer Rouge leaders successfully manipulated the next male generation into becoming instruments of death.

The guide led Walker to a tall, narrow building made of white blocks, with a peaked roof. The inner core of this monument, ten feet square, was made of clear glass windows in wooden frames that went up twenty-five feet on each of the four sides. The Cambodian government, under Vietnamese direction, had constructed this Memorial Stupa at the Choeung Ek Killing Fields.

The glare of the sun blocked the view inside and the glass reflected back like a mirror. As they walked up the steps at the base of the memorial, the angle of light shifted. Even before his brain registered the images, a chill stopped Walker in his tracks. From inside the monument, thousands of human skulls stared at him and they came into sharp focus with his next step. In shades from gray to white, they were stacked on shelves from floor to ceiling.

Upon entering, Walker understood the purpose of the narrow design—to make the visitor feel trapped and mortified. Its architecture ensured a close proximity to the mass of skulls. It replicated in small dosage what the inhabitants must have felt when they were alive at this place. As the guide began his commentary, the space became very claustrophobic. Walker closed his eyes and tried not to think about it, but the vision was etched in his mind.

A small, black painted mark on each skull classified it as to sex and age at the time of death. More accurate identifications could not be made. It seemed odd to Walker that within the monument the skulls were arranged on different shelves according to age and sex.

As the guide described this to him, he handed Walker the skull he held. Walker accepted it as he would have any other inanimate object. The guide asked him to turn the skull around to the cranium and he pointed to the hole in the skull. He explained that this person had died from a blow to the head.

At that point the skull ceased being an artifact and Walker felt death in his hands. Death grasped at him, chilling him. Immediately he handed it back. More than eight thousand skulls watched as he escaped the confines of the stupa, got in the car and drove away.

*

Back at Hotel Samaki, a large group celebrated New Year's by the pool. Young men with a great supply of beer ran around in bathing suits, sang and jumped in the pool. It reminded Walker of a college fraternity party. He sat in a lawn chair and before he had time to take off his shoes, a man sat down on the patio beside him and offered him a beer.

Still stunned by the Killing Fields, Walker didn't believe he could swing into party mode. To be polite, he accepted the beer. The man spoke with a proper British accent.

"So what brings you to Cambodia? Are you a reporter?"

Walker shook his head and said, "No."

"So you work for the UN?"

Walker again shook his head and said, "No."

"Excuse my French, but what the fuck are you doing here?"

"Traveling, on vacation," Walker said in a casual tone.

The man's surprise showed on his face. He yelled to no one in particular.

THE WORLDWIDE SEXUAL ADVENTURES OF WALKER FAYT

"Hey! This sod is here on vacation!" Then he spoke to Walker again. "You really need to fire your travel agent. Cheers!" He dove into the pool.

By this time, Walker had determined that they were British soldiers, assigned to Cambodia as part of the peacekeeping mission. Others came to him too, and through bits and pieces of conversation during their joyous celebration and drunkenness, he pieced together the story.

The British unit had been in Cambodia for a six-month tour of duty. They were shipping out the day after next and heading for home. As many of them wanted to wish their loved ones a Happy New Year and reassure them of their safe return, they lined up behind the only phone in the hotel that could make an overseas call.

From their comments, Walker knew they found it incredible that he was vacationing in a country where they worked. Many didn't believe his story and suspected him of being either a reporter trying to line up an inside story or a nosy UN operative.

The unit's commander, a burly Scot, offered him some advice. "In Cambodia, ya never realla know what's goin' on. Ya ma' think ya doo. But ya dun't. Things are often not as they appear. Keep that in mind; it might just save your life."

Walker turned away from the Scotsman and wrote in his journal.

January 1

Poolside, Hotel Samaki, Phnom Penh, Cambodia

> *An anarchist newsletter used by one of my students for a term paper put forward an interesting theory. The theory stated that any country, no matter how stable or wealthy, was only thirteen days away from total anarchy.*

> *The newsletter suggested that if a particular set of circumstances was put in motion and if the order, timing and disposition were in sync, the thin veneer of civilization and*

social order could be erased. Chaos would ensue. I thought about the riots that happened in L.A. in 1992 after the Rodney King trial. That incident was contained, but what if . . . ?

If the rest of the world is thirteen days away from chaos, Cambodia must be about six hours away. Pain, suffering, betrayal and misery have scarred this land so deeply that it is difficult for anything to take root and grow.

But despite the generations of war and the murder of millions of citizens in gruesome and horrific ways, a gentleness of spirit still abounds. It resides in the people and comes across in feelings of open and genuine friendliness, acceptance and hospitality.

Cambodia's people and their way of life, outside of war, is what I had expected from Thailand. Perhaps the two countries were similar forty years ago before the arrival of millions of tourists to Thailand. I like Cambodia; I can feel its heartbeat and its hope for peace. If only there was a means to lay the anguish of its people to rest.

*

The next day, Haing took Walker sightseeing in Phnom Penh. They visited the National Museum, the central market, the Royal Palace, Throne Hall and the Silver Pagoda. Much of the exterior of these places had survived because the Khmer Rouge wanted to convince the outside world that they respected and wished to preserve Cambodian heritage. Inside they had systematically destroyed most everything.

The Silver Pagoda, covered in over 5,000 silver tiles, each weighing two and a half pounds, remained as one of the unscathed treasures of the old Khmer civilization. Walker lingered over its magnificent beauty and craftsmanship.

Next they walked along the Tonle Sap River, an offshoot of the Mekong River, that formed the eastern edge of Phnom Penh. Many vendors gathered along the concrete walkway, but its atmosphere differed from the rest of the city. Walker felt as if he were at a sleepy beachside resort with all the time in the world. The place along the river's edge seemed to be an unofficial area of cease-fire, a tranquil oasis in a sea of chaos.

At this peaceful reprieve from the rest of the city, women carried big bowls of foodstuffs on their heads, balancing them with one hand. Vendors with scales sold finely etched and crafted gold jewelry. Cheap labor meant that the gold weight determined the price. Other vendors offered eggs, vegetables and fruit.

One pretty young woman with long, wavy black hair, full lips and a bright smile, sold something that looked like a large grapefruit. Haing didn't know the translation into English. Walker bought one and the vendor peeled it for him and offered it in sections.

Because they were on the street, not in a restaurant, Haing accepted Walker's offer of fruit and showed him the traditional way to eat it. Speaking Cambodian, Haing asked something of the vendor. From a container, she poured a mixture of salt and what appeared to be dried, crushed chilies and other peppers into Haing's hand. He broke a section of the fruit apart and dipped it in the mixture, which stuck to the fruit, and then he ate it. Walker did the same. The spicy-hot chili bits, combined with the salt and citrus, refreshed his taste buds.

The next morning, Haing ensured that Walker boarded his flight to Siem Reap. Upon stepping inside the Soviet-constructed propeller-driven plane, Walker gasped for air in the stifling heat. While headed toward his seat, he realized the same American tour group was aboard and he hoped the plane would not be diverted on this trip.

Many of the passengers complained to their guide about the heat and lack of breathable air. They loudly proclaimed that it felt like being in an oven. When the guide returned from the cockpit, he told the group that in a few moments the engines would be turned on and everything would be fine.

As the engines started, a cool, thick mist billowed out of the air-conditioning vents. It did have the desired effect of lowering the temperature and replacing the thin, suffocating air with a fresher alternative. However, it also created a dense fog, so thick that it became impossible to see the person sitting in the next seat.

Panic replaced fear of heatstroke and many passengers blindly tried to find their way off the plane. A voice came over the intercom: "Please remain calm and stay in your seats. This happens occasionally and there is no cause for alarm."

As the plane rolled down the runway, Walker prayed that the pilot could see. The fog in the cabin of this Russian-made plane gave him a tangible sense of how the Cold War had worked its way into the lives of every Soviet citizen. Their country had achieved superpower status through its people accepting a standard of living far below that of their American counterparts.

Eventually the cabin cleared. The 190-mile flight to the north and slightly west took forty minutes and went without incident. Representatives of the Tourism Authority of Angkor met the guests at the airport and arranged buses to transport them to their assigned hotels. The travelers were told that after checking in, lunch would be served at the Hotel de la Paix, as would all their meals, and that guides and drivers would be assigned. Throughout their stay, drivers and guides would remain the same, and tours to the Temples of Angkor would begin that afternoon.

After lunch, Walker waited as all the other tour groups found their drivers and guides and left for the ruins. He began to wonder if being a tour of one had been such a good idea after all. Had they forgotten about him, or was he lost in an administrative shuffle?

THE WORLDWIDE SEXUAL ADVENTURES OF WALKER FAYT

"*C'est la vie,*" he thought and decided to take matters into his own hands. He flagged the next beat-up van used to shuttle the visitors and spoke to the man driving.

"Will you take me to Angkor? Will you be my driver?"

The man seemed a bit confused at first, then nodded his head and waved for Walker to get in. After driving several miles, they passed through the west gate of Angkor Thom, a walled city enclosing a six-square-mile complex. As they zoomed toward the gate, Walker could not get a good look at it. He did notice that the van barely fit through the narrow opening in the monumental sixty-foot door and saw the fifty-four large carved gods on the left and the fifty-four carved demons on the right.

Marvels were everywhere and Walker's excitement built as he thought about exploring such wondrous treasures from the past. At the center of Angkor Thom, they turned south and exited the south gate. They drove another mile and a half and arrived at the entrance to Angkor Wat. The driver held up five fingers to indicate he would be back at five o'clock. That gave Walker almost three hours on his own.

Walker had seen Angkor Wat described as the most awesome, impressive monument ever conceived by the human mind. As he gazed upon the massive stone temple, he would not have argued differently.

The structure stretched beyond understanding, beyond any words to describe it. Spectacularly carved ninety-foot cupolas occupied each of the four corners and two levels. A 160-foot tower formed the center. The whole design was said to replicate a journey into nirvana; the buildings were never meant to be merely a structure bound by the physics of this world.

Walker carried his camera, but he felt it could not capture the mystical essence surrounding him. Slowly he paced the 200 yards along the stone causeway over the moat that surrounded Angkor

INDEARA—A PhD IN LOVEMAKING

Wat to the west gate, the main entrance of the temple. A 700-foot-long carved stone porch welcomed visitors. It was elaborately decorated with carved reliefs and statues. He passed through it and now found himself on a 1,400-foot-long and 30-foot-wide stone walkway leading to the temple.

At the halfway point, on either side, were two ruined structures thought to be libraries. Further along, closer to the actual temple, two large rectangular pools held water. Reflecting in the still water were the temple spires of Angkor Wat.

Walker recognized the photographic potential of the scene and left the stone-surfaced avenue for the parched grass and weeds that surrounded the pools. After he had taken many shots, several small boys gathered around. They competed for his attention by pointing back and forth between themselves and Walker and saying in English over and over again, "Me guide, me guide. . . ."

Intensifying their efforts, they pushed and shoved each other to stand first in front of him. His step in any direction caused them to move with him. Walker thought they were equally able and eager to serve, and had about the same limited English capabilities, so choosing one of the boys to the exclusion of the others would not have been fair. He anticipated that picking one would also mean being hounded by others the entire time. He did not want his first tour of Angkor to be with a chorus of squabbling boys.

"Okay, stop!" Walker yelled. He pointed at each. "You, you, you and you—guides," and then he put his palm to his chest and said, "I have *four* guides."

Excitedly the boys ran around each other and Walker and pushed and teased. These acts were done in friendship and now lacked the previous intensity. The children took turns saying, "I'm guide, you're guide; four guides, yes, four guides."

The boys were very happy and carried a sense of pride at being a "real" guide at Angkor Wat. They moved about the site quickly, showing him things that interested them. They showed him around as they would have done a friend and took him to all their favorite spots. Walker doubted the official tour guides included these places on their itineraries.

Apsara, a celestial dancing girl, had been carved in thousands of places throughout Angkor Wat. In their explorations, the curious boys had found two anomalies among the thousands of carvings and hurried to show him. They took him to an outer wall of the inner courtyard and pointed to a carved figure. They pointed and spoke almost in unison.

"Apsara smiling, Apsara smiling."

As Walker got closer, the boys jumped, trying to touch the mouth of the carving just out of their reach. Until he got very close he couldn't see any difference from the others. Then he saw that indeed her mouth had been carved with a smile, and that her teeth showed.

One of the boys commented very convincingly, "Three-thousand, two-hundred and forty Apsaras—one smiling."

Walker quickly followed them to their next place of interest and again they all pointed and talked over top of each other.

"See Apsara. See Apsara with two tongues."

The lighting on the inside wall made it harder to see. Walker used his flashlight to illuminate where they pointed. This dancing girl looked like any of the others, except at the mouth there were two small notches between the lips. He wondered how these boys had found this unique feature.

"Three-thousand, two-hundred and forty Apsaras—one with two tongues," the same boy as before commented.

As Walker followed his guides to the next boyish spot of interest, he thought of the sensations that a two-tongued woman might provoke. Off one of the inner hallways that linked two rooms, they went through a low doorway. Walker ducked to get into the room. The space inside was about six feet square and twelve feet high.

INDEARA—A PhD IN LOVEMAKING

Light came in from a small opening in the top and from two small entrances on the west and east sides of the room.

All five of them stood inside, looking around. Walker could not figure out why he had been brought here. The boys pushed each other back and forth. One of the boys put his finger to his mouth and loudly went, "Shhh!" As all became still and quiet, the boy struck his chest with his fist and it echoed loudly within the chamber. It sounded as if a bongo drum had been hit. Sound waves reverberated off the walls and Walker felt them ripple through his body.

They all smiled at the effect and each of them wanted to try it. A multitude of pounds, echoes and sound waves filled the space. Sounds blended, crescendos formed, making silent gaps just as loud. Through all the combinations, each person's sound remained distinctive. Sound bombarded them and they smiled at the strange and delightful sensation of hearing as well as feeling the sound pulse.

At the gate tower on the way out, the boys veered to the left and Walker followed. They approached a ten-foot statue carved from a single slab of sandstone. It had many arms and in each hand a different offering had been placed—bits of clothing and paper, dangling ornaments; over the arms brightly colored material had been draped. The boys pointed and exclaimed, "Vishnu, Vishnu . . ."

Vishnu was a Hindu god, the one that Suryavarman II related to as "king-god" when he built Angkor Wat in the 1100s. The boys counted the arms in English and pointed to each one as they did.

"One, two, three, four, five, six, seven, eight—eight arms. Vishnu with eight arms."

Walker wondered if the number of arms represented the beginning of a shift to Buddhism. The eight arms could represent the eight-fold course on the path of truth. As he thought about the Buddhist beliefs of obtaining nirvana by eliminating personal desires and overcoming suffering, a shiver rippled through his body.

He sensed that someone had probed his thoughts. Walker turned and looked behind him.

A woman of Indian heritage stood behind them. In the darkness of the corner, they hadn't noticed her. Walker watched as she clipped a long lock of hair with a small pair of scissors, walked past them and placed it at the feet of Vishnu. As she straightened up, her dark, penetrating eyes pierced him.

"I seek to give thanks for my good fortune."

The woman smiled and bowed her head. When she walked past Walker, the material of her saree brushed against his arm ever so slightly. A thought popped into Walker's head. Ordinarily he would not have been so intrusive with a stranger, but without thinking, he spoke it aloud.

"And what good fortune is that?"

With her back to them all, the Indian woman continued to walk away. Her voice carried to them as it echoed in the enclosure.

"Having met you, of course. We share the same desires, and our paths were destined to cross."

The boys smiled and laughed and made "oooh, oooh" noises as they lightly tapped Walker's leg and pushed him to follow her. "We are your guides. You follow us—we go this way."

The woman's mysterious remark had intrigued Walker. What did she mean, he wondered, that they shared the same desires? He believed she was teasing him with her enigmatic comments. It didn't take much persuading by the boys to follow her.

Outside on the walkway, past the pools heading toward the libraries, they caught up to her. Once beside her, Walker spoke to her.

"Hello, I'm Walker Fayt. What do you mean, we share the same desires?"

"Walker, are you not on a journey that is understood only by you?" He nodded, stunned by her statement. "Then perhaps I have said all that you need to hear. But, I will continue. I am here at

INDEARA—A PhD IN LOVEMAKING

Angkor with the Indian archeological team restoring these sacred sites. That is my work. But I am also on a personal journey."

In silence they walked over the moat, out of the site to the road where his driver waited. Walker gave each of his guides one dollar U.S. To earn that sum they would have had to work in the rice fields for a week. They bowed and thanked him. Each of them held the bill overhead and let it flap in the air as they ran away cheering.

An intensity of purpose and understanding enveloped the woman. Her eyes were very dark, almost as black as her hair, and her complexion radiated a healing color. She spoke once again, methodically, with a distinctive subcontinental accent.

"Treasures of Angkor are coveted the world over and people, including locals, rob these sites for private collectors. Greed is the motivator and money is the temptation. To protect the sites from thieves, the Cambodian Army has the right to shoot unauthorized persons with no questions asked.

"But for the right price, even the guards can be bought and artifacts disappear mysteriously. So the government has granted some of us twenty-four-hour access. If the guards know we are watching, it is less likely that they will steal. The stakes are high because if they get caught stealing artifacts, the penalty is death. Those of us who do patrol are unarmed, so if they catch us watching them—"

"You're in great danger," Walker commented. "You must really believe in your work."

"I do, but it is more than that. It is also my personal journey. The path I have chosen is to avoid future suffering and obtain completeness in one lifetime. Tonight I am going to the temples of Angkor Wat, but not to protect them. I am going to get one step closer to my fulfillment and I wish for you to join me. It is necessary—I have been waiting for you."

Studying this stranger-yet-not-a-stranger's face, Walker thought her to be at peace; she sent out a youthful glow because of it. She looked to be in her mid-thirties, yet her maturity indicated otherwise and he guessed her to be a few years older than he was. She portrayed no harshness, no insincerity, just a loving acceptance of whatever his reply would be as she gazed at him, waiting for an answer.

"What is your name?" Walker inquired, putting off his answer while he assessed the risks of visiting a site where armed Cambodian soldiers had orders to shoot before asking questions.

"On the journey to dissolve earthly desires and rid ourselves of suffering, labels are not important. If you must attach a name to me, you can use Indeara. You will join me tonight?"

"Yes."

Arrangements were made for Indeara and a driver to pick him up in front of his hotel at ten that evening. They parted company as his ride pulled up and honked.

On the way back, Walker asked the driver to stop at the Angkor Tourism office, located in a small building just east of the Grand Hotel d'Angkor. The driver stopped at the large hotel, built in 1928 in French colonial style. Walker's tour package had included staying at this hotel; however, as with so many situations in Cambodia, changes occurred without any explanation.

Walker approached the counter at the tourist office. The uniformed man behind it attended to someone, so Walker waited his turn. When the two were finished, he stepped up to the counter.

"I wasn't assigned a guide today and I wondered—"

"Yes, sir, I know," the man interrupted him. "Your guide and driver will pick you up at nine tomorrow morning at your hotel. Everything is taken care of."

The words were spoken abruptly and without paying much attention to him. The man appeared to be busy arranging papers and reading notes. A little confused, Walker turned to leave and as he did, he said, "Oh? Thank you."

INDEARA—A PhD IN LOVEMAKING

On the way back to his hotel, Walker realized that he had not given the man at the tourist office his name or any other form of identification. However, the man seemed to know not only Walker, but his hotel and the fact that he didn't have a guide or driver. Walker thought, "If a guide and driver show up in the morning, I know the tourists here are being watched more closely than we realize."

At dinner, his fellow countrymen relayed all sorts of information that had surfaced during the day. Speculation on their safety varied the most. Some had been told that the governor of Siem Reap province had personally hired a crack unit of the Vietnamese Army to protect the area. It kept all terrorists at bay. If terrorists caused trouble for the tourists, there were standing orders for the Vietnamese unit to wipe them out.

Others had been told that, since all tourist dollars were split among the rival guerilla factions, they were wise enough not to bite the hand that fed them. Some had been convinced that international pressure for peace in the area kept the truce. Even more far-fetched was the tale of a curse that would befall anyone attacking visitors of Angkor. The stories were better than the food.

More frightening were the reports of the police, the Cambodian army, the Khmer Rouge and the Vietnamese Army—the latter not even officially allowed into Cambodia—dressing in uniforms other than their own and raiding villages and attacking tourists. Dressing in a false uniform had several benefits: the actual loot taken, the ability to direct accusations against an opponent and then, of course, the right to retaliate.

The tourists shared a feeling that things were not as they appeared and that no one really knew the truth. Chaos hung in the atmosphere and seemed to be only a blink away.

Back at his hotel, Walker asked if the showers had any hot water. The man at the reception desk nodded his head. Naked in the shower stall, Walker held out his hand to test the water. He opened the hot water tap to full and a tiny stream of lukewarm water dribbled out. This met a Cambodian definition of a hot shower. The traveler from Wisconsin made the best of it.

Walker slept for a few hours after dinner. Shortly before ten, Indeara and her driver arrived in a faded yellow van. She and Walker greeted each other pleasantly. Indeara moved from the front to the second row of seats so that they could sit beside each other. Wasting no time with small talk, she spoke of matters that were important to her; Walker listened to her beliefs.

She was a Hindu, and she believed in many of Hinduism's early teachings, including reincarnation and the possibility of achieving bliss, the fourth aim in life, by escaping the cycle of death and rebirth. This could be achieved successfully by living the other three aims. Dharma, the first aim, required meeting religious and moral obligations. Artha, the second aim, sought a material well-being and Kama, the third aim, involved the pursuit of pleasure and love.

Walker began to understand the logic in the foundations of Hindu religious doctrine and contrasted it with his own Christian teachings. Physical pleasures and wealth were generally things to be avoided for Christians, because they represented temptations of the Devil. They might not always lead to evil deeds, but they were certainly considered obstacles scattered along the road, sent to test one's faith.

As he listened, Walker thought it ingenious for the Hindu religion to incorporate human nature into its practices. Rather than rely on guilt and fear to control its believers, Hinduism incorporated human instincts toward wealth and sex as part of correct living. Unlike Christianity, Hinduism did not set unconditional rights and wrongs or indoctrinate absolute morality. Rather, the four aims established a guide toward the betterment of each person's karma.

As Indeara discussed fatalism and the interconnection of the past, present and future, the driver stopped at the entrance of Angkor

INDEARA—A PhD IN LOVEMAKING

Wat. A young Cambodian soldier holding a semiautomatic weapon guarded the entry point. He recognized Indeara and let her pass, but blocked Walker's way with the barrel of his gun. Although Walker was a foot taller, his height made no difference in the battle for dominance and intimidation. Indeara said a few words in Cambodian. Her words did not change the soldier's position.

Walker reached into his pocket and pulled out several bills, then illuminated them with his flashlight. He displayed to the guard three U.S. dollars and put a five back into his pocket. The soldier shook his head and pointed to Walker's pocket. With one hand, Walker reached into his pocket and pulled out the five-dollar bill and with the other hand put the ones back in. Expressionless, the young Cambodian soldier snatched the bill and with the end of his gun waved at Walker to enter the site.

Indeara said a few more words to the man in Cambodian. She then turned to Walker and spoke English.

"We will have no more problems tonight. You were very generous. That was more than a month's wages."

"I thought it generous of him not to shoot me," he said, and looked into the heavens. "Look at the stars! I've never seen a sky like that before."

"I have heard that Cambodia has fewer electrical lights than any other country in the world," Indeara responded. "This is the way the night sky used to appear to everyone on earth. Its beauty and meaning are overwhelming. . . ."

After a long pause, while staring into the sky Indeara asked, "Have you heard of the Kamasutra?"

"Only a very little." Walker knew that it had something to do with the art of lovemaking.

"The Kamasutra was the subject of my Ph.D. thesis. In the fourth and fifth centuries, for certain women, Kama, the third aim, was considered the most important goal in life. Love, sex and relationships were intertwined and pursued with religious zeal, creating miracles of the flesh in order to obtain a purity of the soul."

Indeara continued with her explanation. Walker sensed her getting to the point of what she believed brought the two of them together. He let the sound of her voice carry him into the vastness of the universe that stretched out before them. Content blended with connection and he found meaning and truth in her words.

As they walked toward the temple, Indeara discussed the four types of love. The first two were a love of intercourse and a love for the various types of physical contact associated with lovemaking, such as fondling, kissing and oral sex. Another involved spontaneous physical attraction and the fourth type of love was that of a secret admirer or a one-sided attraction. The first two types did not require any emotion between partners and could be perfected by following techniques that had evolved since sex began.

Indeara had studied all the physical instructions necessary to obtaining perfection as detailed in the Kamasutra. She knew the history, purpose, all the do's and don'ts and the spiritual relevance connecting every aspect of every technique to living a correct life. She elaborated on many of the Kamasutra's insights and explained the eight stages of oral intercourse, the proper way of scratching and love biting, the nine ways that a penis could move inside a vagina, the customary noises to be made during sex and the proper way to strike each other.

When she began to describe the more than thirty different positions for intercourse, Walker stopped her.

"I find all this fascinating and rather stimulating. But why are you telling me this?"

By now they were entering the temple chambers. Walker turned on his flashlight again and Indeara replied, as they proceeded inside, "I am getting to that."

Slowly she walked ahead of him, letting the light from his flashlight shine on her as she led the way. The echo off the stone walls allowed him to hear her.

"I doubt you have ever heard of Tantra. It is a mystical sexual cult that began in the second century. It gained popularity as a revolt against the concept of religious and social order, against the unwavering finality of a caste society.

"In both Hinduism and Buddhism, the ultimate goal is nothingness—a complete release of ego. By living correctly in seemingly endless incarnations, the goal can eventually be reached. Traditional beliefs teach that denial and rejection are the best route to erase ego. Tantra takes a different path."

Walker watched the beam of light reflect off Indeara's saree and cast shadows on the stone walls of the temple chambers. Indeara continued speaking.

"I believe that the universe is an example of love's divinity. All that is in it, is an expression of that. Rather than rejecting the ethereal energies of pleasure and ecstasy, I believe they should be worshiped. Walker, do you understand?"

"No! But I'm listening; please go on."

"Tantrism tries to align the human soul with the universal soul, so that release into nothingness can be achieved in one lifetime."

"I think I'm beginning to understand: a shortcut to nirvana," Walker said.

"Nirvana is a Buddhist concept; nevertheless, it's the right idea. Sex and magic can be used as a tool to synchronize human creative energy with universal energy. It can result in the convergence of an eternal substance and eliminate the need for rebirth."

The walls became familiar to Walker; the boys had taken him here earlier in the day. It momentarily distracted him from her words. Soon he drew back to them.

"Lovers' perfection creates oneness, and individuality can be tuned to universal bliss. Long ago we learned that the sexual pulse between a husband and wife cannot achieve the power needed to manipulate the polarity of the universal current into a state of oneness."

"Indeara, are you married?"

"In my culture, it would not be proper for a woman of my class and status not to have wed. It is not important to my explanation of why we are here."

As she continued speaking, Indeara stepped inside the small room where sound could be felt as well as heard. She waved for him to follow and continued to talk quietly.

"Sound vibration can act as a lens, focusing the combined energies into one. I have been waiting for you, and everything is as it should be."

Mystical expressions of sex leading to transformation through dissolution into a universal nothingness were new concepts to Walker. Indeara's descriptions of such possibilities may have been about magic—or just plain old human seduction. Regardless, they had the undeniable effect of making his penis very hard. He turned off his light. In the blackness he heard and felt her words.

"Do not be frightened to worship your erection. From it will flow your masculine energy stimulated by my feminine energy, and when combined properly it will allow our chakras to be poured into the universal bliss. Each chakra is associated with a different part of the body and different consciousness, and is represented by a color. You may experience color bursts as the energy flows from lower to higher levels."

"Yes, I understand this." Walker flashed back to Jordan and remembered the purity of pleasure's color.

"We must start with the five enjoyments: meat, fish, wine, grain and sexual intercourse. Do not be alarmed if during the ceremony I chant and repeat various mantras. It is a necessary part of the ritual. Please do as you wish; you will know what is right."

INDEARA—A PhD IN LOVEMAKING

Walker's lips felt a thin, worn finger pressed against them. It did not surprise him that an archeologist from India working in Cambodia would have rough hands. In the touch, he knew that the hands had done a tremendous amount of hard labor. The finger encouraged him to open his mouth, which he did. Into it she placed a small piece of meat that tasted like chicken. Over the course of an indeterminable amount of time, Indeara fed him the first four enjoyments, accompanied by a very quiet humming.

Anticipation of the fifth enjoyment permeated Walker's body and mind. Blackness shut off the visual, allowing the other senses to dominate. The sounds of chewing, swallowing and breathing were magnified in the enclave of stone. Indeara's humming progressed into song and Walker visualized the thousands of celestial Apsaras in Angkor dancing to the melody.

Walker's gasp reverberated loudly in the room. He hadn't expected the first touch of the fifth enjoyment to be a strong, flowing hand stroke down the length of his erection. His loud utterance had been an automatic response to his surprise.

Song lapsed into chant as Indeara stripped him naked. His skin was sticky from the closeness of the thick, warm air. She applied the prescribed love bites to the backs of his legs, his buttocks and to the insides of his thighs. By licking his hanging testicles, she began the first seven of the eight steps of oral intercourse. Each step was performed with Kamasutran precision. The eighth step involved swallowing or spitting, and it was much too early in the fifth enjoyment for that.

In the darkness of the echo chamber, Walker could hear his soft moans vibrate throughout the enclosure and feel the sounds surround their bodies. The echoes touched them, a caress from the moment just past. The sounds looped together, creating an incarnated message from the material world to the ethereal universe. In a series of physical touches and pleasured responses, simultaneous with a series of chanting and echo reminders, the man and woman strung their essences together in a poetic flow.

Even when Walker opened his eyes, he saw only blackness. Indeara slowly moved her head back, allowing his fully expanded member to slide from the back of her throat to the tip of her lips. As it slid out of her mouth, she curled her tongue up so that its hardened tip stroked the underside of his penis. When it reached her lips, she continued to use the tip of her tongue to press firmly into the opening at the circumcised head. Then she left him.

Powerful sexual tension ran high; it bounced off the stone walls, filling the room. In his blindness, Walker heard Indeara disrobing. He backed up two steps and pressed his sweaty back against the cool, hard wall. Instinct made him press his heels into a ridge in the cobbled floor. With his feet and back firmly in place, he aligned his body at a sixty-degree angle with the floor.

Chanting began and Walker felt the vibration surround him. It teased his erection, making him aware that it stood straight up. He felt Indeara's feet touch his, and then she moved so that she stood with her legs apart with her feet on either side of his and her back toward him. As she bent over and leaned back, she balanced herself by extending her arms upward and back, and pushing her hands against either side of his rib cage.

Indeara lowered herself backwards and enveloped him with her yoni. As Walker entered her, her chanting became a high-pitched yelling and he experienced her both inside and out. The energy of the scream-chant reverberated inside her body as well as outside of her in the room. It sent out a pulsing shiver that entered his penis, traveled through his abdomen, up his torso, pierced his heart, ventured to his throat and released itself through his vocal cords with a thunderous groan.

Balancing against the wall while Indeara rocked herself up and down on his penis required Walker's full effort. If he slipped or gave out, one or both of them could be injured. His having to focus his strength and stamina on not falling allowed the sexual friction to mount far beyond the normal level. Ordinarily a tight, warm, juicy grip in combination with an intense, forceful slip-and-slide would have caused him to explode.

The circumstances allowed Walker to act like a marathoner who had reached the other side of "the wall." He replaced the pain of not being able to continue with a euphoric state of well-being. Secured from the chasm of faltering ability and flung into a maze of glorious possibilities committed to completeness, he began to vocalize a mantra.

Loudly and raucously Walker yelled with all the capacity his lungs would permit. Indeara became her own incantation. Sound became color, pain became pleasure, destiny became reality and the oneness of the universe approached. Nothingness hovered within their grasp.

Walker migrated away from his ego, but snapped back into personal focus when she moved forward and off his emancipated organ. She spoke as if in a trance: "Your creative force must flow into my body and toward my head. We are close. You will come to know."

Indeara took hold of his hands and led him away from the wall. Then she stood on her hands with her backside to his front and arched herself backwards to such a degree that her legs came down and gripped his waist. She moved her legs even lower now, which allowed him to hold on to one of her legs while the other one dangled freely. With the arm that wasn't holding her leg, he locked the inside of his elbow under the back of his knee and lifted his leg. While standing on one foot, he bent forward, gripped her breast and penetrated her vulva.

The position they had just assumed would not have been possible in the light. Visual awareness would have rendered it unattainable. A black vertigo eliminated any connection to earth-bound physics, allowing them to contradict natural parameters. This complicated sexual contortion did not permit much motion, and a loss of balance on either of their parts could have snapped Indeara's vertebrae. The margin of error between disaster and divinity was miniscule.

Indeara chanted again and moved her body up and down minutely by flexing her fingers. Much more powerful were the contractions that she performed internally. Her vaginal muscles gripped Walker's hardened penis in a fleshy vice. He held her breast for balance and flexed his arm up and down slightly. This rotated his leg just enough to move his pelvis, causing a slight in-and-out action with his penis.

Dual mantras resonated in harmony, and this resonation eliminated the need for much external movement. Walker and Indeara were bombarded with sonic pulses that rippled their sweaty flesh. In the black, external stillness an implosion mutated. The Yin force tried to crush the Yang force, while the Yang force tried to expand to infinity to erase the Yin force. Neither was possible. Enormous seismic stresses built up inside their bodies and they teetered on the brink of a tectonic explosion. . . . Then it happened.

The creativity that suddenly radiated from Walker's consciousness flowed more bountifully than the sperm that electrified his penis as it gushed out of his body. He felt powerful orgasms rock Indeara. Later she would describe to him how her chakras had gradually vibrated faster and faster, then linked up, causing the universal flow to rise to the top of her head and then shower out and down, all around her. Existence ended in their screams of earthly cleansing. They evaporated into nothingness.

Unpatterned energy absorbed and released in a purity beyond human comprehension invaded Walker's soul and disintegrated his individuality. Love was everything—light and understanding were the messengers. He became lost in the vastness of a divine love that baptized him in a billion trillion seas of tranquility. As Walker's mind surrendered to the bliss of eternity, the powers of creation overwhelmed him. He was immersed into everything-become-nothing and transformed—digested into a realm of existence centered in both commitment and freedom. . . . Then it was gone.

More accurately, Walker returned. Very slowly, his human faculties crept into his awareness. He lay on the floor, still unable to see. Sand and dirt stuck to his back. The acoustics of the room made it possible to distinguish that two people were breathing. Indeara was still there and alive.

Deep now in silent meditation, Walker began to feel the weight of his human imperfections. He had never noticed them before and their presence now agitated him. Being masked and layered with human weakness and suffering no longer felt comfortable to him and the longer he lay there, the more aggravated he became. Why did he accept a state of imperfection over perfection? What good was it to know that perfection existed when it was nearly impossible to access?

"We now share the substance of a higher existence," Indeara spoke, her voice again trancelike. "It dances in our souls and in our bodies, and that cannot be changed." She then described what had happened within her at the moment of their orgasms. "Together we will watch the sun rise above the horizon and, with that, the ceremony will end. After that, we must never see each other again. You must not try to contact me, nor will I try to contact you. There must be no exceptions."

Walker did not understand, nor did he need to; he just accepted her words.

After a long silence, Indeara whispered to him: "Walker, you are close to your destiny. It waits for you in Cambodia. You have the strength, wisdom and power now to fulfill what is required of you. After that, only you can decide."

Their driver awaited them at the entrance to Angkor. In darkness, they drove to Phnom Bakheng, about a third of a mile south of the south gate of Angkor Thom. The ruins there had once been the first mountain temple of the first city of Angkor. Constructed around 900 AD, it was also known as Indradri, or Mountain of Indra.

With the use of the flashlight, Indeara and Walker climbed the steep path up about 200 feet. At the top, they sat apart on large stones and waited for the day to begin. After about forty minutes, night started turning into dawn. Mist in the jungle appeared like vapors rising off a huge pot of magic potion.

A tiny orange sliver eventually broke the horizon. At a leisurely pace, a giant glowing sphere resurrected itself from the ground; its roundness and brilliance grew with each passing minute. A quarter of it emerged, then half, and soon only its bottom rim clutched the earth.

Views away from the sun offered expansive vistas of Angkor Thom, Angkor Wat and the immensity of the surrounding jungle. Walker soaked up the improbable sight—a fit ending to an incredible night. The last fourteen hours had redefined his definition of the word "incredible."

When Walker looked back, the earth had released the sun. Drifting higher into the sky, it illuminated the jungle and the towers of Angkor Wat with soft, amber-red light.

Indeara came over to where he sat. She bowed to him and they kissed on the mouth for the first time. Their lips held a connection far greater than passion. Passion was too base a measurement to describe the insights that bonded them from the inside out. The heavenly kiss lingered until earthly incantations seeped in to spoil its purity.

"You must leave me now; closure is complete. Go down, and the driver will take you to your hotel. I will stay here and he will collect me later."

Walker stood straight and stepped toward her. She put her hand up, signaling him to stop.

"Go now, please, before it is all ruined. Please, you must."

Walker turned and walked away. Every so often he glanced over his shoulder at Indeara. She kept her gaze on the sun rising in the clear sky above the jungle, and never faced him again.

chapter 14

GOING BEYOND ONESELF
Rescuing Children in Chaotic Cambodia

Walker missed breakfast in order to sleep a couple of hours. Shortly after 9 a.m., a blue van met him in front of his hotel. The driver from the previous afternoon smiled and waved, then pointed to a young man sitting in the passenger seat, indicating that today a guide had joined him. Lek apologized for the mix-up the day before and stated he would be Walker's guide for the remainder of his tour.

A few thoughts crossed Walker's mind: The tourist office did know who he was, and likely knew every other tourist, too; or perhaps they didn't, and this was just a lucky coincidence. He couldn't tell for sure.

Angkor Tourism charged $120 U.S. per day to visit the sights. It was included in the price of his package, and to Walker it was worth it. Most packages were from one to four days, but he had combined two packages and would be staying seven. Due to Cambodia's reputation of being dangerous, he hoped the number of tourists would be minimal and that his stay would be comparable with visiting the monuments of Egypt in the 1930s. He doubted that another chance to visit Angkor, under these conditions, would arise in his lifetime and he embraced the day

GOING BEYOND ONESELF

invigorated with its potential. The events of the past night had also awakened him to all sorts of possibilities.

Angkor Thom was the city and at its center was the Bayon Temple. Walker spent the morning exploring this wondrously eerie place. Like with all the Khmer temples, there were gates facing the four directions. The Bayon's main gate was on the east side of the complex; large artificial ponds straddled the entrance walkway.

On the long outer walls around the first level, the bas-reliefs, or low-relief sculptures, remained in excellent condition. Lek talked slowly, with a unique emphasis on certain words or phrases. It would take some time for Walker to adjust to Lek's cadence.

"The Bayon has three thousand, six hundred feet of carvings, depicting over eleven thousand persons."

In sixteen different areas, bas-reliefs were carved into the sandstone walls. Some depicted multiple-level battle scenes while others showed scenes of normal citizens of the Khmer Empire in the twelfth century. Others recorded specific history, almost like a photograph, of battles with the Cham armies, showing both defeat and victory. In 1177, the Chams defeated the Khmers and they broke and pillaged Angkor. This event was carved into one panel while on another two panels, the Khmers avenged themselves in battle victory in 1181.

It fascinated Walker to be able to see and touch the history of the Khmer people. He ran his hand lightly across a carving of a woman giving birth.

Built in 1181 to 1201 by Jayavarman VII, the Bayon was originally designed to worship the Hindu god Shiva; there were two levels to this temple. Experts do not know exactly when the Mahayana Buddhists added the third level. Lek spoke to Walker about it as they walked along this upper stage.

"On this level you will see forty-nine towers and on those towers there are one hundred and seventy-two faces of the Buddhist god Avalokitesvara."

No matter where Walker looked, no matter where he stood, there were always at least ten or more stone faces watching him, each one four feet high by three feet wide. As the light changed, the huge faces brightened or were cast into shadows. Some faces were above him and others were at eye level, massive stares knowing something that he didn't. Walker felt a haunting, claustrophobic sensation of being ensnared by a people who understood the meaning of life, yet tortured captives through their own ignorance. Each stony face smiled the same thick-lipped smile, adding to the completeness of the people's superiority.

All of the towers and all of the faces of the towers had been carved in pieces and fitted together like a giant puzzle. Walker wondered about the message in their design.

Back at the hotel that offered lunch to the guests visiting Angkor Wat, Walker sat with some countrymen and listened to them complain about the food, the rooms, the transportation and whatever else came to mind. He found it incredible what some of these people expected. They were in one of Asia's poorest countries, a place that had been ravaged by war for the last thirty years and in the seventies, by secret decree of the American president, was savagely bombed by the American military. Most Cambodians were uneducated and simply trying to survive and did not have the capacity to comprehend an American expectation for service and quality.

Several members of the large tour group had ventured off from the designated hotel for dinner the previous night and were now discussing it. A number of private restaurants operated on the road through Siem Reap that ran north to the Angkor monuments and south to Tonle Sap. The tourists reported that one of the places offered hamburgers with real beef. A few of them, Walker included, arranged to meet later that evening and check it out.

GOING BEYOND ONESELF

In the afternoon, Lek took him to the temples of Angkor Wat. Walker had been there twice in the last twenty-four hours and he relished another visit. Lek spoke his scripted words from memory; each description reminded Walker of listening to a tape recording. It wasn't bad, just a little stilted. He surmised that to be granted official guide status, a candidate had to pass an oral test in English or another chosen language about the facts of Angkor. Lek concentrated on pronouncing each word correctly.

"In the year one-thousand one-hundred and twelve to the year one-thousand one-hundred and fifty-two, in the twelfth century AD, King Suryavarman the Second built this temple, Angkor Wat. It was built to honor the god Vishnu."

All of Lek's descriptions were automatic and related to dates, physical dimensions and descriptions of things such as pools, libraries or towers. He did not discuss the history or beliefs of the people who once inhabited the city and its temples. When Walker did have questions along those lines, Lek politely tried to answer, but it soon became obvious that he did not have the training to respond outside the basic facts. On these occasions, Lek smiled and apologized.

As Lek pointed to the many carved images of womanliness, he always said, "Apsara dancing." No matter the number of times Walker saw the figure, it always touched him on a sexual level.

Etched in stone throughout Angkor were thousands of Apsaras. Each represented a perfect female form: small waist, flat stomach, round, voluptuous breasts and taut arms and legs. Always naked except for the jewelry she wore, Apsara enticed the male observer in her dance stance. Carved in fine detail, the decorations on her body included a tiara, earrings, a necklace, bands around each of her upper arms, bracelets, anklets and a waistband that covered her pubic hair and vagina. Every Apsara delighted him and Walker fantasized about being a Khmer king and having all the women around him dress and dance like Apsara.

THE WORLDWIDE SEXUAL ADVENTURES OF WALKER FAYT

As Lek went through one of the doorways from the esplanade to an inner enclosure, he rubbed a carved breast of an Apsara. He turned back to Walker and said, "It is custom; you must do also."

Walker thought it silly and perhaps a bit perverted to fondle a stone carving. As he slid his hand along the well-rounded sandstone breast, he noticed that it was more polished and darker than the rest of the wall. Thousands of people over the many centuries had done what he had just done—touched the smooth, hard, dry and cool breast of a dancing celestial concubine. It felt rather good and he resisted the urge to touch all the Apsaras in a similar fashion.

"Lek, it was good for me. Was it good for you too?"

Lek smiled and laughed a little. "Yes. It makes me wish I were king."

"Why is that?"

"If I were king, I could have as many concubines as I want. They would all be like Apsara." He laughed at his foolish fantasy.

Walker patted him on the back. "That wouldn't be so bad, would it?"

Lek's face held a big grin when he said, "It would be very nice."

On the outside of the central temple compound wall were 800 yards of exceptional bas-reliefs. Much of it was polished by the millions of hands that had touched it over the centuries, and now it looked like black marble, not sandstone. In accordance with Khmer tradition, the American traveler and his guide began walking on the west side and kept the carvings to their left.

Battles, history, kings, soldiers and slaves were all meticulously carved into the wall. Two of the sections Walker found of extreme interest and he spent a long time looking them over. Lek got bored, sat down and smoked a cigarette while he waited for Walker.

The eastern half of the south gallery featured the rewards of the thirty-seven heavens and the punishments of the thirty-two hells. Eighteen armed Yama, or judges of the dead, sat on a bull as people walked toward them. The lower tier marked the road to hell and devils dragged off the wicked people for a horrible torture. Above the Yama were the ones chosen for heaven. They lived in lovely big houses and were served by well-groomed women, children and other heavenly attendants.

The Churning of the Ocean Milk is the most famous bas-relief in all Angkor Wat. As he beheld the scene and listened to Lek tell the story masterfully carved into the stone of the east gallery, Walker turned cold, hard and as still as the stone he faced.

Indra stood on top, overseeing all the activity. Apsaras danced in the heavens. Eighty-eight Asuras, or devils, and ninety-two Devas, or gods, faced off against each other. Both groups craved the tincture of immortality and desired to extract it from the sea. They churned the waters by spinning Vasuki, the massive serpent, that had tightly wrapped itself around Mount Mandara, the mountain in heaven. Vishnu stands on one side of the mountain, aiding in the task, while other deities, Shiva and Brahma, watch.

Eight hundred and fifty years later, the stone wall carvings appeared to Walker as mythological because they no longer represented truth. They amused and interested him, but it was hard for him to believe that they were once taken as truth and that they shaped the lives of millions of people for centuries. In that moment he witnessed the journey from belief to religion to mythology. He wondered how many centuries would pass before Christianity, Hinduism, Buddhism, Islam and Judaism became mythology for the humans of the future to study and romanticize about with quaint amusement.

The tour lingered into the late afternoon, until the setting sun turned the sandstone spires flaming red and orange colors. Each day at this time, Angkor Wat transformed itself into a raging crimson creation; Walker beheld heaven materialized on earth. Lek informed him that at one time, the tops of the towers had been covered in gold. The sparkle must have brightened the jungle for miles.

On the return drive, Walker realized that the official tour had not included the unique Apsaras or the echoing room. He smiled at his special opportunity from the previous day.

Back at his hotel, Walker slept for two hours. Upon arising, he found that the shower dripped even less hot water than the day before. It took longer to get the grime and sweat off his body, but it felt good to do so.

Once cleaned up, Walker met the others for dinner as planned. There was a couple in their sixties from Baltimore and a single woman in her late fifties from Seattle. A current of apprehension ran among them. Being the youngest of the group and now an experienced traveler, Walker took charge and convinced them that it would be safe to walk unsupervised and without a guide. Each of them had brought a flashlight.

After about a ten-minute walk, the string of restaurants appeared. None looked that appealing. The tourists easily distinguished the place that served the hamburgers. Above an open veranda hung a sign, "If you like it killed—we serve it" and in smaller letters underneath it, "Pure beef imported from Australia."

As the visitors approached, everyone noticed several tables full of Western soldiers in green fatigues drinking beer and loudly telling jokes. Young local women hung out on the periphery.

"I don't think I want to go in there," said the woman from Seattle.

The other woman supported her. "I'm glad you said it first, because neither do I." The group turned around and went to the next place, a few hundred feet farther down the road.

This restaurant appeared safe inside, and several people from the tour group were already there. Walker glanced at their food. It appeared no better than that in the hotel. "If you don't mind, I really want a burger—it's been such a long time."

They said they didn't mind a bit. Being with their traveling companions seemed to give them a sense of safety in numbers and

Walker sensed that they really didn't mind if he left them. He bid them good night. It wasn't only his craving for a hamburger that took him next door, but also the thought of hanging out with soldiers on a UN mission. He figured their stories would be more interesting than listening to people complain about the food.

Little light bulbs that hung under the veranda roof provided the only illumination. Walker negotiated the steps and glanced at several empty tables. A man from behind the bar shouted without looking at him: "Take any table you like, or you can have a stool at the bar."

Walker chose the latter, and read the sign written on a ripped chunk of cardboard in black magic marker:

Beer   3 U.S.$

Imported Australian Beef Burgers   4 U.S.$

"What will it be?"

Walker detected an accent, but couldn't place it. He pointed to the cardboard menu and said, "I'll have one of each. Is it really Australian beef?"

"You can bet that you won't have to ask after your first bite. I have one hell of a time getting it here. It brings in the boys on a regular basis." He glanced around, referring to the UN soldiers that filled the place.

Reaching into an old pop cooler, the man pulled out a cold beer and set it on the bar in front of Walker. He called into a back room, "One burger!"

Walker began to notice something peculiar about the bartender's behavior, although he couldn't quite identify it.

Before the burger arrived, a couple in their late thirties entered the restaurant and took the stools beside Walker. She was a tall, good-looking brunette with shoulder-length hair. He stood a couple inches shorter than her and was handsome as well. Both radiated an air of wealth.

During a brief introduction, they revealed that they were Swiss visiting Cambodia on vacation. Without looking directly at them, the bartender intently listened in on their discussion. Soon the couple expressed their hunger and ordered beers and burgers too.

Walker pulled the bartender into the conversation. "So is this your place?"

"Yes, I'm the owner. I do okay. I've been here almost ten years now."

The short, bristled hair was streaked with gray. Darting, cold, steel-blue eyes could not stay in one place and constantly shifted, never stopping anywhere for longer than one second. The man looked to be in his early fifties and in top physical shape.

Walker engaged him further. "So you've seen a lot of shit in your days. Why Cambodia?"

Without any hesitation he responded. "I love it here. There's no law. They say I can't do something, I say, 'Show me the law.' They can't. Cambodia is one place where I can do whatever I want because they have no law to say otherwise."

Peter, the Swiss tourist, jumped in. "Where are you from originally?"

"I'm from South Africa. I have the proud distinction of being the youngest person to do time in a South African military jail. I was fifteen. I lied about my age to get into the army. Once they accepted me, they couldn't throw me out and they couldn't get me to obey orders.

"I didn't agree with Apartheid, but I loved the action. I needed it more than sex. I just had to get as much as possible. My commanders were stupid and they knew I was smarter than they were. My intelligence threatened them and they tried to break me with ridiculous orders. It didn't work, so they sent me to jail and then when that didn't work, they sent me away for psychological profiling."

Elizabeth questioned, "Did it reveal anything?"

The owner's visual surveillance of his premises continued as he spoke and now it included them as well. "That I was a genius, a loner, distrusting and couldn't be counted on to follow orders . . . so they put me in intelligence." He pointed to his eyes as they darted about. "It's now instinct."

The owner's name was Dirk, and for the next several hours as they conversed, he explained how he became disgusted with the policies of Apartheid and could no longer work for a government and army that held such beliefs.

"Status based on race is ridiculous. Everyone is the same. No one is better or worse than anyone else."

Dirk's eyes instinctively flashed in sequence into all three of their eyes to read their reactions as he said, "If you peel away the thin layer of civility, we are all just animals. I know that it doesn't take much to get us there. Given the right circumstances, like a fight for survival, you would all behave like animals very quickly."

Walker thought it strange of Dirk to say such things among people he had just met. Obviously he was an intense person. Walker asked him how he had found his way from South Africa to Cambodia.

At twenty, Dirk said, he had quit the South African military intelligence and headed for action. In the late Sixties that meant Vietnam. For the first few days he wandered around Saigon; eventually CIA agents approached him and wanted to know who he was and why he was in Vietnam. Dirk told them the truth: he was a former South African soldier vacationing in Vietnam. The agents didn't believe him. A couple of days later, KGB agents wanted to know who he was and why he was in Vietnam. Dirk gave them the same pitch; they didn't believe him either.

The day after the KGB had spoken with him, different CIA agents cornered Dirk and wondered why he had been speaking with the KGB. They wanted to know his true business in Vietnam. Dirk

THE WORLDWIDE SEXUAL ADVENTURES OF WALKER FAYT

explained to the CIA agents that the KGB just wanted to know who he was and why he was in Vietnam. He convinced the CIA agents that nothing more had transpired. The agents then asked Dirk if he would like to work for them. Dirk first wanted to know what he would have to do. His instructions were simple: "Get the KGB to follow you around."

That was how it began for the South African. By the end of the war, he had performed many assignments for the CIA. He told stories of running money, weapons and spies all around South East Asia. Dirk showed them an identification card with his picture on it. It read, "If you find this man's body please contact the CIA."

There was no way to know whether any of it was true. The stories Dirk told were usually only found in spy or war novels—but they made for an entertaining evening. As a bonus, the burgers were very good and the beer was cold.

Dirk explained that he was also a "teacher," and from under the bar he produced pictures of his "students." They were teenage boys and young men with high-powered rifles, dressed in battle garb. It now became clear to Walker that Dirk held the distinction of being an elder statesman in the world of mercenaries. He no longer did the missions himself, but trained the men who did. He had become a "teacher for hire."

During the course of the evening, several UN soldiers from various countries approached and asked, "Dirk, where can I go to find some real action?"

The answer was always the same: "Don't ask me, I have no idea. I'm only a proprietor of burgers and beer," but the comment was followed by a subtle grin.

On one occasion after such a request, he responded in his usual way and then he leaned down and spoke softly so that only the three of them could hear. "I wouldn't take on any of them. They come here thinking they're on the front lines. But all they really do is crash up vehicles, drink beer and chase women. It's political; it's all an excuse. Over the last ten years, the UN has dumped billions of dollars into the country to try and stabilize it."

Elizabeth asked, "If you had to live in a city, which one would it be?"

Immediately Dirk responded, "Bangkok! I love it there."

It made sense to Walker that a person of Dirk's character would enjoy a place of jumbled chaos, a city that catered to a wide spectrum of tastes, from subtle to gross. Walker thought that Dirk would also enjoy New York City.

Walker inquired, "How do you ensure your safety, especially when you travel?"

"If there's a sniper out there," Dirk said as he pointed straight out of the bar into the darkness, "with a long-range sight and night-vision goggles, I can't control it or even worry about it. My first priority is always what I can see, what's around me, what I can immediately prevent. From a security perspective, at any given moment the rest of the world doesn't matter. That's why I always carry a gun, even when I travel on airplanes."

Peter spoke up. "How is that possible?"

Dirk reached into his shirt and extracted a pistol. Then he leaned below the counter and, out of sight from the rest of the restaurant, removed the bullets. The gun empty, he handed it to Peter.

"It's a fully functional gun and it's made of plastic. When I go through metal detectors, everything remains quiet, and the bullets—well, that's a trade secret."

Peter graciously picked up the tab for the evening's food and drink. He and his wife were staying at a different hotel and left in a different direction than Walker. The talk of the evening made Walker's journey back to his hotel somewhat unsettling. People passed him on foot and on bicycles. Each time, Walker checked over his shoulder to make sure they weren't attackers. Insights into an existence so foreign, so complicated, so unbelievable made it difficult for him to sleep that night.

Lying in bed awake, Walker heard explosions but thought they came from his imagination. They were loud sounds like thunder, but also not like thunder. After about ten minutes, he knew that the sounds breaking the silence of the night were real. Now it wasn't just his thoughts of the evening keeping him awake, but the explosions. Adrenaline began to rush into his bloodstream. The blasting continued off in the distance, but didn't appear to be getting any closer.

Eventually Walker stopped fearing for his personal safety. The time intervals between explosions seemed to last forever; just when he thought they were over, another occurred. They lasted for about an hour and with each explosion he wondered if anyone had been killed or injured—lives changed forever without warning or explanation.

Several hours later, Walker fell asleep. He slept right through breakfast, which didn't matter because the two hamburgers from the night before kept him satisfied. Lek and the driver patiently waited outside his hotel. They didn't seem in any hurry to begin their day.

Walker spent the morning in two places, one known as the Terrace of the Leper King and the other the Terrace of the Elephants. Both provided glimpses into the Khmer Empire culture of the twelfth century.

In a confined walkway at the south end of the Terrace of the Leper King, archeologists had excavated a terrace from a time earlier than the one built atop. With barely enough room for Walker to maneuver, he could not see the entire scene that had been carved into the wall. By crouching, looking up and then walking back and forth he formed an idea of the carved message.

At the bottom, supporting it all, were nagas. On top of that were four tiers of Apsaras. There were other figures as well, but Apsaras dominated. Unlike at Angkor Wat, they were all seated and the figures protruded from the wall more, with at least half their bodies carved. The carvings were well-preserved and in immaculate condition.

In places the figures projected a greenish hue, which appeared to be a natural coloring, but was actually caused by a moss growing on the sandstone. There were many hundreds of naked Apsaras, each figure different, including breast shape and size. In a strange way, it reminded Walker of the confinement of the Killing Fields monument. However, being trapped by stone breasts rather than human skulls made a huge difference to the pleasantness of the experience. As he stared at the breasts, they all seemed to cry out, "Touch me."

Neither Walker nor Lek could help themselves—an automatic reflex took hold. As they walked along the tight enclave, their hands went out and touched the naked stone breasts of the Apsaras. Fantasies of being king floated through Walker's mind, and Walker guessed through Lek's mind too.

The sunny, warm weather had made visiting the ruins pleasurable. Driving the six miles back to the hotel to drop Walker off for lunch, Lek told him they would be spending the afternoon at Ta Prohm, a Buddhist temple constructed by Jayavarman VII late in the twelfth century AD.

Back in the van after lunch, they headed northeast from Angkor Wat and slightly southeast from the east gate of Angkor Thom. On the way to Ta Prohm, Lek explained that this would not be like visiting any of the other places at Angkor. In Lek's style of giving dates and facts, Walker learned some of the area's history.

In 1431, Khmer power and influence had diminished. The Thai king had captured and ransacked Angkor and the city and temples were abandoned. Shortly afterward, Hinayana Buddhist monks moved in and adopted the temples as a place of worship. Angkor soon gained a reputation as a Buddhist pilgrimage center.

In the 1860s, a French explorer and naturalist, Henri Mouhot, wrote a book about his travels and adventures in Cambodia and Angkor. It created interest in the region and by 1908 investigation, restoration and excavation began in earnest. The effort continued until the outbreak of war in the 1970s. There were purists who believed that restoration disturbed the natural evolution of the jungle. To satisfy the complaints and concerns of this group, officials decided that one monument would remain untouched. The jungle would be allowed to progress and reclaim Ta Prohm unabated.

Along the dirt path leading to the entrance, many children sat and played. Walker soon realized that they were all girls and he guessed that they ranged in age from about six to thirteen. They did not hide their amazement at his height. Extremely friendly and delightful, they danced around him; many of the girls held his hands and touched his clothing. They did not appear to want anything other than to be around him and to practice their English. "Hello," "Have a good day," and "Goodbye," they said, and after each English phrase they giggled, covered their mouths with their hands and bowed their heads.

Inside Ta Prohm, Walker felt consumed by yet another unexpected reality. Vegetation ranging from towering trees several hundred feet tall to moist moss less than a half inch high had invaded and corrupted the sandstone structures. Monuments and carvings were being crushed by the immense, invading jungle trees. Giant roots framed doorways and broke apart beautifully crafted stone edifices. Massive trees grew haphazardly among stone rubble, filtering light through their leaves to illuminate the site in a greenish hue.

The most imaginative set director for some blockbuster jungle adventure could not have come close to matching the real thing. In addition to the visuals, a cascade of bird, insect and frog noises blended together with blowing leaves, making the jungle come alive. Lek had warned Walker to avoid the poisonous, lime-green Hanuman snake, biting red ants and large spiders. Butterflies

GOING BEYOND ONESELF

fluttered in the soft green light, pushing thoughts of these dangers aside.

The main part of the temple measured 100 yards square. Originally this temple lodged more than 12,000 people, including high priests, ordinary priests and choristers required for Khmer rituals. Their home had become a seemingly endless maelstrom of debris, blocked corridors and overgrown rooms. Many spaces could not be entered because of broken stone or jungle growth.

In a courtyard relatively free from jungle habitation, an elderly Cambodian man sat playing a homemade instrument. With its strings and wooden bow, it resembled a violin. The man's clothes were dirty and he wore a hat resembling a fedora, only rounder.

As they got closer, Walker said, "I know that melody; it's played on New Year's Eve in America. It's . . . 'Auld Lang Syne!'"

"It is a very, very old Cambodian song, very traditional . . . played at weddings," said Lek.

"Is he expecting a tip?" Walker asked Lek.

"No, but if you wish, it is your choice." Walker put a dollar beside the man. The musician smiled and bowed while he continued to play.

Lek paused for a smoke in an open terrace and Walker wandered around and took pictures. He doubted that photographs could capture the daunting presence of the real image, but hoped for the best as he snapped a couple of rolls of film.

Ta Prohm stirred in Walker an overpowering spirit of discovery, adventure and magic. Immersed in the ethereal surroundings, he felt baptized by a triumphant Mother Nature and blessed by the elemental energy of the jungle.

*

Still high from the afternoon's outing, Walker skipped dinner at the hotel buffet and opted for burgers, beer and interesting conversation at Dirk's place. The humidity had been bearable for the first time since his arrival in Siem Reap and before leaving for the restaurant, he turned off the big fan that vented directly outside, situated along the back wall of his hotel room.

Walker arrived to a restaurant less crowded than the night before. When Dirk saw him, he waved him in to sit on a stool by the bar.

"The usual?" Dirk asked. It was a bit of a joke, since hamburgers and beer were the only menu items.

"Well, of course," Walker responded jovially. Then in a serious tone he asked, "Dirk, is it possible that I heard bombs or rocket fire last night?"

Dirk didn't indicate that he had heard anything, yet went on to explain. "As you know, Pol Pot, head of the Khmer Rouge, is dead. I can't believe somebody didn't kill him but they didn't. He died of natural causes a few years ago. The news caused a celebration here. I was lying in bed sleeping and heard gunshots—lots of them. I came running out of my room with weapons ready to blaze and found some drunken bastards shooting at the moon.

"Recently two of his right-hand guys have been seeking asylum from international genocide trials. To keep the peace in Cambodia, the current government would spare them going to trial; however, the international community is balking at the idea. Generally speaking, people who have directed the eradication of millions of other people are not let off the hook. To express the Khmer Rouge's displeasure with the international community's decision not to exonerate their leaders, they want it to be known that they can still cause some mischief.

"So you may have heard some of their displeasure last night. Nothing to worry about. It was probably more than twenty miles away. Part of the strategy is to get the attention of the tourists. Was it small blasts at regular intervals or a constant firing?"

"It was small blasts that sounded like thunder. It lasted about an hour."

GOING BEYOND ONESELF

Dirk went into a small room behind the bar and came out hauling a piece of equipment. "They probably used mortar shells and fired them from a device like this. It's mobile and easy to handle and the shells can be found anywhere, if you know where to look."

A young man in green army clothing with a Dutch accent asked, "So, Dirk, what else you got back there?"

"You'd be surprised, I'm sure."

While Walker ate and drank, he listened to Louie, who was from Rotterdam and doing his tour of duty for the Dutch army. In two days his tour ended and he was scheduled to go home. Louie inquired whether Dirk knew where any real action was to be found. Dirk gave his standard reply.

Louie was part of the highly trained land-mine removal team. He told Walker that over six million land mines had been placed in Cambodia. Almost the entire country needed to be swept. His personal rate of progress had been about twenty square feet a day. At a steady rate, they could clear the country in about 100 years. But the task was not that straightforward. Areas that had already been cleared were continually replanted with mines.

Louie told of a horrific incident from five years past when a school bus full of children had hit a land mine on a road that had been cleared and safe for many years. Walker thought it an odd coincidence that Dirk had pictures of the burned-out bus, which he now showed to him and Louie.

Louie hadn't been in Cambodia at that time and told a more recent personal story. In order for UN soldiers and personnel to be accepted into the community and to pump money into the local economy, many units were required to find their own private accommodations rather than stay in camp barracks.

Louie had rented a small private house in Siem Reap and had been living there for about a month; an elderly woman who lived in, cooked and cleaned for him. About five months ago, Louie returned home early from work and he saw a large gathering of people in front of his house. He got rather angry because he thought the maid was having a party and hadn't told him about it. It was no party. She had been killed by a land mine planted in the backyard. Likely it was meant for Louie, as a way to send a grim message to the UN.

The talk turned nostalgically to the Vietnam War. Dirk gave first-hand accounts of some missions, thick with a "glory day" emphasis. Dirk and Louie discussed the Viet Cong's AK-47 assault rifle and what a great weapon it was. Dirk retrieved one from the back room. It had been buried in the mud for twenty-five years, he said, yet it had fired perfectly with only a minor brush-off.

Louie's eyes lit up. "Dirk, what are you doing tomorrow afternoon?"

"I'm here. Why?"

"Can we go out and fire off a few rounds?"

Before Dirk could answer, Walker asked, astonished, "You can just go out and fire a high-powered rifle and nobody is going to do anything?"

"Think about it," Dirk replied confidently. "Who's going to bother us? If you heard shots or machine-gun fire, are you going to go and see what it's all about, or are you going to stay away? Believe me, you'd stay away. Nobody will bother us."

Dirk looked at Louie for as long as his darting eyes would allow. "Sure, Louie. We'll go tomorrow, about two in the afternoon. Walker, want to come along and pop off a few shots?"

Walker hadn't expected the offer and the force of the question hit him as hard as a punch. He had never fired a weapon of any kind and just the idea of doing so put butterflies in his stomach. It reminded him of Uganda and the last time he had held a rifle and the trouble that had ensued. What would be in store this time? The memory quickly erased itself and he responded without thinking. "Sure, okay. I'll be here at two."

GOING BEYOND ONESELF

Louie left for the night, leaving Walker alone with Dirk. There were other people at tables, but none sitting on stools at the bar. Walker sensed that he had garnered a little respect from Dirk in accepting his invitation to fire the weapon. Rather than staying with war, spy and military-operation stories, Dirk turned the conversation more personal.

"There is justice in this universe. I have four children and all of them are girls. Providence knew that any son of mine could never live up to his father's expectations. The son I always wanted was spared from living with that torment. I had daughters, so all I had to do, and still do, is protect them."

"I have two children, both daughters. What about loving them—how does that fit in?"

"Protection. Love. It's the same thing. Just because we're humans, we perceive love as something stronger, or different from the rest of the species on the planet. Do we say that a mother lion loves her cubs, or that a father gorilla loves its baby? No. They protect them, feed them, care for them and teach them. We don't say they love them. Why so for humans? It's no different. We perceive it as different only because the emotions we have are so strong and we have a way of verbally expressing it in language. At an instinctive level, it's exactly the same for all the creatures of the earth, including humans."

Walker shrugged his shoulders. "I can't say you're wrong because I have no way of knowing if you are wrong or right. If you believe it to be true, then it is."

The words seemed to pass right by Dirk; it was as if he didn't hear them. "Speaking of love," Dirk said, pointing to a local girl sitting at a table all by herself, "I know that she's in love with you."

"Yeah, I bet she is. I'm sure that for a few dollars she would accept my love."

In his ever-present monotone and without stopping his surveillance for an instant, Dirk said, "I protect all the women you see in here. I provide a roof over their head and food when necessary, but I'm not their pimp. If the boys don't have a place to go, I will rent them a room. But what takes place between them and the girls, I don't get involved in. Both parties get what they need."

Dirk had just stated that he believed love and protection were the same thing. Walker wasn't about to draw that point to his attention. He suspected that Dirk had slept with all the local women that he protected.

"Her name is Lee. All the girls in here have Western names. It makes it easier." After a brief pause, Dirk continued. "Walker, don't be so judgmental. Last night after you left she told me how handsome she found you and that if you came back in, she wanted me to introduce you to her. I told her I would. Don't make a liar out me; that would spoil my reputation. I know this is personal for her. It's not business."

Walker did not look in Lee's direction; rather, he stared into Dirk's shifting eyes. "Before I agree to even talk with her, I want to know her real age."

Dirk showed no sign of deception when he said, "She's twenty-four, although she probably looks fifteen to you."

Walker believed him. To Walker, the Cambodian people all looked much younger than they were. Haing, his guide in Phnom Penh, looked to be in his late twenties or early thirties, but he was in his mid-forties. Lek looked to be a teenager, but was twenty-nine. The boy guides from his first day at Angkor were actually twelve and thirteen, despite looking seven or eight. So when he finally looked at Lee and thought she appeared to be about sixteen, twenty-four was likely correct.

"Okay. I'll talk with her." Dirk waved her over to come and sit beside the American.

Lovely, big brown eyes looked blankly at Walker and then looked

GOING BEYOND ONESELF

away, showing no hint of what she felt. She bowed her head and slowly glanced directly at Dirk, without changing her expressionless composure.

"I've been in Cambodia a long time and I don't know what it is with these people. They don't seem to feel anything. I suppose they have all been through so much trauma that their emotions have been stripped from them. They have lost the ability to feel anything. Combine that with Buddhist fatalism and nothing remains. They always stay so expressionless. Look at Lee. She shows no sign of excitement. For the last twenty-four hours, you were all she talked about. Now nothing."

Walker suggested a different reason. "In many cultures, stoicism is a sign of high stress. Khmer may be one of those cultures. The people of Cambodia have been under stress for so long, they probably don't remember any differently. It has become ingrained in their collective consciousness. Perhaps in the coming generations, if positive events continue to happen, their collective behavior will change and their expressions will return."

These comments challenged Dirk's view, but Dirk didn't argue it further. Instead he quipped, "Like you said, I can't say you're wrong because I have no way of knowing if you are wrong or right. If you believe it to be true, then it is."

Without debating Walker's point of view, Dirk had one-upped him. Walker simply responded, "Touché!"

Over and over, Lee refused Walker's offer to buy her food or beer. She spoke English better than any of the Cambodian women he had met. In rural areas, often only the boys went to school, while the girls stayed at home and learned domestic chores, so usually the women had no exposure to English. Lee's contact with foreigners made her different from most Cambodian women.

Shy and pretty, she had big dark oval eyes, long straight black hair, high cheekbones, a chiseled chin and a small nose. Like most

THE WORLDWIDE SEXUAL ADVENTURES OF WALKER FAYT

Cambodian women, she was petite, but unlike many of the local women she had a light complexion.

Lee did not ask any questions of Walker. She let him do all the asking. She seemed content to sit there in silence and listen to them talk or listen in on other trivial conversations with some of the other UN soldiers who sparked up a discussion. A mostly vacuous face could not hide her attraction to Walker. Her body language told a truer story. Even so, after forty long minutes of mostly silence and one-word answers, it became a bit tedious. Walker paid the bill, gave his farewells and left the restaurant.

About a hundred yards down the darkened street, Walker heard someone behind him. He turned and in the dim moonlight determined that someone was walking about ten yards back. The person slowed down. Walker turned on his flashlight and shone the beam in front of his own feet and continued on. He became suspicious, but not worried. Not wanting to show any sign of fear, he kept a steady pace. The sound of footsteps got closer and Walker knew that the person following had sped up. Suddenly Walker turned and shone the flashlight beam right in the face of someone only a few steps behind him.

"Lee, why are you following me?"

"I go with you. I stay with you."

"No, you go back to Dirk's. It's not right that you stay with me."

"I not safe alone. Please let me come with you."

"Okay then, I will walk with you back to Dirk's and then you will stay there, all right?" Walker tried to sound as kind as possible.

"You no like me. You no like me," she repeated over and over, bowing her head in sadness and hiding her face in her hands.

Uncertain as to what to do next, he thought of a compromise. "Lee, in my hotel room I have two beds. You sleep in one bed and I sleep in the other bed. Do you understand?"

"Yes, two beds, yes." She accepted whatever he wished.

Walker turned and walked toward his hotel. He slowed his pace, expecting her to fall in beside him. She did not and remained behind him, as any good subservient Cambodian woman would. He stopped walking so that she could catch up, but she stopped as well. He went back a few paces, stood beside her, put his arm on her shoulder and motioned for her to walk with him.

At this late hour they found no one in the hotel lobby. Except for a dim light at the end of the hall, all other lights were out. Walker went to his room on the ground floor just off the reception area. His eyes had adjusted to the dark and he didn't want to strain them by turning on the lights in his room. Nor did he wish to peer into Lee's longing eyes and try to resist them when he rejected her.

In a loving but firm tone, Walker said, "Lee, this is your bed for the night." He eased down on her shoulders with his hands, until she sat on the bed. "That's my bed over there. That's where I'm going to sleep and you're going to sleep here. You do understand?"

Even in the darkness, he could sense her disappointment and lack of understanding. Her voice filled with rejection the one-word response, "Yes."

Lee waited until he had prepared himself for bed and was lying in it before she lay down herself. Once they were both still, noise and movement occupied the room. Something wasn't right. At first Walker thought it came from outside; he soon realized it came from within the room. With tension rising in her voice, Lee called out: "Something in room!"

Walker's heart skipped a few beats and his breath stopped as a shadowy black figure flew through the air toward him. It grabbed hold of his neck. One or two seconds of confusion and terror seemed like forever, then he realized that Lee had jumped across the open space from her bed to his.

There was no other person in the room, but something moved about. Walker reached for the light switch. As Lee understood his movement she cried out, "No!" Too late, the light from above his bed flooded the room, and grasshopper-like insects bombarded them.

They knelt on the bed as the onslaught of bugs ricocheted off the light, the wall and them. The impact of insects against bare skin hurt, especially the ones that hit in the face. Lee bravely reached up and turned off the light and the assault stopped.

Turning off the fan had allowed the invaders to come through the vent. Understanding this, Walker left the bed and turned it back on. The blades began to whirl around, slowly at first and then faster and faster. Next he picked Lee up and carried her back to her own bed. He didn't want her to be attacked again when he turned the light back on. Putting his face to the wall, he flicked the switch and with equal force the bugs flew toward the light. Quickly he moved away, with only a few insects hitting him.

With his hiking boot, Walker proceeded to squash all the pests as quickly as he could. They were larger and darker brown in color than American grasshoppers. In death they made a crunching sound. To rid the room of the infestation required seventy-two such crunches.

A late night had been made even later and it took a long time to settle down after the bug incident. Despite a persuasive argument and a visual check, Lee could not be convinced that another invasion would not take place. She refused to sleep in her bed alone. Walker had his doubts about her fear, yet had no way to disprove it. Impatience and weariness gave way to acceptance and he agreed to sleep in the same bed.

Walker surrendered himself to Lee's wishes. She dominated all the sexual pleasuring and did not permit him to initiate any of the activity. He could not help but participate; his sexual arousal ensured that. Her pleasure came from pleasuring him. He understood this and did not attempt to satisfy her in any other way.

The tender aggressiveness Lee played out was based on her understanding of what she believed he wanted. She believed that he did not care about her needs, and she performed for his complete satisfaction. On a certain level she was correct, and she chose to focus and act upon it.

Lee gently pushed him back on the bed and fanned his face with her hands until he cooled. Then she caressed his face and hair with soft delicate strokes and playfully rubbed his lips and inserted her finger inside his mouth. She fanned, caressed and stroked different parts of his body.

As Walker drifted into sleep, Apsaras filled his vision. Physically there was only one girl, yet in his mind there were many and they danced across his body, intent on fulfilling his every need. Desires and wishes that had not been formulated in thought were extracted from his body by her touch and transformed into purposeful motion.

The Cambodian woman kissed, licked and gently bit all parts of Walker's body. Rhythm, comfort, pleasure and trust sent him close to sleep. He may have been asleep when she began to kiss, lick and suck his flaccid penis. Warm lips and a hot probing tongue soon changed his condition. Her spittle made his penis slick and she wrapped her hands around it and forcefully encouraged it to stiffness.

Tightening her grip at the base of his hardened dick, she stroked harder and faster and flicked her hot tongue across his purple head. Intensity ramped up to the point of finality. Her sensitive, instinctive touch understood, and she took it deeper inside her mouth. Persistent in its pleasuring desires, her tongue still stroked the muscular organ inside her mouth.

Without aim or accuracy and without intent or motive, Walker's semen shot to the back of Lee's throat. Walker was certain that they had both selflessly fulfilled each other's desires. He sensed that their sexual truths would dance until the darkness became dawn.

THE WORLDWIDE SEXUAL ADVENTURES OF WALKER FAYT

*

Lek did not appear unhappy when Walker informed him that he wished to tour the ruins only for the morning. Walker thought it unlikely that Lek would inform his superiors of the change in schedule. If he did, they might interrogate him about Walker's whereabouts. He assumed Lek would rather spend the time peacefully smoking, sleeping or, better still, surprising his wife with an afternoon visit.

They began at Preah Khan, a temple built in the late 1100s as a Hindu place of worship. Indications of later Buddhist dominion over the temple was evidenced by the deliberate removal of carved scenes depicting Hindu deities and epics, scratched away centuries ago. The two also went to the Preah Neak Pean, a temple dedicated to an intertwined naga. It was located in the exact center of a massive basin in the earth that had been used for purification rituals.

On the way back to the hotel for lunch, Walker smiled to himself, remembering some of Lek's phrases during the morning tour. The slow, carefully worded comments replayed in his mind. "Over here you can see one person more." He chuckled, remembering Lek pointing to a phallic symbol and trying to pronounce the English word, but speaking it the way it would read in Cambodian. "You know, *pallic* . . . it mean penis."

They arranged a nine o'clock pick-up for the following day. Lunch seemed empty with the large tour group gone and no other people to replace them. Walker arrived at Dirk's at about 1:45. The proprietor was nowhere to be seen and the place looked deserted. Louie drove in with a white UN four-by-four a few minutes later. Then Dirk appeared from the back carrying a large, old wooden box and greeted them both before going into the room off the bar. Out he came with two AK-47s and a couple of pistols.

"Ammo is a bit dear, so I might have to charge you a few dollars,

GOING BEYOND ONESELF

depending on how much you want to pop off." Walker and Louie nodded their acceptance.

They traveled for a few miles on a narrow road through the jungle. Louie drove while Dirk gave directions from the passenger side. Walker bounced along in the back seat, not following the conversation in the front. It focused on the history and performance of the weapons they were about to shoot. After a sharp right turn, they went left into a wide bend where the jungle gave way to an open space. Obviously it had been cleared for a specific purpose and Walker decided not to ask about it. Regardless of the possibilities, the space made an excellent place for target practice.

Louie's training allowed him to quickly inspect, load and test the weapon and he stood ready to fire. It frightened Walker even to touch the rifle or the ammunition. Dirk signaled to Louie that he could begin firing, and with the wave of his hand, bursts of loud gunfire filled the air.

Dirk suggested that Walker start with a pistol, and he loaded one up and handed it to him. Hesitantly Walker aimed at a distant tree and fired. The gun kicked back and he shot a few more times without knowing whether he had hit the tree target or not. Dirk shouted to be heard above the sound of gunshots.

"It doesn't take much to kill a man. All you have to do is squeeze a trigger. It's not that hard, is it Walker? You don't have to look into his eyes, see the blood or hear the air escaping from his lungs. They make it so easy for you."

"Shooting and killing are light years apart," Walker shouted back. He wanted to be sure that Dirk understood that he didn't buy into the South African's sentiments about a savage animal dwelling just beneath a thin layer of humanity.

"Really? Sure thing!" Dirk handed Walker a loaded AK-47 and showed him how to aim and hold it.

Raw power exploded into Walker's shoulder as he pulled the trigger.

THE WORLDWIDE SEXUAL ADVENTURES OF WALKER FAYT

Physically Walker easily absorbed the shock. Mentally he wasn't sure he was prepared to fire an assault weapon. Why had he accepted the invitation? What personality trait wanted to succeed at blasting targets a hundred yards away? He could not answer the questions he asked of himself.

Over the next couple of hours, they all fired both the rifle and the pistol. In between shooting episodes, Dirk patiently showed Walker aspects of both guns. Walker learned how to hold the weapons in order to achieve an accurate shot. He also learned how to load and unload them, how to clean them, how to safely check the working parts and how to carry them when not in use.

As a teacher, Walker recognized Dirk's great ability to instruct. He was efficient and his methods were effective. Louie wasn't interested in much other than shooting the rifle and practicing his accuracy, although again he mentioned his desire to find real action. Dirk didn't bite at his plea for a referral to a regional military contact. Walker believed that if Dirk gave his recommendation of someone, there was no doubt that they would be accepted into a militia group.

They were back at Dirk's place at about five o'clock. Walker felt weary yet exhilarated from the afternoon's expedition; Louie seemed less tired and Dirk didn't appear affected at all. Louie said he had some things to do before leaving the next day, but would be back that night. Walker hung out by himself, sipping on two complimentary beers.

After about an hour, just as it got dark, Louie returned and announced that he had officially moved out of his house and was ready to fly home the next morning at "zero-eight-hundred hours." An American woman in her early twenties accompanied Louie. She was neither attractive nor unpleasant; it was just that nothing about her made her stand out. They sat at a table by themselves, wanting to be alone on his last night.

GOING BEYOND ONESELF

Louie had been bringing Crystal around for a couple of weeks, Dirk gossiped in a quiet voice. The two dated, in a strange sort of way, he said. Crystal came from a super-rich family. Her father owned the majority of the shares of a Fortune 500 company on the New York Stock Exchange and was the company's president and CEO. Dirk couldn't remember which company, nor did he seem to care.

"It's rather sad. She has to run away from home and become a UN groupie to get attention. Her family and friends are probably worried sick. It's just what she wants. Now she can impress them with her stories of danger from a faraway land and can thrill all her rich friends with stories of the soldiers she has fucked. I'm sure her reputation as a commando-fucker will bring her lots of attention. The things people need to do to get noticed by the ones they love." Dirk shook his head and said no more.

Lee arrived and sat with Walker at the bar. Although she displayed little emotion, she seemed pleased to be around him and remained as silent as the night before. Several times Louie came up to the bar and mentioned to Dirk that he didn't have a place to stay that night. Dirk ignored him the first two times and on the third time replied, "I have plenty of room and you can stay if you wish, but she can't," and he tilted his head toward Crystal. Louie got the message.

Walker thought about offering them the spare bed in his room. But it would be awkward, trying to sleep in the same room with them on their last night together, probably their last night together ever. In their desperation to find a room, they'd accept it if offered, he thought.

Walker anticipated that Lee would follow him back to the hotel again and insist on staying the night. Tonight he wouldn't resist if she did. He thought it would be disrespectful to her to have another couple in the room with them. He knew she wouldn't complain

THE WORLDWIDE SEXUAL ADVENTURES OF WALKER FAYT

if he decided to do so. However, he did not wish to dishonor her and remained silent about the spare bed.

The night proceeded much the same as the previous one, except that this time Walker and Lee left together and remained side by side the entire way to the hotel. Sexual activity followed the same pattern as the night before. Lee dominated, based on her belief of what he wanted, and he let her do it, believing that was how she obtained her carnal satisfaction.

*

Walker's last scheduled day at Siem Reap was spent touring the ruins in the surrounding areas with Lek and the driver. In the morning they went to Preah Ko and Lolei, many miles from the main monuments of Angkor. Along the remote, bumpy, dirt road Walker couldn't help but think of the grisly images of the school bus that had run over the land mine.

The monuments they visited were built two to three hundred years before the main temples of Angkor, around 900 and 1000 AD. Unlike the earlier towers, these were made from bricks, not carved of sandstone. Rows of brick towers were built to honor the relatives of various kings, mostly their fathers, mothers and grandparents. The dying king must have assumed that the tradition would continue and that his son or grandson would one day build a monumental brick tower to deify his life on earth.

Many of the towers had inscriptions in Sanskrit written atop and alongside the doorways. Lek explained that most of the script had not been deciphered. Their meanings were lost long ago and remained a mystery to modern-day scholars.

Many children gathered at these monuments and it pleased Walker to see them playing instead of working in the nearby rice fields. He played hide-and-seek with some, as others dashed about wanting to attract attention in their own way. Big smiles, laughs and whistles filled the air. Against one of the walls an old woman sat silently watching all that transpired. As Walker ran after a young boy, they almost stumbled over her.

They stopped at precisely the same moment and looked at the woman's stump. The leg was gone from just above her knee—not that uncommon a sight in Cambodia. The effects of exploding land mines and Khmer Rouge torture remained visible throughout the country.

The boy's eyes became sad. He looked up at Walker, said "Pol Pot" and slid his finger across his throat, at the same time making a cutting sound. Sorrow and grief for the people of Cambodia filled Walker's awareness. He realized that most of his life had been lived with his head in the sand. His understanding of humanity's ruthless side had always been historical and academic. Witnessing first-hand pain, misery and human tragedy discomforted him to his roots. He lost a piece of his innocence as he saw the harsh reality reflecting in the young boy's eyes. They walked away slowly and then resumed their play.

Walker spent his last night in Siem Reap much the same way as he had the previous ones—at Dirk's eating burgers and drinking beer and hashing over Dirk's old war stories with Lee at his side. Near the end of the night, for a moment, Dirk became personal and told Walker that he had converted to Buddhism twelve years ago. As proof of his faith and dedication to it, he had become a monk for six months. He showed a picture of himself with his head shaved and wearing a monk's burnt-orange robe.

Dirk explained that reincarnation made sense. He did not believe that a human being could achieve all that needed to be achieved or learn all that needed to be learned in just one lifetime. Multiple lives were necessary. It made sense to Walker that Dirk would believe such concepts. Judgment based on one lifetime would not be kind to Dirk. It did not surprise him that Dirk had converted to a faith that was less definitive in its rules and where more than one chance at a successful life was granted. He understood why Dirk longed for another shot at humanity, for a set of circumstances far different from his current lot, with different lessons to be learned and other burdens to carry.

Walker shook Dirk's hand about nine o'clock that night, never expecting to see him again. He felt grateful for Dirk's acquaintance and told him so. Dirk let it pass without acknowledging that a compliment had been delivered. Walker sensed that Dirk had appreciated the comment, even if he did not have the ability to express himself.

To further complete his last evening, Walker wanted to ensure that Lee experienced self-worth from something more than pleasuring a man. He decided that before the night was over, she would be demonstrative in her sexual satisfaction. When, back at his hotel, she resisted his advances and tried to get him to accept her pleasuring, he forced the issue. Soon she acquiesced to his domination and let him disrobe her.

Walker kissed the back of her neck, then moved down her back and lingered kissing her buttocks. He rolled her over and worked his way up her stomach to consume her small breasts. His tongue crossed back and forth between delicate tenderness and savage passion.

Everything about Lee was slight and Walker's size emphasized it. When she was lying on her back, her breasts almost disappeared into her chest and her little dark nipples stood erect and hard. He paid relentless attention to her nipples. Lee sighed and moaned and rubbed her hands between her legs. He felt her body tremble as her fingers glided across her clitoris. Then he slid his tongue down her sweaty torso until he reached her small, light patch of pubic hair.

Lee's body heaved, and she spread her legs as Walker moved farther down. He pushed his face into the pink fleshiness of her womanhood, then inserted his pointed tongue far into her vagina.

GOING BEYOND ONESELF

She dripped with a wetness that tasted delicate and sweet. As Lee cried out in delight, he moved away slightly and gently used his fingers to spread her labia, exposing her swollen clitoris to the air and his approach. Again he alternated between soft tenderness and hard passion.

Prolonged, delicate strokes from Walker's tongue and lips produced an extended orgasm. After a minute or two, a time of recovery, she broke all of her upbringing, training and traditions and made a request of her male partner. "Fuck me . . . please."

Readying himself to fulfill the request, Walker stripped naked and put on the condom that he had set out. It did not seem possible that such a tiny woman could handle what he possessed. Drenched in sexual excitement, however, she took it all. At first he pumped sensitively, not wanting to hurt her in any way. After a few moments, she turned the intercourse into a frenzy of wild roughhousing.

Lee rolled him onto his back, straddled his penis and rode it deep into her body. Kneeling at times, squatting at other times, she played his stiff cock like a musical instrument until she reached her second orgasm. Then, still wanting more, she went to her hands and knees and begged him to enter her doggy style. Walker rammed his battle-weary, beaten, sore and engorged dick in and out of her. After a dozen strokes holding her bony hips from behind and slamming his pelvis against her slender butt, he came with a great shudder.

They fell asleep with her wrapped in his arms, lying on his chest. It seemed almost the next instant that Walker awoke to the light of day. Lee was not around. He looked at his watch that lay on a small table beside the bed. It was 7:30. Lek and the driver were scheduled to pick him up at 9:30 and drive him to Siem Reap Airport for an 11:30 flight back to Phnom Penh. He used the next half hour to shower, dress and pack.

After breakfast, Walker sat in front of his hotel and waited for the driver. Leaving Siem Reap and then Cambodia the next day filled him with mixed emotions. He did not particularly wish to depart, yet at the same time he looked forward to getting back to the amenities of Bangkok. He realized how far he had come: a month prior, Bangkok had represented a place of chaos and now he viewed it as civilization.

Walker planned ahead. He would collect his other bag held in storage at the hotel in Bangkok, stay a few more days and make arrangements for his next destination. He had decided on Australia.

Basking in the bright sunshine, he sat on the front steps of the hotel and thought about Lee. What had made her leave? She had not done so the other mornings they were together. He thought that perhaps she felt ashamed at having allowed herself to indulge in her own sexual gratification.

Walker wished for a chance to say goodbye to her. With that thought in mind, he glanced up and saw her running down the road sobbing, tears streaming down her face. He jumped up to meet her, thinking that the joys of the previous night had turned into today's trauma. Prepared to comfort her and make the necessary soothing comments of an emotional goodbye, he stood with his arms ready to embrace her.

When Lee fell into Walker's extended arms, he felt something other than lover's sorrow from her. It dawned on him that the Cambodian people buried their emotion in stoicism and that she would never openly express her feelings toward him. Quickly he realized that another issue caused her to quiver against his body.

Amidst tears, gasps for air and broken English, he pieced together a story. The Khmer Rouge had kidnapped Lee's younger sister and eight other young girls. They would be subjected to rape, assault and malnutrition and be forced into prostitution to raise money for their captors. The girls would not survive long under such conditions. Her sister was only thirteen; a few of the other girls were younger than that. Lee begged Walker to help them.

Walker's intuition told him he must assist her, and he stilled his mind for direction. He could not do it alone, he quickly realized; he picked up his bag and began walking to Dirk's place. Along the way, he tried to gather as many facts from Lee as she could manage. At the same time, he thought about the confusion that Lek would be plunged into. Under the circumstances it was an unfortunate necessity.

Walker could have left a message for Lek at the front desk, but that would have cut his lead time with the authorities. By leaving no trail, he extended the period before which an official search would begin. He envisioned that Lek would first have the room checked. When there were no signs of him and it was obvious that he had packed and left, Lek would go to the hotel where the meals were offered. Then he would go to the airport, assuming that Walker had found another driver. Boarding passes would be counted and finally the plane would be searched.

At this point, Lek would inform his superiors at Angkor Tourism of a missing guest. There would be a scramble to double-check Lek's information and, once it was verified, the army and other Cambodian government agencies would be informed and a search would be mounted.

Walker guessed that was at least three hours away, maybe more, and he planned to make the best possible use of that time. This was Cambodia—perhaps he could buy the girls' freedom and still be on time for take-off. If not, then he needed Dirk's expertise. Things were quiet at the restaurant and Lee showed him Dirk's private room. He banged on the door.

Dressed only in boxer shorts, Dirk swung the door open. Inside was sparse: two chairs, a dresser, a bed and a door to a bathroom. A white sheet covered a young woman from the restaurant. Dirk did not look amused.

"What is it?"

Before Walker could answer, Lee sobbed and babbled in Cambodian. Dirk glared into Walker's eyes with his cold blue stare. It lasted much longer than his normal look at anything. Then he spoke while continuing to stare.

"This doesn't concern us. Why aren't you on a plane out of here?"

"I'm going to help. If you're not, at least give me a gun and some bullets."

"Don't be a fucking idiot. Just because you got a little sucky-fucky doesn't mean you're her hero. Getting killed for her sister is just plain fucked. This is no goddamn game. Wake up, asshole. You're not that committed, and this is way over your head."

Adrenaline pumped through both men's veins; Walker could see Dirk's systems tuning into assault mode, all of his senses priming for performance. But Walker couldn't tell whether it was aimed against him or the captors. He challenged Dirk's manhood to find out.

"I'm going to give life back to those girls. Are you with me, or are you all talk?" Walker turned and headed toward the restaurant.

"Hey, Rambo!" Walker stopped and looked back as Dirk continued. "You're so fucking lucky that these guys are enemies of the people I currently work for."

"And if they weren't?"

A slight smirk broke across Dirk's face, yet he remained silent. Walker didn't know how to read it. Either it meant that if the kidnappers were his current employers there was no way Walker would be going anywhere, or that, employer or no employer, Dirk had his principles and would be doing it anyway.

In a flash, Dirk dressed and loaded a blue van with weapons and ammunition and devised a tactical plan. He put Lee in charge of the restaurant—she sobbed "thank you" many times as they prepared to leave. Tears rolled down her cheeks as they drove away.

GOING BEYOND ONESELF

frightened him because, despite their beliefs and their prayers, millions of them had still died in battle.

Courage above fear, courage in his beliefs, courage in his necessity swirled together like the winds of a hurricane. Walker touched the aquamarine stone that hung around his neck and he seemed to drift into the center of an eerie calm. Being used and betrayed by the woman who gave it to him still stung. Yet for some unknown reason he had not discarded it. Treasures had been unearthed and polished in order to add a stepping stone to his path. He now used its properties to mine the courage he so desperately needed.

Connecting epiphanies and insights with thoughts and actions from his past focused Walker's attention into a point of clarity. Following his truth had led him to this event, and Indeara had proclaimed that he had the strength, wisdom and power to fulfill his karma. Success or failure, life or death would measure its completion. Now everything made sense. He had arrived at his purpose and his fate.

The twenty minutes passed, and Walker's fear began to lift. Every cell in his body seemed tuned to the frequency of fulfillment. Distractions outside his purpose did not exist. Universal love flooded his being a million times with each breath, slowing the pace of his reality into eternities per second. He kept checking his watch to reconfirm that more time hadn't elapsed.

Weapon in hand, Walker made it to the edge of the clearing. Just as Dirk had explained, there were two large huts off the ground and a smaller one about eighty feet behind them. Outside the hut, one guard sat on the ground, leaning against the wall. He appeared to be asleep. Two rifles stood upright along the bamboo wall the hut.

Logic suggested that he might be able to sneak up on the man and secure the position. In his acutely aware state, he held no place for rational thought; instinct told him to follow the plan. Walker stayed hidden and set the sights of his rifle on the man's chest.

THE WORLDWIDE SEXUAL ADVENTURES OF WALKER FAYT

An explosion pierced the tranquility of the jungle with a deafening boom and rocked the ground and air as one side of the communications hut shattered into splinters and began to burn. Flames rose into the sky, then black smoke too.

Walker's target pounced to the ground, grabbed a gun and crawled on his belly inside the hut. This had not been planned for and the enormity of Walker's next move gripped him like a noose. With each passing second the tension mounted and he raced over options not previously discussed. He waited and waited. After about a minute, two men emerged from the hut. The man without a gun grabbed his and they ran toward the explosion.

Walker could hear shooting and sensed confusion. Another grenade went off in the jungle area in front of the shacks. A vehicle with armed men drove off toward the explosion. He crawled along the ground, focusing only on his destination.

Before Walker got to the opening of the hut, the stench of human urine told him of people inside. He heard muffled cries and moans. As he cleared the doorway, he saw streams of light shining through the bamboo strapping and, huddled together against the back wall, many small bodies. When he entered, all their sounds stopped. His fear paled in comparison to the terror that consumed the children. He slung the rifle around to his back and let it hang by its strap. He put out his hand and smiled.

"Hello, I am your friend."

As Walker came closer, many of the girls cowered tighter against the wall. The smallest of them, and probably the youngest, reached out and grasped his hand. She was so innocent and so gentle, he thought. He pulled her up from her hell, off the damp stinky dirt, and held her tight to his chest. She rested her head against his shoulder.

Outstretching his other hand, Walker coaxed the other girls to move away from the wall. None of them budged. Leaning over, he gently tugged at their arms. They pulled away, whimpering. Still holding the first girl tightly, he felt the pounding of her heart against his chest, and decided to trust his instincts. He headed for the door.

As he left the shack with the small Oriental girl in his embrace, she said something in Cambodian. Her words prompted the other girls to follow. Once outside, they clutched onto any piece of Walker's clothing that they could grab hold of. At a steady walk, then a slow jog, he led them to the path in the jungle. Its narrowness did not allow them all to keep their hold of him, so some let go and followed behind. Seeing this as an advantage, he began to run.

Dirk's warning had been right. The distance through the jungle seemed to take forever. Gunfire and the pounding of his heart dominated his hearing. Every so often he glanced back to see if everyone followed. Finally the jungle broke and a two-prop plane glistened in the sun. The roaring engine and whirling propellers blanketed all other sounds.

Three bodies lay still on the ground beneath the plane. Walker ran as fast as he could and pulled the clinging girl from his body and set her through the doorway of the plane. He motioned for the other girls to hurry and one by one he picked them up and tossed them in the open door. The last three girls ran toward him.

Three men at the edge of the jungle fired their weapons. Walker seemed to see the bullets discharge from the guns, travel toward the girls and ricochet off the ground at their feet, creating dust pellets. Engaging his weapon, he returned fire and witnessed all three of the men dive toward the ground. He had no idea if any of them were hit or if they had only taken cover. When he looked back, the first two of the girls were climbing into the airplane. Another lay on the ground about twenty feet in front of him, screaming, with blood gushing from her leg. She seemed to be screaming out of fear of being left behind more than out of pain.

As Walker made his way to the wounded girl, gunfire resumed.

THE WORLDWIDE SEXUAL ADVENTURES OF WALKER FAYT

He dropped his rifle and replaced it with the girl. Picking her up, he ran toward the plane as it moved away from him, gaining speed.

Two steps into his run, the shooting closed in on his position. Dirt flew up around him as bullets hit the places he had just stepped. One bullet whizzed through his legs and others by his ears. At a full sprint, he reached the opened door of the moving plane. With one hand he grabbed the rod that ran from the wing to the body of the plane. One foot dangled while his other foot stepped onto a rung. With one arm he lowered the limp girl inside the fast-moving airplane. A powerful jolt struck him in the back. Air pounded from his lungs and stunned him into unconsciousness.

The sounds of bullets hitting the body of the plane and either passing through or deflecting off the metal frame revived Walker. He reached out and pushed as many heads down as he could. Shortly they were out of range and the only sound was the roar of the engine. Slowly gathering his wits, Walker checked the leg of the girl who had been shot. The bullet must have just grazed her or rebounded off a rock. The wound showed a lot of blood, but the bullet wasn't lodged in her leg.

Walker moved to retrieve the first-aid kit from his backpack. He was sore and exhausted, and it pained him to get the straps off his shoulders. His eyes widened at the sight of the black hole in the center of his pack. He opened it up and pulled out his camera; the steel-case body had been blown apart. Without pausing for reflection on how lucky he was to be alive and how ironic Dirk's instructions had been, he unpacked the medical kit and did the best he could dressing the girl's wound.

Moving up to the co-pilot's seat, Walker plunked himself down. Dirk tilted his head, raised his eyebrows, widened his eyes and confided. "I didn't think we'd get this far, but now that we have, here's the second part of the plan. Before I go on, you look no worse for wear. Did everybody make it?"

GOING BEYOND ONESELF

"We've got nine. I hope that was all of them. One of the girls is injured and will need a doctor. Put that into your plans."

Walker, who in the past minutes had reached down far past his everyday mind, beyond his ego, now found himself experiencing a state of divine love, drawn from a reservoir available not only to him but to all of humanity. Transformed into a spirit of providence, he sat and watched the jungle rush past below them and listened to Dirk's plan.

*

In the second part of his scheme, Dirk—who had lived up to his own billing and proved to Walker he wasn't just hype—had set in motion a series of events that played as beautifully as a Mozart concerto. Masterfully he had done it from the shadows without anyone, other than Walker and a Thai general, ever knowing or discovering his complete involvement. His plan involved calling in military favors, playing international politics and manipulating the media.

While they were still in Cambodian airspace, Dirk had gotten on the plane's radio. With the use of some highly restricted code words, he had been connected directly to a Thai general who controlled northeast Thailand. Apparently Dirk and the general went back a long way and he owed Dirk some favors. They had arranged a landing at a remote army base along the Thailand-Cambodia border, south of Surin.

Neither Walker nor Dirk had risked their lives only to have the girls end up on the streets. Without the proper attention, they could have easily wound up on Patpong Road or even worse. The Red Cross operated from a refugee camp near the base and through the same general, Dirk had arranged for treatment and placement of the girls.

Through diplomatic channels, Dirk had gotten Walker a meeting with the American ambassador to Thailand, as well as with his wife and two teenage daughters. Attacks on U.S. embassies had raised fears with many foreign diplomats and Dirk had advised Walker that by exploiting this insecurity, he stood a better chance of getting them onside with the plan. It had worked. The ambassador and especially his wife were sympathetic because of delicately placed references to their daughters and how lucky they were to be safe.

Fear may have been the ignition, but political astuteness accelerated the engine. Once revved up, there was no shutting it down. The ambassador had recognized a great story when he heard one. He could shine some glory in his direction as well as make the U.S. look good in the international media.

Walker had guessed rightly that the more attention focused on the event, the less likelihood there was of it going awry, at least in the short term. In the midst of the fanfare, he had discovered that Lee's sister had been among the girls they had rescued. Once the story broke internationally, all the parties had tripped over themselves to grab the spotlight.

American and Thai government agencies had battled over who had the right to place these girls in good homes. The international press had interviewed several Red Cross workers. Their concerns had focused on the treatment of the girls and the progress of their placements. The Cambodian government had used the incident as rhetoric against the Khmer Rouge. The affair had helped support the position of those who were against the exoneration of Khmer Rouge leaders. The United Nations tribunal looking into Cambodian atrocities had reiterated its plea for justice.

Walker had entered Thailand illegally; however, when he had flown into Bangkok aboard a Thai army helicopter, he had been officially admitted to the country with diplomatic hoopla. Throughout the ordeal, with help from the Thai general and the American ambassador, Walker and Dirk had maintained their anonymity from the international press. Dirk and Walker both wanted it kept that way. As long as they stayed in Thailand, however, that became harder to manage. From the background, Walker had watched the events unfold and the story gain momentum. Dirk had quietly disappeared.

Compliments of the U.S. government, the ambassador had offered Walker an airline ticket to anywhere he wished to go. Walker appreciated the offer, but also understood that having Dirk and him out of the picture allowed the ambassador to maintain his position as spokesman for the story.

Two days after the ambassador's offer, Walker took off from Bangkok International Airport bound for Sydney, Australia. He needed to rest, and Sydney, being far from anyplace else, seemed like a good place to go. Once settled in the plane, he got out his journal to write.

January 27

En Route to Sydney

> It began when I was a teenager—a feeling that I would someday be called upon to perform some deed involving a greater part of myself. At sixteen and seventeen, I remember dwelling on it. Instinctively I knew this deed would involve danger and threaten my life. Somehow I knew that my actions would be a gift provided in total disregard for my safety, sanity and previous life experience. It would be a test of my worthiness, and if I achieved it, I would then have the right to call myself a complete human being.
>
> The only person I ever told about this precognition was Marlene. I remember mentioning it to her shortly after we were married. She responded in a loving, but rational way. In one of her psychology courses she had learned that many people have similar notions, but few are willing to admit to them.

THE WORLDWIDE SEXUAL ADVENTURES OF WALKER FAYT

Marlene thanked me for sharing it with her, then told me that some researchers believed such thoughts represented the recognition of our individual potential—an understanding that there are higher levels beyond our current consciousness. She believed that it was a way for my subconscious to express fulfillment of my future. This included our lives together and a family that was yet to come. After a while I passed it off as American hero-worship—too many John Wayne movies. I had forgotten all about it until today.

These premonitions from my youth have now blended with my epiphany from mid-life; all predestined outcomes have been satisfied. The reason for my journey has been discovered.

chapter 15

DEATH OF A FATHER
Home Again, and a Dark Detour into Ménage à Trois

Walker arrived in Sydney completely spent. He had planned to rest for a week before heading out to explore other parts of this vast country. Australia, at ninety-six percent the size of the continental United States, was big and Walker wanted to immerse himself in the experience. He wished to see everything from the 1,250-mile-long Great Barrier Reef to the deserts of the outback in the Northern Territory to the misty isolation of Tasmania.

The exhausted traveler spent the first twenty-four hours sleeping; he took only brief breaks for room service and the bathroom. On the second day, he went to the American Express office to check for any international messages. It surprised Walker to find a message from Marlene. He stood stunned as he read the words telling him of his father's death. A massive heart attack had claimed Roger the day Walker had arrived in Sydney.

The funeral had been tentatively scheduled for three days hence, but that depended upon locating the only son. Walker thought that if his father had died a week earlier, only after the funeral would he have found out about it. The notion of missing the funeral distressed him and he called his mother immediately.

THE WORLDWIDE SEXUAL ADVENTURES OF WALKER FAYT

Walker's mother, Jessica, hid her grief by focusing on how happy she was to hear from him. She mentioned the package from Thailand and the many nice postcards he had sent. Eventually he mentioned the funeral. Roger had been her husband for the last forty-seven years, and Jessica began to break down and cry.

Walker heard relief in her voice when she came to understand that he would be back for the funeral, that none of the arrangements had to change on his account. In her bitter grief and shock, she seemed unstable and her condition concerned him. In thirty hours, he could comfort her the way she used to comfort him. She had always been close by when, as a child, he had been awakened by a nightmare and needed comforting. It seemed a long time before he'd be home.

January 30

Kingsford Smith Airport, Sydney, Australia

I have swelled and crested, risen as the next wave, the next generation. I am ready to crash onto the beach, to make a temporary mark in the sand. Millions have reached the beach before me and millions will come after. Each wave is linked and each wave is important. My moment is now—I feel the creative force in me that is existence curling into form and then breaking into white water. I mix with air and light at the apex of my individuality and then meet the sand. Next will come the final fizzle into non-existence and a return to the sea of eternity and oneness.

My father has died. Unlike the Khmer royal families of ancient times, my family doesn't build towers to honor our parents. Our custom is that the son gives a eulogy—words to capture a father's life; in this case, a life so connected to my own, it is impossible to measure its influences.

DEATH OF A FATHER

The route home would take Walker from Sydney to Honolulu, Honolulu to San Francisco, San Francisco to Chicago, and Chicago to Appleton. During the first section of the trip, mixed emotions and memories surfaced. In his weariness, the somber ones seemed to stand out and linger longer than the positive ones.

Walker thought about life's progression. His grandfather on his father's side had passed away when Walker was nine. He remembered being sad not for himself, but for his father. He didn't know his paternal grandparents that well and remembered thinking at the time, "Old people are supposed to die. It's no big deal."

As Walker contemplated his grandfather's death, he recalled old feelings. As a nine-year-old, he had been more frightened than sad. He came to the realization that if his dad's father had just died, then someday his own father would die. The next year when his paternal grandmother died, he went through the whole gamut of emotions again, worrying about losing his mother.

When Walker's maternal grandparents passed away, the Fayt family lived in Toronto and they had to travel to Milwaukee for the funerals. The services happened a year apart, when Walker was in grades ten and eleven. On both occasions, he missed several days of classes and he remembered explaining to the vice-principal that he had been away for a funeral. Both times the vice-principal had responded by saying, "A funeral only takes an hour; why were you gone for days?" Walker had answered simply, "It was out of town."

As a teenager Walker didn't want to display any weakness. Showing grief, pain, sadness or even a flicker of emotion about the death of his grandparents, he believed, would make him appear weak. So he left out the detail that it had been his grandparents' funerals he had attended. Being frightened at the possibility of losing his parents did not seem manly. So he buried any such fears until he wasn't aware they existed.

First his grandparents, and now his father. Walker's own mortality hovered around him like a bad dream. He was next in line. Distant memories from his childhood refreshed themselves in haunting clarity.

Between the ages of four and six, Walker remembered on numerous occasions staring into the sky and putting himself into a trance thinking about whether he was mortal or immortal. Paradoxical concepts filled his young mind. Since he lived, someday he must die. He wondered why that was, and he thought about the difference between being alive and being dead. In this self-hypnotic state, long periods of time passed and he grappled with what it felt like to be dead. During these times he remembered pinching his body to ensure that he still lived. He could not believe it would ever be otherwise and he became transfixed by a sense of immortality. During and shortly after these episodes of life-and-death searches, he had always felt strangely wonderful.

Upon achieving the age of reason, at around seven, these internal journeys into what it meant to be alive or dead stopped. From about age seven through ten, Walker remembered trying to induce his life-and-death trances, without success. On such occasions he could only conjure the memory of what it had been like; he never actually made it back to that place.

Since turning eleven, that place and all its wondrous sensations had never once crept into his consciousness, not even as a memory. Now as he approached San Francisco en route to his father's funeral, he rediscovered the memory of it. He marveled at the mind's ingeniousness at storing and retrieving memories.

In Walker's early twenties, he understood the notion of doing battle with his own death. He envisioned that his death hovered over the back of his right shoulder, always present, stalking, waiting patiently for its chance to strike. The superstition of throwing salt over one's shoulder must have had its basis in the notion of keeping death at bay, he thought.

DEATH OF A FATHER

At first the concept of death hovering nearby frightened him and caused many bone-chilling shivers in those lonely moments after a nightmare or a terrifying movie. Eventually it developed into an uplifting concept and provided him with a sense of enthusiasm. If his death lurked behind him ready to strike, then he could look forward and live life to the fullest. He realized that he could not dictate the time and place when his death would attack him, and he decided not to worry about it. Instead he chose to focus his attention on his life and allow his mortality to become a source of constant inspiration.

During moments of inner strength, he turned and challenged his death; he planned skirmishes that would be arranged on his own terms. These duels made him stronger in life and he believed they prepared him for the time when death would ultimately conquer him. He stopped these encounters at about twenty-two.

Now in mid-life, Walker knew that to achieve happiness on the journey into old age, he needed to reassess, re-engineer and restructure his life path. His mortality once again provided the impetus for doing so. During the flight from Sydney to San Francisco, he wrote the first part of his father's eulogy in his travel journal.

January 30

Somewhere over the Pacific Ocean—en route to Appleton

Eulogy: Working Draft

(Introductions—Acknowledge Mom, girls, Tracy and family and friends)

It is with sadness and joy that I stand before you today. Sadness because a man that I love and respect is no longer here to guide me. And joy because I'm able to celebrate a life created and lived to its full potential.

I believe that in the moment before we pass from this life to

THE WORLDWIDE SEXUAL ADVENTURES OF WALKER FAYT

the next, whatever each of us believes that to be, our life in its completeness will be reflected back to us. In that instant, all that is important to us is held before us in its totality. In this stage of final self-judgment, I believe that the only thing we will value as eternal will be the relationships in our lives.

Material possessions, money invested, career accomplishments will all be deconstructed and will vanish. What will remain is the intangible nature of our relationships. There is nothing that we can do now for my dad, Roger. Funeral services, in whatever form they take, are for the living. All of us are gathered here today in recognition of a relationship—either directly with him, such as family, friends and business associates, or in support of someone who knew and loved my father.

My daughters, Petra and Amy, have many of their old friends here, and many of my former colleagues from the high school are here as well, and it brings me great joy to see strong relationships in force.

At times we think we control events; we do not. What becomes important is how we choose to view them. Although my loss is great, at this moment I choose to see it as an opportunity to reflect on the many significant relationships in my life and as a chance to make them even stronger.

I have no way of knowing when my time will come. When it does, I want the quality of my relationships to be strong, so that I can enter the next life healthy. I hope all of you see this as an opportunity to do the same. Think of it as a way of celebrating my father's life in order to make your own richer. I know he would treasure such an act as a gift to his memory.

I will now take some time and speak about my father's life and some of the important relationships that I know he cherished.

(Complete later)

DEATH OF A FATHER

Marlene waited at the baggage carousel as Walker entered the arrivals area of Outagamie County Airport. He hadn't expected her; he had planned to take a taxi to his parents' house. Shock and uncertainty, joy and sadness rocketed through his mind and body. The sight of her stunned him into inaction. She stared with tears in her eyes. Except for some redness around her eyes, she looked very good. He dropped his bag and she walked slowly toward him, gradually opening her arms up to give him a hug. She spoke softly: "Walker, I'm so sorry."

They embraced tightly and rocked back and forth for several minutes, not saying a word. Their tears soaked each other. When the intensity of their energy exchange reduced to the point where she could speak, Marlene whispered, "Walker, I haven't forgiven you. At times I hate you, at times I can forget you, but I still—" She didn't finish.

Backing away, Walker's former wife looked him up and down, managed a smile through her tears and definitively stated, "Walker, you look like shit—and you don't smell that good either. We have to get you out of here; you're an embarrassment."

The comment broke the ice and they both chuckled. Walker quipped, "You look beautiful and I don't want to ruin your reputation." He sniffed his armpits, saying, "I agree, I am an embarrassment. Let's get the hell out of here."

Marlene insisted on carrying his daypack and noticed the bullet hole and inquired about it. Walker passed it off as being "a long story" and said he wanted to discuss more important matters about home.

On the way from the airport to Walker's parents' house, Marlene updated him about the heart attack and then about the funeral arrangements. She then spoke about Jessica and the difficulty she was having dealing with her loss. The twenty-minute drive did not allow enough time to discuss all the crucial matters that needed to be dealt with. Marlene stopped the car about five minutes from the house so they could talk more. By her change in tone he knew she had something both difficult and important to say.

"Walker, before you face anyone, there are some things that you need to know that you probably aren't aware of."

Walker's throat became instantly dry and he swallowed deeply, trying to get relief. Marlene hesitated, not knowing how to continue.

" . . . I know that you have been to Africa and I'm sure that almost everyone in the country does as well. The rest of the country may not care, but the people in Appleton sure do. And . . . well . . . some of them may be downright hostile. Many of them feel insulted and betrayed."

Walker had felt exhausted, jet-lagged, emotionally drained, grief-stricken and nervous all at the same time. Now dizziness waved through his head and he felt faint. He had no idea what else could be coming. He spoke lightly, "I don't get it; you'll have to explain."

"When you were on safari in Uganda . . ." Still he stared blankly. " . . . it was all taped and a U.K. television tabloid made a show out of it. Do you remember any of this? It was you—wasn't it? Because it certainly looked and sounded like you."

The weary man mustered enough energy to nod while she went on. "Well, a U.S. television show picked it up and broadcast some segments of it."

The reality of it all seemed to pass him by, so Marlene continued. "Footage of you fighting over a woman; the recorded conversations of you explaining the need to seek sexual experiences; the noises of you two having sex played loud and clear. On top of that, they hooked into the whole racial thing. . . ."

Walker felt stretched well beyond the point of being able to get upset. Emotional feelings and rational thought bundled to form a strange mixture. He believed in himself and if people loved him and were really his friends, they would believe in him and seek truth before judgment.

Marlene continued. "I taped it. You should watch it before you see anybody. I also got a video of the BBC show. It runs about fifteen minutes and is even more damning than the piece that ran in the U.S. If I was able to get a copy of it, I'm sure other people in town could have. After the national spots aired, the local media picked up on it. If anyone in town didn't know you before, they certainly do now. Walker, you're infamous."

Walker put up his hand to stop her from going on. "How are Petra and Amy handling it?"

"Amy—well she's Amy; she seems to take everything in stride. She definitely wants to hear your side of the story before she believes any of it. True or not true, I don't think she'll be that hurt as long as she gets to talk to you about it. Petra—well, that's a different story. Don't be surprised if she doesn't talk to you for a long time."

Walker sighed and contemplated the idea of having caused so much devastation in his daughter's life. His destiny ensured that he would save nine girls from a gruesome existence, yet it also ensured that he devastate his daughter by other events that led him to that point. How could he ever get her to understand? Perhaps he could not, and that pained him deeply.

The traveler turned his gaze back to Marlene and changed focus for the moment. Walker had spent more of his life with her than not, and he still loved and cared for her. "Marlene, how about you? How are you coping?"

"What I said to you at the airport is true. Despite that, I think you should know . . ." She paused for a long time and he knew her words were difficult to select. "I was at a medical conference in San Diego . . . and it just happened. We've seen each other a couple of times since then."

Walker cut her off with a wave of his hand. "Marlene, say no more. You don't owe me an explanation. You're a beautiful, intelligent, vibrant woman in the prime of your life. I didn't think about this happening, but I should have expected it. Please, no worries. "

Deep in the pit of Walker's stomach, it felt as though an atomic bomb had exploded. A giant mushroom cloud filled with radiation quickly expanded throughout his body, delivering a deadly sickness to each cell that it reached, poisoning him at the molecular level and eliminating his chances at a healthy life. He hid his distress as best he could.

The brilliant, light-filled insights and the joy of following his epiphany to its conclusion overlapped now with Walker's realization that he had been blind to the many consequences of following it. He wanted to combine opposing realities into a unified source of well-being. To do so, he needed to reconcile these two polar forces. At the moment, he could only manage a simple request.

"Marlene, please take me to Mom's. I'm sure she's getting worried."

*

Amy returned from UCLA and, without question, decided to stay at her grandmother's house. Petra's decision to stay at her mother's condominium was just as decisive. As usual, Marlene's assessment of their daughters' actions and states of mind had been accurate.

Many friends called on the telephone and offered Walker short condolences. He suspected there was more to the uneasiness in their voices than just searching for words to express their sympathy at his loss. People were nervous, not knowing whether he knew that they knew about his transgressions.

Walker decided not to watch the tapes that Marlene had provided. When he approached his friends, relatives and former colleagues and students, he did not want those images and sounds swirling in his head. If people specifically asked him about it, he would deal with it. Otherwise he'd ignore it and try not to let it interfere with relationships that he wished to renew.

The silent approach worked with his mother. In her withdrawn and grief-stricken state, she did not have the energy to address other issues. On the day before the funeral, Walker's sister Tracy came to the house. She apologized for the absence of her husband and two children. From her lame excuses, he understood that his brother-in-law, niece and nephew did not want to see him. She hammered the point home when she commented, "And Mom, they all said to tell you that they'll see you at the funeral," and made no mention of seeing Walker.

After that comment and others, Walker could not ignore the mounting tension any longer. Away from their mother, he and Tracy did not mince words. She accused him of betraying the family and all they believed in. She declared that his actions created so much stress for their parents that they had induced the heart attack. She invoked as much guilt as possible in her vicious verbal assault.

Amy heard the raised voices and came to investigate. As soon as she determined the situation, she jumped to the defense of her father.

The day before, Walker and Amy had spent hours talking late into the night. They had discussed many topics, ones that ordinarily would be welcome and routine. Under the pressing circumstances, they eased into more difficult areas. Eventually he described for her the insights that he had received earlier in his life. She seemed to identify most with the one about living life with no regrets and with no skeletons in the closet, because it had struck him while he carried her home from the playground sobbing.

This connection to her provided an opening to discuss the epiphany that had put him on the path of divorce and driven him to leave Appleton. If she had asked about the women her father had been with, Walker would have told her. He was grateful that she did not. He also revealed to her his involvement in the Cambodia story and his belief that it had been the reason for everything. His destiny lay in saving those girls, he explained.

Only two weeks earlier, the rescue and placement of the Cambodian girls had been the hottest media story in the U.S. Amy found it hard to believe that her father had been at the heart of the story. She was filled with a sense of love and pride for him, she said, and she wanted him redeemed. She wanted everyone to know and she planned to go to the media.

Walker calmed her down and asked that she respect his wishes for anonymity. He explained that he wished to reclaim the broken relationships in his life. To help him do that, he offered to take both Amy and Petra on separate trips of their choosing. It would be a perfect chance for them to get away and reunite. Walker wished for the trips to happen soon and hoped they could be scheduled around spring breaks.

Amy would accept the invitation and Petra would not, Walker suspected, and he needed Amy to act as a mediator. Perhaps she could convince Petra to embrace the idea. Amy suggested that if Petra knew the whole story, she might entertain the idea of going away with him. He agreed that she could tell Petra, but no one else. Amy consented.

Walker could feel his younger daughter's love and admiration for her father as she defended his honor against her aunt. Many times he could see the truth about Cambodia on the tip of Amy's tongue, because it would have sealed her argument, yet she refrained and it made him proud of her.

Tracy left upset. She loved her brother and knew there were missing pieces, yet she could not bring herself to trust her intuition about him. Instead she clung to the belief that he had betrayed the family, which then justified her negativity toward him.

*

Jessica sat in the first pew of the church, with Walker beside her. Amy sat beside him, between her father and her aunt. Other family members refused to sit in the front row and the rest of the pew remained noticeably vacant. In the second row sat Tracy's husband, Bill, her eldest, Bill Junior, and her daughter, Tammy. Petra and Marlene also sat in the second row.

Roger and Jessica had been popular in their church for many years and were respected members of the community, but this couldn't have accounted for the number of people attending the service. The church was filled to overflowing. Walker believed many of the attendees came to see how he would handle himself, rather than out of respect for his father.

Walker sat holding his mother's hand. He provided as much comfort as he could, but realized no amount of consolation could lift her burden of grief. Listening to the minister, he thought that no words either of the minister's making or from the scriptures could ease the loss to his mother or the family.

Then the time came for him to address the congregation. He could hear people holding their breath and feel the weight of their stares against his back as he left his mother's side and approached the pulpit. He turned and faced them, raised the microphone, took out his prepared speech, cleared his throat and began to speak.

Walker delivered his eulogy with force, conviction and compassion, and tears rolled down many cheeks. Some openly sobbed as he raised the emotional connection with his charged words. He saw tissues being passed around everywhere. Small teardrops fell from his eyes as he recounted stories of his youth and how much his father meant to him.

Among the stories were the times his father had taken Tracy and him to hockey games at Madison Square Garden. He spoke of the special loving bond between his mother and father. He mentioned Roger's reputation for being a brutally tough negotiator while at the same time remaining honest and operating with integrity. His approach had garnered the respect of his business associates.

With the skills he had been given, Roger had done his best to raise his children, Walker said, and he publicly absolved his father from any mistakes he may have unwittingly committed in that role. In a private place, Walker healed the associated childhood wounds. He knew the full extent of his father's love, and for the moment, he needed nothing more. He was proud to be his father's son.

The cold trip to the cemetery stripped away the strength Walker had gained from his speech. Each family member dropped a handful of dirt on top of the coffin. Jessica had neither the vigor nor the will to participate.

At the reception the family hosted in the church basement, the room filled with people and the effort of conversation drained Walker's energy. He had not anticipated how difficult this part of the day would be for him.

When his parents had first moved to Appleton, his father had needed a lawyer and Walker had recommended his friend, Jerry McIntyre. It turned out that Roger liked Jerry, so Jerry had handled Roger's legal needs throughout his retirement. Early in the reception, Jerry approached Walker.

Away from everyone, Jerry cleared his throat, straightened his tie and tugged on his collar. Acting as a professional, not as a friend, he told Walker that his father did not approve of Walker's recent life choices. It seemed that Roger no longer trusted Walker's judgment and had removed him as the executor of his will. Jerry had been asked to fulfill that role. He apologized and said that he was only following Roger's wishes.

Jerry said he had scheduled a meeting for the upcoming Monday, at ten in the morning, to go over the contents of the will. Preferably all family members, including Marlene, should attend. Attendance wasn't absolutely required, so if Jessica wasn't up for it or if the girls needed to get back to school, it didn't create a problem. Jerry had set a similar meeting with Tracy, Bill and their children for Monday afternoon.

Walker and Jerry shook hands without ever speaking as friends. Jerry had handled Walker's divorce and now his father's will. Lawyers were so immersed in people's unpleasantness, Walker thought, their high fees didn't surprise him.

Throughout the afternoon, condolences were genuine, but the comments of "Good to see you back," "Hope you can stay," and "Let's get together soon," all seemed like pretenses. Underneath, much remained unsaid. People conveyed messages to Walker with their eyes, though. For the most part they said, "I know that if it weren't for your father's funeral, you'd be out fucking women. You are on the way to hell."

Walker spent most of the reception with his mother, helping her socialize. Bonds of mother-son love helped both get through their expected roles.

On a trip to the refreshment table to get an orange juice for his mother, Walker carried an empty glass for the refill. Turning around in front of him was Ann. She held a drink in one hand, and as they noticed each other, both said "Hello." Ann acted sweet. She didn't display any contempt toward him; she actually behaved quite the opposite. She complimented him by saying the history department wasn't the same without him and that enrollments in the courses he used to teach were down.

Ann joked about television journalism and said the real story was probably much more interesting. Ann had been the first person, outside the family, to mention the incidents of Uganda. In a strange way, Walker felt relieved because of it. She lightly touched him on the arm and invited him to dinner. She and her husband, William, would be delighted if he accepted. They settled on arrangements for the next day.

As Walker had anticipated, many of Amy's and Petra's friends were there and he thought that since neither of them came home that frequently, they would want to spend time with them. It surprised him that for much of the reception Amy, Petra and Marlene huddled together in discussion. As the reception wound down, Amy delightedly informed him that she and her mother had convinced Petra to go away with him.

Amy also delivered some bad news. Petra was leaving for Ann Arbor in the morning and she did not want to see him or speak with him before she left. Walker desperately wished to thank her for agreeing to go, but she had left with friends without saying goodbye.

Jubilantly Amy picked up the conversation again and told him where they had decided to go. Her enthusiasm lifted from Walker the burdens of the day. Deciding had helped convince Petra that she should do it. Both their choices made sense to him. Living in California, Amy wanted to go skiing and picked Whistler, British Columbia. Enough snow had fallen in Michigan to last Petra a lifetime and she picked the tropical climate of Costa Rica.

The day after the funeral, Amy left for UCLA. None of Walker's old friends or associates called or dropped by; he spent his days alone recuperating and reading while his mother rested. Once a day, he waded through the snow to the Fox River that ran along the back of his parents' property. He strolled on the frozen water, making deep footprints in the snow. On each of these walks he made at least one snow angel, an activity that helped him mask his mounting depression.

While traveling the last seven months, there had always been a new challenge to keep Walker on edge: unfamiliar settings, different cultures and languages, and constant meetings with new people. Being back home under extremely emotional circumstances and witnessing his mother trying to cope with her loss depressed him. Rejection from family and loss of support from friends made it worse. He knew he could call Marlene and she would accept him. Somehow that didn't seem fair to her. Perhaps in time he would go to her, but not just yet.

Walker wished for acceptance and for just one of his old friends or colleagues to reach out to him and call him. Brooding over the situation sank him deeper into melancholy. The only light that shone through all the darkness was Ann and William's invitation to dinner. Other than the reading of the will, it remained the only event in his life currently planned for. Ever since Ann had asked him over, it seemed that he counted every minute while waiting to go. Three hours before he had to leave, he started getting ready.

If this had been a year ago, it might have taken Walker thirty minutes to prepare. Today the three hours didn't seem long enough. While getting ready, he got panicky and wished he had given himself more time to prepare. How had he let the time get away from him?

Walker had stored most of his clothing at his parents' house before he had left on his journey. He quickly put on a dark navy suit with a smart black knit sweater underneath it. He thought that perhaps he had overdressed, but he didn't want to take the chance of being underdressed on his only outing. He arrived fifteen minutes early and, not wanting to appear anxious, parked around the corner and waited until the scheduled time. With one minute to spare, he drove to the house and parked in the driveway.

As a gift, Walker had brought a bottle of Bordeaux—a nice wine deliberately chosen from a region of France nowhere near the area he had come to know so well.

It was a Friday night and Ann had dressed for it too. Walker suddenly felt more comfortable in his choice of attire. She took his arm, whisking him out of the cold, and quickly closed the door behind him. Shivering, she rubbed her hands together. He presented her with the wine. She accepted it, then stood tiptoe and kissed him on the cheek in thanks and helped him off with his overcoat.

As they entered the living room, Ann explained that William had just phoned. There had been an emergency at work and he'd be late and insisted that they start without him. He would try and join them later, but they shouldn't count on it. She joked about William working too much and didn't understand how money could ever really create an emergency. William was the chief financial officer for a large paper mill.

Ann asked if they could try the bottle of wine that he had brought. Walker agreed and she requested that he open it for her. She sat on the couch and he chose a chair on the other side of the coffee table. They drank one glass each while chatting. She let him in on little snippets of gossip about other teachers, students and even some parents.

Tight black pants and a sweater showed off Ann's hips and attractive breasts. Normally this would have reminded Walker of the night he accidentally pressed his hand against her breast a few years ago. Tonight, in his depressed condition, it did not.

Sitting cross-legged, Ann slowly rotated her dangling foot. Her shoe had an open toe and he could see that she wore sheer black stockings and had her toenails painted a bright red. Her auburn hair, red nail polish and red lipstick created a provocative contrast with her black outfit.

Ann mentioned that they might as well start dinner—the sound of William's voice suggested he wouldn't be home any time soon. There were three places set on the dining room table. Ann seated Walker at the head of the table and she sat in the spot closest to the kitchen. She joked about leaving the third place set, just in case William showed up.

"I remember you saying that you were a meat-and-potatoes man," Ann said, as she patted his hand. "I hope you still are, because I've prepared roast beef, mashed potatoes, Yorkshire pudding and gravy. And for dessert, it's my specialty—a homemade apple pie."

DEATH OF A FATHER

Refusing Walker's offers to help, Ann did all the preparation and serving while he sat there feeling a little helpless. Then the roast arrived and she asked him to carve. It had been eight months since he had been served an American home-cooked meal. His mouth watered and soon he was experiencing the delicious tastes.

With just the two of them there, dinner proceeded quickly. Shortly after the main course, the wineglasses were refilled and the conversation turned to Walker's trip. After about fifteen minutes of hearing various stories, Ann wanted further explanations on his reasons for going. She seemed deeply interested in knowing how he had come to realize that he had to seek sexual experiences, and if he had had many successes in his quest.

Ann had been a colleague, not a friend, so discussing these matters was awkward for Walker. Ann didn't appear uneasy at all. The more he opened up, the more she wanted to hear and she continued asking questions and often shook her head in amazement at his replies.

When Ann expressed her belief that he had done a courageous thing, at first this confused him, because he had not revealed to her his role in the rescue of the girls. Then he realized that she referred only to his decision to leave his former life and travel.

Ann cleared away the dishes and came back to the dining room. She rested her hand on his shoulder, bent over close to his ear and asked softly if he wanted coffee with dessert. Rich coffee aroma drifting in from the kitchen filled Walker's nostrils, and he accepted the offer.

Their knees and feet had touched many times during the course of the meal, but never for very long. With the slightest brush, one of them quickly moved away so that they no longer touched. During dessert, it seemed to Walker that the touching happened more frequently, that it lingered longer and that they pressed against each other just a little harder. Walker didn't attribute too much to it and he actually enjoyed the little inadvertent contacts. As the conversation about his trip engaged her, she leaned closer toward him.

At the end of a funny story, while they both smiled and chuckled, out of the blue Ann quipped, "Do you remember that time a few years ago, at the spring Mardi Gras?"

Walker looked puzzled and when he didn't respond, she continued. "Oh, you must. We were at the bar and I turned around and my breast went right into your hand."

Amidst all the murky weight of the past week, Walker dug out the memory. Having it replayed caught him off guard and his jovial mood ended. He tried to recapture some of the humor from moments before and break the building tension.

"You know, my high-school buddies had a name for that kind of stuff. We would have called it a tit-of-hand incident."

"Don't you think it's strange that for all those years afterward, we worked together every day and never mentioned it?" She looked at him for his reaction.

Shrugging his shoulders, Walker gave the impression that he didn't have the answer. Underneath his knit sweater and jacket, his body temperature increased. Ann continued to stare. In his uncomfortable disposition, he rested his hands on the table. Ann moved her hand over until it lay on top of his.

"I thought with your recent encounters that you may have gained some insights into matters like these." Walker remained silent as she wrapped her fingers around the top of his hand in order to hold it. Ann squeezed it slightly and said, "You know, Walker, there are times I can still feel your hand pressed against my breast."

Ann raised his hand to her chest and placed it on the exact spot where he had accidentally touched her many years before. Her nipple felt semi-hard and it reminded him of the last time he had touched it.

Without the strength to resist, and needing comfort on many levels, Walker accepted guidance to the bedroom. Only an hour and half had gone by since he had first walked in the door. Ann didn't hesitate in undressing and stood beside the bed in black, sexy underwear. Seeing Ann in her bra, panties, garter belt and sheer stockings pushed aside his fears about being discovered by her husband.

During one of their kissing frenzies his jacket came off, but other than that he remained fully clothed. Ann crawled onto the bed and put her hand down the inside of his pants. She proclaimed in a sultry voice, "I've waited for this a long time. Ever since you first touched me."

While kneeling on the bed, she unbuckled Walker's belt, undid the top of his pants and slowly pulled down the zipper. The pants went round his ankles and he kicked off his shoes, stepped away from his pants and removed his socks. His stiffness bulged beneath his white Jockeys. Ann moaned as she rubbed her fingers down the length of his penis. With a little devilish gleam, she looked up briefly, then tucked her fingers behind the waistband and slid the last barrier to pleasure down his body.

With one hand resting against his hip for support and the other hand clutching his hard dick, Ann guided the end of his penis into her mouth. She worked it for several minutes while he held the back of her head and rocked it back and forth, letting her know the right speed. The heat trapped beneath his sweater needed to be released and Walker let go of Ann's head, pulled off his top and tossed it away.

She tugged at his naked body to lie down while saying, "It's not going to end with only that."

As Walker lay flat on his back, Ann reached into a drawer attached to the headboard and pulled out a condom. Tearing open the package, she hurriedly put it on the end of his penis and rolled it down to the base. She moved so that she straddled his midriff, raised herself up and guided his erection through the crotchless panties and into her vagina.

Being inside Ann felt good after the events of Walker's week. Sliding in and out as she moved up and down drew him completely into the physical sensations of the moment. Nothing else mattered and Walker absorbed himself further and further in the act of sex. Ann became tired of pounding and went to a low crouch on her hands and knees.

To stay thrusting and inserted, Walker now needed to do the work. Closing his eyes, he rocked his abdomen up and down, feeling the warm, wet softness glide around his penis. Reckless abandonment befell him; his body desperately ached to be released from the week's memories. Pumping harder would bring him closer to freedom, he thought.

At times the end seemed near, but then it fell away in an illusion. Walker longed for the elimination of awareness, but it would not come. His agony transformed into sexual propulsion, which only prompted Ann to resume her thrusting. He heard a faint scream. In his deep journey for release, the sound seemed far away and barely perceptible to his ear. Ann had yelled, "Yes! Yes! Now! Do it now!"

Walker pumped with all his force, venturing farther into his inner world, trying to find the right passage, trying to unhook his turmoil and depression in one act of ejaculation. In a brief moment of external realization, he noticed he was no longer inside her. Then he pulled back to his inner world with no memory of the external.

Then once again Walker pushed out to the external reality. This time his sojourn lasted longer and his awareness was clearer. Ann smeared lubricating jelly between her legs. His internal universe reclaimed him and he searched again for his orgasm.

Recaptured in the carnality of her vagina, Walker returned from his inner crusade without success. A bolt of energy ripped through his body and told him that something wasn't right. Was he dreaming? Was he hallucinating? Without stopping his pelvic thrusts, which were his only connection between inner and outer existence, Walker struggled to break free. He attempted to shake her off him, but the weight would not shift aside. He felt movement along the thin fleshiness between Ann's vagina and anus. He screamed out in shock—a third person fucked her ass at the same time that he fucked her vagina! Walker still needed a release and he plummeted into a crazy rage to get it. Nothing mattered; he would give up everything, even his sanity, just to come.

Again Walker heard faraway shouts. "It's okay, Walker! It's what William and I both want!"

Walker found himself kneeling behind Ann, holding her hips as he jammed his cock in and out of her vagina. Weirdness didn't discourage his single intent on release. While he slammed back and forth, William held his fingers in a circle on her labia. Walker's penis slid along William's fingers with every in and out motion.

Remnants of homophobia, left over from high school, were not as strong as Walker's need for orgasmic salvation. His purple-and-red throbbing head swelled from the activity. William applied more patches of lubricant to Ann's buttocks and rectum. He then grabbed Walker's penis.

No man had ever touched him this way before and Walker never imagined he would ever allow it to happen. In a state of suffering torment, he helplessly watched as William rubbed jelly all over the condom covering his stiffness. Then William gripped Walker's penis and guided it into Ann's anus.

Slowly Ann pushed back, allowing a deeper entry. William ensured that Walker held still while she determined the pressure and depth. Once it felt comfortable, Ann moved back and forth. Again William made a circle with his fingers so that he could feel Walker's cock slip along his fingers in and out of his wife's ass.

THE WORLDWIDE SEXUAL ADVENTURES OF WALKER FAYT

Mortality/immortality, life/death, sanity/insanity all blended together, trapped inside the walls of what Walker had thought was a journey of self-fulfillment. He had fallen into someone else's experiment of lust and he needed to escape. Misery and rejection had taken him here, and he needed the evening to end so he could get out of there. His only way out was his own emancipation, he quickly thought to himself.

Walker pulled out of Ann, ripped off the condom, wiped his penis clean with a sheet, got off the bed and stood at the side of it. Ann turned around, still on her hands and knees, and immediately began sucking his cock. It looked like it might explode from the inside. Balancing herself with one hand, with the other she held one of his buttocks and forcefully sucked along his steely shaft.

William removed his condom and fucked her vagina from behind. Enjoyment radiated from every cell of Ann's body, heating the entire room. Walker placed his hands on the upper part of her back. It felt like a flattop grill with the gas turned on full.

William screamed, "I'm coming!" and Walker felt Ann's body shake as it received William's hot shots of sperm. Her hand and mouth motions jerked with each burst, and Walker's penis felt the heat inside her mouth increase. It added to the stimulation and he sensed imminent release. Ann increased the pressure to his penis and intensified the stroking. At last Walker's longing ended. He exploded with a burst of energy as intense as a wildcat escaping from a cage. He felt his come being sucked from his testicles, up his shaft and into her mouth and throat. Walker let his aftershocks trickle into her open mouth.

In breaths as deep as if she had just set a world record in the hundred-meter sprint, Ann gasped, "God, is it ever great with two men! I can only imagine the sensation of having a man in every orifice!"

No one spoke while Walker dressed. Ann and William lay on top of the bed, stroking one another. Throughout the whole encounter,

DEATH OF A FATHER

Ann's underwear had stayed in place and she still looked sexy. She radiated and glowed with satisfaction.

Walker opened the door of the dark bedroom; light from the kitchen invaded his eyes. Ann's voice came from behind him: "Thanks for the wine. . . . Can we see you again?"

"Thanks for dinner—no," Walker said in a tone that suggested disappointment in himself. In the foyer, fitting his arms through the sleeve of his overcoat, he felt someone's help. It was Ann. She looked vibrant and alive, sexier than when the evening had started.

"Can we still be friends?" she asked.

"Yes, I don't see why not."

Ann rose up on her tiptoes to kiss his cheek and Walker bent over to allow it. She was still burning. Her lips were fiery against his skin as her heated body leaned against him. Her hot breast once again pressed against the back of his hand as they kissed.

"I'm not through, you know. I'm so worked up I might be able to go all night."

Walker reached for the door handle and Ann caught his arm. "Walker, it isn't going to be the same without you. It's still early. Are you sure you won't—" and as she said, "—come back in?" he shook his head.

*

Over the weekend, Walker reflected a great deal on his encounter with Ann and William. He thought that he had understood the sexual motivation of all the other women he had been with on his travels. Life's struggles, challenges and goals had been worked into the fabric of their intimate desires and needs and projected back in their sex.

Walker had not known any of these women prior to being sexually intimate with them and their sensual releases had allowed him to peer into their souls and understand them. On many occasions this had happened with just one act of lovemaking. Did his insightfulness get blocked with Ann because he had already known her for years? Did prior knowledge of her life outside of sex prevent him from seeing her sexual predisposition? It created quite a conundrum for him.

Perhaps Ann needed to have as much attention focused on her as possible, Walker thought. Her comment about wanting to feel three men inside her simultaneously rang loud in his mind. He thought that she might enjoy a dozen men at a time—maybe more. Where did the upper limit of her fantasy collide with reality? Her job ensured that attention got focused on her. Three classes a day meant that at least sixty people watched her. Was she a bottomless vessel for attention?

What childhood relationships and parental influences created this need in her, Walker wondered. Then he turned his thoughts to William. He could not imagine a husband wanting to watch another man have sex with his wife. To participate actively went w-a-a-a-y out there. Walker didn't attempt to analyze what might have driven William to such behavior.

Regardless of the couple's predispositions, Walker knew that he had allowed himself to be enticed into their sexual drama because he had been weak and depressed. He also realized that he wanted no part of it. He could accept their friendship, but he sensed that friendship was unlikely if he refused their further sexual advances.

Monday morning arrived quickly. With Walker behind the wheel of his father's Oldsmobile Delta 98, mother and son drove to Jerry's offices in downtown Appleton. As they headed past the college to the other side of town, the clear, cold air and shining sun made for a pleasant outing. Walker looked around with renewed eyes. Appleton had been his home for the past twenty-three years. It remained his home.

DEATH OF A FATHER

Marlene waited in Jerry's reception area as Walker and his mother arrived. A pleasant young secretary showed them into a small meeting room and offered them coffee. They all thanked her, but declined. After a few minutes, Jerry came into the room carrying a file folder and he shook hands with them all.

Today Jerry acted more like a friend than a lawyer. He paid special attention to Jessica and behaved very congenially toward her. He mentioned her good standing in the community and church, and how much he had enjoyed working with Roger since the two of them had settled in Appleton.

Jerry seemed in no rush and the pleasantries continued for about fifteen minutes before he got down to business. When he began, he stated that Roger's wishes were fairly simple, but that some of the administration would be difficult. Roger had intended to leave inheritances to the people who were most important to him. Jerry proceeded to give details of the will.

The family home and all its chattels were left to Jessica, along with a trust that had been set up that would generate an after-tax annual income of $60,000. There was also a $2 million fund to pay for Jessica's medical needs, should they arise in the future. Four other trusts had been set up, one for each of the grandchildren. Each trust had sufficient capital to generate income to cover all college expenses. Tracy and Walker inherited portfolios worth in excess of $2 million each. To show appreciation for the admirable job Marlene had done in caring for his son and raising two fine granddaughters, Marlene received $300,000 in U.S. government bonds.

Marlene didn't need the money, but receiving recognition from a man she loved and respected brought tears to her eyes. Walker sat stunned. Money was not his forte and he had no idea that his father had been that wealthy. Roger had never lived extravagantly; he had always been frugal. Other than living in a lovely home, he had given no indications of possessing great personal wealth.

THE WORLDWIDE SEXUAL ADVENTURES OF WALKER FAYT

Walker had never operated under any assumption of getting inheritance money. He and Marlene had always lived within their means. They provided for the family, paid their mortgage and saved what they could for retirement. He had counted on his teacher's pension to pay for most of what he needed later in life.

Walker felt overwhelmed. Now he would have to learn something about investing. His father had often tried to get him to take an interest in the financial markets and had tried to teach him various aspects of personal financial management. Walker had never showed an interest and eventually his father gave up. He found it a bit ironic that what his father could not get him to do while he lived, he would force Walker into after he died.

Not only did Walker have his own millions to invest, Roger had appointed him trustee, along with Jerry and Marlene, over his daughters' scholarship trusts and Jessica's medical fund. It made Walker's head hurt to think about it. But he gave thanks to be blessed with such challenges. Jessica didn't seem a bit surprised. Obviously she knew of her husband's financial holdings.

Back at home, Jessica told Walker that money didn't matter much to her as long as she was comfortable. What mattered were faith, family and community. As he had done since arriving, Walker made dinner for them. They enjoyed themselves reminiscing about the good old days, when they were a young family and living in New York City.

After his mother retired for the evening, Walker called Marlene on the phone and asked if he could come over to discuss a few things. He sensed her nervousness, but she accepted. It wasn't long before the doorman at the condo called up to Marlene, asking if she expected a visitor.

Walker stood at her door and knocked lightly. Under his arm, a cylindrical container held the gift he had purchased in Bangkok. He remembered tearing up the shipping slip with her address and replacing it with his parents' address. Now the timing was right to give it to her.

Marlene opened the door. "What is that under your arm?" The package acted as a perfect icebreaker and she focused nervously on it. After a pause, she said, "Come in, please. Welcome."

Walker's descriptions of the markets of Bangkok and his extensive search for just the right gift allowed them to maintain emotional neutrality. He only revealed to her that he wanted to give her the gift in person. The notion that it might have caused her pain to have received it directly from overseas he kept to himself.

As he handed her the cylinder, Walker said, "Marlene, I want you to know that I too appreciate all the things that you've done for me and I'm proud of the way you have raised our daughters. Your influences on them are wonderful and important. When you look at this piece, I hope it will remind you of these things."

Marlene gazed at the dancer painted on the fine Thai silk and tears welled in her eyes. "I absolutely adore it!" she whispered.

Walker sensed her reaction was not because of the gift itself, but because a man she loved and respected had thought about her in his travels and had taken some time to find a gift that he knew would please her. By purchasing this gift and delivering it to her in person, he expressed his tenderness and love. Marlene's tears involuntarily dropped onto the fine silk weavings.

During their conversation, Walker thanked her for persuading Petra to travel with him. Marlene explained that the turning point happened after a private conversation between Amy and Petra. Marlene wondered whether he knew what Amy had said to change Petra's mind. Walker indicated that he did, but let it drop without any further explanation.

After about forty minutes, Walker decided it was time to leave and excused himself. Marlene offered her assistance in planning the trips with the girls; she asked if she could make some of the arrangements. Walker indicated that he had more than enough time on his hands to handle the details. Then he realized that Marlene wasn't trying to lessen his burden—she wanted to be involved. She needed to feel connected to the people she loved. He realized he did not want to shut her out, and suggested a time on the weekend when they could meet and plan the journeys.

Neither of them knew how to say goodbye, which created an awkward moment as Walker stood at the open door of the condo. Should they hug? Should they kiss? Should they shake hands? Walker decided on a little wave and she returned it as she closed the door behind him.

The next day when the phone rang at Walker's mother's home, it was Ann calling to ask him over for dinner for the coming weekend. William didn't have to work. Walker declined the invitation. Two days later she called again.

This time, Ann explained her and her husband's motivations for the night the three of them had spent together. For quite some time, she said, both she and William had wanted to bring another man into the bedroom. In a small, conservative city, such attitudes were not openly accepted, rather they were feared as being evil and deviant. Ann and William were frightened to act on their desires, because if they were ever discovered, the community would chastise them. Acting out their fantasies could strip them of their employment and social status.

Isolated in their lust and frozen in their fear, they did nothing about their desires. The TV show featuring Walker's exploits had fascinated both of them. Romantic notions of being in exotic places and fulfilling erotic fantasies consumed many of their private discussions. It fueled their sex life and rekindled their desire for a second cock in the bedroom. When they found out that Walker had come back to town, it had put them in a constant state of arousal.

No matter how hard they tried to satisfy each other, afterward they longed for that missing element.

From the time Walker had touched her breast many years ago, she had fantasized about him being with the two of them, she said. The mystique of his sexual endeavors had added to her appetite for him. Ann revealed that William had hidden in the closet, waiting for them. Prior to his participation, slots in the door had allowed him to witness everything.

Walker listened to it all, trying to understand the situation. Still he did not. He refused for a second time to join them. She then worried about privacy and he gave his assurances to tell no one. Ann was disappointed that he had rebuffed their advances. She expressed relief that he had no intentions of revealing their secret.

On Saturday afternoon, Walker and Marlene met as planned. Each of them had purchased guidebooks on Central America and Costa Rica and he had even found a large map. They spent time reading about the different places of interest. As they read separate books, they would interrupt each other to read aloud about a place that sounded particularly good. Then they looked it up on the map.

Planning the ski trip was much easier. Walker wanted Marlene to feel part of it, so he prompted her to call the 1-800-WHISTLER number. When Marlene hung up the phone, all the arrangements had been made and she said, "You guys are going to love it. It sounds fabulous."

Marlene joined Walker and Jessica for dinner and the three of them enjoyed the conversation, which centered on the upcoming trips. Walker could tell that it pleased his mother that he and Marlene were together and getting along so well. When Marlene left, she and Walker kissed each other on the cheek.

On Sunday afternoon, Ann called again. She said that William was at work—for real. In a seductive tone, she said, "Walker, I'm lying on the bed in a sexy pink bra and panties with a garter belt, stockings and high heels. I'm thinking of your large, thick cock and how good it would feel if it were sliding in and out of every hole I can lubricate."

Walker listened as her breathing increased and she exhaled her words. "Walker, can't you feel me, can't you taste me, can't you smell my excitement? It's all for you. Listen to this . . ."

He heard wet, slick, rubbing noises, and then, "You know where it was. Wouldn't you like to be down there with your tongue buried inside me? Walker, just you and me. Think of it . . . think of me. I promise it will be like nothing else you've ever had."

Walker sensed her sexual intensity rising hotter than anyone he had ever been with; he felt the fire of her body projecting through the phone line. It stiffened his penis and he touched himself as they spoke. He almost said, "I'll be right over," but instead said nothing.

Tasting Ann on his tongue, Walker let his answer hang momentarily on his lips. From some unknown place he hardly recognized, Walker said, "No, Ann. This must end," and he hung up the phone.

chapter 16

ELLIE—DOCTOR, HEALER, LOVER
In the Coast Mountains of British Columbia,
Tracking Down the Male G-spot

Walker and Amy had scheduled to meet at Vancouver International Airport in southwestern British Columbia. They had booked their flights to arrive as close together as possible. Walker arrived first and in the hour before Amy's plane touched down, he strolled around the airport. In all his travels, Walker had never seen a more beautiful terminal building. He was impressed with the display featuring native totem poles and cascading water, and he particularly enjoyed a 20-foot-long sculpture of native paddlers sharing a canoe with mythological creatures.

Back at customs, Walker saw Amy waiting in line. When she cleared customs, she saw her Dad and rushed to him and greeted him with a big hug. He could feel her excitement and it contrasted with his apprehension.

Walker had never skied anywhere other than the bunny hills of Wisconsin. The thought of graduating to a mountain after so many years of absence made him nervous. Leaving Appleton, he had felt fine. In Chicago, tension had started to build and it increased with his arrival in Vancouver. He assumed it would only get worse as he got closer to the top of the mountain. For Amy's sake, he buried his uneasiness as far beneath the surface as he could.

The bright, sunny day seemed to create cheerfulness in the people they met. The young woman who worked at the car-rental counter smiled and said it would be a great drive. "Enjoy the sunshine while it lasts," she encouraged. "On days like this, Vancouver is the best place in Canada to be."

Amy navigated while Walker drove. They noted that Vancouver had decided against the use of multilane expressways, as she directed him through the city streets using a map that came with the car. Beautiful vistas of water and land unfolded one after the other: colorful Granville Island with its huge Public Market building, False Creek with its waters lined by condominiums and high-rises, then English Bay, where freighters sat quietly at anchor, and the huge, forested peninsula known as Stanley Park. Driving across Lions Gate Bridge spanning the entrance to the enormous harbor, they took in the residential areas of North and West Vancouver climbing up the sides of the snowcapped mountains.

The two holidayers decided to enjoy the glorious weather and stopped for lunch at Horseshoe Bay. From a sidewalk restaurant facing the pocket of a harbor, they watched as a giant ferry took on pedestrians and vehicles bound for Nanaimo on Vancouver Island. Sailboats and powerboats of all sizes and colors filled the marina and behind them ranged a backdrop of calm water, snowy mountains and a deep blue, cloudless sky.

Spring-like freshness filled the air. Over the span of their short stay, the grass seemed to turn greener and the buds become anxious about opening. Amy took his arm as they strolled back to the car. She mentioned an article that referred to Highway 99, the Sea to Sky Highway they would be traveling, as the most romantic drive in the world. For the first time Walker saw his daughter as a beautiful young woman and no longer his little girl.

Thirty minutes north of Horseshoe Bay, Amy concurred with the magazine's rating, commenting that indeed it had been the most beautiful drive of her life. The icy blue waters of Howe Sound below and the craggy mountain cliffs above expressed, for her, a spirit of bountiful life filled with richness, peace and beauty.

Concentrating on the winding road rather than the scenery didn't provide Walker the luxury of being able to agree or disagree with her. He marveled at the way the pavement appeared to be an insignificant scratch on the side of the rock. Signs indicating upcoming road curves carried squiggly configurations that did not seem possible, but proved to be true. Other signs indicated "Hazard – Falling Rocks. No stopping for the next 400 meters." Meshed wire kept loose rocks on the towering sheer wall from cascading down on them.

They passed large black-and-yellow striped gates that could be swung down to stop traffic in poor weather conditions or in the event of rockslides. Walker found driving strenuous in the perfect conditions of dry asphalt and unlimited visibility and hoped never to be on the road otherwise. Climbing and descending along its mountain perch, the road seemed as if it were designed for alpine sheep. At times the water loomed far below and at other places they were level with it.

During his travels in Africa, the Middle East and Thailand, Walker had been on roads much more dangerous than this, but never as a driver. After he got used to the up, down and around, he actually enjoyed it. Amy thought a speed limit of eighty was totally insane. Her dad explained that the postings were not in miles per hour but in kilometers per hour. He also informed her that the temperature would be given in Celsius and not Fahrenheit, and that the gas prices would be on a per-liter basis. None of it made sense to her.

In Squamish, they stopped for a washroom break and a cold drink. Overlooking the town they admired the 2,300-foot, near vertical facing of solid gray granite, called the Chief. This spectacular formation had already stood for thousands of years before man had had a chance to gaze at it and marvel at its dominance. Staring up at its sheer walls mesmerized them and Amy indicated her desire to come back in the summer and hike the trail to the top. She imagined the sensational vistas of Howe Sound and surrounding mountain ranges she would find up there.

North of Squamish, at a viewpoint on the highway, they stopped for a photograph. Father and daughter linked arms and asked a couple from the U.K., returning from a ski vacation in Whistler, to take their picture with Walker's camera. The mountain range behind them was one of the most impressive he had ever seen. Covered with glacial snow and ice, the peaks of the Tantalus Range glistened in the deep blue sky. From there onward, the road wound its way north through canyons and valleys, steadily working its way up to Whistler's altitude of 2,000 feet above sea level.

After checking into their adjoining rooms at the Westin Resort and Spa, Amy and Walker made plans to go out to dinner. Many fine restaurants lined the quaint village, all within walking distance of their hotel. Choosing one became difficult. Amy suggested French cuisine, but Walker declined, stating that he did not care for French cooking and that he didn't like the wine much either.

During an Italian meal, they looked at a trail map and planned where they would ski the next day. A gondola operated right outside their hotel and it would whisk them up Whistler Mountain to the Roundhouse Lodge at 6,100 feet above sea level. Looking at the trail map more closely, Walker realized that another chair lift carried skiers over 1,000 feet higher, to Whistler peak. At the top, close to 5,000 feet of vertical drop, all skiable, awaited. Thoughts of it brought butterflies to the pit of his stomach.

Amy had brought her ski boots and would rent skis and poles; Walker would rent all his equipment. Their decision eliminated the hassle of traveling with bulky luggage. It also meant they could try the latest in high-performance equipment: shape skis. Amy excitedly told him about trying a pair for a few runs while skiing in California.

Sensing his nervousness, Amy reassured her father that no matter how high they went, there was always a beginner's route down. She pointed out all the green trails on the map. Walker remembered from his skiing days that green circles meant beginner, blue squares intermediate and black diamonds advanced. He pointed out several places on the map that had double black diamonds. He had never seen that symbol before. She explained that those runs were for experts only, and if the conditions were good she hoped to try some of them. He didn't have to come along.

*

By the end of the second day, Walker skied blue runs and felt more confident about his abilities. The shape skis made a significant difference in that carving turns was easier. Amy's ability astonished him. She flew down any run in all types of snow conditions. It didn't matter to her; she tore it all up.

After four days, they had skied Blackcomb Mountain twice and Whistler Mountain twice. Their pattern had been consistent: a balancing of her exuberance with his reluctance. In the mornings they would get up early and be among the first in line. For the price of a buffet breakfast at the Roundhouse, Fresh Tracks gave them the privilege of going up before the lifts opened to general skiing and riding. Once ski and avalanche control had determined that the terrain on Whistler Mountain was safe, they gave clearance and guests could glide though snow that had fallen during the night and be the first to make tracks.

After each day on the slopes, Amy and Walker would go back to the hotel, get out of their ski clothing, change into their bathing suits and relax in the hot tub. The hot water, propelled against their sore, stiff muscles and joints, provided relief and helped them recover for the next day's skiing.

Once physically revived, they would do a little shopping and then go out for dinner. During these times they shared personal conversations about important matters. They glimpsed each other's motivations, dreams and ambitions and this allowed them to draw close to each other. If their relationship was to be fulfilling, Walker knew he needed to recognize Amy as an adult woman, and not his little girl.

Blending the physical challenge of skiing with personal connections and interest in each other strengthened their relationship in ways beyond measure. Walker felt closer to her than ever before. As a child, she was bound to him out of need and necessity, not by choice. Knowing that she now chose to be with him filled him with love and appreciation.

*

On their fifth day of skiing, Amy and Walker reached the top of Blackcomb and saw a thick mass of cloud and driving snow closing in. They headed down, hoping to avoid it, but could not. Walker lost sight of Amy. Above the tree line, with no protection and no reference points, he quickly became disoriented. He had no experience with such harsh conditions and the sensations that came along with it overtook him.

As Walker froze with fear, white vertigo consumed him. He couldn't sense motion. Nausea set in, making him light-headed. He couldn't distinguish up from down, sideways from backwards, or whether he faced up or down the slope. Blinding whiteness made seeing his feet impossible. He didn't know if he stood still, slid down or had fallen over a ledge. He trembled with fright and dizziness and he felt totally alone and helpless.

Instinctively Walker crouched down to determine if his skis pushed the snow in any direction. As he bent over, his feet came into view and he saw the slight motion of his skis brushing and dragging the snow. This ignited panic and he fell into the snow, not wanting to move another inch.

Once Walker was secure in the knowledge that he no longer moved, the intensity of the white vertigo eased and his dizziness and nausea lessened. But he became dreadfully worried about Amy. He did not possess the energy or ability to move, but desperately wanted to find her. He wondered whether she had stayed above him or skied down in an attempt to find him in the void. He had no way of knowing, and very few options for action.

In the white blindness of wind, snow and cloud, time passed slowly. He had, on occasion, fantasized about climbing to the top of Mount Everest. Time and money had always been a constraint. Since receiving his inheritance, the notion of paying to get on an expedition that took inexperienced customers to the top of the world came to him more and more. Despite the numerous books and articles recounting recent disastrous and fatal attempts to make the ascent with inexperienced climbers, Everest still enticed him—it was the idea of going to a place on earth where so few had gone.

Being twenty-two thousand feet lower than the top of Everest and trapped in his own little mountain nightmare now convinced Walker otherwise. Imagining a wind twice as strong, air three times as thin and temperature forty degrees colder brought a harsh reality to his fantasy. His current conditions were bad enough and tested his resolve to the limit. He sat in the snow and waited for rescue.

Outlined in the fringes of whiteness, like an angel sent from heaven, a figure appeared in the cloudy abyss. As it floated down and stopped just above him, he recognized the form as Amy. He involuntarily babbled, "Thank God! I don't know where we are! I don't know how long I've been here! I don't have a way down!" He then realized the extent of his fear.

"Dad, it's going to be okay. I remember this part of the hill from when we were here the other day. A bit farther down, the trees start and you'll get your sense of direction back. Are you hurt?" She clicked out of her skis and sat down beside her father; he shook his head. She continued speaking. "I didn't think I'd find you until the bottom. It's a bit freaky up here. If we stay close, do you think you can follow me down?"

"I'll try; I don't see any other choice. Waiting for a break in the weather could take too long and I really want to get down." He leaned over in the snow and hugged her. "I don't think I've been happier to see anybody in my entire life! It's a miracle that you found me. I feel much better now. Take it slow, I don't want to lose you again."

From Walker's perspective, it seemed that Amy had no trouble negotiating the white nothingness. With her in front of him as a point of reference, he managed his speed and direction. Deep snow caused him to lose his balance several times. She kept an eye out and stopped when he fell.

Finally trees appeared, providing Walker with guidance and eliminating his disorientation. On the cut trail, visibility cleared, the driving snow stopped and the wind calmed. To Walker it seemed like a different universe. They skied down a run devoid of people, covered with a foot and a half of fresh powder.

The trauma of his previous condition made Walker appreciate the relative ease of where he was now. In this state of mind he got his fat, shaped skis to glide and plow through the powder like never before. His legs still shook, but they handled the motion of making fresh tracks in the deep snow. He found the sensation exhilarating. In only a few minutes and with the difference of only a few hundred feet, he migrated from his worst skiing experience to his best.

ELLIE—DOCTOR, HEALER, LOVER

Skiing the fresh powder tired father and daughter more quickly than skiing the groomed runs, and Walker and Amy stopped often to rest. On each occasion, Walker looked up the hill to see the mass of cloud that had been his nemesis. He acquired a new respect for the mountain.

*

During dinner that night, Walker wanted to try to transfer his knowledge and insights about life to his daughter, so that she would not have to learn them through the hard lessons of experience. He almost believed it could be done through touch, and several times over dinner, he took her hand and squeezed it. But he understood that his wisdom would only go so far to help her, and that she had to look within to find what she needed to complete herself. Still, he wanted her to have access to the enlightenment that he possessed, so that her journey might be eased.

Pulling her hand away, Amy asked, "Dad, did you ever fall in love with any of the women you were with?"

Suppressed memories of Selena gushed to the surface. "Yes. But it was based on a false pretense. I believed I loved her, and she used me to obtain what she wanted." Walker winced slightly as he continued. "There was never anything there for me. A woman entrapped me with a spell of love and entangled me in her web of deceit. It sends shivers down my spine to remember her tight grip over me. I could have easily let her consume my energy to make her stronger."

"It sounds diabolical. I'm sorry it had to happen to you. . . ." After a long pause, Amy asked, "Does that mean that Mom is your only true love?"

"Yes."

Amy swallowed heavily. "Is there a possibility that you'll get back together?"

"I don't know. A lot has happened between us and I can't say what's ahead. In the back of my mind, I believe it's a possibility. Is that what I want to happen? At this point, I honestly don't know."

Amy flushed slightly as she spoke. "I'd like to see you and Mom together, but I also want to see you happy. I can still feel the child in me. It's silly, I know, but with you guys split, I feel insecure. I try and pretend differently, but the feeling won't go away.

"I can't help but wonder whether I caused your divorce. I know it's not logical, but it's there. I worry that if it happened to you guys, it'll happen to me after I've been married awhile. If my parents weren't capable of finding solutions to stay together, then how will I? I feel angry and ashamed that you and Mom split. I haven't begun to understand all these childhood notions that live secretly inside me."

To break the tension, Walker smiled and said, "I didn't know you were so heavily into psychology. I thought you were planning to be a business major."

Now he better understood how deeply his divorce from Marlene had affected his children. Amy had thought about it a great deal and had chosen to perceive and approach it differently than Petra. Walker spoke in a serious tone.

"Amy, I wish I could tell you that we're getting back together. I'd love nothing more than for that piece of you to be safe and secure. But I can't say, and that's the best I can do for now. I'm sorry."

Walker was finding his daughter mature beyond her years; he found brilliance in her approach to life. He was continuing to learn from his children, he thought to himself. They were such a blessing in his life.

A question had nagged at Walker ever since his visit to England, and he asked it now: "Amy, as a child were you ever abused, sexually or otherwise? Or for that matter, has it ever happened to you as an adult?"

"No. Dad, it hasn't. I've been fortunate. I've never been in a situation where I felt overly uncomfortable. People I've been with have always respected the word 'no.' And as a child, nothing ever happened. Thanks for asking. Is there a reason?"

"Nothing specific. It's been haunting me because of some of the things I've seen on my travels."

She lowered her eyes and said, "Sounds like you've been through some horrible stuff."

"I believe it's all been worth it. I've also been witness to some incredibly good stuff. It's just different sides of the same coin. It all depends on where you choose to look. I've learned that one from you."

Walker had never admitted to learning from his daughter and Amy looked up with widening eyes at the compliment. They spent the rest of evening together. He retold some of the more positive events of his journey, like capturing the poachers, diving in the Red Sea, trekking in Thailand, visiting Tim and his family, attending her second cousin's wedding and exploring the many spectacular ruins.

By the end of the night, father and daughter were giddy from all the honesty and the adventure talk. In this atmosphere of bold confidence, they decided to try snowboarding the next day. A good night's sleep didn't change their determination to try something new, and they rented boards and boots.

During the morning lesson they were told it would take three or four days of riding the snowboard to grasp its feel. After lunch they tried a run, without an instructor, down a green slope. After quite a struggle to finish the run, and falling many times, they called it quits for the day. Walker's wrists, shoulders and tailbone could take no more abuse. Amy's younger body was more forgiving and she was up for staying longer, but decided to leave with her father.

At the end of previous ski days, Amy had talked her father into skiing out to the bottom rather than taking the gondola down. To motivate her father into skiing out, Amy had said, "Death before download!" Today she said nothing. Walker and Amy rode the Whistler Village Gondola down the mountain back into the village.

Soon after arriving at the hotel, Walker and Amy treated their wounds by relaxing in the hot tub. Most of the guests still skied, leaving the spa and pool area relatively quiet. In a couple of hours it would be crowded. They sprawled out, letting the water from the propulsion jets hit as much of their bodies as possible.

An attractive woman lounged in a recliner patio chair by the pool. Her jet-black hair was knotted into a thick single braid that ran the length of her back. She wore a sleek, one-piece purple suit that contrasted nicely with her dark complexion. Her eyes danced and sparkled as she glanced at Walker from time to time. Their eyes met briefly several times.

Walker had no intention of flirting or doing anything overt that would upset Amy. Regardless of his intentions, he could not conceal his attraction to the mature-looking woman.

After about ten minutes, the jets in the hot tub went silent and the water fizzed to a stop. Amy finished the last of her cold drink and spoke a little louder than before.

"Dad, I'm really beat. I'm going back to my room to relax. I don't feel up to dinner tonight. Do you mind if we skip going out for one night?"

"Not at all, if that's what you want." As she stepped out of the tub and picked up her towel, Walker asked, "Are you all right?"

She smiled, "I'm fine. I just need to chill, that's all."

"O.K. If you change your mind, call me. Otherwise, we'll meet early for Fresh Tracks."

Amy nodded her acceptance and turned the jets back on for her father. "See you tomorrow, Dad. Have a good night."

Walker's daughter walked to the locker-room door, pushed it open, looked at the woman looking at her father, then stepped through the door. A minute later the woman by the pool raised herself out of the lounger, walked toward the hot tub, tested the water with her toes, and stepped down the stairs into the swirling heat.

"Your daughter is beautiful. Is she a model?"

Walker usually only saw Amy's inner traits, such as intelligence and enthusiasm, yet he knew her to be beautiful. Her attributes of a slender, tall figure with curly, dark hair and deep blue eyes were almost invisible to him. He never really thought about how others viewed her.

"No. Amy goes to UCLA and is a business major."

"Your pride in her shows. It is good for children when their parents are proud of them."

Walker asked, "Do you have any children?"

"Yes, I have a teenage son. And I'm proud of him too, but for reasons much different than yours."

By the time the hot-tub timer had run its course, Walker knew many personal details about Ellie's life. She was a native North American of Kwakwaka'wakw heritage. She appeared to be in her late thirties and for most of her life she had lived in Alert Bay, a small community on the island of Cormorant, off the northeast coast of Vancouver Island.

Ellie's community recognized her as a healer. After her husband died from complications of alcoholism, she decided that she wanted to learn more of Western medicine and culture. Influences of Western society had killed her husband and she did not want to see that happen to her son or others of her native community. Ellie's mother raised her son Darrel while Ellie completed university and medical school.

People from Ellie's community rarely went to university and she was the first from it to become a medical doctor. Now she walked between two worlds. In her practice, she administered both Western and traditional treatments. She did not see them as being in conflict;

rather she allowed the two systems to work in harmony. She did what she believed worked best for the patient.

Ellie advised Walker that it wasn't healthy to stay in a hot tub too long, as it caused dehydration. Acknowledging her warning, he left the tub. Her heritage, background and story intrigued Walker and he found her personal energy attractive. As they dried off, he asked her out for dinner. He did so on the condition that if Amy changed her mind, it would be a party of three.

Ellie smiled and tilted her head slightly and said, "I would be honored if Amy decided to join us."

An hour before dinner, Walker called Amy to see if she had changed her mind about going out. She hadn't and asked if he planned to go without her. He joked about his need for sustenance after such a hard day and left it at that.

Walker had nothing to dress up in and put on a pair of black jeans and a dark, collared shirt. His sensitivity to his informal attire eased when they met in the lobby. Ellie wore blue jeans and a bulky sweater. They smiled and joked about how lucky they were that Whistler was such a casual place.

Over sake and sushi, Ellie and Walker exchanged more information about themselves. He told of the recent death of his father and of his intention to fortify the important relationships in his life. Without giving too many details, he described his unexplained drive to travel and how he believed it connected him to a higher purpose. He did not mention his involvement with the Cambodian rescue.

Walker found it difficult to explain why he had believed it necessary for him to be unattached when he set out on his journey and why a divorce seemed to be the only option. Ellie seemed to intuitively understand his vague comments. Walker sensed that she somehow saw past his words to his instincts.

The native woman explained that the loss of her husband became a motivating factor in her life. She turned disadvantage into advantage and used the negative memories as inspiration to see her through her goals.

"With each challenge I meet, new ones continually arise to keep me engaged. Many of the Kwakwaka'wakw people, especially the elders, are skeptical of Western treatment and if it were not for my subtle influences, they would reject them outright. Many Westerners treat me as a bit of a quack. If I were not an MD, many people would think that what I prescribe is nonsense."

Intimate conversation continued as time quickly evaporated. Before it seemed possible, they were standing in the hotel lobby, neither of them wanting to say goodbye, but knowing they must. Ellie invited him to go snowshoeing with her in the morning.

Walker apologized. "I've promised to go skiing with Amy in the morning."

Ellie raised her eyes and said, "I saw your bruises when you were in the hot tub. My advice is that you give them a day to heal. Snowshoeing is a gentler activity. You should give your body a break."

"You're the doctor! Besides, I know I need to give myself a break. I've been going six days straight, and snowboarding did me in." Walker paused, thinking about what to do, then he said, "I'll meet Amy in the morning to see how she feels about it. I'll give you a call early and let you know."

At 6:30 a knock came on his door. Amy stood dressed, ready to go skiing. He couldn't possibly disappoint her and decided he'd cancel snowshoeing with Ellie. He decided not to even broach the topic.

"Good morning, Dad. Remember when I said I wanted to do some double blacks on this trip? Well, I'm hoping to do that today. Last night I met a ski patroller and today is his day off. He offered to take me out so we can carve some turns in the steep and deep."

Thoughts jumbled and swirled in Walker's head and before he could sort them out and say anything, Amy continued. "I know we had planned to go up first thing this morning, and if you still want to, I can cancel on Simon. It's just that—"

Her pause hung in the air and confused Walker even more. Collecting his fragmented ideas, he said, "I think it's great. Go challenge yourself . . . but who is Simon and when did you meet him? I thought you stayed in last night."

Amy put on an amused look. "I stayed in about as much as you did. Don't think I didn't notice the attraction between you and that woman by the hot tub. I knew if I left you two alone it would lead to something. You didn't go out to dinner alone and, as they say, three's a crowd."

Walker smiled and shook his head in disbelief while she continued to answer his questions. "I met Simon at a restaurant last night. He's been with ski patrol for the last three years and knows all the good places to go. Besides, he seems like a nice guy and he's cute too."

"Are we meeting for dinner, or is three a crowd?"

Amy laughed and reached up and gave him a kiss on the cheek. "We'll meet at 7:30 in the lobby. See you then. Have a good day. . . . Are you skiing today?"

"No. I'm giving my board-battered body a break and going snowshoeing."

". . . Oh, I understand." Amy smiled and waved. "Have a good day."

It was before seven when Walker went outside to enjoy the fresh mountain air. Cloud cover hung low in the sky and muted the dawn's light. The village appeared to be trapped under a gray, cottony blanket. Outstretched before him, the world wallowed in shades from black to white. Dullness had wrung the color out of existence.

Tree trunks and branches appeared as light shades of black amongst all the snow, which clung in heavy clumps to the trees and covered the ground. Buildings of various shapes seemed to be painted in all the shades of gray. Walker wished he had brought his camera, so that the color film could have captured this black-and-white scene. It struck him that the world seemed simpler, easier to understand, less complicated. Some of the finer details had been lost, but that wasn't necessarily a bad thing. It remained beautiful.

Simplicity did not remain for long. With the brightening day, colors became increasingly detectable. The world again became complicated. He went to the hotel's dining room, ate breakfast and called Ellie to arrange a time for snowshoeing. Before leaving his room, Walker wrote in his journal.

February 19

Whistler, British Columbia, Canada

> There are times I wish I had the ability to see the world as black and white, the innocence to know there is an absolute right and wrong, a this way or that way, a heaven and hell. It would be a blessing to be able to accept a two-dimensional reality.
>
> Over the course of my lifetime I have been exposed to religious teachings. I was raised as a devout Christian, strongly influenced by family, church and community. From the time I can remember, reading the Bible and understanding its words were important to me. Yet I do not believe. Despite all my desires and prayers to believe, I do not. Ministers, family and friends have advised that I try too hard or I think too much. They say, "Let go of yourself and allow the power and love of God to fill you with faith." In all my years of trying, it has not worked. I have not been blessed with the gift of faith.
>
> My family and friends seem to be good Christians and I have followed their rituals, hoping that some day I would be struck

with the rays of faith. I go to church, I pray and I follow the Commandments to the best of my understanding and ability. On the outside, I appear as a faithful Christian. I do not consider myself a hypocrite because of the religious activities that I do. I'm open about my non-belief in them.

I do not partake as a pretense of faith or as insurance against the possibility that all of it is true. I do it out of consideration for the people I love. It makes my family and friends more comfortable when I participate in their religious activities. My going along, in some ways, seems to make them stronger in their faith. So I do it because I love them.

Being denied conventional religious faith makes life more difficult in some ways, but in many ways more interesting. Having sought and found a purpose for my life, I now find creation and love in every quark of energy in the universe. Somehow I know that all of it is divine, and that I have access to its power. Getting to this point has taken many years and has been an awesome journey.

The tides of the universe are changing, and as they change, they are shifting the way the waves meet the beach. I feel connected to those changing forces, attuned to the frequency of their vibration. I know there are many others who also feel this. Altering the focus of an entire species takes tremendous effort, yet it is happening. As more and more people converge on this aspect of truth, the swell will become bigger and stronger.

In time, this swell of change will become a tsunami washing over humanity, affecting attitudes, beliefs and activities for centuries to come. Organized religions will have difficulty adapting to the changing times. They may not be able to reinvent themselves to accommodate the concept that all the power in the universe resides in the individual. Humanity's flow will submerge *religions that remain tied to the notion of a divine master who has the power and willingness to summarily pass judgment on a human soul, sentencing it to either salvation or damnation for all eternity. Soon such concepts will not be acceptable; humanity's truths will be different ones from today.*

I am truly grateful for my chance to surf the waves of change and discover myself to be an indispensable part of a constantly changing humanity.

They met in the lobby at nine. Ellie knew of a local shop that rented snowshoes and Walker needed winter boots as well. The equipment differed from what he had expected. His own image of snowshoes was big, wooden, beaver-tail-shaped frames with string-gut webbing. The shop gave him snowshoes made of metal and plastic. The toe of the winter boot went into a pivoting crampon cup attached to the frame of the snowshoe. Straps over the toe of the boot and around the back of the heel attached the snowshoe to the winter boot. This modern design provided traction with a slight bend of the leg or foot.

Walker drove as Ellie gave directions to a place away from the village and the activity of the ski hill. They donned the snowshoes and walked away from the car and into the woods. Soon they were encompassed by the serenity of the forest. It was quiet and peaceful; light snow fell around them. When they stopped to enjoy the tranquility, Walker could hear the snowflakes as they landed on the water-resistant fabric of his jacket.

In the privacy of the woods, Walker thought about skiing and the requirement to constantly concentrate and assess the immediate surroundings. Equipment, lifts, technique, direction, snow conditions, terrain, other skiers and riders all provided a lot of stimuli. A successful run required all of these stimuli to be coordinated and processed. By contrast, snowshoeing felt like a liberation of the senses.

Freed from the tightness and weight of ski boots, he felt loose and mobile. His pains from the past week left him as he paraded through the mountain woods.

They used existing trails and also made their own paths through deep, fresh snow. Making new tracks was harder going and at times, their cardiovascular levels built up to that of a workout. At other times, they maintained a slow pace, allowing them to talk as they walked.

Ellie's native heritage interested Walker and they spent much of the time speaking about the history of the Kwakwaka'wakw people. In the early 1900s, the Canadian government outlawed the potlatch, an important gift-giving ceremony central to the customs of her community. At the time, officials came and forcefully confiscated the masks important to the ceremonies. It was an attempt to break their spirit, she said. In the late 1970s, the government realized the error of its ways and returned the masks to the community.

In a small clearing, Ellie stopped and reached into her pocket and pulled out some raisins. She asked Walker to take off his glove and she filled his palm with the dried fruit. Black-and-white birds chirped in the nearby branches. She motioned for him to hold out his hand, away from his body. As soon as he did, a bird swooped down, landed on his hand, gobbled some raisins into its beak and flew off. Soon another took its place. He felt its small talons grip his fingers for support while it ate from his hand.

Ellie did the same and he watched in delight as other whiskyjacks scooped up their breakfast from her hand. When there were no more raisins, they moved on and she asked, "Walker, have you ever studied history from a social perspective?"

"No, not really. It's mostly been from a European discovery point of view, in a political and economic context. Why?"

"I've come across a theory that suggests once a culture or people have been conquered and assimilated, five generations later their ideals resurface and become prevalent in the culture of the victors."

Walker thought about the comment for a few moments before speaking. "Interesting. I've never heard that theory before. I'm sure there's a PhD thesis in there somewhere. Do you believe that the ideals of your ancestors are working their way back into society?"

"Yes! I see it everywhere. The environmental movement has been born from the ways of my people and other native peoples from around the world. Native North Americans lived in harmony with the earth and the universe. They were a part of it like everything else is a part of it. If we were to disappear, which almost happened, there would be very little evidence that we were ever here."

Ellie pointed in no particular direction and continued. "Completely opposite are the European attitudes. They need to tame the land, defeat it and mold it to their desires. In doing so, they destroy the environment in a reckless and naïve belief that they are smarter than Mother Nature. They think their ways are sustainable and that they can fix their problems with more complex technology.

"I cry at the damage that has been done. With every species that goes extinct, we are that much closer to eliminating ourselves. If the human race does not adopt the harmony and respect that my ancestors had for nature, then nature will stop respecting the human race. When this happens—"

Ellie did not finish and Walker understood and believed her sentiments. He put his bare hand into hers, squeezed it and said, "We have to believe that the ways of your ancestors are not lost in the modern world, and that they will find a way to prevail again."

Crystal-clean snow and fresh, pure air filled the woods. In such a place, it was almost possible for them to forget that there were problems needing attention. Walker thought that connecting with nature was a fundamental need for human beings. Their mental and physical health depended upon it because matter, in all its human form, could not be unlinked or deemed independent from other matter in the universe.

During lunch and later in the spa, they continued their discussions. As they conversed, Walker sensed a growing physical attraction flowing both ways. While in the hot tub, Ellie examined Walker's purple-and-black bruises. They were still sore to the touch. Walker complained that his tailbone hurt the most. She informed him that bruised tailbones required a long time to heal. Light-heartedly she commented, "To be completely sure it isn't seriously injured, I'll have to examine it more closely."

Walker caught the innuendo and responded, "Well, I believe that will have to be done in private, will it not?"

Ellie smiled and responded in kind. "Well, of course."

Walker mocked a groan and feigned distress. "I think that I may be hurt real bad. I should have this looked at immediately."

Shortly they were in her hotel room, where to Walker's surprise, the pretense of a medical examination continued. Ellie had him strip down to his underwear and lie face up on the bed. She then applied a native holistic ointment to the dark bruises and tender spots of his body. It had a strong but wonderful smell; she said it would help with the tenderness. She had made it herself.

"Now it's time to examine your damaged tailbone. Roll over, please . . . and remove your undergarment," she said in the tone of a medical examiner.

After he had complied, Ellie touched his upper and lower back and then the back of his thighs and buttocks. In the process, her touch changed from that of a doctor or healer to a lover. Her caresses became gentle and purposeful, with the intent of causing arousal. She kissed his back and legs and licked the crease where the legs ended and buttocks began.

Ellie worked her way up his back to his neck, and when she

reached his ear she whispered, "Men have G-spots. It's near your tailbone. Would you like me to find it?"

Without moving or opening his eyes, Walker whispered, "Uh-huh."

Momentarily she left the bed. When she returned, he felt two lubricated fingers sliding up the crack of his bum. They stopped and applied a little pressure to the swelling around the bottom vertebrae. Involuntarily Walker's body stiffened, but he refrained from expressing his discomfort.

"My, my, you are sore. I think this will take your mind off it."

Her hands now pressed against the inside of his thighs, spreading his legs farther apart. Next she applied warm lubrication around his buttocks and over his anus. Circling his anus with her well-oiled fingers, she slowly inserted one into his rectum. She moved it around, making the opening comfortable to the foreign penetration.

The only other time he had had a finger up his ass was during a prostate examination. It had been an uncomfortable moment for both him and his doctor. In the current context, it felt completely different. In a state of relaxation, having it done by a beautiful woman in the form of sexual stimulation made the activity erotic. Perspective was everything.

After a few moments of pressure and penetration of one finger, Ellie inserted a second. She stroked a spot that catapulted a surge of ecstasy throughout Walker's body. Quickly she backed away, saying, "I don't want to rush things for the uninitiated. You'll have to be eased into it."

Gently Ellie began stroking the spot again, this time with a little more pressure and a little longer. Walker moaned—he had never known any part of his body to be so sensitive. Before this moment, he would not have believed that men had a G-spot. Briefly he wondered what created such intense physical pleasure. She skillfully caressed it again.

After only three touches, the prone man's penis went rock-hard. For many minutes Ellie continued her subtle magic. Each stroke intensified his arousal; powerful pleasure bursts rippled through his body. Ellie also decreased the amount of time between strokes. Eventually she maintained a constant caress. The intense physical pleasure could not continue indefinitely and in its defense, Walker's body responded by ejaculating sperm. As it did, she ceased rubbing. Slowly she slid her two fingers out of his rectum and along the crack of his buttocks, as he lay limp.

Several minutes went by before Walker moved and rolled over. With his eyes opened only as slits, he asked, *"What did you do?"*

"I found your G-spot. The most sensitive part of a man's body is his prostate gland. I just gave yours a little attention. I can tell it was your first time. You're no longer a virgin."

Walker remained motionless as he watched her undress. Ellie's body was firm and proportioned, with sizeable breasts and hips. She bent forward so that he could suck her large dark nipples to firmness. He took one nipple in his mouth, and pinched the other between his fingers. He delicately fondled her clitoris with his other hand. Her wetness stuck to his fingers as he proceeded into her vagina with his probing digits. Heat from her body warmed him and the smell of her excitement filled his nostrils.

Straightening up, Ellie crawled forward until she kneeled with his head between her legs. Using a pillow, Walker propped up his head, to take pressure off his neck without losing the position of his tongue against her genitals. He searched deep inside her with his tongue. Tightly pinching and twisting her own nipples, she sighed as he used his hand to spread her labia. Juices flowed out of her body and onto his face as he softly and skillfully tried to give her as much sexual satisfaction as she had given him. Delicately he swirled his tongue on, over and around her swollen clitoris.

Eventually Ellie's body also reached its limit for regalement and it shuddered in orgasm. When he continued to pleasure her, she rolled into a fetal position and whispered, "No, no, I can't take it any more. You have to stop. That was so good."

For the rest of the afternoon and into the early evening, they remained naked. Tenderly they talked and a couple of times made love in more traditional ways. Time passed quickly, turning light into darkness. Walker had to go; he needed time to shower and change before meeting Amy for dinner. He extended an invitation for her to join them.

"Walker, you have only one night left with your daughter and it's important for both of you to spend it together privately. If I'm there, or if you are expecting to come back here afterward, it will hurry you and tarnish your precious moments together. I'm leaving in the morning. If you want to see me again, please come to Alert Bay. You'll have no trouble finding me; I live in the blue house on top of the hill near the airport."

Ellie remained naked when he left and they passionately kissed goodbye. As they did, he squeezed her tight and then ran his hands down her long braid. That was the last of her to touch him.

At dinner, Amy and Walker struggled to get a conversation going.

"So, how did you and Simon get along?"

"We skied. So how did you and—"

"Ellie."

"Thank you. How did you and Ellie get along?"

"We snowshoed."

"It was your first time. How was is it?"

"You're right, it was my first time. It was incredible. Beforehand, I wouldn't have believed that I would have enjoyed it so much. I just had to go at it with the right frame of mind."

"What are we talking about?"

"Snowshoeing!"

"Oh yes, I almost forgot," Amy said, smiling and nodding.

Their final day of skiing turned out to be a glorious one. Standing on top of the mountain seemed like standing on top of the world. In every direction, the Coast Mountains sent white jagged peaks into the rich blue sky. Walker and Amy decided to ski both mountains on their last day: Whistler in the morning and Blackcomb in the afternoon. From the top of both mountains they marveled at the view of Black Tusk, a hardened volcanic core left after a mountain had been worn away thousands of years ago by the last Ice Age. It stood straight up from the top of a mountain: a massive, black monolith.

The sight of it made Walker contemplate a different perspective. From a human viewpoint, things appear so permanent. Upon altering that outlook to a longer term, like a historical or geological era, he realized that permanence was relative. He and Amy traded turns having their picture taken with Black Tusk in the background.

*

As they said their goodbyes at Vancouver airport, tears rolled down Amy's face. In their final hug, father and daughter absorbed as much of each other as they could. Walker couldn't believe how much he desired to hang on to her and not let go. Amy boarded her plane for L.A. and, soon after, Walker found himself in the air too, headed back to Appleton.

chapter 17

RECONCILIATION
Foes Become Friends in Tropical Costa Rica

Walker had two days in Appleton before he was to leave for Costa Rica; both were filled with preparations and visiting. He had the photographs from the Whistler trip developed and spent a few hours one evening with his mother and Marlene, showing them the pictures and providing various explanations and stories. It surprised Marlene to see him and Amy on snowboards. Jessica didn't even know what they were.

On the day before he left, Walker thought it best to get an international driver's license. As he sat in the AAA office waiting for the paperwork to be completed, his thoughts went far back, to the very beginnings of Appleton. His connection with Ellie had made him more aware of native peoples, who had also played a role in the founding of his own community. Local history stayed on his mind as he drove through town.

Before the Europeans had arrived, Menominee and Winnebago tribes had built villages along the Fox River and Lake Winnebago. The trapping and fur-trading activities of these native settlements attracted the Europeans; French explorer Jean Nicolet is credited as being the first white man to visit the area, in 1634.

THE WORLDWIDE SEXUAL ADVENTURES OF WALKER FAYT

In a region northeast from the Fox River, from the 1630s to 1663 the French warred with the Iroquois for domination of the fur trade. This war spilled over to other regions, affecting the economics and politics of the entire New World. The Algonquins, as traditional foes of the Iroquois, were pushed out of their territories around Lakes Erie and Huron and into current-day Wisconsin. Immigration of Algonquin and Outagamie (Fox) tribes put pressure on the ecology and food supply for the area around the Fox River. A war broke out between the local tribes and the new arrivals.

In the end, the Fox tribe gained control and set up tolls along the river. When the French and Iroquois war ended in 1663, the fur trade flourished. By 1713, the French had become impatient with the tariffs and tolls and for the next twenty-five years warred against the Fox tribe and their allies, the Winnebagos. In an effort to break the tribe, in 1733, the French burned to the ground the last of the Winnebago villages on the lower Fox River.

In 1761, the area came under the control of the British who, like the French, were only interested in the fur trade and not land titles. After the American Revolution, however, priorities changed and by 1850 the American government had procured all native land in Wisconsin.

Local history and its effect on human development of the region lingered in Walker's thoughts for the rest of the day, as he prepared to leave for Costa Rica in the morning. At ten after eleven that night, the phone rang. It was unusual for anyone to call after 9:30, and Walker picked it up hesitantly.

"Hello?"

"Is this Walker Fayt?" It was a woman's voice with a British accent.

"Yes, who is this?"

"The same Walker Fayt that captured the poachers in Uganda and saved the girls from the Khmer Rouge in Cambodia?"

RECONCILIATION

The remark shocked him. The voice sounded distant and somehow different than a normal telephone line or cell phone. He raised his voice.

"Who the hell is this? Is this some kind of joke?" As he said, "I don't find this very funny," she spoke over top of him, causing a delay in the voice connection.

"Before you hang up, please listen to what I have to say. I'm calling from a satellite direct-link phone from Machu Picchu in Peru. Do I have the right Walker Fayt?"

"I don't know, convince me."

"Now I know it's the right one. Hi, Walk. It's Taylor. Remember me?"

Walker stayed completely silent.

"Oh, you do remember. I'm calling to say that I'm sorry. My producers sold the Uganda piece to a U.S. TV tabloid without my permission. I'm sure no one watches those things or takes them seriously, right? You're not saying anything. Okay, I'm sorry if it caused you any trouble. I didn't mean you any harm. I was just doing my job, you know. And now I'd like to right my wrong. If my hunch and sources are correct, I can do that."

Again Walker remained quiet.

"Are you still there? . . . Hello? . . . Okay, just listen, then. I'm quite sure you're the American that rescued those girls in Cambodia. I'd like to do an exclusive interview. If you agree to do it, I will retract and set the Ugandan story straight. I know it can't be completely fixed, but I'll agree to try and fix it any way that you wish.

"I must admit at first I saw my hook as the reformed safari sex guy who changed his ways, foiled the sex trade, and saved the lives of young girls bound for prostitution. After giving it some thought, I didn't think you'd buy into that." Taylor paused, ". . . Would you? . . . No; no, you wouldn't.

"So I'm offering a complete retraction on the Ugandan story at the beginning of your interview on what happened in Cambodia. I've already got guarantees from my producers in the U.K. and from the people in the States to air it edited to my specifications. It's a huge story and every news agency in America will want to interview you once it breaks. Once it airs in both markets, you can do other interviews if you wish. That'll be completely up to you.

"You get to restore your reputation from any damage the safari story caused and get to be seen in a well-deserving hero's light. I know that I'm making it sound as if it's all for you. Neither of us is that naïve.

"Think about it. If I found you out, other reporters will too, and be on to you shortly. You might as well get something out of it. Others might offer you money, but I can offer to fix your reputation. Do we have a deal?"

Walker spoke confidently. "What if I wasn't involved in the Cambodia rescue? Would you still be willing to run a retraction?"

Now Taylor turned silent. Walker let the pause linger in space for an extended time. "… I didn't think so." Just as he was about to hang up, he changed his mind and said, "What are you doing at Machu Picchu? A story on UFOs and wild sex with aliens?"

"Yeah, something like that." Taylor laughed. "I know you won't believe me and I don't blame you. I want to change the type of stories I do. Your story on the rescue of those girls would help me change direction. I'm tired of the crap, but my ratings are so good, there's no way they'll let me change my story angles.

"I want to do credible stories. They'll still have to be sensational—that won't change—but the content can. Help me with that. I know what trouble my program must have caused you. In a way, you'll help to ensure that it doesn't happen to others. I know the interview will be a big success and once it is, it'll give me the latitude to avoid the salacious ones."

"Okay."

RECONCILIATION

"Okay? Fabulous! Brilliant! As soon as possible, I can be in Wisconsin . . . the day after next. You're in Wisconsin, aren't you?"

"I am now, but tomorrow I'm in Costa Rica. I'm going there to be with my daughter to try and fix up a little mess that your program caused. Taylor, you have no idea. I'm still very skeptical and don't trust you one little bit. So the interview must be done on my terms or it's not going to happen. I'm not going to let you do it to me again. Do we have an understanding?"

"Yes."

In that one word that traveled through space from South America, bounced off a satellite and returned to earth and was transported to Appleton, Walker heard that Taylor needed him to get what she wanted. Only this time she needed him to get what she really wanted and not just what her television show wanted.

They spent the next fifteen minutes talking about the retraction and the conditions of the interview. They also planned when, where and how they would meet. It would be in three days, on Costa Rica's Caribbean coast in one of the stops on the Fayts' itinerary—a small town called Cahuita.

*

Petra flew from Detroit to Miami. She arrived first and waited for Walker at the connecting gate for their flight to San José, the capital of Costa Rica. When he joined her, she offered a cold, "Hello." She stiffened and recoiled when he tried to hug her. Walker felt the pain and anger that she carried and that he knew it was not healthy to carry. For her well-being, he needed to regain his stature with her. He didn't know how much time that would take.

During the two-hour, thirty-minute flight, they spoke little. Walker asked how things were going at school and how her midterm exams went. She answered briefly and remained distant in her thoughts. Petra did not ask him much, other than whether the trip had been preplanned and how much flexibility they had in the itinerary.

Walker felt like he was walking a tightrope. He tried to keep her engaged, yet at the same time he needed to keep his distance. He believed that a delicate mixture of both would eventually lead to her opening up and letting off some of her steam. He decided not to tell her about his meeting with Taylor. If it happened, it happened, and he would deal with it at the time. If it didn't, then he might be pushing buttons unnecessarily.

Walker remembered how vicious Petra had been throughout her early teenage years. He thought to himself that, somewhere between the ages of fourteen and eighteen, some young women become like poisonous snakes. In order to defend themselves and to protect their territory, they coil and hiss. They warn of a deadly danger as they prepare to strike. When they do strike, their bite has a nasty sting and the poison quickly spreads throughout the victim's system. It is paralyzing and can be difficult to survive.

The only antidote to such attacks, Walker knew, was a focused commitment to a principle: unconditional love toward the person whose fangs were filled with poison; see the world through her eyes until she understands that there is no danger and no need to strike.

Marlene, as with most mothers, had been the primary and preferred target of the deadly strikes, although no one could claim safety from a seemingly unprovoked attack. For several years Walker and Amy had tiptoed around Petra, hoping to avoid her venomous bite. Marlene did not, which added to the number of confrontations between them.

Despite the attacks, Marlene's integrity and principles held together. Her unconditional love and support for Petra never wavered, and with skillful application, it prevailed. As Petra matured, love and respect for her mother gradually returned.

Walker now saw the wisdom in Marlene's handling of Petra's

teenage years. If he had followed Marlene's lead and faced the brunt of Petra's pain with love, caring and understanding rather than avoided it, perhaps there would be fewer unresolved issues between them now. She might be more willing to try and understand him rather than to judge him.

Suddenly Walker realized that he had fallen into an old pattern of behavior in his reactions to Petra. Rather than stand his ground and absorb her pain, he was darting away from her strikes. That forced her to take the full shock of a missed hit. For her sake, he chose to change.

If they were ever to have a successful relationship, Walker realized he must truly understand his daughter. He had failed to see the world from her perspective and needed to find the real source of her difficulties. Walker now saw that any effort he made to absorb and understand Petra's pain would help provide her with the strength and protection she needed to understand him.

As he sat beside her on the plane, this bit of wisdom provided a breakthrough. Walker's desire to enhance the important relationships in his life became stronger than ever, and he felt his chances for success had just gotten better.

*

Father and daughter went out to dinner on their first night in San José. Although located just ten degrees north of the equator, the city sits three thousand feet above sea level. The night air was crisp and chilly—but Petra acted colder than the air temperature.

Walker did not force any issue and did not probe what bothered her. He kept the conversation focused on the trip. He and Marlene had done the research and Petra seemed satisfied to go along with their choices. Her input into the route had all been through Marlene.

On their first full day, they picked up a Toyota Camry from Avis.

THE WORLDWIDE SEXUAL ADVENTURES OF WALKER FAYT

It came with a standard transmission, which meant that Walker would be doing all the driving. At the appropriate time, he would seize the opportunity and teach his daughter to drive a standard, he thought.

They drove north on a good paved road to National Park of Poàs, to see one of the largest and most impressive volcanic craters in the world. Unfortunately clouds covered the area and views were severely limited. Disappointed at not being able to see the crater, they headed down to the town of Sarchí, southwest of Poàs. En route they saw several open-back trucks loaded with red beans.

Petra pointed and said, "Dad, do you know what they're carrying?"

Walker thought they were freshly picked coffee beans, ripe but not roasted, but wishing to get an opening with her, he replied, "Well, I'm not really sure. I'll pull up and you can try your Spanish. Ask the guys on the back of the truck."

"No, I don't want to. They'll never understand me. My pronunciation isn't that good."

"It's going to get us through this trip. My Spanish is nonexistent."

Walker pulled the car to a place where she could yell out the window. "Go ahead, ask them."

Petra put her head to the window and yelled over the rushing air, "What's in the back?" and pointed to the red beans. She turned toward him and they both laughed.

The men heard her, but they looked confused. She tried once again. *"Qué es?"*

They yelled back, "Coffee!"

Petra leaned back in the car and said, "It's coffee. It's raw coffee beans. We'll have to take some back to the States."

They spent the rest of the day visiting the artisans' shops of Sarchí, a town famous for its finely detailed, hand-painted miniature ox carts. People from all over the world bought them and shipped them home. Petra found one that she could not resist.

RECONCILIATION

On the mountainous roads back to San José, impatient drivers in both cars and trucks did not wait for a straight stretch of road to pass, they passed on curves. Walker found it nerve-racking to watch vehicles blindly pull out and try to gain momentum as they went uphill and around other vehicles.

By the end of the day, he discovered that the standard transmission gave him better control of the car than an automatic would have, and he too used the gears, his driving skill and his intuition to negotiate "Hail Mary" passes around the mountain curves. He only did so when an extremely slow truck blocked his progress. Each time, Petra just shook her head without making any verbal comment.

In the morning they headed for the Caribbean coast. They traveled a major highway all the way from San José to Limón, the most important Costa Rican port city. The route ran northeast for about thirty-five miles before heading southeast for the coast. About sixteen miles outside San José, the highway traveled high in the mountains through Braulio Carrillo National Park. Dense and green, the "cloud forest" stretched out from both sides of the highway as far as the eye could see. Low-lying clouds blanketed parts of the jungle, making the terrain look ominous.

The landscape remained unscathed for about fifteen miles and at one point as Petra stared out the window, mesmerized by the magnitude of nature unspoiled by human development, she commented, "It's beautiful."

Once they cleared the mountains the road straightened, making the driving much easier. It took almost three and a half hours, including a couple of stops, to travel the 105 miles from San José to Limón. From Limón, Cahuita was another twenty-two miles south along the coastline. The small fishing village rested on the north fringe of Cahuita National Park. Eight miles farther south was the Panamanian border.

THE WORLDWIDE SEXUAL ADVENTURES OF WALKER FAYT

They pulled up to a small rustic hotel two blocks from the center of town and close to the park entrance. Walker got out of the car and smiled at a large black man with long groddybeads, wearing a muscle shirt, sandals and cut-off shorts.

The man did not smile back and in a thick Caribbean accent he said, "Hey mon, dis your car?" Walker nodded. "You be stayin' awhile?"

Hesitantly Walker responded as he watched the man check out Petra as she got out of the car. "Yes, a couple of days."

The Cahuita resident nodded and looked back at Walker. "You be needin' anyt'ing, mon—" and he put his hand on his chest and smiled, "cum 'n' find me."

Without understanding the man's intent, Walker politely said, "Yes, thank you, I will."

When the villager had walked far enough down the street, Petra said, "Dad, that guy wanted to sell you drugs."

"No! It's a small town. He was just being friendly."

"For someone who's a world traveler, I can't believe how naïve you can be."

After they had settled into their rooms, they went to a small family-run restaurant near the hotel. In a coastal fishing village, fish seemed to be the best choice on the menu. Halfway through dinner, from the front of the restaurant, they were interrupted by a voice calling out.

"Walk!"

Taylor came over to their table and Walker introduced her to his daughter. Petra reacted worse than he had anticipated. As he tried to explain, she imploded into a silent rage. Taylor's politeness, enthusiasm and her stunning looks seemed to fuel Petra's anger.

Before long Petra exclaimed, "This is too fucking much," and stormed out of the restaurant.

Walker got up to go after her when Taylor advised, "Give her

RECONCILIATION

some space; that's what she needs right now. Nothing you say will help. It'll only make it worse."

"I hate to admit it, but I think you're right."

Walker and Taylor watched Petra march down the street toward the center of town. Her brisk stride indicated that she remained very angry. Despite being worried, Walker knew that she needed time to cool off before he approached her. Taylor ordered something to eat and they finished their dinners together.

As per Walker's instructions, Taylor traveled alone. All the equipment she needed to conduct the interview—video cameras, recording equipment, lights, generator, cables and so on—was packed in the back of her four-wheel-drive rental vehicle. Her producers had been against her coming to Costa Rica without a crew, she said. They perceived her as the on-air, good-looking, well-endowed bitch not capable of handling any of the technical details. She knew better and this provided her the chance to show them and her crew otherwise. While Walker went to find Petra, Taylor set up for the interview.

Not knowing the village and not knowing where Petra had gone, Walker headed toward the loud reggae music that blasted from a building a couple of blocks away from the restaurant. Each place he passed looked more unsavory than the next. Finally he located the source of the music and went inside.

In the dim light of the bar, Walker observed that most of the tables were empty. He scanned the premises and in the far corner of the room a couple of tables were pushed together and some people were gathered there. He saw Petra. She sat with a group of Caribbean men. Shot glasses, both empty and full, littered the table.

Walker started toward the table and on his way over, saw Petra take a drag off a joint. When she saw him, she put on a fake smile and offered some to her father. Holding his outburst just below the surface, he shouted over the music, "No thank you, Petra. Are you safe in here?"

She yelled back, "What the fuck do you care? You've got what you want for tonight. I want some fun too."

Without using force, he could not remove her from her seat. Nor would she listen to him if he tried to explain. He doubted that her new friends would allow him to join them. All the men around the table seemed to understand the situation.

The man who tried to fix them up outside the hotel earlier sat next to Petra. Walker looked directly into his eyes. During that moment, Walker peered into his soul and knew that he was a man of integrity. Walker's voice became very pure, concentrated, so that there would be no misunderstanding the consequences if the man did not comply.

"My daughter doesn't want to talk to me right now, so I'm leaving her in your trusted company. I know you will look after her and see her safely home. Do we have an understanding? Do I have your word?"

The black man stared back at Walker and replied without hesitation, "Yes, mon. She is wid me. She be safe. No problem, mon."

Walker trusted his instincts and believed the man's word. Although Petra refused to look at him, he shouted so that she could hear.

"I'm trying to imagine what you're feeling right now. I wish you would tell me, but I know you can't just yet. Petra, I want you to know I love you more than anything in the world. Please look after yourself."

Walker left the bar shaking. With troubled, measured steps, he made it back to his hotel and got out his journal.

RECONCILIATION

February 25

Cahuita, Costa Rica

The only event in the universe that I can control is how I choose to feel or react to situations that attempt to govern me. This choice is made moment to moment. The rest of the universe is chaos and beyond my control. René Descartes wrote, "I think, therefore I am." I would carry this a step further: "I choose how to feel and react, therefore I am."

Selecting positive, loving thoughts is at times difficult. My thought patterns were established long ago and are so deeply entrenched that it does not seem that I have choice in my reactions. The stimulus around me seems to govern my thoughts and feelings by the law of cause and effect. To react in a way that I know deep inside is right is especially difficult at times when the negative thoughts and feelings (the ones that I perceive as unloving) are powerful and almost overwhelming.

When I'm successful in selecting positive thoughts, feelings and reactions, the universe changes for the better. It becomes harmonious and everything in it is as it should be. This capacity for divine empowerment exists in every individual. Trusting the purity of the soul's intention to be positive is the key to salvation.

I wish for my daughter Petra to understand this; it would help her in her journey toward personal fulfillment. To the best of my abilities, I will try to guide her in a direction that allows her to love herself, so that she can then learn to love the ones around her. Emotionally she is badly hurt and her healing may not come quickly or easily.

No matter how much she strikes out, I will not let it change my reactions toward her. I will not give up on the daughter that I love so much.

THE WORLDWIDE SEXUAL ADVENTURES OF WALKER FAYT

On the sandy beach just inside the national park, Taylor, with help from locals, had set up the spot for the interview. The setup resembled a small outdoor studio complete with chairs, lights and a bonfire for added ambiance. Two stationary cameras and sound-recording equipment were in place. Quite an incredible set had been established in a relatively short time.

Walker did not feel like being interviewed and tried to postpone it to another time. Taylor was leaving the next day and so it had to be done that night. For the next several hours, Walker answered questions, gave minute details of what happened, described his feelings and captured as best he could his motivation and the emotions he felt during the Cambodian rescue ordeal. They talked about the reasons for his anonymity and she pressed him to reveal the name of the man who masterminded the operation. He would not give it, nor any hints as to Dirk's identity.

The firelight and crashing surf added texture to the content. The interview took on an intimate flavor. Walker's concern for Petra interwove itself as unspoken subtext. He never mentioned it directly except near the end of the interview, when he reflected that in following his epiphany he had saved complete strangers in a foreign land but had deeply hurt loved ones at home. Walker looked directly into the camera and asked, "Where's the justice?" and then added, "I'm not sure it was worth it."

Taylor recorded several hours of material, though she only needed twenty minutes. From experience, she knew that television audiences did not want to see heroes absorbed in self-doubt. His final comments would definitely be edited out. The lights went out, the cameras stopped rolling, the sound equipment was switched off and for the next three hours they sat on the beach and talked quietly.

Six months earlier, Walker had poured his heart out to Taylor and she had covertly recorded it and used it as material for her television show. For a reason he could not fully grasp, this time it seemed different and he found himself confiding in her again. On this occasion, she seemed less interested in the women he had been with and more interested in him, and what he had come to understand from his experiences.

Walker spoke of his father's death and the profound effect it had had on him. He tried to be as coherent as possible when he spoke of his mixed feelings for Marlene and the confusion he suffered trying to piece it all together. Eventually the talk came around to Petra and how it troubled him to see her in so much pain.

When the conversation began to exhaust itself, they gathered up the equipment in silence and packed it into the sport utility. By the time they finished, dawn began to break the darkness. Walker's long emotional outpouring had ebbed into a shared peacefulness. With their wells of personal protection drained, the bonds of honesty held them together. Walker had never told such things about himself to anyone. Nor, he guessed, had anyone ever told so much about themselves to Taylor. They were bonded by this unique experience.

Taylor suggested that they get into their bathing suits and go for a walk along the beach—watching the sun come up and taking a swim would be rejuvenating. He agreed. Before meeting her, he knocked on Petra's door. There was no answer. He opened the unlocked door and went inside. It smelled of stale alcohol. Petra lay sound asleep in her bed.

As Walker and Taylor walked south along the beach in the national park, high-tide waters broke onto the shoreline. Waves erased their footprints from the sand. Rising waters left only a small beach between sea and jungle. Often they climbed over fallen trees or walked around a thicket of bushes and grasses outcropped into the water.

They had walked a fair distance and Walker felt her arm linked to his. He didn't reciprocate or act as if he cared. After the words they had shared during the night, somehow it seemed natural to be walking arm-in-arm. Dawn brightened the morning sky, but the sun had not yet breached the horizon. They swam. The night of confession made the waters feel like a baptism. It was cool enough to be refreshing, yet warm enough to enjoy without shivering.

They had stopped at a spot that evoked the idealized image of a deserted island. A palm tree hung low over fine white sand. Logs had washed up, making natural chairs and backrests. Glowing rays of the birthing sun reflected across the water and onto their faces, painting the world a magnificent rosy hue.

Physical beauty and emotional connectedness fused together, creating a setting that did not seem of their world. The setting created a moment of weakness, and Taylor confessed a fantasy.

"Walker, have you ever seen the movie *From Here to Eternity?*"

Taylor didn't need to say more. He understood the reference and the context of the scene. In the movie, released in 1953, Burt Lancaster and Deborah Kerr kissed passionately and tumbled on the beach as the scene faded to black. At the time, sex on the beach could not be shown to audiences and the two actors had pushed the bounds of social acceptability with even their modest level of provocativeness.

As in the movie, Taylor and Walker were two beautiful people in a beautiful setting, drawn together without limitations. Walker looked at Taylor for the first time as a woman open to possibilities between them. The setting may have triggered her fantasy, but their shared intimacy had been the aphrodisiac. Her job, her personality, her history had ensured a lack of such moments. Intimacy and not the beach sexually stimulated her, Walker understood.

By most standards, Taylor dialed in as a perfect ten and undoubtedly by those same standards she was the most attractive woman ever to have propositioned Walker. Images of the first time he saw her in her safari clothing—the jungle temptress outfit—flashed before him. The moist lingering sensation of pressing his fingers and

RECONCILIATION

hand into the yielding fleshiness of her vagina and ass, saving her from a grave fall, returned. Walker saw her piercing, cold blue eyes in a different light. At the moment they didn't seem so cold and penetrating, rather clear and naked.

The wet stretchy fabric of Taylor's swimsuit stuck to her body like a second skin. Cool dampness hardened the nipples that protruded from her firm, large breasts. Her tight, flat stomach and narrow waistline accentuated her curvy hips and taut long legs. Between her slightly parted legs, a delicate mound pushed out against the confinement of her bathing suit. Standing before Walker, she pulled back her shoulder-length wavy blond hair, wet from the salty water of the Caribbean. Then Taylor smiled, and began moving her stunning, five-foot-nine frame toward him.

Time in paradise collapsed around them and they pressed their bodies together and kissed. Walker could not believe the passion that stirred from inside her. She had always seemed like such a frigid bitch, too gorgeous to think lovemaking required any participation on her part. Her probing tongue felt like an inferno seeking a cooler place to escape its own heat.

Taylor's exploding fantasy escaped into Walker's body, creating rapid arousal in him. She grabbed his face with both hands and tried to suck out a lifetime of kisses from his mouth in one breath. As she did this, she briskly rubbed her mound into his hardened cock. As they fell into the sand, the sun breached the horizon along the water, blazing the world a brilliant crimson.

Peeling the straps of her one-piece suit off her shoulders, Taylor exposed her glorious, voluptuous breasts to the morning light and to the attention of Walker's lips and tongue. She wanted more than this and she pulled her suit completely off. Reaching for her tummy pack, she unzipped it and removed a condom. She pulled Walker's trunks down, tore open the packaged sheath and quickly rolled it over his erection.

THE WORLDWIDE SEXUAL ADVENTURES OF WALKER FAYT

With their feet in the water and their heads in the jungle, they tangled in the dance of sexual rapture. Salty surf swirled around their feet and legs as Walker's ass went up in the air, then down as he thrust his hardened penis as deep into her as he could.

Fast and hard he pounded, without regard for anything but release. Building and building, their sexual joining approached its known conclusion. Walker heard Taylor calling his name, softly at first, then louder. In the act of sexual coupling, no woman had ever bellowed out his name with such perseverance and intensity. It excited him to know that she enjoyed it as much or more than he did.

Walker pumped so hard, they sank into the wet sand. Added to the cries of his name, she slapped his back, then hit him with her fists. No woman had ever seemed to relish it more. She yanked his head up by the hair and yelled, "Walker, stop! There are people!"

Walker opened his eyes. Standing on a jungle path only five feet away was a group of elderly tourists. Men and women in shorts and T-shirts with wide-brim hats and binoculars stood nervously around them. Some had passed by already and others hesitantly waited their chance to move around the unexpected findings on their early morning bird-watching outing.

Bare ass to the sunshine, Walker lay still, trying to ensure that his body covered as much of Taylor as possible. Once he had been still for awhile, he looked straight ahead and watched hiking boots tentatively and delicately step around them. He dared not look into the faces of the people that passed. As they stepped by, he sensed their hesitancy, embarrassment and perhaps a little envy.

Lying there, as Taylor covered her face with her hands, not wanting to be seen—or worse, recognized—Walker let the sad reality sink in. She had not called his name in joy, but in panic.

When the last of the bird-watchers had moved into the bush and out of sight, Walker pulled up his shorts. By this time his soft penis had slipped out of Taylor. She hurriedly got back into her bathing suit.

Overtaken by the events of the previous few minutes, they sat in stunned silence with their backs against a fallen tree and stared out into the Caribbean. Taylor smiled and giggled.

"I guess some fantasies are better left as fantasies. The reality can never be as good."

"You're right. And this is one that was never meant to be."

In a mocking tone, Taylor uttered Deborah Kerr's famous line from the movie that had promoted her fantasy. "Oh, I never knew it could be like this!" And then in a more serious tone: "Actually, it's too bad. It was going so well."

They glanced at each other and Taylor stared at him with her deadly blue eyes and said, "You have got to promise me that you'll never tell anybody about this. If this ever got out . . ." She pushed him lovingly, but hard, with both hands. "Promise!"

"I think I saw somebody with a video camera, and I'm sure they were recording us."

"Quick, we have to go find them and kill them if necessary," Taylor joked, getting up. Walker remained seated and calmly laughed at her alarm.

"You shit! There was no fucking video camera," she said.

"How does it feel to be on the other side of exploitation? Not so nice, is it? No, there was no video, at least none that I saw." After a short pause, Walker said, "I believe we are done here. Let's get back."

They had breakfast together. Finally, with sufficient pressuring, Taylor secured Walker's word that he would never reveal to anyone what had happened that morning. After breakfast, as Walker sat in the shade in front of the hotel, the British broadcaster went to her room, in the same hotel where Walker and Petra were staying, to view her tape. She wanted to be sure of the quality and had a little video monitor on which to play it back.

Around ten o'clock in the morning, the man who had been left in charge of Petra's safety sauntered over. He shook his head as he spoke to Walker.

"Hey, mon! Oooh, did she tie it on lest night. Barly goat 'er back, mon," and he shook his head some more. "How's she doin' tis mornin', mon?"

"She's still sleeping." Walker got up and extended his hand and they shook. "Thanks. What you did was kind. You're a good man."

"No problem, mon. I heave daughters of me own. I know. When dey are as fine as Petra—" he shook his head side to side. "If she not been wid me, dare could haf been trouble."

"Yeah, I know. Thanks again. What's your name?"

"Thomas."

The Cahuita resident began to walk back to the village center, then turned around with a big grin, showing a mouth full of white teeth. "If you be needin' sum stuff, mon, cum see Thomas. He fix you up real good."

Petra, having woken up hung over from the night of abusing herself with alcohol and ganja, appeared on the steps of the hotel. Walker did not reprimand or advise her in any way. He let her be. She still needed his love and support, but as an adult she was beyond the limits of his supervision.

"You look pretty rough. Is there anything I can get for you?"

Petra did not answer.

"You know, I'm really delighted that you decided to come on this trip with me. Costa Rica is just fabulous."

"Is that woman gone?"

"Taylor? No. She's reviewing the material from our interview last night. I think it went quite well. You know, she's planning to clear up the bullshit from Africa."

RECONCILIATION

In disgust, Petra turned to go back to her room.

From inside a nearby hotel room, Walker heard Taylor call, "Petra, I think you should see this."

"What is it, bitch?"

Walker wanted to jump out of his seat and scold his daughter, but he held his first reaction back and chose to say nothing. In the quiet of the coastal village morning, he heard Taylor's voice speaking.

"As much as I'm open to the possibility, I'm not romantically involved with your father. If you want to understand what kind of a man he is, I think you should see some of the things he said last night. Look behind his words and you'll see his love for you. Please, it's worth your time."

*

After Petra had seen the entire interview, she sought out her father. Her face was wet, and she wanted to be hugged. It seemed to Walker that she was his little girl. The hug began her healing process. Tears that had flowed when Petra watched the interview returned now. She told her father that his expressions during the interview had revealed to her that his courage to rescue the girls stemmed from his love for her.

"I understood how your love could not be segregated so that I could harbor my own piece of it. It is a part of you, and cannot be divided from your other parts."

Taylor left later that day for San José. She wanted to get back to England to get working on the show, so that it could air as soon as possible. She and Walker agreed that he would review a copy of the retraction and edited interview before it aired, and if he had any problems or suggestions, she would try and get them incorporated into the final cut. They also discussed the possibilities for a romance between them, and agreed that it was not meant to be.

*

THE WORLDWIDE SEXUAL ADVENTURES OF WALKER FAYT

Walker lay relaxing on one of Costa Rica's Pacific Coast beaches a week later, reflecting on some of the experiences of the last ten days.

While driving back from Cahuita, Walker and Petra had been flagged down by police with radar guns for speeding. Other cars were also waved over, but they didn't stop and sped on by. Inside the little roadside station, the police wanted the fine to be paid immediately. Walker showed a $10 American bill. They shook their heads and pointed to his wallet. When he produced another $10, they smiled and nodded their heads.

Back in the car and on the road, Petra began to chuckle and asked if her father knew why none of the other cars had stopped. Walker replied that he had no idea. On the way out of the station, she said, she had noticed that the police did not have a vehicle to pursue cars that didn't stop voluntarily.

Next came the memory of their visit to the volcano of Arenal. Several times a day, the ground shook and rumbled. Billowing out from deep inside the earth, a mushroom cloud of ash and steam rose high into the air. It disrupted the clouds and blue sky around the peak. At the base, they immersed their bodies in hot streams that flowed off its slopes. While bathing, Walker lost the car keys. For about an hour they searched frantically. They tried to come up with another plan if they could not find them. Eventually Petra spotted the keys on a rock at the edge of one of the streams. She saved the day.

Then Walker's thoughts jumped to the cloud forest of Monteverde. There they spotted the beautiful and elusive quetzal bird. On the same clear day, they climbed a peak and enjoyed a view of both the Pacific Ocean and the Caribbean Sea with just a slight turn of the head.

On the trip to Monteverde, whenever they asked for directions they were given the same response. The person would say *"directo"*

RECONCILIATION

and point straight ahead. Inevitably in less than a mile there would be a fork in the road. When the only people they saw were traveling by donkey, Walker became concerned. Even in the remoteness, when asked, the locals pointed straight ahead.

Over one of the ridges, they came to a path that had deteriorated into not much more than a steep slide of rock and dirt. Driving down the slope terrified Petra. At least Walker could feel whether the car slipped out of control or not. Miraculously they made it to the bottom and continued on.

After several more miles, the road ended at a river. It continued on the other side, but there was no bridge. Petra threw her hands up in the air and pointed back the way they had come. Getting down the rock slide had been extremely difficult; getting back up it would be impossible. Walker knew they could not go back.

Petra and Walker surveyed the river. It wasn't that deep and the bottom seemed hard enough to support the weight of the car. Getting up the steep embankment on the far side with only two-wheel drive, however, presented another complication. Nothing more than their belief that they could do it if they worked together got them through the river and on their way. By the time they reached their lodgings at Monteverde, their nerves were shot; they'd been pushed beyond the edge of tolerance from completing the last of the very rough road in the dark.

Other guests were already dining and the hosts came out to greet Petra and Walker in the parking lot. The wearied travelers were told that their reservation had been misplaced and that there were no rooms for them. Petra burst into a flurry of frustration. Walker calmed her and the hostess down and sorted it out. They did have reservations; somehow there had been a mix-up in names.

Still shaken from their drive at dinner, Walker and Petra ranted about the bad road conditions and that people should be warned to come in only four wheel-drive vehicles. The other guests politely listened but didn't concur with their sentiments. Finally one man spoke up.

"The roads were bad, but they weren't that bad. I made it in just a car."

Walker and Petra looked at each other and then after a pause she said, "Really? So what did you do when you came to the river and there was no bridge?"

Immediately the other guests, the hosts, as well as Walker and Petra, realized that the American father and daughter had come to Monteverde via a different road. Or perhaps it was just a donkey trail.

On the way back, they found the right route—a fairly well-maintained gravel road. On a flat stretch that extended for many miles, Walker taught Petra to drive a standard-transmission vehicle.

Currently they were staying at a picturesque site on the Pacific Coast, just a few minutes' walk from Manuel Antonio National Park. Perhaps the most beautiful park in Costa Rica, its lush jungles, white sandy beaches and abundance of wildlife were unmatched. In two days they had seen howler monkeys, two-toed sloths, a multitude of birds and white-faced monkeys.

Walker's thoughts came back to the present. Peace and tranquility had surrounded the two of them at the beginning of this day, their third in Manuel Antonio National Park. Then, while lying on the beach, after a great morning of body surfing, Petra began to confide in her father. She revealed that while at university she had gone through a couple of bad relationships and had reached a point where she believed that "all men are assholes."

Admittedly some of her anger was based on what Walker had done to Marlene and indirectly to her. Petra felt betrayed and it added to her conviction that men could not and should not be trusted. In an atmosphere of honesty and with her guard down, the words poured out. Through held-back tears, she confessed she had been a victim of date rape.

RECONCILIATION

Instantly an overwhelming desire struck Walker to avenge the assault. His blood boiled with rage, sending him to the verge of erupting with a demand to know who did it—he'd "kill the fucking bastard." Then all the wisdom from his travels melded together in his consciousness and he stopped himself. Rather than react in the lofty pronouncements of his old patterns, he chose to focus on matters of importance in the moment—Petra's emotions. He listened with love and concern.

It had happened on campus at the time when the divorce was being finalized, Petra began. She desperately needed to talk to her mother about the rape. But in Marlene's emotionally fragile state caused by the sudden breakdown of her marriage, Petra felt she couldn't add to her mother's burden. And she knew if she told Amy, then Amy would tell Marlene. Petra felt abandoned in the time of her greatest need, and she placed the blame directly on her father. From her perspective, it had been selfish of him to leave his family as he did and his timing could not have been worse. It left her with no support just when she needed it most.

In his deepest nightmare, Walker could not imagine his heart sinking any lower than it had just done. A dark reality had surfaced—but at least he now understood what had been causing Petra so much distress. Her wounds had been inflicted by many sources and on many levels. That was her truth—and now he had heard it.

Walker further helped her healing process with a small truth of his own. "Petra, if I had known, I wouldn't have gone. You'll have to choose whether to believe me or not."

"I believe you. I know it's true. But if I had said something and you hadn't gone, then those Cambodian girls wouldn't have been saved. It's better the way it has happened. We still have time together. Things will be better now. Thank you for this trip."

chapter 18

EPIPHANY FULFILLED
Accepting the Unfolding Universe

March 22

Appleton, Wisconsin

"The road to hell is paved with good intentions."

This statement was first uttered over eight hundred years ago, and since then many people worldwide, of differing faiths and beliefs, have earnestly repeated it. By doing so, they have promoted the idea that, during so-called "Judgment Day" rulings, what one intended to do isn't enough to get them into heaven.

By contrast, the principles of modern law require action as well as intent for a guilty verdict. The convicted person must have the mental capacity—which includes intent—to commit a crime, and they must also physically have done it.

If the aphorism at the top of this page is true, then all those with pleas of mental incapacity, inability, lack of intelligence, bad timing, poor judgment and all the other human weaknesses—as well as those dealing with forces of the universe beyond their control—are bound for "hell."

EPIPHANY FULFILLED

Of all the people who have ever lived and all the people who have yet to live, most will be filled with good intentions. For many human reasons, those good intentions become waylaid, or they turn out to be misguided notions; either way they don't lead to good actions—or sometimes any action at all. Sentencing all these people to "hell" cannot be my truth.

My journey has taught me that if there is such a thing as "Judgment Day," it is right here and now, in this moment; and it is a time when each person passes judgment on themselves.

Walker strolled along the Fox River at a favorite place of his and Marlene's, unsure of what would happen next. Though past issues, ideas and events of his life seemed to have tied themselves together, it still felt as though they could unravel again. As he reflected on the last nine months, a rush of memories of all the places he had been, all the people he had met and all the things that he had done, flooded his consciousness.

Walker stood in a very familiar location by the river and now it seemed foreign to him. Through breaks in the ice he watched the water flow by, and he thought of himself, and all human beings, as "work in progress." No one is ever a completed individual. And even though he craved all the limitless possibilities to be his truth, yet that was impossible. The ongoing choices he made created the unfolding universe.

Different realities fabricated from choices not yet made were like road maps to his future. Would he reconcile with Marlene? Did either of them want to? Was he on the right track with his daughters? Could he settle back into his previous life in Appleton? Would Taylor's interview and retraction make him famous and set him on a course of interviews and speaking tours all over the world? Would he go to Alert Bay and see Ellie, or give Tanya a call when she returned from Saudi Arabia? These and so many other possibilities swirled around in his thoughts.

"I choose how to feel and react, therefore I am," he thought.

Financial independence gave Walker the kind of freedom that most people only dream of, although he did not believe it to be an important factor in creating his future self. Fulfilling his epiphany did not lessen his desire to see the world, but increased it. Regardless of his other choices, he would continue to travel. He pushed back these noisy, consuming thoughts and stood quietly in the moment.

On this bright, sunny spring morning, life and hope for renewal filled the air. Walker looked out along the river. Except for a few places where the current moved swiftly, the water remained frozen. Many ducks congregated in the largest section of open water. Despite the cold temperature, they seemed happy and thankful for a place to swim.

**Keep up to date
with Walker Fayt:**

w w w . w a l k e r f a y t . c o m

THE WORLDWIDE SEXUAL ADVENTURES OF WALKER FAYT

BY MITCH RHODES · ISBN 1-894694-01-5

ALSO AVAILABLE AT YOUR LOCAL BOOKSTORE

U.S. ORDERS		CANADIAN ORDERS	
___Copies @ $14.95US	$_____	___Copies @ $19.95CDN	$_____
Shipping [1st book]	$6.95US	Shipping [1st book]	$7.00CDN
Add $4.25US for each additional book	$_____	GST 7%	$_____
Total enclosed	$_____	Add $4.25CDN for each additional book	$_____
		Total enclosed	$_____

OVERSEAS ORDERS
(Payment in U.S. Funds)

SURFACE (allow 8 weeks)		AIRMAIL	
___Copies @ $14.95US	$_____	___Copies @ $14.95US	$_____
Shipping [1st book]	$7.50US	Shipping [1st book]	$14.00US
Add $4.25US for each additional book	$_____	Add $7.00US for each additional book	$_____
Total enclosed	$_____	Total enclosed	$_____

Make your check or money order payable to:
New World Solutions Inc.
103-4338 Main Street, Suite 980
Whistler, BC • V0N 1B4 • Canada
or order online by email: orders@walkerfayt.com
or from the website: www.walkerfayt.com

Shipping information

Name _____

Address _____

_____

City, State/Province _____

Zip/Postal Code _____

Phone _____

Email _____

Credit card orders only

Visa or Mastercard? _____

Card number _____

Expiry date _____

Name on credit card _____

Signature _____

THANK YOU FOR YOUR ORDER!